DETOURS

EMMA GATES

WELLS STREET PRESS

Copyright © 2014 by Emma Gates

ISBN 978-0-9888906-6-4

Cover design: Derek Murphy

Printed in the United States of America

DETOURS

ONE

C LARE'S RITUAL at the Chicago River, weather permitting on her way to work, was to lean on the bridge railing and look northeast, where shipping lanes flowed through long Great Lakes, out the skinny old St. Lawrence Seaway to the wild grey Atlantic and beyond.

Today's icy December sky was spitting white dots and dashes by the time she entered her building on LaSalle Street.

The elevator operator stepped forward to indicate an open car and said, "*Sun Times* says more snow due tonight."

"I hope O'Hare stays open," she said. "I'm on an eight o'clock flight."

The next man who followed her into the elevator turned to ask, "Where are you going?" He was a chatty blond whom Clare saw occasionally in the building.

"Kuwait City."

"*Where?*" He grinned his disbelief. "How come?"

"Educational trade show. Biggest in the Middle East."

"Middle ... East ... " he repeated, as if she'd said "Middle Earth."

She smiled without elaborating. She was all for making friends, but prior conversational attempts had convinced her, educating this young man would just wear her out.

Late that afternoon a telex came in from EduGulf headquarters: the final list of event attendees, many familiar to Clare from past trade shows. But one name jumped out, in an

1

addendum at the bottom, and glowed like black neon against the flimsy yellow paper:

EDUGULF U.S. PARTICIPANTS INVITED TO FIRST NIGHT RECEPTION, HOME OF **JAMES LOWELL GOODENOW IV**, NEWLY APPOINTED U.S. COMMERCIAL ATTACHE, GULF COOPERATION COUNCIL, AMEMB KUWAIT CITY.

Newly appointed? No wonder she'd had no warning.

Snow was falling thickly now and lights were coming on in the highrises around her. Transported by memory and by the silent tumble of flakes, which evoked the most poignant parting of her life, she let herself lean back to remember.

HE WAS at the front of her line, for French classes, during registration. Everything else—the swampy humidity of Indiana University in late August, other students jostling the line, echoey noise, and her own freshman confusion—faded when she saw his sharp profile. For sure *he* was no freshman.

He wore a white oxford shirt, sleeves folded below his elbows, when everyone else wore baggy tees, and his hair fell in glossy black waves, not the frizzy halo or lank ponytail of other boys. His right hand whacked a stack of data cards against his left palm. She heard this echo of impatient awareness as the only sound in the world and studied him as its only inhabitant.

How would it feel to receive his crackling attention?

Not that she knew how to attract it: he was exactly the type who'd *never* looked at her in high school, three months and forty-six-and-a-half pounds ago.

Clare's new friend Ginger glanced ahead to see what Clare was staring at. "*Oh* yeah. Let's take what he's taking."

"Who you rubbernecking now, Ginger?" asked Lee, next to them. He lived on the first floor of their small co-ed dorm, which was precocious for 1972 Indiana: girls up, boys down, Resident Assistant on the lookout to catch fraternization after midnight curfew.

"That preppie up there," Ginger said. "The sexy one."

"That's Lowell." Lee's Hoosier twang broadened in pleased

recognition. "He was in our Paris group last year. Poli Sci grad student. Good people."

"Here he comes." Ginger nudged Lee. "Introduce us."

The impatience Clare glimpsed in Lowell's stance had dissolved into a stroll—long legs encased in faded jeans—by the time he ambled by. His hair swung over his forehead as he shuffled his registration cards. When Lee caught his arm he glanced up. His face was as captivating as his profile had promised: large eyes, straight slope of nose, long lips tilted slightly.

"Hey Lee." His quiet voice held a soft Southern hint. "Bone joor, mone frer," he mocked an American accent. "What're you up to this year?"

"Trying out French House," answered Lee.

"*Frrench* House." Lowell's expression was straight but Clare imagined a suggestive smile behind the slow way he said this.

"Yeah. We're s'posed to speak French all the time."

"Lee? In Paris, I only ever heard you speak French after a couple rounds." A dimple appeared at the side of Lowell's curving mouth. "And it wasn't exactly what I'd call ... *conversation.*" Ginger and Lee laughed.

"We'll help him practice," Ginger said. "We're in French House too."

"Ginger Harris, Clare Meredith," Lee said. "Girls, this is Lowell Goodenow."

"Pleased to meet you," Ginger said. "Do people call you "Good?" For short?"

As he focused on her his dimple sharpened. "Some call me *very* good, Ginger." Gin-jah. He surveyed her slowly, from auburn curls to pink toenails. "Depends what I'm doin."

Then his gaze moved to Clare's Earth shoes, traveled up her body, stopped at her stare. His light-sparkled grey eyes, fringed by thick black lashes, invited her to dive all the way in. She was used to a lonely fog blinding guys like this to girls like her. But there was no fog between them as he looked straight into her eyes.

She got so lost in his curious gaze that when the line shifted, propelling Ginger and Lee forward, she stumbled right into Lowell. His hand steadied her arm and sent a hot current through her. His hint of smile had vanished. She could not summon the wit to smile either.

"Clare." Cleh-ah. His accent made her name unique. The line shuffled again. Lowell dropped his hand, leaving a cool space when he walked away.

FOR WEEKS, Clare had anticipated going to EduGulf, but right now she didn't even want to leave her office. She surveyed the confident order she'd created: detailed map of her territory, telexes stacked in clear IN and OUT trays, massive dictionary of business Arabic anchoring a peach-colored pile of *Financial Times*. A seasonal poinsettia brandished its red-velvet cheer on her windowsill and a jar of cinnamon potpourri scented her serene space.

She reached into her lowest desk drawer, which held a pack of desperate cigarettes, lighter tucked into the wrap. Point of pride: they were stale from infrequent use. But she lit up a deep soothing drag and felt relief with the first exhale.

Lowell Goodenow.

Not again.

TWO

WHEN CLARE first walked into her one senior-level class, Tuesday-Thursday Advanced French Conversation, she saw only Lowell. He was leaning back, legs stretched in front of his chair, and his rolled workshirt sleeves showed tanned, lightly muscled forearms and a slim gold watch. She made herself slide into the seat beside him. When he looked over, a corner of his mouth rose in recognition.

"Clare." Cleh-ah.

He knows me. A week had passed since they met.

"Lowell." His name was whipped cream in her mouth, rich with sugar and vanilla, and she could not help saying it like a mantra.

"You remember me," he said.

As his gaze intensified, his dimple appeared, and she felt the warmth of his observation pouring down her fan of hair, generating heat as if his regard were summer dawn on a ripe field. Did he sense the steam rising? She concentrated to keep her gaze on him steady, and to hold still, when inside she was squirming like a new puppy seeking approval.

Ginger took the seat next to her and leaned past Clare to grin. "Hi, *Good.*"

He laughed. "Hey, Ginger." Gin-jah.

The instructor, a stern young Frenchman, called the class to order. "Turn to the person next to you," he told them in French. "Interview them about their family background and why they study French."

Lowell angled toward her. "Mademoiselle Clare, please tell

5

me, how many brothers and sisters do you have?" His French was fluent, without a trace of Southern.

Why did the instructor insist on such personal information?

"I have, eh, I had ... two older brothers. I have an older sister."

"And why do you study French?"

"To get out of college fast. It's an easy major." Someone had left eraser crumbles on the desk and she brushed at them before tucking nail-bitten fingers into her hot damp palms. She studied her hands to avoid looking at him.

"Easy? You must be good at languages."

"I am. But I hate to study," she confessed in a small French voice—and she wanted to snatch the stupid words back as soon as they left her mouth.

There was a pause before he asked, "Where did you grow up?"

"In Merrillville."

"Where is that?"

"It's north, eh, north of the Indiana. Not far from the Gary." Staggering through a simple French sentence? But it wasn't this question: it was him. She searched her memory. *Moulin.* "My Dad worked in the ... windmill."

"Moulin?" he repeated.

Wrong word. She leaned toward him, close enough to savor a whiff of aftershave or cologne, a clean watery fragrance summoning a plunge into some clear summer lake. She whispered in English, still looking down, "Steel mill."

"And how will you improve the world, with your French?"

Had Lee told him she was an activist? She glanced up, meeting his keen look, as he went on, "What will you do when you graduate next year?"

"Next year ... " Because she'd placed into this upper-level class, he assumed she was a lot older. Good. A worldly grad student wouldn't be impressed by a naïve freshman. "I will continue my work for peace and justice."

"An idealist," he murmured. "*Moi aussi. Formidable.*" He was an idealist too. *Flirt back! Seize the day!* But how? She could barely muster her questions for him.

"And you, Monsieur Lowell, your family, your French?"

6

"I grew up in Virginia. I have one younger sister. I study French to work, effectively, in Senegal next year."

"*Senegal?*"

"It's on the west coast of Africa, south of Mauritania—"

"I know where it is—"

She wanted to ask, 'why Senegal?' but the instructor said, "*Alors,* introduce each other to the class."

When it was their turn, Lowell dipped his head, indicating she should start.

"Monsieur Lowell is from Virginia, he has one sister, and he is going to … join the Peace Corps?" she guessed.

He took his time, smiling at her with those flashing eyes and deep dimple, before he said, "Mademoiselle Clare is the youngest in her family, who live near Gary, and she is an idealist … with a good imagination."

When class ended, Lowell took her hand briefly, as he stood. His fingers were warm and ink-stained. "*Enchante, Mademoiselle. A tout alors.*" He walked out.

In the next few classes, Lowell nodded when he saw her and Ginger, but the instructor mixed the students so he and Clare did not sit together again.

Meanwhile she was developing camaraderie with her French House mates.

Clare had been lonesome at home the last two years, older siblings gone, so she loved dorm life: the instant friendships, the mix of music, the freedom to sit all night in the lounge playing Hearts and Crazy Eights and Indiana Euchre; getting addicted to vending-machine Coke, trying weed and wine, and exploring every possible subject, sometimes even in French.

She and Ginger discovered a mutual love of Leonard Cohen and Bob Dylan. Ginger's guitar and alto voice were in perfect harmony with her own soprano on dulcimer. They started practicing so they could perform for French House gatherings.

Her only dissatisfaction—aside from not knowing how to get closer to Lowell Goodenow—was her dorm-mates' political indifference. Mystifying: most of them had traveled internationally and should, she thought, be more aware.

"What's *with* you guys?" she demanded one Friday afternoon in mid-September when they were hanging out in Ginger's room.

"I'm asking for *one hour* of your time to raise awareness on campus. We need as many people as possible to come out, to show this administration—"

"It's Friday, Clare," Lee said lazily. "We know you have a special personal mission, and we respect that. But it's the *weekend*." He started rolling the second joint. "Listen to this Humble Pie song and have another toke before you go." He turned up the sly snickering that kicked off "Thirty Days in the Hole."

Clare unfolded herself from the floor. "I'll make my voice heard for all of you."

"Yeah, cheri, tell em." Ginger closed her eyes.

STILL PUZZLED by their apathy, Clare walked over to the quad where about two hundred students were gathering. The day was perfect for a demonstration: bright blue sky, air smelling like fall, breeze warm on her skin. Arm-banded marshals threaded through the group, handing out signs, calling to passing kids.

The Student Mobilization Committee leader, Steve Henderson, raised his bullhorn. "We'll march through campus to the square. Grab anyone to join us. Stay off the sidewalk for the lie-in unless you wanna get busted. The man told us we're okay on the grass."

Steve lowered the bullhorn and grinned. "Grazin in the grass, can ya dig it!"

Everyone applauded.

Their chants echoed against the university's stately limestone buildings as they wove around Showalter Fountain and passed the observatory in the woods at the edge of campus. Clare waved her sign—PEACE NOW—and shouted until she felt hoarse. As classrooms emptied for the day, the weather enticed about another hundred students to join, and Steve led the crowd across the street that separated campus from town.

A couple of policemen waved them toward the town square, anchored by the limestone courthouse with its statue of a Civil War hero, enveloped by well-kept lawns on four sides. "Stay on the green, kids," an officer said as they marched past.

The boy next to Clare—shaggy-haired, scruffy, in a tattered army jacket—made a face. "Who the fuck's that pig think he is,

8

telling us where to go?" He shook his sign at the policeman and shouted, "Hell no, we won't go!"

"Hell no, we won't go!" the students repeated.

"ROTC off campus!" Steve shouted.

The scruffy boy yelled louder, "Ho, Ho, Ho Chi Min, NLF is gonna win!"

Clare sang above him, in her clear soprano, "Give peace a chance!"

"All we are *saying* is give peace a *chance*," everyone moaned as they swarmed the square. Steve's bullhorn was proving ineffective against their increasing noise, as they drew a curious audience and responded to the attention with renewed vigor.

"Go hide in your classrooms!" cried an angry-faced older man, standing in the doorway of a grocery store across the street. "Cowards!"

"Fuck you!" shouted the boy next to Clare.

She nudged his elbow and reminded, "*Dialogue* with the people."

"Redneck assholes don't deserve it." The boy held his sign up with both hands, high, and brought its wooden staff down hard on a curbside mailbox, where it made a noisy, satisfying ring. "Fuck no, we won't go!"

"Fuck no, we won't go!" roared the crowd, and banged signs on newspaper stands, on the heavy chain railing that surrounded the lawns, on the courthouse steps. But the mailbox resonated best, loudest, as the shaggy-haired boy kept smashing.

Clare was pushed into him by eager kids. Her sign slammed against the mailbox too.

Steve mouthed into his bullhorn but nobody could hear him above the din.

"Break it up!" Clare's upper arm was suddenly gripped, and a policeman was scowling at her and shouting, "Break it up now! Get outta here!"

He yanked her so roughly she stumbled to the curb. Her sign flew onto the windshield of a parked car and she stopped her fall by slapping both hands on the hood.

The policeman bawled, "Hands *off* the vehicle!"

A marshal pulled Clare to her feet. He hissed, "Split before you get busted." He snatched her sign from the windshield and shoved her toward campus.

"But—"

"Just go!"

She lurched across the street. It was only seconds since they reached the courthouse. She barely noticed passing a blurred line of hostile, and supportive, shopkeepers and students. She didn't recognize Lowell until he was right in front of her.

"Clare?" Cleh-ah? He frowned past her where, she saw when she turned, the marshal was wading back into the now-chaotic crowd.

"C'mere." He took her right hand, and she was surprised to feel a sharp stab on her palm, as if he'd stung her.

He led her through a dark storefront. Inside, Neil Young's "Heart of Gold" and the reek of beer greeted her: uh-oh. She didn't have a fake ID. She'd get carded and thrown out. But Lowell propelled her forward.

"I'll get you a beer. You look like you could use one." He indicated a booth at the window where another guy sat. "My buddy Troy, visiting from Boston this weekend."

She sank. She pressed her lips in a semblance of smile at his friend, felt her mouth folding, and was suddenly afraid she might whimper from shock.

Troy leaned forward. "You're safe." Straight red hair brushed a shoulder as he turned to look at the street, where police were scattering demonstrators. "You were lucky. That copper was aftah you!" She folded her arms tight to calm herself. "Low was outta here like a shot. He was afraid you were gettin busted."

"No cause to bust me."

"Destruction of property," Lowell said as he glided into the booth next to Clare and set a mug in front of her. "Mailbox, newspaper stand, parked car. Looked like you were gonna hit that cop, too." He leaned close—too close; it was unnerving, feeling so helplessly attracted to him—and sniffed. "And, pardon my presumption if I'm mistaken, Mademoiselle, but you stink of dope." His slow grin lit up his eyes. "Coulda been one ugly bust."

Troy reached to bring a piece of her long hair to his nose. "Smells like good stuff. Where's it from?"

"You guys were ... just sitting here, watching?"

"It went down fast," Troy said, mild. "Not that I'd be out there with ya. You'll never hear me rooting for the Cong. I don't support your cause."

Lowell finished a sip. "Neither do I."

Getting angry was easier than allowing her unsteadiness to show: from the sudden havoc of the demonstration, from the way these guys felt so out of her league, but most especially from Lowell's proximity. "How can you not? It's an *illegal* war, an internal struggle in a country where we're not wanted. Our aggression there is wrecking our relationships all over the world. If you didn't have student deferments, you'd be up for the draft. You've *got* to care!" She heard the wobble in her voice and, to stop herself, took a long cool gulp of beer. She wasn't much used to it, but this tasted good.

Lowell said, "I didn't say I don't care."

And then Troy said, "I'm not deferred, babe, I did my time in Nam. And Low's gonna work to make sure we stay outta illegal wars."

Oh?

"Yeah, you heard me. I'm a vet. Done thinkin about it, too, so don't even ask." Troy drained his mug. "Although I suppose a vet could get laid fast if he acted halfway open to the Movement. Plenty of cute sympathetic chicks." He tilted his mouth in another grin, and looked her over, thoroughly. "Am I right?"

"*No.*" Mortified, she turned her attack to Lowell, who was shaking his head at Troy in a rueful, familiar manner, his lips suppressing a smile.

"*Lowell.*"

"Mademoiselle." He lifted his beer in a mock toast.

"I don't mean to trash your career goals, but the Peace Corps is *hopelessly* colonialist. It's basically a government mouthpiece. I meant to tell you that after class, sometime, when I got the chance." *If I ever worked up the nerve.* "I mean, you might as well join Up with People."

Lowell's laugh shook him close enough to lean on, were they better acquainted and she bolder. His cool-lake scent induced her to close her eyes and breathe in deep. She made herself grimace instead. "I'm *serious.*"

"I know, I know. Your commitment's plain to see." He was

11

still laughing. "I'm not laughin at you, Cleh-ah. It's just—I'm joining an even more blatant government mouthpiece than Peace Corps. The Foreign Service."

The Foreign Service. The *State* Department! "But, but ... in class you said you were an idealist! How can you *possibly* work for someone like *Kissinger*?" Everyone knew Nixon would promote the current NSA chief to Secretary of State after the election.

"Well, it'll be awhile before I report to him directly," he said, sarcasm keeping his grin broad. "I'll be startin at the bottom of his heap."

"He's a war criminal!"

Smile erased, he set his mug down as if anchoring it into the table. "Depends whose point of view," he said slowly. "I don't approve of everything he's done. But he wants to solidify our influence in the world, and he's willing to do bold things to accomplish that."

"Like invade Cambodia and Laos!"

"Like getting Nixon to visit China, and finally talking to the Russians again."

"So we can expand our imperialist agenda right along with theirs." She slammed down her own mug. "Preserve the balance of fucking powers."

His expression tightened. "So we can, just maybe, negotiate to avoid unnecessary wars in the future."

"Negotiate to divide the planet into haves and have-nots."

Troy slid his lanky body out of the booth. "I'm gonna book, Low, can I take your Vette?"

"Course." Lowell tossed keys.

Good riddance. But Troy was a veteran. He deserved respect. "I'm sure your service was meaningful, Troy." She reached out a hand, wanting to tell him about Joe.

But it was Lowell who took her hand, turning it palm up, and she noticed a freaky trickle of blood on her wrist. "That's deep." He dabbed at it with a napkin. "You got yourself a nasty splinter from that sign."

Troy laughed. "Looks like your service was *meaningful,* too, babe."

THREE

HER HEART thudded as Lowell gripped her splintered palm. She lifted beer with her other hand and gulped.

"Easy now." Lowell tugged with steady fingers.

She winced at the flash of pain.

"Got it." He held up a sliver of wood. "Better go wash this." He got out to let her move. She struggled from the booth and stood on legs that felt insubstantial.

He put a warm hand on the middle of her back. "Should I take you home?"

His touch made her hitch a sudden sharp breath.

"You seem kinda shaky." His hand slid around her waist, making her feel shakier. "Want me to call a cab?"

Keep holding onto me.

"No, I'm okay, let's have another beer. I'll be right back."

She found her way to the bathroom to scrub the puncture in her palm.

She glanced in the mirror, wiped her flushed face, then stood to study herself.

Who was she now? She'd taken off The Weight with clear intent, to transform herself before college; but how was she supposed to *use* her new body to seduce Lowell as this unexpected siren in the mirror, full-grown and hungry, was demanding? What did *he* see when he looked at her? She never wore a bra, so erect nipples advertised her disequilibrium like warning lights under her thin red sweater. She combed wet fingers through her mass of hair and shook it over her chest as a cover.

Oh fuck it, like he's even noticing I'm female. To him, I'm just some hippie protester. And he was a straight arrow aimed directly at a successful Establishment target. Obviously, she could engage him as a political challenge, something she believed she knew how to do ... if she could keep her head straight in his distracting presence.

The bar felt different when she walked back to their booth. The mouth-watering smell of baking pizza mixed pleasantly with beer. Couples huddled, lamps glowed on tables, and the music was now live—a girl on a stool was playing guitar, singing "One of Us Cannot be Wrong," a Cohen favorite, in front of the corner fireplace. Good voice. Clare hummed along, in harmony, asking to be let into the storm.

Lowell stood as she returned to their booth. "You okay?"

"Yes." She sat across from him. "I like this place."

"First time here?"

"My first time in any bar."

"For real? How old are you?"

Being in Advanced French probably made her seem mature to him. She looked older, too, with her height and stubbornly robust figure. She wanted to appear worthy of his serious attention and this desire surpassed, in the moment, any potential consequence of misrepresenting her age.

"Nineteen." End of next year: soon enough. She tossed her hair in a careless, sophisticated nineteen-year-old move, and barely missed throwing her mug off the table. "Nearly twenty."

"I thought you were older. How come you're in Advanced French?"

"I placed into a high level when I started college."

"You *are* good at languages." His gaze flicked to the bartender and wait staff. "Seein as you're underage, we'd best get outta here." But he took another long sip as if they had all the time in the world. "Tell me how you got political."

She tried to look *into* him, to see if he could receive her story with the seriousness it deserved, and he frowned and leaned forward. "Clare?"

She concentrated on keeping her voice steady. "Two years ago my brother Joe was killed in Vietnam. He was a helicopter mechanic trainee, and he was attacked trying to fix a bird on a hot landing zone." Saying it shocked, even after repetition, and she felt the familiar chill which came with this recitation.

"At first we thought, oh, noble death in the cause for freedom, to preserve our way of life, all that bullshit the government tells us, about soldiers' deaths.

"But I decided there was *nothing* noble about it. Joe got drafted right out of high school. He was in the wrong place, at the wrong time, and he died because our fascist government made a mistake. At least, a mistake for the average dumb American grunt. The military-industrial complex is just fine. War's such good fucking business."

When she raised her eyes he was nodding slowly. "When you mentioned him in class, I wondered what happened."

She'd talked to him, about Joe, in French class?

"Our interview," he clarified. "You said you *had* two brothers—"

Her throat closed.

"Thank you for telling me," he said. "I can't know exactly how you feel, but I can imagine angry. And sad."

They shared a long stare. Few people, outside of family, held her gaze like this when she talked about Joe.

"Refill?" a waitress called, passing their booth. Her eyes narrowed on Clare and she stopped. "Did I get your ID?"

"We're just leavin," Lowell said, pulling money from his pocket to add to Troy's bills.

Outside, they faced each other as sunset cooled the breeze and washed the square in gold and purple. Light slanted on the lawn where a few signs lay trampled; gleamed off the weathervane copper fish, greening with age atop the courthouse; and illuminated blue glints in Lowell's hair. He broke their silence. "How far to your famous Language Units?"

French, Spanish, German and Russian Houses shared twin double-winged dormitories next to each other. "It's about six blocks, east on Seventh, across from Graduate Housing. Where do you live?" *Probably not in a dorm.*

"Out past Tulip Tree. You're on my way."

Their legs moved in sync on the sidewalk, jeans belling slightly as they stepped. He was a couple of inches taller. She wanted to take his arm as it swung in rhythm next to hers so they'd rock in unison down the street like a choreographed couple. Music might suddenly play. But he kept a distance between them, the distance of not-yet. Or, maybe, not-ever.

"Lee's been fillin me in on French House," Lowell said

easily. "He says y'all don't really speak French, you just drink a lotta French wine."

"He's lying! All we can get is Boone's Farm." She loved his little chuckle. "Tell me about France."

"Paris is very picturesque, and the people are appealing, but it's a big city. Hard to make close friends. Tough usin French all the time."

"You sound fluent."

"Living in language was hard work. Gave me a headache."

"Lee says you're in Poli Sci."

"Finally finishing my M.A. thesis."

"What's it about?"

"Oil-based emerging economies."

Would it intrigue him if she mentioned Yevtushenko's poem about the Siberian plant? But maybe he'd think she was showing off. "You know Yevtushenko?" she blurted anyway.

"Heard of him."

"He wrote a poem about a power plant." She added, "I mean, Bratsk was hydroelectric, not oil. And the Soviet Union's not exactly emerging. But you might like the poem anyway."

His scrutiny, as they kept walking, made her feel itchy all over. "Interesting," he finally said.

They entered the woods, passed the gazebo surrounding the Wishing Well, and crossed in front of Adam and Eve, a naked bronze couple who reached for each other in what Clare saw as a mystery of virginal yearning, doomed by their sculptor never to touch.

She stopped, out of habit, to admire the statues. Lowell's standing right beside her felt as powerful as if he were the magical lover she'd dreamed of since she was old enough to fantasize. There was a nostalgic campus legend about being near the Wishing Well House, something about a co-ed being kissed at midnight ...

She peeked over at him.

He was watching her too. "You really hate to study?"

It was so hard to look into his eyes and try to converse. She dropped her gaze and shrugged. "I just want a diploma."

"So ... you have a goal, as a French major?"

"I'd like to travel ... "

16

"Why not chaperone a student program? Free ticket, some babysitting."

"Well, I'd rather just work my way through, you know, hitchhike, stay in hostels. After the Revolution."

"The re-vo-*lu*-tion," he repeated, contemplative. "Tell me, Clare, how'd things get so riled up all of a sudden, out there on the square?"

"Well, I mean, it was like ... " She raised her palms. "Marshals lost control of the crowd. There was this one jerk who started it and people joined in. You know, they're angry—*we're* angry, Nixon doesn't want to listen to us!"

"And bustin up Bloomington mailboxes is gonna make him? What's next, a march on President Ryan's house? Maybe *he* could end the war for you."

Steve Henderson had suggested this move, as an act of speaking truth to power, but most kids in the SMC sort of liked the genial university president, and it was concluded he was probably sympathetic to their cause so there was no reason to bother him.

"The SMC isn't skilled in crowd management, but it's all we've got here. The Revolution has to start somewhere."

He glanced at Adam and Eve, then back to her, with his now-familiar half smile. "You look to me about as innocent, of real revolution, as they do."

"Well I'm *not*, Lowell. I've been in this struggle a long time. I know exactly how things'll go down."

"Oh yeah? Lay it on me." His hint of amusement became a frank grin. "The way you spit out 'military-industrial-complex,' and your labelling our government as fascist, makes me wonder if you're just recitin' dialogue, like we do in class sometimes." He tapped her arm with a light forefinger. "I'd like to hear more from *you*, not just movement rhetoric." He stepped close so his hand cupped her shoulder. Heat sank in.

Her pulse jumped and she reached for her framework of familiar political discourse. Maybe his charm was deliberate? He might be the type Nechayev warned of, in his "Revolutionary Catechism": a bourgeois intellectual who would try to talk a Revolutionary out of her convictions, seduce her with glib chat.

"C'mon, don't just look at me, tell me what you're thinkin."

His voice was low and his eyes still teasing as he shifted a little closer.

She pulled up easy rote like a shield against his confusing warmth. "For revolution to succeed here, to combat our government's delusions of grandeur, we need to review homegrown models like Nechayev's."

His hand dropped as he stepped back. "*Nechayev?* Jesus please us, he was crazy!"

"On the contrary. His ideas represented new ways of fighting repression from inside corrupt systems. But I'm surprised someone like you even knows who he is." Most Establishment types wouldn't. Of course, Lowell was in Poli Sci.

"And just who the hell are *you?* Young Socialist Alliance? SDS?"

She shook her head. The nearest Young Socialist Alliance group was in Chicago. She'd wanted to join them in high school but didn't have a way to get to regular meetings on time.

"Don't tell me Indiana's Student Mobilization Committee is so sophisticated it's preaching Nechayev. I had a class with Steve Henderson. Not the world's brightest political light, in my book."

"I'm self-taught."

"Huh." He looked at her awhile. She tried to keep still. He mused, "The self-taught revolutionary, from Merrillville Indiana, who hates to study—unless it's Nechayev's Catechism, or maybe Yevtushenko. Why not Pasternak or Solzhenitsyn? And of course Mayakovsky. You must be into the Russian Revolution."

"I love Mayakovsky." Again, she was surprised by what he knew. "You're smart."

His confident grin took this as banter. "Not half as smart as *you* seem to be, baby." He laughed softly. "You're quite a gal."

She couldn't hold up her end of their stare.

After a moment he turned away, and they moved on toward Seventh Street under the shadows of trees. The air held the headiness of first-fallen burnished leaves trod to sweet fragrance under their feet—no wonder it was so hard for her to breathe.

"So, Clare, you think political change can only be achieved by anarchy? Not by democracy?"

"Oh, like the way it's working so well here now … "

"I think our policy's changing, based on public opinion against the war."

"Too late!"

"You know the Administration's looking for ways out." He suddenly sounded tired, of the subject or maybe of her company, she feared.

She tried to re-establish rapport. "Why do you want to be a diplomat?"

"To change the negative view some other countries have of us."

"So you agree Vietnam was a mistake."

"I think our initial involvement was fucked up." He sighed. "And complicated. There have been miscalculations, ignorance for sure, terrible losses, we all agree. But it's so beyond our supporting the South now, and I don't see black and white when it comes to the geopolitical power balance. And no matter what you think, there *has* to be balance. Black and white is a dead-end for diplomacy."

"So what's your goal?"

"In ten years I want to be ambassador to a major country. Secretary of State, ten or fifteen years after that."

Wow. She'd never met anyone with his kind of ambition. She wanted to stretch out their conversation, but they were already at the French House corner.

"Why Senegal?"

"Entry-level opening I've been told of, at the embassy. I'll go into training in January."

"January?"

"Yeah. This is my final semester." He gestured to the spread of lawn in front of several stubby cinder block structures. The Jordan, Bloomington's meandering stream, wound its shining way around them. "Language Units, right? One's called Aydelotte?"

"This little pink building." January was only four months from now!

He faced her. Under the streetlamp he looked as surreally beautiful, and as far away, as the three quarter moon appearing over the corner high-rise quadrangle of Graduate Housing. "Y'know Clare, we prob'ly can't change each other's minds.

19

Politically speaking."

Why'd she carry on like a fanatic about Nechayev, of all dreary topics, in the romantic woods? Of course he wasn't going to be her magical lover! Maybe not even a new friend. Just an Establishment enemy, leaving soon. No loss, really; no reason for the ache blooming in her chest and pulling her mouth all the way down to her Earth shoes.

"But let's continue this conversation. Not now. I've got work."

"On a Friday night?"

"I've got another thesis chapter due Monday." He suddenly took her right hand and looked where he'd removed the splinter. "This seems to be okay." His thumb circled her palm, leisurely, making her shiver, as his smile moved up her body to her eyes. "Clare. I have never met *anyone* like you."

He lowered her hand and gave her shoulder a pat. "I have to go, but we can talk again. If you like. G'night now."

She watched him walk swiftly to the corner, check the light, cross, vanish into the shadows beyond Graduate Housing. His sure-footed stride would be perfectly at home no matter where in the world he went. She felt herself falling as she followed the energy he left behind, as surely and deeply as bronze Eve would plummet after bronze Adam, were he to suddenly plunge into the WishingWell.

FOUR

S HE KNEW she *shouldn't* feel bent out of shape over him. A more experienced girl wouldn't obsess over some guy, however foxy, who smiled and said hey when he saw her next Tuesday in French but who didn't seek her out, as if they hadn't shared such profound dialogue after last Friday's demonstration. Profound to her, at least.

Anyway, just because he said he'd never met anyone like Clare didn't mean he *liked* her. He probably thought she was a weird novelty, bringing up scary Nechayev, branding herself a wild-eyed anarchist stuck in 19th century Russia.

Anyway, she was cozy in French House, occupied by her part-time library job, somewhat absorbed in her studies. And her SMC cell was planning an action on the nearby naval weapons depot. She was plenty busy without pining over some soon-gone preppie.

Anyway, he probably had a girlfriend, or several; he was so magnetic, with his lit-up eyes, sultry low laugh, luxuriant hair, and the strong fluid way he walked. He must have girls constantly falling at his feet.

This glum conclusion was reinforced Wednesday night, when she and Ginger were roaming the campus woods, smoking. She wanted to duck out of sight when she saw Lowell and an exquisite-looking dark-haired girl walking toward them on the path. He stopped.

"Nice evenin for a toke." He glanced down at the girl by his side. "Sylvie, meet Ginger and Clare." He took a relaxed hit off the joint Ginger handed him.

He offered it to Sylvie.

She shook her head. "I do *not* do *drugs*."

"Good weed." He breathed out slowly and handed it back to Ginger. "Thanks."

21

Ginger squinted at him as she inhaled. "Why'ncha come with us," she suggested in a voice made gravelly with smoke. "We're headin to a wild party."

A lie: they were going to buy munchies at the convenience store across Third Street and smoke more on the way back to French House, where they'd go to Lee's room to hear the new Leo Kottke record and get higher. This was not a wild party and Ginger knew it.

"*Wiiild,*" Lowell repeated, laughing as if he knew it was a fib. "Just exactly how wild do you gals get?" His gaze swept Clare like a sunburn.

Sylvie didn't laugh. "My sisters are expecting us."

"Bye," Ginger trilled, taking Clare's arm and starting down the path. "Have fun."

"Say hey to Lee for me," Lowell called after them. "Thanks for the smoke."

Clare felt she and Ginger were pounding through the trees, whose leaves flashed by in the lamplight, and she realized she was panting: it *was* good weed.

"Why'd you say we were going to a party?" she gasped.

"To see how he'd react! He'd come with us if he was alone."

"He thinks we're hippie freaks, Ginger, he thinks I'm some militant *extremist.*"

"That's what interests him."

"He's *not* interested!"

"Sure he is. Didn't you see how he looked you over? You weren't paying attention. You were too sto*oh*ned." Ginger laughed and ran. Clare hurried to catch up.

"Seriously, you think he might like to hang out with us?"

"Let's flip a coin for him. Or share him. He seems openminded."

Share him? What was *this* supposed to mean? It sounded so raunchy, Clare couldn't even picture it, but getting used to new ideas—like Ginger's—was part of college, she supposed. Ginger was from New Jersey. East-coast people were more direct than Indiana people.

Ginger navigated them into the store across the street. "But supercool guys can be so arrogant. Hard to get. Expecting you to make all the moves."

He's not arrogant.

They picked out Bugles, Jiffy Pop, Good'N'Plenties and a big Hershey's chocolate bar. At the checkout counter Ginger suddenly announced, in a voice too loud for Clare's liking, "How does a contest grab you? Let's see who gets him first."

"*What?*"

"Dare ya. If you want him, don't fuck around, go get him!"

"Right on," murmured the long-haired clerk.

"He's ripe," Ginger went on as they plunged through the woods again. "He needs a good lay if he's been trying to get any from Sorority Sylvie."

"She's so pretty." It hurt, seeing petite Sylvie as his type. "Just like a doll."

"Too right, a Skipper doll! That's not a body. *We've* got bodies, and he was scoping em out! They're probably not even dating. Betcha a nickel bag one of us balls him."

"I'm not betting that. Yuck!"

"Hey, one-night stand. He'd be *perfect* for losing your virginity."

No way could she put Lowell in that category, disregarding his radiance, allotting him no more importance than "first ball." As if she had a ghost of a chance to ball him! As if he even saw her. A feeling of loss dashed her enjoyment of the evening, and she went to her room early.

In bed, she banished the image of him with Sylvie, or with Ginger, and imagined him gazing at her the way he had last week in front of French House, imagined his warm hands teasing her body, his long lips on hers, imagined stroking his lush hair and holding him close. She wanted to stare a long time into his light-filled eyes. She could almost taste his kiss, sucking her own lips, squeezing her eyes tight. Alone, in the dark, she could pretend he was hers, and when she touched herself, she made her fingers his.

How embarrassing to see him in class next day, especially when he glanced her way and, seeing her looking at him, lifted a corner of his lips and lowered one eyelid in a slow exaggerated wink. At least he couldn't read her mind.

But he came right to her desk when class was finished.

"So how was last night's wild party? Tell me about it over

coffee?"

Ginger, next to her, answered for both of them. "Let's go."

They dawdled at a picnic table outside the student union. Ginger and Lowell did most of the talking, because Clare could not rouse enough brainpower to bring up politics. His nearness, his scent, the way his hands moved made her giddy; he wore a red plaid flannel shirt whose cuff she wanted to surreptitiously stroke.

She was shocked when he took her hand and laid it palm up on the table, probing with warm fingers where she'd had the splinter. "Looks like you healed up."

Ginger's inquisitive stare insisted on an explanation.

"Clare's antiwar wound from last week's demonstration." He kept his hand on hers and smiled, teasing, into her eyes. She felt the familiar, loathed heat of her too-common blush and, as she always did, dropped her head so her hair hid her red face.

Lisa, a buxom, outspoken Linguistics regular at the cafeteria's grad school dining table, came up behind Lowell and covered his eyes with both hands, pulling his head back so it was pillowed in her ample cleavage. "Hey goodlookin, guess who?" she sang.

His hand dropped from Clare's when he twisted around. "Lisa, hey."

"How was France? Far out?"

"Rigorous."

"Not enough wine, women and song?"

"That's not exactly why I went." After a few more minutes' chat, he checked his watch and stood. "Gotta go," he said. He glanced again at Clare and she stared back, immobilized, before he sauntered away.

Ginger turned to Lisa. "You seem to know him pretty well."

"Not nearly as well as I'd like to. What a stone *fox.*" Lisa licked one finger, pressed it on her bare arm, and made a hissing noise. "Ssssteam."

Ginger smirked. "We're seeing who gets him first."

"You have the hots for him too?" Lisa lifted surprised brows to Clare. "But you didn't say a word to him, even when he was looking at you! *And* holding your hand!"

"He didn't mean anything by it," Clare muttered. "And I

didn't agree to a bet."

"If he's touching you, he's flirting, you lucky kid."

"I think he was just being ... " she did not know how he was being, or why, or how she was supposed to respond. "Just ... toying with me."

Lisa leaned forward with the manner of someone who loved to give advice. "No. I've watched him in action, not with me unfortunately, and that's how he comes on. He just reaches out and takes what he wants."

"But "experienced only" applies," Ginger teased. "She's so cherry."

"So get experienced," Lisa told Clare. "Ask him out next time you see him."

"And game on!" cried Ginger, grinning.

"You mean ... for a date?" She'd have a heart attack.

"Not like 1955," Lisa said patiently. "Just "Hey, wanna hang out?" He'll know what to do."

Hey, Lowell, let's hang out, Clare practiced to herself. Let's hang out and talk politics.

"His Dad's with the State Department too," Lisa was telling Ginger. "Lowell came out here to 'experience the heartland,' he said."

Ginger laughed. "Sounds like a politician."

Clare remembered his ten-year-plan. And his twenty. Let's hang out and talk diplomacy.

"He'll go far, you watch," Lisa concluded.

"Watching him is a pure turn-on," Ginger said, sly.

Bold Ginger probably *would* get him. She had enough verve to hold her own as an A student, a double major in French and Spanish, and as a notorious partier; she'd spend all night drinking or smoking and get up three hours later, sharp for her morning classes. She was a year older than Clare and she'd already had six lovers, whose names she kept on a list she and Clare laughed over one day. But it wasn't funny to imagine Lowell becoming lucky number seven.

FIVE

CLARE WAS looking forward to the Language Units party the next night—the corny idea of a harvest moon hayride seemed the perfect opportunity to get really stoned.

But seeing Lowell walk up made her anxious. At least he was alone.

"Hey *Good*, this outing's for residents only," Ginger said, giving him a friendly nudge. "Unless you wanna be *my* guest?"

"Sorry, Ginjah, Ah'm Lee's date." He linked his arm with startled-looking Lee's.

On the hay wagon, a straw-bedecked flatbed truck, Clare found herself lodged between Lee and Lowell. Ginger was on Lowell's other side, and she launched into serious flirtation—flipping her hair forward to twist curly strands, brushing against him. Clare heard Lowell laugh. *Oh well.* If she were a guy, she'd fall for vivacious Ginger.

Clare breathed in country as they rattled out of town, and looked at the moon peeking above the treetops, its lush hugeness an illusion she knew would shrink into a high cold orb as night fell. She watched it sail the next few minutes, so absorbed she did not notice, at first, a change in pressure on her right side. She turned. Lowell was leaning in, watching her.

"Beautiful moon."

She nodded.

"Like your hair." Heh-yah. He took a lock, wound it around his forefinger, held it up to study its pale gleam. He didn't seem to notice how rigid this little touch made her. "Now's our chance to continue the conversation we started last week, Clare."

"Oh, definitely," she answered quickly. "I mean, I think you certainly need some re-education." *Stiff as a schoolmarm!*

"You go right on ahead, darlin, I'm all ears."

Darlin? "Okay, um, last time, we were talking about

Nechayev."

"Mmm-hmm. I looked him up again, y'know, after our chat. Maybe someone over there from Russian House has read him too, and all three of us can start a new party." His languid snicker resonated inside her. His leather jacket smelled good enough to lick.

"Well, look, I don't think *everything* he wanted, in his time, is appropriate for ours."

"Lotta revolutionaries think ideas like his are just fine right now." His finger still rolled her strand of hair. "His tactics—he didn't call em guerrilla warfare—are gettin adapted into just about every militia crawlin outta global liberation movements."

She tried to sound crisp. "Freedom fighters *have* to use extreme means to make statements. The avant-garde, you must know as a student of political science, sometimes deploy methods that outsiders can't understand."

"You really support violence? I mean, of all Nechayev's messages, that's the one Lenin got." He let the strand unwind in a long ringlet.

"Lenin had to free his people from years of oppression and poverty."

"So he led em straight into civil war."

She straightened up. "Engineered by colonialist powers in Europe."

His tone sharpened. "Russia was destabilized by what Lenin became—a ruthless dictator. And Stalin took over from there. Now even you would have to agree, Clare, that was a *real* fascist government."

"Russia wasn't stable under the *czars*. Lenin gave her a chance to breathe free!"

Lee thrust a jug of Ripple into Clare's hands. "It's obvious you two are made for each other, but would ya shut the fuck up, enjoy the friggin hayride, and let the rest of us get a buzz on?" He nudged her. "We want you and Ginger to start the singing at the bonfire."

"You sing?" Lowell asked. He passed, to Ginger, the Ripple Clare handed him. He reached for another lock of Clare's hair, brushing against her neck, freezing her. "You sing about blowin up the Stock Exchange?" He wound her hair all the way up on

27

his hand and tugged once. "Hmm, Clare the Red?" She felt his warm fingers on her cheek, felt a debilitating mix of enchantment and alarm.

"Actually, last year I wrote a musical comedy, based on the life of Lenin." *I did* not *just say that.* Nobody but her brother Andy knew about her musical, "Vladimir," because she suspected her twisted sense of humor would amuse very few. What possessed her to tell Lowell?

His laugh, warm with delight, shook her as he leaned close and dropped her hair. "The life of Lenin!" He laughed again. "Clever. Sing me a number."

She started quiet, but as she sang on, he started humming, and then Lee joined in, and Ginger leaned forward for a rousing finish:

"Give my regards to Moscow, remember me to our Red Square,
Tell all the gang in Petrograd that I will soon be there,
And give my regards to Kerensky, tell him I'm on my way
Yes give my regards to old Kerensky, hope he's ready for my May Day!"

"That's what your pal Lenin was thinking on the train from Finland," Lowell guessed, still laughing. "Gearin up to oust those damn ole lily-livered White Russians."

"You gotta do this for Russian House," Lee declared. "They're gonna freak."

"Who's Kerensky?" Ginger wanted to know. "What was the May Day?"

"Go on, Red." Lowell sat back and grinned.

So she sang a few more, like "He's a Grand Old Czar," and "Roll Out the Cossacks" and "Never Give up Your Reign, Dear." It was gratifying to have the whole truck listening, and clapping when she stopped.

"You oughta perform this at the comedy club in town," Lowell said. "I wonder what the SMC-ers would make of your musical, darlin, somehow they don't strike me as very humorous. For sure none of em appreciate how funny you are."

She laughed. He was right—she'd never sing to the SMC. "They'd hate it!"

"Do that again."

"Sing another?" She'd written more than twenty.

"Laugh. You got *such* a pretty laugh." He was studying her mouth.

She stopped laughing.

"How come you're a French major when you like Russians so much?"

"French is easier." Merrillville High didn't offer Russian. She'd have been starting from scratch at IU. "I did look into a free college in Moscow, where they'd teach me Russian, but their preference is students from Africa and Latin America."

"Let me guess ... hard core party-liner like you? Patrice Lumumba Peoples' Friendship University. They must have a hell of a fight song, doncha figure?"

He kept surprising her. "How do *you* know about it?"

"Why, Mademoiselle, I'm sure you're aware Russia's of some interest to the diplomatic community. Peoples' Friendship is a training ground for exporting Soviet-style revolution." His grin made this statement flippant. "So why didn't you follow up? I'm sure they'd have loved to nab an applicant from the Enemy of the People. Destroy the system from within, et cetera."

"My mom wouldn't let me," she had to admit.

"Thank you, Clare's mom." He captured another hank of hair and spilled it from hand to hand like a Slinky. "I like your hair." His accent seemed to come and go with selective application. "We may never *harmonize* on Mother Russia, y'know, Red, we might just have to drop the rev-o-*lu*-tion and move on to ... other topics."

She was sliding, sinking, willing toward him. She tried to rally her inner schoolmarm. "Lowell, we had a revolution *here*, remember, and good reason for it. I'm sure it wasn't cleaner than freedom fighting anywhere or anytime since."

"Precisely why I don't think we need another one." He slid his arm around her. "Let's agree to disagree about this, hmm, let's be ... *friends*."

"So ... you're not really interested in ... "

"A smart person, like we established you are last week, must know exactly what I'm interested in." She felt his lips brush her ear, making her shiver, as he whispered, "Tell you what. I'll be open to your campaign if you'll be open to mine." His low chuckle vibrated against her.

"That sounds like a Dylan line," she whispered back. " *"I'll letcha be in my dream if I c'n be in yours."* You know that one?"

"I do."

"Let's hang out," she finally remembered to say.

He pulled her closer. "Let's."

She allowed herself to settle under the disturbing comfort of his arm, and after what felt like about three hours her pulse finally slowed enough for her body to enjoy the sensation even as her mind, busy scurrying from one set of possible outcomes to the next, sped twice as fast.

SIX

AS SOON as she got used to resting against Lowell, the truck stopped, and everyone piled out to unload the keg, snacks and instruments. They made a bonfire. Clare and Ginger sang in French, Russian House made Clare sing more numbers from "Vladimir," and others sang in Russian, German and Spanish.

After the singing, the group broke into smaller bunches to eat, drink, and talk. Lee led a select few to toke in the woods, away from Teaching Assistants who were supervising the outing. Clare looked for Lowell, but he was talking to their French instructor, so she wandered along after Lee. She didn't smoke. She wanted to keep her mind clear in case Lowell reclaimed her shoulder on the way back, in case he decided to kiss her, in case ...

Ginger poked her out of her reverie. "You don't win til you've actually balled him, you know, so don't be looking so smug."

"Shhh!" She waved away the joint Ginger was holding out.

"Come on, Clare, everyone knows about our bet."

"Ginger! It's *not* a bet. I never agreed!"

"My money's on you, cheri, he's got a thing for blondes." Lee plucked the joint. "Leastways, he did in Paris. *Tojours les blondes.*" He started singing in French, with a bawdy growl, "*Auprès de m'blonde ...* "

She was ready to slap him.

Jenny, a French House senior they were friends with, came up behind Ginger and Lee, and used both elbows to shove them. "Shut up, you guys, leave Clare alone and let her get to know Low on his own merit." She gave Ginger a reproving look. "I think it's crude to make that kind of bet. Immature. Dehumanizing."

"If I don't share any winnings with you, Jen, your conscience

31

can stay clear." Ginger twisted her hair on top of her head and took another deep hit. "Looks like I'm not gonna get laid tonight. I'm just gonna get totally wasted."

Lee said, "You know *I'm* always at your service, Ginger."

"I'm not *that* horny, Lee, eew, it'd be like doing it with my brother!"

"You are such children." Jenny wandered off toward her boyfriend.

Ginger gave an exaggerated sigh but brightened when she looked through the trees at the group around the fire. "That German TA, now ... hmm, d'you s'pose he speaks any English?"

"Let's go find out," Clare answered.

"The way he looks, I don't need him to actually *speak*," Ginger said as they approached. "Go get your man, Clare, before that Spanish hussy nabs him."

Lowell was stepping backward as the Spanish House girl advanced. Clare smiled at him, when she sat down with the circle around the fire, and he made a neat sideways move, nodded to the Spanish hussy, and was sitting beside Clare in moments.

"No secret what y'all were doin in the woods, Red, we got a contact high just breathin over here," he informed her. "International TAs think it's funny, but that one American was worried." As he spoke he was smoothing back her curtain of hair and sliding a sure arm around her. His hand flowed on her tee shirt inside her jean jacket, and spread wide on her waist so his thumb was just an inch from the bottom of her breast, pounding her heart so hard she was sure his hand would bounce away any second.

"I didn't smoke. I didn't really feel like it."

"So you're just high on life, hmm."

"High on *you*." Tightness in her throat made this sound husky, sexier than she knew she could sound; her rebellious inner siren had nudged aside the schoolmarm and was thrusting forward, insistent on being heard.

His hand smoothed more firmly and his quiet laugh heated her ear and deep inside. "I'm high on you too." His thumb grazed the underside of her breast. "Come home with me."

Charges from her ear and her breast coalesced into a bright red river of mindless heat.

She had to pull away to breathe. "I guess I *should* know the enemy. But I won't agree with you. We'll argue all the time."

He kissed her cheek, soft and lingering and disarmingly sweet. When his lips lifted he whispered, "That's why you're so interesting, Red."

On the ride back to campus they sat next to their French instructor, with whom Lowell started a lively conversation about life in Paris, the riots of '68 and the future of the student movement in Europe. Clare added her opinion about Danny the Red but her attention was offset by the way Lowell hugged her.

Soon they were all climbing out in the campus parking lot, hauling gear away, making plans to go for pizza.

Lowell turned to her. "D'you want to get pizza with everyone?"

Be bold. "I'd rather be alone with you."

"I'll fix you a snack, we'll have some wine, talk about more dead Russians." He led her down the street. His Corvette was what she would have imagined he would drive, if she thought about cars: sleek, black, built to seduce. He handed her into the leather bucket seat and she sank, boneless, as the engine roared to life.

"Can't You Hear Me Knockin" blared out and he turned it down, a little. "I'm on a Stones kick right now, but I have other stuff. Pick what you like." His hand indicated the 8-track tapes stacked in the console between the two front seats. "With your voice, Clare, I wonder you didn't go into the music school here. They say it's as good as Julliard."

Her voice?

She took it for granted, even though it was what she was known for, in high school, before she'd launched the underground newspaper, broken the dress code, and started the Merrillville War Moratorium Project.

But at thirteen, her only goal was to join Madrigals, whose angelic-faced girls wore fabulous medieval outfits at some performances, cream skirts and sweaters at others. The boys, equally polished, made Clare daydream, but they never saw past her heft. By the time she was a junior, eligible to try out for the ensemble, she thought Madrigals were as square as Lawrence Welk. She could admit, now, she'd also dreaded looking out of place next to the others: the biggest girl. She tried to never let herself think the word "fat."

"Music majors work too hard," she declared. Madrigals would've snapped up Lowell. She could just picture him starring in the line of smooth boys, crooning in a snowy shirt and red cardigan, or caroling in fanciful satin and velvet. "How about you, Lowell, do you sing?"

"Sometimes, to myself. I like all kinds of music."

"What interested you, say, back in high school?"

"When I was a kid? I was crazy about polo, but I went to school in New England and didn't take my horse. I played soccer. Rowed crew. Climbed the White Mountains. Chased town girls. Read."

"New England?" His *horse!*

"St. Paul's, in New Hampshire." They passed Tulip Tree Housing, wound through the wooded area beyond, by the Conservatory. "Ever been to New Hampshire?"

She didn't want to seem some untraveled hick. "I've been to Chicago."

"I'd like to see Chicago. Maybe you can show me around." Would he want to see the undergound newspaper presses she visited when she was setting up her high school rag, or the SDS office at the University of Chicago, or the food co-op place where her sister used to shovel granola?

"I guess I could take you to the top of the John Hancock building, that's one of the world's tallest, and look over Lake Michigan."

"Play tourist, huh?" He pulled up in front of an apartment building just past the trees.

"I'm not much of a Chicago tourist. I'm a region rat."

"A *what?*"

"Calumet Region. Illinois state line to Gary." Merrillville residents liked to think they lived safely south of the 'rat' moniker but she liked the tough way it sounded.

"Clare the Red region rat." He stopped the engine and got out, reached to help her stand.

"We could see Marshall Field's Christmas windows."

"A revolutionary who likes Christmas? You're funny." He continued chatting as if they were friendly acquaintances instead of about-to-be lovers.

She stumbled on this thought, and on the curb, where he encircled her waist with a firm arm. Weren't they going to be lovers? Wasn't that why she was here with him? Shouldn't she tell him she was a virgin, like, right *now*?

Instead she blurted, "What did you like to read?"

"I'm a history fan." He gave her a little poke. "Unlike you, I enjoy studying."

"I read. Just not for class." Her voice sped up as he got closer. "I actually read a lot—"

"Shh."

"What?"

"I'm into readin *you* now." He spread his fingers through her hair, brought his mouth to hers, so fast she didn't have time to think much anymore.

His was the softest touch her lips had ever felt, sipping up, down, over, coaxing to slide his warm tongue into her mouth. This kiss was so much better than her first, with slobbery-bitey Bert Wilson back in Merrillville, she had to shut her eyes to savor it. He pulled her tight against him and she stroked, at last, his hair, coarser-feeling than it looked, slippery in her fingers. His hands skimmed down her back, following the seam of her jeans to curl underneath, tugging her into his heat and rubbing where she ached.

She dragged away.

"What's wrong, Red? I'm a good host."

"No."

"Would you feel more comfortable in your dorm room, baby?" He smoothed her hair with the fingertips of one hand, while the other ran firm up and down her spine, and the brightness of his eyes, staring into hers, outshone the faroff moon.

She tried to see past his beauty, gauging her chances of surviving a casual liaison.

"No."

"No?" He widened his eyes playfully. "You want me too, darlin, don't tell me no."

"Don't call me darling." She stepped out of his reach.

SEVEN

CAUTION QUICKLY narrowed his eyes and mouth, draining their warmth.

"I can't just—" She felt her face flaming, of course, and hung her head so hair obscured the crimson she knew was staining her cheeks even in the moonlight. "I can't just be some ... easy lay you'll forget about tomorrow. That'd *kill* me, Lowell."

"Now how'm I gonna see those Christmas windows if I forget about you tomorrow?" Although his comment was amused, his voice stayed aloof. "Let's walk awhile, okay?" He indicated the path. "I won't touch you." But when she started walking beside him, she was trembling and, with a shrug, he put his arm around her. "Keepin you warm, that's all."

They strolled. "What a moon," he remarked. "I didn't expect Indiana to be so pretty—I thought it would be flat. Virginia's like this in autumn too."

His renewed travelogue allowed her to speak. "I'm too into you to just want a one-night-stand, Lowell, you have to be careful with me—"

"I'm a gentleman, Clare," he interrupted. "I'm always careful." The hint of humor under his smooth voice was so light he might not have intended for her to hear it.

"Please don't make fun." She detached herself. "I need you to understand."

"I understand you want me to chase you longer. Is that how you like it? Sort of a ... game." His tone was conversational, but his face was in shadow and she could not read his expression. "I know every step and all the rules, hell, I prob'ly made up half of em, but I didn't think I'd have to play with you. I thought you were different. "

He thought she was a loose hippie chick. "But I don't just go with any old boy ... "

"I'm not any old boy, and so far, we're goin exactly nowhere, not where we both really want to go." His laugh was gently mocking. "Be honest."

"I'm not experienced at this ... game, you call it—"

"So play a little more, and if you still wanna quit, then I'll quit too." He stepped close to kiss her again. His mouth was so sure he connected at once to that rushing river inside, making her rise to him and hug tight so they locked as the kiss deepened.

He lifted his mouth then and stepped out of her grasp. "Quit?"

"N—not just yet."

He folded her against him, ratcheting up her excitement, but his kiss was soft this time and his tongue teased hers so gently she heard herself moan a little before he pulled back.

"Quit now, Clare?"

She shook her head and clung limply.

"C'mon. I don't live far."

"I don't know if I can walk," she exhaled. "My legs feel so weak—"

"I *knew* you were hot." He hugged her against his side.

"But only for you, Lowell, I don't want you to think—"

He wheeled her into him for another avid kiss, hard now with insistent hunger.

"Don't wonder what I *think*," he muttered afterward. "I'm into you too. Feel." He took her hand and slid it inside his leather jacket, pressed it flat against his thudding heartbeat under his warm shirt. She felt his pulse speed up when she rubbed her hand over his torso, beginning to explore. "Since I met you."

"I didn't think you noticed me," she said in a small voice.

"We noticed each other. Registration."

She nodded, thrilled by his acknowledgement.

"You're kinda shy, aren't you. But you kept lookin at me, so after our talk last week I decided to come get you. This dumb hayride turned up just in time."

At his apartment building he ran with her up a short stairway to the second floor, twisted a key into a door at the end of the quiet hallway.

His living room was large, in shades of blue and beige, with a sofa and two easy chairs grouped around a glass-topped coffee table and fireplace. The carpet was thick and soft. Plants hung precisely in the draped windows, books lined the shelves, big candles on the coffee table stood smooth in tall holders. The only vestige of student-hood was the music crooning from an FM radio station whose light bars flickered on a stereo system in the corner. When he raised the volume, Jethro Tull were singing "Reasons for Waiting," her favorite of their songs, as if on cue.

"No blacklight posters? No waterbed?" she quipped, trying to hide the tension stiffening her in this adult room.

"I outgrew all that a long time ago." He shrugged off his jacket and walked into a kitchen tucked half out of sight at the end of the room. "You like white wine or red?"

"White, I guess." She perched on the edge of the plush couch and buttoned her jean jacket all the way to her neck. Jethro Tull eased her, a little, as did Little Feat when they took over with "Sailin Shoes."

He brought in a tray with olives, cheese, crackers, and two glasses. He sat beside her, handed her the one with white wine and clicked it with his own red.

"Cheers, baby." His smile was relaxed and playful now, as if they shared the same knowledgeable anticipation. "I'm glad we finally got here."

Studying him this close felt like the most daring thing she'd ever done. She saw clearly, as he looked at her, what made his eyes so unusually bright: splinters of white fractured his dark grey irises. The wine was green-scented, icy, fortifying her smile.

He set his glass down with a conclusive little clink. "C'mere." His hand beckoned as he leaned into the cushions. She turned to him, unable to keep what she knew must be a scared look from crossing her face.

He lay back so his wavy hair spread, revealing a boyish cowlick springing awry onto his forehead. "C'mon, Clare, get next to me."

His eyes gleamed, half closed, as she edged near, propping one hand on the couch back and letting the other rest on top of his chest where his steady heartbeat felt safe. She examined his face, feeling free at last to really absorb: lip creases, beard stubble, long eyelashes, faint scar on his forehead she outlined with one fingertip. She leaned close and crunched a few bonfire-smelling strands of his shiny hair between her teeth. He shifted and she pressed him still.

She explored his mouth, copying the way he kissed, letting her tongue play with his. Then she sat up and spread hands over his geography, exploring his hard and soft contours, gently touching for the first time the hot ridge between his legs and feeling a rush of power as it jumped in her palm.

"Mmm."

She was so excited she couldn't tell whose sigh this was so she stroked him again, slow, watching his chest rise and fall, his brow wrinkle, and his eyes peel open fretfully. Then she kissed him over and over as long as she'd been wanting to since she first saw him, finally letting herself lie completely on top of him, arms wrapped around and face buried in the warmth of his neck. She hugged tight as his hands stroked her bottom and pulled her into him in a slow rock.

After some time of blissful embrace, while Crosby Stills and Nash, Janis and then Jimi wailed softly in the corner, he rolled her over and kneeled on the floor beside her as she lay flat on his couch. He unbuttoned her jacket and slid warm hands under her tee shirt to touch her so lightly, so slowly yet so thoroughly it felt like he had thirty fingertips.

"Your skin's so soft, Clare." He leaned to give her another long kiss, then moved his lips slowly along her chin and neck before lifting her shirt to suck each breast by turn. She was so busy absorbing new sensations, and clutching his hair, she couldn't keep track of his errant hand unzipping her jeans and pressing wide over her belly and further, inevitable as ripples following a stone thrown into a pool she'd only probed alone. His finger curled, tugging her into urgency. She could feel how slippery he was making her. *Too much!* She couldn't just ... explode at his first contact. She shot her modest hand under his.

He lifted his head from her breasts to send her an amused glance and, keeping his eyes on hers, he moved his mouth to her cupped hand which he pulled away. He flicked his tongue on her as accurately as her own finger when she did this, in a rythmic nudging, but her jeans were not low enough for her to thrust as freely as she felt madly, helplessly compelled to do, modesty forgotten as she started to pant.

He stopped as soon as she grabbed his head. "Want me to quit now, honey?"

"No," she choked out.

He licked his lips, slow, and smiled mischievously. "Let's get more comfortable. I want to see what I'm doin when I make you come so's I get it right all the next times." She felt her face burn as hot as her insides and half-shut her eyes. Was this how it was, having sex, were people this explicit? He drew the jacket from her arms, unrolled the tee shirt over her head, and slid her jeans and panties down so easily that a tiny observer, stuck deep in a corner of what was left of her mind, noted these actions were deft from long practice. She tried to suck in her stomach.

"I *knew* you'd be this lovely." His low admiring voice allowed her to relax and open her eyes to watch him peel off his shirt. His torso was strong and smooth-looking save for a cluster of dark curls trailing, narrow, from between his nipples into his jeans. He started to unzip his fly.

"I'm not ... protected."

"I've got it." He pulled her to stand, walked with her into a small bedroom. "Bathroom's there if you need it." He indicated a doorway in the corner. "Hurry back."

She dashed in to pee; splashed water onto her face and between her legs, not daring to look in the mirror. She took a huge gulping breath and finally found the courage to say, back in his bedroom, "Lowell. I've never."

"Never ... " He glanced over as he rummaged in the nightstand drawer. "You don't want me to use this?"

"Never had sex," she whispered.

His head shot up and the foil package he'd taken fell to the carpet. He dropped onto the side of the bed. She slid her hair over herself as she sat beside him.

"That's why you wanted to stop—" She sensed his stare burning the side of her face. "But then why ... " She felt his body rise in a long intake of breath and sink away as he exhaled. Moving her head, she saw him cross his arms. "I thought I read you right."

"You did." She leaned into his warm shoulder and snaked her arm around his supple-feeling waist. "I'm ready, Lowell. I choose *you*. I just need to know what to do."

"Why me, Clare? Why now?"

Suddenly she remembered Ginger's smutty challenge. She hoped Lee hadn't passed it on, in some vulgar barroom joke, to reach Lowell's ears. Would he talk about it if he'd heard?

She decided to just hug him tighter.

"I've never been with a girl who wasn't ... experienced—"

She pushed him flat onto the bed.

He pulled away to say, "I'm not into promises—" Funny how his accent disappeared. "But I know what I want. Are you *really* sure what you want with me?"

"Now who's thinking too much," she teased, bravely, because as soon as he spoke, her wishes, dreams, and fears sprang like Pandora's winged creatures to cruise the dim bedroom. She willed them away by crawling on top of him, kissing him over and over, and sliding around, pressing here and there, until he groaned. "Quit now, Lowell?" she whispered.

He rolled her to his side and she got lost in his hungry eyes. He leaned on an elbow and waved his free hand between them. "You help me learn you, and I'll help you learn me." His finger outlined her profile and lingered on her lower lip so she nipped it with greedy teeth. "You may not like to study, Clare, but I'm going to research every beautiful inch of you."

He pushed that finger deeper into her mouth, to circle her tongue, and shifted her so his other hand could stroke the length of her hair, grip her bottom and slide underneath, and inside, where she felt such a sweltering ache. He murmured hot into her ear, "I was wondering exactly how long your hair really was, how far down your back. But I knew you'd feel just like this, honey. So ... luscious and willing."

But his blandishments made her twist her head from his finger and let her observant little voice speak up. "What happened to your down-South accent?"

"Oh tha-yat." He disconnected and stood, to undo his jeans and send her a spirited grin. "Ah don' need it on you no mo, now do Ah, Sugar." Su-gah.

EIGHT

THE DELIGHTS of learning each other kept them awake until early morning.

A far-off ringing woke her, and Clare felt Lowell uncurling to get up and walk into the living room. She heard his low voice.

"I can't talk now." He laughed. "Sorry." Then, "I'll call you later."

Had to be a girl. Maybe Sylvie. At least he hadn't used his Southern. But here was another lesson, a painful one, because she was tingling all over from their endless night caresses and didn't want him parting from her to talk to some other girl. She huddled deep into the comforter he'd covered them with, feigning sleep, when he came back in.

His fingers peeled back locks of hair flung across her face and his lips pressed against hers. "Clare. I have to go, but I can make you breakfast, if you want to get up now."

"It's too early," she moaned, blinking at the sight of his tousled hair, beard-dark chin, sleepy eyes and kiss-swollen lips. She needed a taste. A gulp. All of him. "Come here, Lowell."

He rolled into her for another embrace. "My close friends call me Low."

"I like saying your whole name."

"Whatever you want." Slowly he disengaged and stood. "I've got work today. What do you like in your coffee? Or would you rather stay here and sleep some more?"

"I want to get up with you." She struggled out of bed. "I like cream, no sugar."

"No sugah, Sugah." He ran his hand down her back. "There's a robe on the bathroom door if you want to use it."

She wrapped it on, grey velour that smelled of him, and wandered into the living room. Last night's snack tray, which they'd revisited after the first lesson, was gone, and the table

42

clean. "You're really organized."

He came back with a pair of coffee mugs. "I've got to be, I'm so busy—" he stopped when he saw her, set the mugs down, put an arm around her. "What's wrong?"

"I'm okay." But her voice quavered.

His arm tightened. "But what."

It was a relief to heave the huge sigh keeping tears at bay. "I don't ... I don't know how I'm supposed to act now. I can't even remember who I am."

"You are smart, funny, sexy Red Clare." He kissed the top of her head. "The region rat minstrel."

"Why can't we just stay here together?"

"I wish we had more time too, honey, but I'm booked at the library."

She supposed she couldn't just leap on him, declaring her mad love, insisting they go back to bed. She sipped her coffee and tried to compose herself, to come up with some small talk, the kind he was so good at, putting people at ease. "Your place is really nice. I didn't know grad students lived like this."

"I was sick of dorms after prep school. Lived alone most of college."

"You live in a different world from me," she confided.

"You've had other kinds of adventures."

"Last night was my best adventure."

He raised his coffee mug in salute. "I'm honored to be the first, Clare, in what I know will be a long line of ardent admirers."

"I don't want a long line. I just want you."

He leaned to kiss her and she kept his mouth busy until he finally pulled away. "I really do have to go. My carrel's reserved."

"Okay." She tried to speak brightly.

"You want to shower first? Or come in with me?"

She shook her head. She didn't want to wash him away.

She dressed in her clothes from yesterday, surprised they still fit, as if she were the same girl. This was like landing on the moon without a spacesuit. Or like "The Wizard of Oz" where everything turned to Technicolor. What to do, what to say, how to bind him to her?

She studied his bookcases for clues. There were political and

43

philosophical titles, along with spy novels and chess guides and a stack of worn Marvel comic books. There was a board game called *Diplomacy* and a *Y Ching*; funny, he didn't seem the *Y Ching* type. It cracked with the newness of never-read as she opened it and a note fluttered out. "To the Superior Man – love, Karen." She replaced it, fast.

She picked up a framed photograph at the end of a shelf. A teenaged Lowell, helmeted and in uniform, sat astride a black horse on a playing field. The grass was as glistening as the people milling behind him. In one hand he hoisted a trophy cup, with the other he held a mallet across his knees. What a gulf, between her careful middle-class upbringing, and the aura of privilege reflected in this photo.

"That's Midnight." Lowell spoke behind her. Longing spiraled as she saw his wet curls, smooth-shaven cheeks, white fisherman's sweater.

"Mah horse," he clarified broadly, misreading her stare, grinning like the boy in the photo. "My team won at polo that day."

She'd never seen the game. "Croquet on horseback."

He laughed. "Yeah, sort of."

"Do you still play?"

"Not here. There's no time. And Midnight's back East." He glanced at his watch. "Want me to drop you at French House?"

She nodded sadly.

The morning was crisp and bright, perfect country drive weather: how they'd fly through autumn in his fast car, finding a secluded road, a hillside meadow to spread a blanket. He'd make a meandering, meticulously thorough, agonizingly slow picnic of her, just like last night, until she was stunned with heavy unfamiliar pleasure.

Too bad he'd rather go to the library. The Stones echoed her mood as they sang, dolefully, about comin' down again.

Too soon, he pulled up in front of the pink buildings. "La Maison Francais, Mademoiselle."

"Merci." She tried to sound as detached as he did.

"How can I find you later? D'you have plans tonight?"

Yay! "Well … dorm parties, I guess you can come along—"

His grin dismissed dorm parties. "I'd rather take you to

dinner. Eight? I'll call you."

She got out, shut the door, and turned to say something more through the open window, something foolish about being glad to have met him, but he was gone. She stood on the pavement and watched his car vanish around the corner.

The empty lounge looked as strange as if she'd never seen it before. She was rarely up this early on a weekend. And her room, upstairs, was bleak compared to his place; her lumpy bed a cold solo mess. "Too much." A sob rose and died in her throat as she buried her face in her pillow, not even trying to identify her churning emotions. She slept.

At noon there was a pounding on her door. "Meredith, if you're in there, it's lunchtime!" Clare opened the door to Ginger, who seemed to spring in, holding a joint that she lit up immediately.

"So tell me!You stayed at his place, right, didja *do* it?"

Clare blinked.

"You look like you're so in loooove."

It was not cool to be in love. A lover was one's old man, and you were together until you weren't on the same wavelength anymore, and then you parted. No hassle. Getting hung up was unhip. "I don't know."

"Well, you win! Far out. But I don't have your nickel bag prize." Ginger passed the jay. "How was he?"

Clare let smoke dissipate in a twirl on the ceiling, unable to describe her yearning.

"That good, huh?" Ginger grinned. "So … was it just a one-night-stand?"

"He's taking me to dinner." Saying this out loud confirmed it was real, didn't it? She wasn't sure of anything except need: skin and nerve and fiber. She sucked in a toke.

Ginger's hug startled her. "I give up. I know you really dig him."

Clare felt good in the cafeteria with her friends around the table, seeing the sunlight streaming through the big windows on her fellows: Saturday leisure noisily apparent, long hair springy, faces lit in lively rapport with one another, wholesome in their jeans and workshirts. She'd never felt so fond of them. She'd never seen the beauty in this ordinary cafeteria.

45

At the same time she was seeing Lowell bent over his books, black hair falling, an intent frown on his wonderful face. He must be thinking of her right now, too, so his eyes were lifting to gaze dreamily out the library window, and his long lips were rising in an amorous smile ...

Ginger interrupted her with a bowl of chocolate ice cream. Clare pushed it away. She hadn't been able to swallow more than a couple of bites of her grilled cheese. She turned to Jenny. "Let's go for a country drive!"

So they piled into Jenny's car, wound around the meandering hills, howling with laughter at nothing and sharing a bottle of very cheap brandy. She could only have been happier if he were beside her. When she thought of last night, and the night ahead, she lost her breath.

Back in the dorm, the girls' floor phone was ringing. Clare ran to answer.

"Hey Clare, this is Lowell." His lazy voice pulled her tight. "I forgot, there's a party at my thesis advisor's house tonight—lots of Poli Sci people—okay with you if we skip dinner?"

He was breaking their date—bored with her already!

Or maybe it *was* the stupid bet, and now they were even, and now he'd try Ginger.

"It's kinda formal, so we have to dress up, if you want to come with me. The party's around eight thirty. I can get you after I go home and grab a nap."

"You're still at the library?"

He laughed. "*Some* of us work here."

She filled their sudden little silence, boldly, speaking low and quick into the big black receiver. "Lowell. I've been feeling you, all over me, all day, I am just ... *aching*."

His exhalation was a thrilling echo of his night-time melodic sighs. She clutched the phone and felt moisture collecting in her mouth, over her skin, between her legs.

He finally spoke. "Me too. So ... soon."

Ginger peered out of her doorway. "Lover boy?"

"I'm supposed to get dressed up. We're going to a professor's house."

"What a drag!"

"Will you help me?"

46

Ginger knew clothes and makeup, even in these days of faded, torn garb and bare faces. While Clare showered Ginger found Clare's only dress, packed by her mother, a rose-colored shift that skimmed her breasts and hips. Ginger twisted Clare's hair up, with tendrils curling by her face, and added touches of makeup. She lent Clare gold hoop clip-on earrings and a pair of black heels. Clare had not worn hose since seventh grade.

"Funny, doing this for some *guy*," she joked, borrowing Ginger's electric shaver.

"Not for some guy, for *you*, so you look the way you want to right now."

They trooped into the bathroom to admire, in the full-length mirror, the glowing young woman there. Ginger nodded in satisfaction.

They heard a male voice outside calling Clare's name. "There he is. Go—Miss Foxy." Ginger pushed her out.

47

NINE

LOWELL WAS standing in the hall, and when he turned she savored seeing his expression blur, for a few seconds, with the heady stupor she'd been wandering in all day.

Kissing was like drinking after a long thirst. She hung against him while he squeezed. When he finally let go she tried to act cool. "Don't you want to see my room?" She nodded toward her door, still covered with its Orientation cartoon, a goofy chipmunk holding a balloon saying "Je suis Clare."

"If we went in there now we'd never leave."

The professor's house was on a hill lined with cars. Lights blazed in the windows and laughter sounded from the open front door. Clare felt suddenly nervous, and wanted to say she changed her mind about the party, but Lowell was already waving at someone on the path.

Once inside, he said he'd get drinks, and she watched him cross the room.

He shone. Not only for her.

His charisma was in his walk, in his manner as he listened attentively when stopped by a number of people, in his voice with its tone of Virginia blue blood, even in his sleek black blazer and light blue shirt. She ran her thumbnail along her teeth, seeking out its rough places, but yanked it down when he came back with two glasses of wine.

He handed her the white. "Let's mingle awhile and then we can go."

They joined the loudest group, who were arguing about the '72 Presidential election six weeks away, and—of course—about Vietnam. Clare recognized Steve Henderson from the SMC, and remembered he was a Poli Sci major. Lowell called him less than a bright light. She didn't know Steve well enough to know any better, even though he was her cell captain.

48

"—to make our *voices* heard because the system makes our *choices* for us. That's why a total boycott of this so-called election will make more of a statement than so-called voting. Democracy has been co-opted in this country, so we *have* to be subversive, the only real role open to us is total subversion—"

"—that's where you are so wrong-headed!" One of the Young Democrats—Clare forgot his name, they'd been hounding the SMC at every meeting—tried to shout Steve down. His voice was hoarse and desperate. "You're just handing this election to Nixon if you don't participate in the democratic process—"

"What *process*?" Steve laughed. "You're duped! It's pathetic."

"You might wanna let him finish his sentence, Steve, let us all hear him out." Lowell's voice was so mild in pitch that both combatants leaned toward him to hear. "You need to understand the system in order to manipulate it. If you ignore it, it'll roll over you. And my guess is you're already feelin kinda rolled."

Steve eyed him. "We're not dead yet, man."

Lowell turned to Clare. "The courthouse busts must've brought you down."

"We're regrouping." She couldn't tell him about their plan for the naval weapons depot; the core cell was sworn to secrecy.

Steve, recognizing her, nodded. "There's a groundswell of resistance we're just beginning to tap," he said. "The people here are realizing what's in it for them, to show strength in numbers, to personally contemplate civil disobedience—"

"Or *un*civil," Lowell inserted, with so charming a smile that the group laughed.

"It's not too late to get out the vote on this campus, if we work together," the Young Democrat said ardently. "A vindication of the decision to let eighteen-year-olds vote!"

"They might elect the mayor here in town. That'd be a fine grassroots start," Lowell told him.

"You don't think we can elect McGovern?"

Lowell patted the Young Democrat's shoulder. "I'm not one for tellin fortunes." He nodded across the circle. "I'll leave that to you, Steve, and the SMC, y'all got surefire predictions." He took a sip of wine.

A white-haired man approached. Lowell said, "Clare, meet

49

our host, my Department Head and thesis advisor. Dr. Simmons, Clare Meredith."

Simmons smiled. "Let me borrow your date for a moment's thesis discussion, Miss Meredith, thanks." He led Lowell away. "I read your latest chapter. I think, with a bit of editorial guidance, it might work as a submission to *Foreign Affairs* ... "

She watched them walk off. Lowell was so at home in this setting. A tickle of uneasiness made her feel she was not, in spite of knowing Steve and the Young Democrat, who were now deep in the kind of dialogue Clare did not need to revisit. She wandered to the little bar area, where she'd seen another familiar face; one of the bartenders was in her Anthro class. He said hello and refilled her glass.

"Who's that fine Mrs. Robinson?" she heard him ask the bartender next to him.

"Simmons' guest, visiting prof from France," said the other guy. "She's helpin direct traffic tonight, so watch what you're doin with the booze. Nice piece, eh?"

Clare saw a sleek blond woman in black come from the kitchen, followed by a trio of boys bearing trays, whom she pointed toward different parts of the expansive first floor. She looked over the setting like a queen. Suddenly her face lit with pleasure and she strode swiftly across the room, toward Simmons and Lowell.

The woman embraced Lowell in the French manner, kissing both cheeks. Clare watched his eyes and smile widen, watched his hand stay on her waist as they chatted a few moments, and slide down to pat her bottom as she moved away.

So *this* was the competition. She slumped against the wall and stared at her glass. Its yellow liquid tilted until her helpful Anthro classmate reached over to lift and top it off for her. How many women was Lowell seeing? How convenient for him, when he attached himself to the Language Units hayride, to have Clare so willing.

Just last night! His practiced voice! "I'm into you too. Feel," pressing her hand to his heartbeat. "I knew you were hot." Hot now, certainly—hot with shame. Sudden nausea made her set the glass down on the edge of the bar. The Anthro guy grabbed it just before it fell.

"You okay there?"

She lifted her eyelids, with effort, to meet his eyes. "I need a washroom."

He pointed. She was grateful to find the bathroom empty. She dashed inside, thinking she would be sick, but brought up nothing. She'd barely eaten today. The woozy feeling subsided as she ran cold water over her hands, brought them to press against her flushed cheeks, and on top of her feverish-looking eyelids.

After a moment she took a deep breath, frowned at herself. It was still hard to know what she really looked like. But right now, she saw she was easily the equal of any pretty girl, if she erased the shocked look in her eyes. She blinked a couple of times and practiced a smooth, flirtatious smile.

She went back to the bar table and asked Anthro for more wine.

"Sure you're okay to keep drinking?"

She used her new smile. "I'm not drunk, I just had a nasty surprise. My boyfriend's other girlfriend is here."

"Bummer." He flashed a come-on grin. "You need a new boyfriend."

"You may be right."

At the buffet table, suddenly ravenous, she collected a plate of shrimp and ham rolls and tiny quiches. She found a place to eat and drink at the end of a long couch, letting the party swell around her, finishing her wine. Just as she was about to bat her eyelashes toward the bar, to see if Anthro would notice she needed a refill, Lowell walked around the corner.

"Sorry I left you, Clare. He needed to bend my ear. You ready to go?"

"Go where? This is a nice party. I was just going to have some more wine." She held her glass up and tried her eyelash-batting on him. "Please?"

His eyes narrowed slightly as he studied her a moment. "Sure."

She watched him stroll away. Last night she'd been in command of his every move, as his touch and gaze and whisper asked, "Does this feel good? Show me." His certainty ensured her entranced acceptance. But now his confidence underscored the vast distance between them. She ached for last night.

51

"I figured you'd still be deep in the rev-o-lu-tion over there with Henderson." He sat beside her and held out a fresh glass. She didn't take it.

"I saw you with her."

"Who?"

She jerked her head in the direction of the striking woman who, she realized, had a chignon much smoother than her own, as fashioned by Ginger. Clare reached up, pulled out the pins, and let them fall to the polished wood floor. Her comforting hair hid her face again.

"Aimee." He turned back. "She's with the IU Paris program, but she's here this semester, teaching modern French political movements for the Poli Sci department. You should sit in on her class sometime, Clare. She's as radical as you are."

"You're very ... familiar with each other."

"We got together in Paris, yeah, but her husband's here, so we haven't really kept in touch since she arrived."

Her hands knotted in her lap. "Did she get married since you were ... together?"

"She was married then." He set her glass down. "I just came for Simmons, so I'm ready to go if you are. We can still get dinner."

Sitting stiff in some restaurant seemed way too formal for the conversation she needed with him. "Let's go for a drive instead."

"Whatever you want."

They drove through the woods outside Bloomington. He put on The Moody Blues. The lush strains of "Nights in White Satin" filled the space inside the dark car and seemed to spill onto the moonlit trunks they passed. Clare shivered, struck by the beauty and by the strangeness of the evening. It should have been a relief to be alone with him at last, but: *he's too old for me, too sophisticated, too rich, he sleeps with older married women, he's leaving too soon ... and I'm too far-gone stoned in love to care.*

"How did you get involved with ... Amy." She didn't even like saying the name.

"She came on to me, she's good-lookin, I figured she was a main chance for cultural immmersion." His smirk told her he was only partly kidding.

"So you … used her."

"We used each other."

"And you knew she was married—"

He shot her an amused glance. "I think sex should be enjoyed without rules."

So glib, yet so certain. Lots of people felt this way: free love. If it feels good, do it. Love the one you're with. Change partners. But she couldn't stand him having sex with anyone else, not now. "Maybe this isn't right for me." She heard the hesitancy in her voice and tried to will it away. "Maybe it's … all wrong?"

"Too late."

"What?"

"You should have decided that last night, when I asked if you were sure."

He was right. She'd had a chance to back away, but now their night was emblazoned on her, impossible to undo. "So marriage, to you, isn't important? You don't respect it?"

"I'm a cynic," he said lightly. "My mother had an affair with the Argentine trade commissioner ten years ago. She lives in Buenos Aires now. My dad's been the target of every socialite in D.C. They don't care about *him*—they care about his money and real estate. Marriage is just one of society's order-preserving institutions, like religion, don't you agree?"

Imagine having your mother take off when you were, what, twelve; she didn't know exactly how old he was. "It must have been hard on you when your mother left. Didn't you want to go to Argentina with her?"

"I was already at St. Paul's."

"How often do you see her?"

"As little as possible."

Cold! "So … you won't get married."

"Sure I will. Wives are useful in the Foreign Service. Marriage is considered a sign of stability." His laugh belittled the idea.

She stared out the window.

"C'mon, Clare, Engels debunked the whole marriage and family thing as simple division of labor. Just a wealth-preservation scheme." He added, clearly mocking, "You call yourself a revo*lu*tionary, you're into Nechayev, you *dig* that, right?"

"I'm in love with *you*, not with Nechayev," she snapped, then clapped hands over her mouth. Jesus Clare, *terminally* unhip! she exclaimed to herself.

He kept quiet, eyes on the curvy road.

She flipped tapes in the console, found Cat Stevens. "Moonshadow" described, perfectly, the loveliness of the woods looming from either side of the winding highway, the way the headlights splashed autumn color into brightness. *I wish I'd lose my mouth, or at least find a way to keep it shut around you.* But she couldn't.

"Lowell."

"Mademoiselle."

"How many girls—women—are you seeing right now?"

"One. You."

"What about Sylvie?"

"Who?" After a second's frown he shook his head. "She asked me out a couple times. I told her I'm not interested."

"So ... " What conclusion would ease this anxiety?

"Let me ask *you* something, Clare. Are you going to give us a chance to enjoy each other, explore what we started, have some fun?"

"But how do you *feel* about me?"

He laughed. "Want me to pull over and show you?"

"Tell me."

"I'm ... flattered you care about my opinion," he said, measured, still not looking at her. "But in my experience, early declarations are ... unwise."

"So you think, what I said, about being in love, you think that's just—"

"Moonshadow" ended. He reached to pluck Cat Stevens from the tape deck, glanced down in a hasty review, and pushed in the Stones' "Sticky Fingers."

"I think that kind of talk is just a reaction to your first time," he said finally, so quietly she barely heard him over the opening chords, struck like blows, of "Brown Sugar."

TEN

BACK IN his bed they exchanged only heated murmurs as, all night long, their exploration progressed. Toward dawn they slept curled together, damp and exhausted. She felt completely part of him and believed, from his focus, that he felt the same, that his body's declaration was truer and more binding than any words could possibly be.

The next day was rainy and, after picking up some of Clare's books and a change of clothes at her dorm, they stayed at his place. It was a slow afternoon of pleasure, of foraging in his refrigerator, of belated desultory studying. The gloomy weather was offset by the warmth of lit lamps and fire indoors. When the windows grew dark she watched him highlight his book. *I want to be here with you forever.* He looked up as if he heard this.

"Gettin late, huh." The grey in his eyes seemed to mist over when he fixed on her and his eyebrows drew together in a perplexed black line. He blinked and shut his book. "I guess I should take you back."

Outside French House, he switched off the ignition and turned to her. "How about next weekend, Clare? We can go out, or I'll cook. Stay with me again."

She flung her arms around him and squeezed, hard.

He drew back a little, beginning to laugh, but she stopped his mouth with hers, fervently, so he deepened the kiss, searching, heating her again. He paused to stroke her cheek and run his thumb over her lips. She bit, and he let out a whoosh of breath.

"Clare." His laugh was unsteady. "Tomorrow, you free?"

She nodded.

"Okay then." He got out and took her to the door. "I won't come in with you now. But tomorrow."

SHE WENT to the campus clinic to get on the Pill. They saw each

55

other several times a week, when Lowell was free and Clare got off work at the library or out of her SMC meetings. After a couple of tumbled sessions in her dorm room they met at his apartment: "I don't appreciate Mr. Dylan and Mr. Guevara breathin down my neck," Lowell joked, of her posters.

He taught her to play chess and savor bourbon. She helped him perfect his pool game, at the student union, and filled in his gaps on old Mother Russia and Marx's dialectic. They drove into the flame-colored fall hillsides and hiked in the woods, often stopping for the succulent picnics of each other Clare had envisioned their first morning together. He took her to see Firesign Theater, and The Grateful Dead, when they came to Indianapolis. She took him to see Yevtushenko when the poet spoke on campus.

At the Language Units variety show, he sat with Lee and Jenny in the front row, and yelled "Brava!" at the end of hers and Ginger's set. He presented them with two bouquets: pink roses for Clare and yellow daisies for Ginger.

Clare attended only critical classes, studying just enough to get by, daydreaming when she was not with him: exuberant romantic fantasies that always culminated in his declaring that she *must* come with him to Senegal.

But although their sexual journey deepened with each meeting, and in spite of his use of droll endearments—he came up with 'sweet pea' and 'dollface' as well as his occasional 'sugah'—he never spoke of romance or of their relationship. They argued instead, often and animatedly, about history, about current events, even about Dylan lyrics and especially about what he, archly, continued to call "your revo-*lu*-tion."

"So what's the next step for the mighty SMC, Red?" he asked one Sunday afternoon. Of course they were in bed. Sunday was their time of luxurious ease.

"Some of us are going to D.C. to protest after Election Day."

"Even if McGovern wins? Heavy, Clare, way to back The Man against the wall."

"Not funny. You know he doesn't stand a chance."

"I'm sure *your* vote'll put him right over the top. Yours and that Young Democrat's. Victory is all but assured on the way to the dialectic."

She couldn't admit she'd still be too young to vote in November. "Stop teasing."

"Don't get mad at *me*, babe, I'm just the messenger."

She was tempted to tell him about the next local SMC step toward the Revolution, their action on the depot, to get his opinion on its potential impact, but she'd been sworn to absolute secrecy. It made her feel uneasy to keep something so important from him, as it made her skin prickle when any discussion approached her real age. She let him assume she was a sophomore like Ginger, and made vague comments when he talked about classes or professors he assumed she'd know. But these small omissions couldn't matter, now they were so tight; she knew their love was strong enough to withstand the truth if she ever decided to reveal it.

Throughout these weeks she lost more weight, living on coffee and wine and the occasional dorm meal after a joint shared with friends. The simple dinners Lowell cooked for them usually went uneaten until hours passed. Relishing her new ethereal look, she enlisted Jenny and Ginger to take her shopping, and spent a whole paycheck on two long paisley skirts, a gold velvet jacket, and a pair of delicate maroon suede boots, thinking of how he'd admire, briefly, the colors and fabrics before he took everything off.

"I thought you were against male domination, Clare," Jenny teased, twitching the edge of the jacket. "But all you ever talk about anymore is Low."

"Aw, leave the kid alone, she's in love for the first time." Ginger's defense made Clare smile. "Let her enjoy it if it makes her happy."

"Listen to the *luv* guru," Jenny said in a hippie voice. She poked Ginger. "Luv guru added *how* many to her list so far on campus?" The list was legendary now in the Language Units and, they suspected, far beyond.

"I speak from wisdom, my children," Ginger intoned. "Many profound experiences."

Jenny gave Clare an old ID so she could go to the bars with Lowell, Ginger helped her pick out makeup and a particular vanilla-scented shampoo, and Lee indulged her passion for information by recounting what he remembered about Lowell in Paris.

"We kidded he was CIA," he told her one afternoon when neither had class. "He didn't hang out much with the rest of us. He used to spend time with a French family, friends of his dad's, he said. He spoke French all the time."

Clare suspected the "family" was Aimee.

"He's had lots of girlfriends, the two years I've known him," Lee went on. "But never for very long. And none as unusual as you, Clare."

"You mean a pinko peacenik. Thanks, Lee." She smiled at him anyway. "Sometimes I feel sort of insecure because he's so ... sophisticated—"

"He seems to be very attentive to you right now. Don't worry about his playboy past. I never knew him to be a jerk."

She had to laugh at this faint praise.

Sometimes they ran into each other on campus and walked awhile holding hands, letting her feel blissfully coupled for the first time ever. She enjoyed the considering glances of other girls although she knew this was shallow. One afternoon she waited to surprise Lowell after the senior Poli Sci class for which he was the Teaching Assistant. She felt a little self-conscious as the group of older students left the classroom and went past her in the hallway. Lowell finally came out with a beautiful girl who, of course, was laughing up at him.

But at the sight of Clare, his eyes widened as if he were waking up. She lifted her chin, smiling a little, feeling heady self-assurance. The girl, after a glance at Clare, left them in the deserted hallway.

Clare plunged one hand into his hair and massaged his head the way he liked. Then she led him out of the building and down a tiny alleyway where a tall limestone wall and overhanging, fading autumn trees hid them from passersby. She shoved him into the wall to kiss him, excited by her dominance, but he gripped her in such a vigorous hug she lost her breath. He swiftly undid layers between them, cupped her under her coat to swing her against the wall, and thrust until their rhythm caught fire. She was so aroused it took her only seconds. She clung, sobbing into his neck, as sensation flared raggedly though her.

Afterward they leaned together, panting, gazes locked.

Somewhere nearby a boy was singing about knockin on heaven's door. His voice grew stronger as he passed through the trees a few yards away.

Lowell swayed slightly, singing along in a whispery undertone, telling mama to put his guns undaground since he couldn't shoot them anymo'.

Then he lifted a piece of Clare's hair and rubbed it between his fingers. Kissed it. She took his face in her hands and tried to telepath some kind of sacred message words could not convey. He gazed back, eyes unguarded pools, humming a little as the boy's voice receded. She felt his fingers tremble as he wiped the tear streaking down her cheek.

But after they stumbled away to fortify themselves at the Student Union coffee shop, she could tell, by the way he hid behind an uncharacteristic cigarette, he was backing off from the emotion of their alleyway moment. She clanked the spoon in her coffee with sad stabs as elation and certainty evaporated. *Who am I kidding. There's no holding this love, no way of getting him to acknowledge it, no way to ensure it lasts.* He looked remote, feelings concealed behind his perfect features. *Let me in!*

Lowell caught her glance. "Whatever it is, I don't think I want to hear it," he said calmly. "I don't fight."

"What do you do?"

He let smoke wind up between them. "I split."

"Is that always so easy?"

"So far, yeah."

"Then go ahead," she muttered. She dabbed her eyes with a Kleenex, lit one of his cigarettes, feigned interest in the glassed-in bowling alley.

"You don't mean that." He reached across the booth to take her hand. "We just had a great fu—a great time, why are you playing this game?"

"What are you *talking* about?"

"Tears. Getting mad. Playing cool." He sighed. "Clare, what we have is so simple. So good. Let's keep it like this."

"I agree!"

"Then what's wrong?"

But how could she make him understand when she barely

59

understood? "I just—I want you *so much*. I can't think of anything else, I can't eat, I can't sleep, I can't concentrate—" she closed her eyes to shutter their pleading. "But you're so beyond me, so far away—"

He slid out from his bench to sit beside her. "I'm not far away."

He pulled her close to mutter into her ear. "And I want you all the time too, Sugah. I'd have you again right now if we weren't in front of the entire union." His hair, uncut in the six weeks they'd been together, tickled her neck. She leaned away to look at him, thinking he was deliberately avoiding her meaning, but losing her will to argue with the hot-metal of his eyes and the insistent pressure of his closeness. *At least I'm sure of him when he's inside me,* she thought just before he kissed her.

ELEVEN

A FEW nights later she was taking a break at the library cafeteria. She'd been there since six and it was now ten, and she was so tired she was moving in slow motion. She was trying to put in overtime during the week, since she'd almost stopped working on weekends. The final stages of the SMC action were underway, which meant extra cell meetings, and she was even cutting those short to be free for Lowell.

The library job felt tedious now, as much of her time did, away from him. She no longer scanned eccentrically titled books, learning odd bits about all sorts of things, musing over so many wonderful words. Now she raced through the stacking impatiently.

It was better than working in the cafeteria, she supposed, watching the cashier yawn as he totaled up her yogurt and tea. She took her tray to a corner table hidden behind some plants because she didn't want to make conversation with anyone—her head was pounding, her throat hurt, and she hadn't washed her hair in a couple of days. She'd get through the next two hours and then collapse into bed.

A noisy group arrived to sit at a table beyond the plantings, and when Clare recognized Lowell's voice a current of agonized yearning shot through her, taking her by surprise. If this was love why did it feel so desperate? She wanted to rush over and fall into his arms, but she probably looked like a zombie and anyway, it must be a study group; she heard them discussing whose notes were most complete and when their next meeting would be. Then their talk turned idle, interspersed with laughter.

She heard Lowell's warm chuckle and peered through the ferns to watch him. His back was to her. The girl next to him, a long-haired girl with a ravishing profile, had her arm draped on his chair back. She seemed to be telling a series of jokes—Clare couldn't hear her low voice clearly—because after nearly everything she said the group chortled. And the girl did too, throwing back her streaky blonde hair and running a red-nailed hand through it as gold bracelets chimed up and down her wrist.

Resentment and envy swamped Clare. Who the fuck was that girl, putting her hands all over Lowell and making him laugh? *I don't do that enough. I'm too in love to be amusing. No wonder he's paying attention to someone else. Obviously she's more fun.*

And a lot better-looking. Clare glanced down at her bare, bitten nails and raggedy jeans. She never wore jewelry, had only just started using a minimum of makeup, paid no attention to styling her hair. She was not heavy anymore, but she'd never be a sleek stunning knockout like the blonde handling Lowell right now.

How could she possibly keep him, when he was always surrounded by flirting girls? They *flocked* to him.

This excluded-feeling pang was familiar from the worst days of high school.

Suddenly the sight of yogurt made her sick. She'd go back and get a slice of that rich, gooey-looking chocolate cake. It seemed the millionth time she'd resisted, way too often in the last six months, dammit, she deserved one fucking piece of chocolate cake. *With vanilla ice cream. And a bottle of Coke.* She pushed her tray away and waited for Lowell's group to leave so she could go back to the line without them seeing.

Maybe she'd just eat some M&Ms from the vending machines instead—she got up and went to the little alcove where the machines and telephones were. She stood, debating whether to get Peanut or Plain, when arms squeezed from behind her. She whipped around to see Lowell smiling as he ran his hands down her body.

"Hey dollface. I saw you sneakin back here." He reached in his pocket and picked through change. "Your candy's my treat. Big spender."

"I'm working. My break's over." She did not keep the bitchy note from her voice. "You can go back to that girl you were with."

"Girl?" He pulled the lever to drop a dark Hershey bar onto the tray. He knew her favorite. "I'm with people from Statistics."

"You had your arms around each other."

He stopped unwrapping the chocolate. "You're wrong. Debi's friendly, but that's her. Not me." His eyes held an unfamiliar icy glaze. "I'm with *you*, Clare. And if I want to be with someone else, I'll *tell* you first. As you should tell me, if you dig some other guy."

"But she's obviously so into you—"

"But I'm not an asshole. I wouldn't cheat on you. Don't you know that?"

She bit her lip to keep it from trembling.

"Let's talk. Then you can get back to work." He went with her to the corner table, waving at his group over the plantings. "Listen. Maybe we shouldn't see so much of each other. No, don't give me that look, it's not because of Debi." His short laugh chilled her further. "I think you're taking our—thing—too seriously."

"That's no reason to stop seeing each other—"

"Yeah, if it's making you miserable. Paranoid if you see some girl near me. Sad I don't feel the way you do—"

"Why are you with me?"

Caution tightened his features.

She leaned forward and repeated in an urgent whisper, "I mean it, Lowell, just why are you with me when you could have anybody else?"

"You're more interesting than anybody else. But I don't like this ... possessive attitude. You want to lock us into some—" He drew a boxlike shape between them. "Why aren't you satisfied with what we have? Why isn't this enough?"

"How can I make it last?" Tears burned her eyes and she knuckled them away.

"We're here *now*." His exasperated tone just maddened her. "Why future-trip—"

"We don't have a future. You're *leaving!*"

"You always knew that." The ice, in his voice now, implied: *don't get in my way.*

A sudden survivor's instinct made her stand. "I've got to get back to work," she said, putting all the cool she could muster into her tone. "Sorry about my mood, Lowell, I'm just tired. I think I'm coming down with a cold."

"You do look wiped out," he murmured. "Maybe you should knock off work for now."

"I can't, not til midnight." She smiled at him and patted his shoulder briskly. "See you tomorrow in French."

She left him and walked, head high, past his study group. Debi eyed her and twisted around to see where Lowell was. Clare didn't look back.

TWELVE

IN HER section she worked mechanically, glad of the mental and physical effort it took to manipulate the long cart through the stacks and find the right locations for the books, glad that in the impersonal library hush she could not give in to her impulse to throw herself on the floor and wail louder than a fire alarm. Wail and scream and gnash her teeth and rend her flannel shirt.

But goddammit, why did this *have* to feel like the end of the world?

College was supposed to be the place for her activism to solidify, at least that's what she'd planned, when she decided to accept the tuition break the Linguistics Department came up with for her last spring. Until then she'd been ambivalent about college since she truly didn't like to study. But she'd figured, finally, it would be an arena to deepen her political experience; an arena more challenging than volunteering for McGovern's campaign, or throwing in her lot with the underground *Rising Up Angry* or *Seed* crowd in Chicago, sleeping on random floors and selling newspapers on the street with unknown hippies. She didn't have enough cred to get a living-wage job in the Movement.

And so here she was, at college, supposedly to hone her organizing skills.

Ha!

The ladder of SMC politics was shaky for girls, certainly, but she hadn't even *tried* to climb since falling in love.

She hadn't yet picked up the extra carpet samples they'd use to throw over the barbed wire surrounding the depot, and that was her only job on the action planned for November, an easy job, neglected for two weeks already, when all she had to do was borrow Jenny's car and drive to the rug warehouse.

He made her forget fucking *everything*!

She sniffed fiercely, swiped her sleeve across her leaking eyes, and shoved the cart around a corner.

But fine. They'd break up. If the SMC didn't distract her from him, she could try to actually get into her classes. She'd ignore him in French and concentrate on the subject. Her grades were the worst ever: her mind had melted as soon as he first smiled at her.

Was she really just some conformist chick hypnotized by sex with a handsome guy? Mesmerized into craving his strokes on her quivering body, his every leisurely kiss and lick and suck and nibble and—but the *hell* with him! Let stupid Debi have him! Let her clattery bracelets snag his hair and her horrible nail polish leave streaks on his light blue couch.

She yanked the cart so hard a big book thudded to the floor. She kicked it viciously under the stack, then, guilt-struck, swooped to retrieve it so another worker wouldn't have to.

Halfway through her fourth cart, she realized the floor was deserted. The lights blinked, signaling closing time. She hurried to the service elevator, descended, stored her cart and punched out her time card in the employees' lounge.

She came out of the building, pulling on her gloves, and ran straight into Lowell. Joy and fury and a terrifying hopeless surrender flooded her when she saw his casual smile. She'd never be free of this love. *Never.*

"I'll give you a ride, Clare, okay? You shouldn't be walking alone at midnight." They walked to his car, parked under trees in the furthest space. As they got in, the lights in the library went out, and they sat for a moment looking over the quiet campus spread onto the hills below.

"Let me pick you up when you work late," he said, starting the car.

"But I thought we're seeing *less* of each other." She made her voice sarcastic.

"Well—how bout I don't *look* at you, Sugah."

"Okay—I won't look either—I'll just—" She leaned over, switched off the ignition, unbuttoned his peacoat, unzipped his jean fly and reached in to caress him. He laughed softly as she bent to take him in her mouth. His fingers twisted in her hair.

She'd learned exactly how to make him writhe with

pleasure—and now this feeling of control felt like conquest since he was hers completely when he came, sighing. His essence tasted sweet. How about if she just held him down forever with her mouth? No more breakup talk would be possible. Another image came, strange, a baby growing from her lips like a Peter Max flower, seeded by their love. Real love, despite his reluctance to name it.

"Clare." His breathing slowed. "You drive me crazy." He lifted her into a tight hug. "I can't stop seeing you, sweetheart."

What relief to hear his bewilderment. "Scare me like that again and I'll *bite* you."

"No you won't," he whispered hot into her ear. His tongue darted, making her shiver, as he pressed under her denim skirt to ease agile fingers inside. "You don't have to go to your dorm, do you? You can sleep at my place."

They didn't sleep, of course, until much later. Some time in the night she woke alone, throat burning, head aching. She went into the living room where Lowell was at his desk typewriter, surrounded by books, draped in the black Moroccan dress he wore since she had taken his bathrobe. She had a sensation of great distance as she watched him. *This is his real life. I'll never be more than just a passing distraction.*

As soon as this thought crossed her mind, she rejected it, and he looked up as if he heard her heart increase its determined beat.

"Did the light wake you?" He stood and took her in his arms. "Mmm. You're so warm." He kissed her, slid his hands under her robe, then drew back and looked in her eyes. "Too warm, honey, this feels like fever."

She sank onto the couch and closed her eyes. "D'you have some aspirin?"

"Sure." She heard him rummaging in the kitchen and returning. "Drink this."

"What *is* it?" She spluttered after one burning swallow.

"Whisky sour. Old family fever recipe."

"What are you working on?"

"A sample position paper on our oil policy with Saudi Arabia."

"Saudi Arabia." Whiskey sour made its boot shape waver on

the map in her mind as he pulled the throw around her and sat close. "What's your position?"

"I'm recommending King Faisal cut a better deal. In return, we give him increased access to advanced technology, by facilitating joint ventures in the private sector."

"You wily politicians, always trying to manipulate the markets."

"It's called *bilateral trade*." He grinned. "Not manipulation."

"Always in bed with big business." She closed her eyes again and curled under the throw.

She heard him chuckle. "Rather be in bed with you, Sugah."

"C'mere." She scooted to let him slide behind her and reached to bring him inside, slowly pushing back with languid rolls, ratcheting her feverish feeling until they combusted together.

She awoke hours later, hearing a key in the lock, blinking against the light.

"Feeling better?" Lowell asked, dropping his books onto the phone stand. He came over to push the hair from her eyes. "You're still sick."

"We've got French today, right?"

"*Merde.*" He continued in French, "Take a nap."

The rest of the week was a cosy lull she wished could last eternally. He picked up her class assignments, bought cold medicine, and made a big pot of soup. They spent long afternoons in bed.

He told her about growing up in hilly northern Virginia, where his abiding concern had been horsemanship, until his mother Lydia's departure. He brought out a photo of the intact family: Lowell was younger than his polo photo, but fit her image of the polished Madrigal boy, lips curved and eyes shining. His father was an older, even more suave version of Lowell, and his little sister sparkled, white teeth in a big grin, long straight black hair in a velvet band. Lydia looked like Elizabeth Taylor; moody and almost too beautiful.

"When she left, she ruined us. That was the worst time I've had in my life," he confessed. "I don't think I ever got over it. I'm still angry at her, tell you the truth." He put the photo onto the nightstand.

Clare's most recent struggle, against her weight, felt too raw to confide. Her worst time, before Joe, was her father's death of cancer when she was ten. Lowell's intent focus, and his warm arms around her, made it easy to talk about Dad.

"You've been through such loss, Clare. Makes me realize I've been lucky, never to lose someone close."

"Your mom?"

"She didn't die."

"But her long absence from you … "

"It's better that way." He turned the photo facedown and pulled the comforter around them. "Tell me more about Joe."

"He was my best buddy. He kept me company after Dad died." He'd been her champion during the savagery of junior high, when mean kids teased her mercilessly about her weight. After the misery of a long school day, she'd come home and find Joe just arrived from high school, rooting in the cupboard for his snack. They'd watch The Three Stooges and eat Saltines and ice cream. He never hinted about diets the way the rest of the family did. "He made me laugh. He was always on my side."

"You said he got drafted right after high school."

"He hated to study." Her laugh came out with a sniffle. "We had that in common. He had no interest in college but there was no money for it either. And we didn't know enough to get him to Canada, and he wasn't the type to go through the hassle of being a conscientious objector. So he just went off to basic like a good soldier."

"He *was* a good soldier, Clare, you can feel proud of his courage in service. Troy's told me plenty about how it was over there."

"Yeah. I know." She pushed her face against his neck and let the tears fall into his pillow as he stroked her back.

"How'd *you* get money for college, honey? I mean, other than your library job?"

"The Linguistics Department gave me enough to convince me to come here."

"What great luck for me," he said in French. He wrapped her into a long kiss.

When he let go he said, "I'm not the good brother Joe was. I'm not close to my sister."

"How come?"

"She's so young, and I've been away so long. How could I possibly relate to a sixteen-year-old girl?"

You relate to this seventeen-year-old just fine. She bit her lip. But she'd be eighteen in two weeks. *Don't think about it.* She changed the subject.

After five cocooned days, he took her out for a buffet brunch. "You've lost so much weight."

"Too many sleepless nights these past weeks." She pointed. "Your fault."

"But you never eat, honey. Have more bacon. Have some pancakes."

"Oh, I can eat. You should have seen me a few months ago. I used to be kind of, ah, overweight." Last year she'd have consumed the entire buffet. "You wouldn't even have *looked* at me last year." It scared her to think so.

"I wasn't on campus for long last year, but if I'd met you, I'd have looked."

"What made you notice me when we did meet?"

"I noticed your hair, of course, and I liked how that Grateful Dead tee shirt fit you."

"You remember what I was *wearing?*"

"No bra, baby." He wiggled his eyebrows in a playful leer. "Funny-looking shoes. No makeup. Great mouth. Deep eyes." His smile faded, and his eyes widened, darkening as his pupils expanded. "The way you ... looked at me." A sudden sigh lifted his whole body.

He's in love too. The idea silenced her.

THIRTEEN

THE NIGHT before Election Day, she told Lowell she had to meet with a study group for a Soc project.

She hated lying to him.

She dressed in jeans and a black sweater and pulled a black wool cap on her head, stuffing her hair underneath.

In the truck, her cell-mates passed black shoe polish to cover every piece of skin that showed, not forgetting the backs of their hands. The half-moon light was strong.

"Once we get over, we have twenty minutes until the guards circle back," Steve reminded them. "When the time's up, I drive away. I'm not waiting for any stragglers. And remember the most important thing—"

"You get caught, you're on your own," everyone chorused.

"None of you ever heard of the SMC. Second most important thing—"

"If you don't have time to write, just splash the paint."

Steve turned off the truck light and engine so they coasted down the little hill outside the depot. The facility loomed bigger than Clare remembered, more forbidding, but she put that down to nerves. Steve parked under a stand of trees.

After climbing out, they relayed paint until they each held a can, over one arm, paintbrush taped to the top, carpet sample rolled under the opposite arm. The maneuver was awkward, but they'd decided each was better off carrying individual gear. Going over would be hard, with full cans and carpet, but they'd dump the empties afterward to get away fast. Steve made sure only the most nimble were in the cell. She was proud of her hard-won physical strength, proud to have been chosen.

They'd practiced on fences around town until they were all comfortable scaling the diamond-paned chicken wire, but it was different at night, with the paint can dangling from her wrist, bumping painfully against her arm, and the rolled-up carpet sample threatening to slither away every time she moved.

Still she managed to hold on, flip the carpet, and haul herself over the barbs. She held back a whoop of laughter as she found her footing on the other side and quickly scrambled down.

She ran to the side of the depot building, ripped off the paintbrush, and used its filed-down edge to pry open the lid.

KILLERS, she wrote in red paint letters, as big as she could make them. STOP THE BOMBING. U.S. OUT OF VIETNAM. U.S. OUT OF CAMBODIA. U.S. OUT OF LAOS. What a grim pathetic refrain it was, really. Wearily repetitious. STOP THE WAR. PEACE NOW. She ran around the corner, wrote some more, checked her watch. Time to go. She set the can down silently and raced back toward the fence.

As she ran, she heard a noise behind her that sounded out of place, unrehearsed, a musical glass smashing that lent speed to her flying feet. Quick, quick, up the fence again, to scale the top.

The carpet piece, jostled by her ascent, dangled precariously over the edge, about to slide to the other side. No! She snatched at it, caught a corner, yanked it toward her.

She saw the others scrambling down to the ground and running off to the truck. Why was she the last one? What the fuck had been that crashing noise? They'd agreed not to break any windows, tempting through it was, because they didn't know the alarm system.

Suddenly a light shone on her from below, and she heard a voice shouting, "Halt!" But she couldn't halt. She was balancing on the carpet swatch, just about to get her feet over the side of the wire.

"Halt! I've got orders to shoot intruders!"

Everyone knew that, if caught, they should practice civil disobedience: go limp and get dragged. They would not help the police state make arrests. They would slow down the system, drain resources, be uncooperative. Everyone knew that students did not get serious sentences in university towns. But they hadn't rehearsed what to do if they got caught on top of the wire.

Her carpet swatch slid away. She reached for the fence below the barbs, trying to wedge her feet into the wire diamonds, but something was hooking her in place, something snagged. Her sweater, dammit. She struggled, watching the light get closer, seeing clearly now the guard below as he stopped to lift his rifle. *Fuck!*

"Okay, okay, let me get down from here." Could she outrun him if she landed on the other side? Of course, he could shoot right through the chicken-wire fence.

Anyway, she was too high up to tug her sweater free and drop. She'd break a leg for sure. She wriggled more vigorously, trying to unhook herself, and she slipped.

There was a slash, deep into her sweater and under her arm as she slid down, a raking burn like a seam ripping open that made her gasp. She collapsed against the fence, clinging now, trying not to move, making her hands into claws. She willed her sobs of fright and pain not to shake her loose.

Out of nowhere came a picture seen on a childhood friend's bedroom wall: Jesus, crowned with thorns which looked just like barbed wire, bleeding from his side, hung on the cross. She hung on the fence. Her head fell back and her hat, pushed to its limit already by her bunched hair, sailed off on a gust of wind.

"It's a goddamn girl up there!" Another guard had joined the first. "Fuckin-A!"

"Get down!" shouted the first one. "Get down or I'll shoot!"

"I can't get down. I'm stuck," she moaned. Now her hair, blowing loose, wove onto the barbs in a wispy light tapestry. She jerked her sweater with one final effort and felt herself, at last, falling free.

The ground was not as far as she feared, but it still jarred every bone as she tumbled. Her head rang alarms in a dozen places where strands of hair had been ripped away. And her left side, God, *blazing*. She curled into a ball against the pain, not even caring when she was surrounded by guards and then by police. It was easy to stay limp, but when they started to pull her, the tears in her side seemed to gape open. "I'll get up, don't drag me, I'm cooperating," she gasped. "I'm not resisting."

Rough hands shoved her into the back of a squad car. She huddled, glad to be out of the cold, wondering why she kept shaking as she pressed her left arm into the worst of the pain.

The car sagged as a hefty policeman got in front.

73

The scratched plastic barrier separating them obscured his face, but his southern Indiana drawl came through loud and clear. "I hope you got a rich daddy to hire you a rich lawyer, baby. You're gonna pay bigtime. Federal ordnance facility attacked during wartime, that's treason. And there's your B and E, defacement of property, and disturbin the peace, we're talkin serious prison. Maybe even cap'tal punishment."

"What peace?" she managed to stammer. "What fucking *peace?*"

"*Now* you got your harassing an officer," came the pleased reply. "Cursing in public. We got you nailed, you and all your yippie friends."

"I don't have any friends. I was alone."

He just laughed, a rich laugh that might have tickled her under other circumstances. "Oh, we'll find em. You're gonna have plenty of comp'ny down to the jailhouse tonight."

She pressed her left arm tighter. Her teeth were chattering. She lifted her right hand to swipe at the cowardly trickles of tears streaking down her face, and stared, confused, as her palm came away black. The shoe polish. For some reason this struck her as amusing and she let out a snicker before she could stop it.

"Think it's funny, huh? Bet your folks're gonna think this is real funny too. Yep, my guess, they're gonna think it's funnier'n Johnny fuckin Carson."

Her mother, God, Mom would have a *cow.*

It had been bad enough when Andy decided he would dodge the draft by getting himself declared unfit. He'd dropped acid before his induction and raved through his intake about Joe's death in Da Nang, and about Nixon, Kissinger, Ho Chi Minh. It worked—they finally threw him out, tired of him—but as a 4F he was essentially unemployable. He'd been lucky to be accepted into an MA program in California.

More tears joined the first. *Mommy, I'm hurt.*

"That's right, cry over your spilt milk, baby," said the policeman, but he didn't sound so jolly now. "Whatcha got on your face, anyhow, is that dirt?"

"Sh—shoe polish."

"If that don't beat all." He cleared his throat. "There's some Kleenex on the floor by your feet, you wanna clean up some."

Leaning over was agony. She could not reach the floor.

"What'sa matter?" The rearview mirror glinted as he tilted it. "Them guards hurt you? They tolt me they dint fire no weapon." Anxiety exaggerated his accent.

Nobody wanted students shot, not after Kent State and Jackson State in 1970, nobody wanted a repeat of that mess; certainly not at a well-endowed Big Ten school.

"No. I got caught on the wire."

"The war? That barb war?"

She nodded.

"Shee-yit." She heard squawking noises, a crackling, then his voice again. "We might need us a medic look her over before we book her. Perp's got herself injured."

She leaned into the sweat-smelling backseat, shuddering in little cyclical spasms, feeling her loose ends unraveling like her hair up on the barb war.

Like when she and Joe had cracked open a golf ball to see what was inside, and it all sprang away, simple rubber bands waving off into streams of spent energy. She tried to hold on to her own wavy-elastic core.

FOURTEEN

THE OFFICER helped her out when they got to the courthouse, where the police station was in the basement. Clare felt better, standing. She could at least breathe. She managed the stairs with only two stops.

"Didja call in the ambulance?" The policeman asked a woman sitting behind the front desk.

"Not yet. She hurt bad?" She eyed Clare with distrust.

"I'm okay." She couldn't handle the drama of an ambulance. Maybe it was just a scratch.

The clerk pushed a clipboard toward her.

Clare filled out the form with a trembling hand and collapsed onto a nearby bench. She was too rattled to remember not to offer personal information: nobody carried IDs, in order to slow the state's process if they were caught.

"Jamie, problem," the clerk called to the officer who'd brought Clare in. "Your perp's a minor. She's gotta go to juvey and they ain't open anymore here tonight."

Jamie lumbered to the counter, coffee in hand, a disgusted look on his broad face. "Shee-yit, you're a minor? You're doin treason and you ain't even eighteen?"

"A week later, we'd've had her." The clerk turned to Clare. "You're gonna need to call your parents to come get you. We'll deal with the court tomorrow."

"I can't call my parents. My dad's dead." Having to blurt this, in the glaring blandness of the station, which smelled of pencils and burnt coffee, seemed the worst thing to happen so far. "My mom's upstate, she can't come get me."

The clerk folded her arms. "You get a phone call. We got the right to hand you into custody of the state, detention center in Indy's still open, Jamie'll drive you. Unless you have a responsible adult pick you up. Don't be callin on your hippie

friends or none of them dope-smokers over to the dormitories."
Her smile was unpleasant. "We'd let you go with a university
administrator, I'm sure they'd welcome bein woken up. Or
maybe a teacher, now, that'd be fine by you, right Jamie?"

"A teacher, one of the professors, that's right." Jamie sipped
his coffee, good humor restored. "With an ID, of course."

Oh shit. "What if I don't know their phone numbers?"

The clerk reached under her counter. "That's why we got
phonebooks." She thudded down a volume Clare recognized
from the lounge phone at French House. She thought, wildly,
through the roster of her teachers, on none of whom she had
made an impression in the huge lecture halls where she took
mostly freshman requirements. Maybe the Advanced French TA?
If she could tell this story without making herself sound like an
Indiana Danny the Red? But foreigners were afraid of American
police. And his English wasn't strong. He wouldn't work.

There was, of course, only one person she could call—
because he was a TA, even if not for one of her classes—but
how could she tell him about this? If Lowell found her broken,
busted, if he discovered she'd lied about her age and hidden the
SMC action? He would never again look at her with the bemused
yearning he let show at their brunch following her week of
illness. She'd been overjoyed to see that soft expression on his
dear face. If she had to call him—no. She'd lose him forever.

"Turn me over to the state. There's no professor who can
pick me up."

"I don't know about that," Jamie said, peering at her. "Seems
to me you thought of one just now, I seen it. You better make
that call. You don't wanna spend your time at the Ind'anaplis
detention til your mom can come down. I was you, a college
student, I'd wanna keep up with class. I'd wanna keep my mom
from springin me from juvey."

He was right. This was a break. His bloodshot eyes, set in
baggy circles, suddenly twinkled with kindness that made her
throat ache. She got up and reached for the phone the clerk
plunked onto the counter.

"Goodenow." Lowell's greeting was annoyed. He hated
interruptions when he was in his thesis zone, sometimes not
answering the phone at all, and she knew he was under pressure

now to finish. At least he sounded awake.

"Dr. Goodenow, this is Clare Meredith, I'm one of the Poli Sci students you TA for?" She took a deep breath. It hurt. "I have a huge favor to ask. I'm at the police station, in the courthouse, and I need a responsible adult to pick me up. My mom can't come because she's upstate. I got caught defacing the naval weapons depot outside of town in an antiwar action."

There was such silence she thought he'd hung up. "Um, Dr. Goodenow?"

"I guess this was your so-called Soc project, huh." He sighed. "Of course I'll come. Are you okay? Normally they'd just have you post some bail and let you go."

She pressed her lips tight together, then said, "They won't let me go on my own." Jamie and the clerk were standing right beside her. "They said they have to give custody to the state, because I'm a ... a minor."

"A *minor*. But you're twenty, right, that's what you told me?"

"Not just yet, actually. I'll be ... eighteen next week."

"Eighteen ... next week? Next *week*!" Another long pause. "Jesus Christ." At last he continued, in a dry neutral voice, as if he really were her TA, "Sounds like you lucked out on any serious charges. This time."

Too choked to speak further, she handed the phone receiver to Jamie.

Lowell arrived looking every inch a professional, shaved, hair brushed severely back, in a formal jacket and slacks. She hadn't seen him in shiny shoes since the night of his advisor's party. He didn't look her way as he dealt with Jamie and the clerk, who responded to his crisp authority with a deference that might otherwise have amused her. He spoke to them in clipped tones without a hint of Southern.

It was over in five minutes.

"I'd advise a stern lecture, Professor," Jamie said, as Lowell turned to her bench. "These kids don't have no idear how the world works. You tell her she's lucky to get off like this. It don't mean they won't be pressing charges, but she'll have an easier time of it as a minor. Community service. Prob'ly have to powerwash the depot down, if they let her back in there."

"She was alone?" Lowell might have been speaking of a

stranger. He did not meet her eyes as he appraised her dishevelment.

"She wadn't the only one. We found a bunch of paint cans, carpets, and at least two sets of tracks leadin from the broken windows, not hers, cause her shoes're clean."

"The Navy ordnance facility, that's federal."

"Yep. It's gonna come down real hard on the ones behind this, and we're thinkin she can tell us just who they might be, if we plead her time down."

She unclenched her teeth long enough to spit out, "*No.*"

A cold, unfamiliar smile did not light Lowell's features. "She's pretty stubborn, officer, my guess is she won't give them up. But I'm sure they'll be easy to find."

"Well, Professor, she's all yours. Oh, by the way, she might've got herself tore up a little on that barb war."

Lowell frowned. "Barbwar?"

"Just so you know, none of us touched her, none of the guards neither."

Lowell looked directly at her, finally. She shrank from the distance in his eyes. "*Touched* her?" He turned to Jamie and asked, glacial, "What are you saying, officer?"

"Just forget it, Dr. Goodenow, I snagged my sweater, it's nothing. Can we go?"

Lowell shrugged. "Fine. Miss Meredith."

She pulled her arm tight into her side as they trod upstairs and went out into the quiet square. His Vette was parked in front of the bar where he'd sheltered her after the demo.

She tried, hell, she had nothing to lose: "Hey *Perfesser*, if the bar's still open, drinks on me, for springin me from the pokey." She would have loved a beer just then, but more, she would have loved to have him cuddling her in a warm booth by the fire.

He rounded on her so swiftly she had to step back.

"You lied to me. Give me one reason, *one,* why I shouldn't let them toss you into juvey, and why I shouldn't rat out those fucking SMC *assholes* who left you all alone."

"One: you care about me too much."

He shot her a bitter look and yanked opened the passenger door for her. When she tried to bend, to climb in, her side clamored.

"You're bleeding!" She saw, glancing down, a dark stain soaking her sweater under her arm. *"That's* what the officer was talking about! He has to call us an ambulance." He ripped off his blazer and wrapped it around her.

"I don't want to go back in there."

"But this looks so bad, honey, what the hell happened?"

Honey. That's better. "I got scraped on the barbed wire. Barbwar."

"If this was just a scrape you'd be marching around the courthouse claiming police brutality." He reached in to push the passenger seat back. "We're going to the hospital." He helped lower her into the car. "I'll get you there as fast as I can, honey, hang on."

In Emergency, Clare was slathered with a topical anesthetic and her side was cleaned up, revealing a six-inch string of red teardrops, three of which needed stitches with a welcome shot of painkiller.

"You were lucky," said the tired-looking young doctor on call. "You could have really done a number on your breast or under your arm. Next time"—he interrupted himself with a short laugh—"don't let there be a next time, okay?" He tossed her shredded sweater into the trash. Her tee shirt underneath was blood-splotched but wearable, with Lowell's blazer over it. "No showers for ten days, sponge baths okay, back in two weeks to get the stitches out." He peered at her. "What's that on your face? Makeup?"

"Shoe polish."

He shook his head, resignedly, and pointed to a sink in the corner. "Might as well wash up now, since once the Demerol wears off you won't want to move." He scribbled on a pad. "Keep these drugs to yourself and let your profs know you need a couple days off. And no more stupid sorority pranks." Clare had made up a story to cover her involvement in the action.

In the waiting room Lowell was walking around in the same small circles he paced when he was stuck on a thorny thesis sentence. When he saw Clare his impatient frown evened out, a little, and he strode over as if she were some task he would dispatch in the quickest possible way.

He patted her back, a brisk touch that would have suited a

dog, or a child. "I'll take you to French House." He helped her back into the car. "Is there anyone you need me to call? Your mom maybe?"

She shook her head slowly. The Demerol was distancing her not only from the stinging in her side but also from how she must quickly erase their formality. She should tell him how frightened she was, and how sorry to have dragged him out in the middle of the night, fudged the truth about her real age, hidden so completely the SMC action.

If she could talk, maybe he'd say how he was feeling too, and they'd mend the space gaping between them. But, apparently, her seconds on the wire divided past and present as if a millennium passed while she was up there, caught by streaks of moonlight and pitiless flashlight from the startled young guards. She was speechless.

But in the lounge at French House she told him, "Come up with me. The RA's asleep by now." She put her cheek on his. What ease, if she could just stay close to him.

"It's past three in the morning."

"That never stopped us before."

"You need rest. So do I." He moved away. "Can you get upstairs?"

"All right." Disappointment and, more, a distressing sense of opportunities lost, was almost waking her. "I *wish* you'd come with me."

Dark circles underscored his eyes' bleakness. "We'll talk." He patted her back again. "Get some sleep."

She walked up one step at a time, measuring each tread, heavy as cement, too numb to cry. She curled on her bed and wrapped his blazer around her. Sleep swooped in, offering comfort as Lowell would, she knew, if he were beside her.

FIFTEEN

LOWELL CALLED the next day to ask how she was feeling, and to give her the name of a lawyer he thought she should use instead of the SMC-recommended student legal defense organization. But she didn't see him again until Thursday, in French, where she forced herself to get to class in hopes he would be there.

He looked older to her, careworn, as if he had been under the same pain, and detached painkiller spell, as she. His smile was barely a lifting of his lips.

"You doing better?" he asked after class. "Let's get some coffee."

They walked out of the building but did not wrap arms around each other as usual: when she tried to circle his waist, he stepped smoothly out of her grasp. "Why didn't you come see me?" she asked.

"I've been thinking about you, Clare. Of course. But I decided to wait, until you were back on your feet, to have a serious conversation."

This sounded bad. They walked off campus and into town. "Let's try this place." It was a nondescript diner, devoid of the romantic atmosphere she'd prefer. At least he chose the most isolated booth. At least the sun was trying to shine outside.

"Does Henderson know what happened to you?"

This was not how she would have begun their reunion. "No."

"He didn't bother to find out why you didn't come back with the rest of the group? He didn't even call you?"

"He probably assumed I got busted."

"He doesn't check up on his people?"

"It's not like we're personal friends." She wasn't going to spell out exactly how the cell worked. "We—in case of trouble, we keep each other out of it, if we can."

"I figured you'd maintain their secrecy."

"Of course."

"Too bad you were the only one who got stuck. I hope, at least, you're thinking about quitting after this?"

She'd thought about it. She hated the way they'd left her alone on the wire, even though she knew why it had been necessary; but she'd be cowardly to give up after a simple scrape. So many had suffered so much worse. "Not until the war's over."

"Nixon got re-elected while you were recuperating, I'm sure you heard."

"I know." She'd tried to sleep the news away. That it was no surprise did not make it less painful: the death of a long-cherished collective dream.

"Too bad *you* were too young to vote. Might've made *all* the difference."

She flinched from the jeer in this statement.

"Getting our troops out is his first priority," he continued. "I predict peace talks will start next month. You oughta be able to lay your burden down right quick."

"Why are you so angry?"

He gave a little disbelieving laugh. "You have to ask?" He shoved the glass containers of salt, pepper and sugar together in a tight consortium that apparently displeased him, for he began at once to re-arrange them. "You tricked me."

"I didn't mean to—"

"Why the hell would SMC sponsor such a dangerous stunt, anyway?"

As if speechifying would deflect his fury, she began to stammer, "To show how easy it is for the state's arsenals to be penetrated. To thumb our noses at the security apparatus."

"Bullshit, Clare. Henderson knows those guards can shoot trespassers. Shoot to kill, it's a federal armory, for Christ's sake, they're allowed to! Henderson probably figured on big headlines, that fucking opportunistic asshole, probably hoped one of you *would* get shot. Jesus!"

"I'm angry you got into this." The saltshaker spun, spilled. He knocked it upright.

"It was a *paint* job, Lowell, it's not like we firebombed the place," she muttered.

"But that's how things escalate when assholes are in charge. Do you see yourself as a *Weatherman?* Is that what you want?"

She wasn't sure, yet, Weathermen was where she wanted to go. "Sometimes the avant garde has to take a direction that—"

"Avant garde!" He was glaring now. "You and your damn Nechayev." Color rose over his cheekbones and his breathing got fast. "Those guys who killed the Olympians in September probably started out with what *they* thought was civil disobedience, and look where it led."

SMC weren't *that* radical. Nobody in the States took the Movement that far; the only time there'd been death at Movement hands, at UW Madison two years ago, was accidental. SDS had not figured anyone was in the building at the time, but a young research assistant was killed in their bombing of the "Army Math" facility.

"That's what your precious revolution actually means."

She shook her head, frowning.

"And did you stop to think how your mother, your family, would feel if you'd been hurt worse? If you'd been *shot?*"

She had to look down. When she'd spoken to Lowell's lawyer contact, yesterday, she'd asked if her Mom had to be notified. He said he'd look into it: since her birthday was so close and since, as he put it, "the wheels of justice move slowly," there might be no need. She really didn't want to have to confess to Mom, who had more than enough to worry about, how she'd screwed up a simple protest her very first semester of college.

"*I'd* probably make that call. Not a nice way for me to meet your mom."

"You don't have to act so ... *parental,*" she murmured.

He leaned forward to hiss, nastier than she would have believed him capable, "Then don't call me to bail you out next time you get yourself the fuck in trouble."

The waitress came by, asked if they wanted pie, but Lowell waved her off. He took out a pack of cigarettes, lit one, then stabbed it into pulp in the ashtray. "I keep seeing you on that fucking wire. You were stuck and I was oblivious."

She had to meet his eyes, acknowledge the shock there, put

her hands out to cover his, clenched on the table. "Lowell ... this had nothing to do with you."

"You mean it's none of my business?"

"No—"

"You put yourself at risk and it shouldn't *matter* to me?" He jerked his hands away. "I thought we were close. I don't understand—" He dropped his head, shaking it. "But I'm not like this. This isn't me." When he looked up she saw coldness overtaking outrage as his frown evened out and his flush faded. "This isn't me, Clare."

"It's you," she insisted, trying to stifle the fear she felt rising in her chest, burning like bad weed, making her heart race. "We *are* close. You and I are together."

"We are not together. You lied."

"I *had* to hide the action from you."

"This isn't just about your war-defeating death-defying derring-fuckin-do *action!* Why'd you pretend to be so much older when we first talked?"

"What difference does it make? Nineteen, seventeen, did you care?"

"Yes! It would have made a difference to me. I made assumptions, about you—" He shrugged his jacket on. "You gave me no choice. I guess so you could win your bet, huh, the one you and Ginger had about me. Some bet! Hope it was worth it."

"Oh *no*—"

"I laughed when I heard about it!" He exploded a breath like a little bomb. "But I had my eye on you, anyway, as you know, so I figured I'd get lucky fast on that corny hayride. I thought it was *funny*. But not now." The dazed look in his eyes made them more distant. "I don't know who you are now. I guess I didn't then, either. My mistake."

He stood. "Usually in these circumstances I say 'we can still be friends,' but I don't feel that way about you. I'm keeping my distance. I ask you to keep yours."

"No, oh *no*—"

He drew his shoulders up as if shrinking inside his jacket and shook his head, once, quickly. Then he turned and walked away.

85

Sixteen

WEAK SUNLIGHT outlined his back, as he left, in a wavy fashion like an old Western saloon bad guy. Leaving. Leaving her.

The waitress came by, intentional pad in hand, obviously wondering if Clare was going to keep taking up space in her station.

"Chocolate cake," Clare said. "With vanilla ice cream. And"—she couldn't remember what time of day it was—"coffee. Black."

When the cake came it looked like some kind of alien life form, a wedge of wet dark brown, quivering under her gaze. How had this ever been a comfort? She slurped the coffee too fast and burned her tongue. The ice cream didn't soothe but was at least a numbing spoonful in her vacant mouth.

I need drugs, she thought, weed whites and wine just like in "Willin" by Lowell George of Little Feat—how weird, his *same first name!* She listened to the song in her mind for awhile. *Willin. Willin. Lowell. Oh Lowell.*

"Miss?" An aproned, white-hatted man stood by her booth. The waitress hovered behind him. "Time for you to pay up and leave."

Focus. The weak sunlight had faded to black. She must have slumped here all afternoon. He'd left his cigarettes and the pack was empty, ashtray full. The coffee was cold, ice cream melted in a white pond, cake untouched.

"Okay." She felt the smoke in her mouth and all over her shivering body—she'd never smoked a whole pack before!

She pushed herself out, remembered she had to give money, and fumbled in her purse for some bills. She cranked out a smile but didn't get any in return. The waitress and cook seemed to stand back like spectators at a state funeral as she staggered out.

What a creepy place. I'm not patronizing your establishment again, sir.

She made her way to French House and stopped at the lounge entrance, peeping in like a stranger, remembering how, long ago, she used to join the Hearts game in progress as if no entry fee of normalcy were required.

"Clare?" Jenny came up. "You look really bad."

"Oh, I just want to play Hearts. I'm okay."

"Did you eat when you took your meds today?" Jenny spoke behind her to Lee. "Get some water. Get crackers and cheese from the house fridge."

"I want weed whites and wine."

Jenny laughed. "Okay, after you get something in your stomach, I've got a great bottle of red upstairs."

"Where's Keith?" Amazing she could pull this boyfriend's name from memory.

"He's got a game tonight. Where's Low?"

"He's got a game too!" This sounded so funny, she didn't know why Jenny wasn't laughing, was leaning in to study her face.

"What happened, Clare? You look like you're about to pass out."

"He broke up with me." She remembered, just in time, that nobody was supposed to know the truth of the depot action. She'd told her friends she'd tripped on an unsecured cart, at work, and was taking painkillers. "It's over."

"Over, why, sweetie, can you tell me?" Jenny helped her stand and move toward the stairs, and this was good, close to bed and the oblivion of sleep, but Jen's "sweetie" sounded too much like what he'd say and she could not hold back her broken sobs and it hurt so much, still, in her side that she had to stop and lean on the cinderblock wall. What a bummer for the Hearts players who turned to observe her grief.

"Come on, upstairs, you can make it." Step by step they advanced. Jenny walked her to the room, whose "Je Suis Clare" cartoon, a bit raggedy-looking now, made her tears flow free.

"I want to start again. I want to go back. I loved every minute here."

"We love you too, Clare." Lee came in with a plate of snacks. They shared Jenny's red as Clare obediently ate the cheese, crackers and apple slices, and drank a big glass of water. Lee brought cards so they could play their own Hearts on her nunlike bed. Mr. Dylan and Mr. Guevara observed from their poster vigils on her wall, dusty from neglect, but still keen-eyed.

Her tears and intermittent shaking didn't faze Jenny and Lee, as they shot the moon and switched to Euchre and took turns handing her Kleenexes. Ginger showed up, took one look, and returned with a bottle of tequila and her guitar.

"*Hay unos ojos que si me miren,*" she sang in Spanish, making her voice warble *ay ay ay* like the mariachis she'd told of long ago, when the air was warm and the ideas were new, and Clare was in love not just with *him* but with all of it.

After a time her friends collected their offerings, turned out the light, and crept away. She curled into a ball on her bed and mourned. At least she had his blazer, permeated with his scent, to blot her tears.

In anguished clarity, she saw his body stretched with one arm flung over his eyes, his deep relaxed breathing causing his chest to rise and fall. How delicious his skin was—firm, smooth, always warm. She never resisted her impulse to smother him with kisses after lovemaking, and he would smile so affectionately, his eyes half-open, catching her lips with quick teeth when she lingered on his mouth.

Often her kisses would rouse him again and she would lick down his body to take him in her mouth, reveling in his sighs as he grew harder and his hands tightened in her hair. Then he would surround her with caresses of his own, melting into her until she was lost in sensation. Frequently he gave her such exquisite pleasure she had the impulse to bite or scratch him. That always made him laugh.

Sometimes climax left her in tears and he would rock her in deep communion until her quaking stopped. She remembered the weekend it seemed they'd each come about ten times, and still couldn't stop even though they were both sore, and when she asked him if it was possible to die from too many orgasms, he reached for her again and said, "Let's find out."

How could they have been so close and now so far apart?

But he had been her only lover; maybe this ecstasy was commonplace for him, since he'd been with so many women.

Maybe she was nothing special. But if she was nothing special why had he wanted to be with her over and over? They'd been snug for weeks now, weeks of love so profound his eyes had echoed her feeling, that day at breakfast.

But maybe that was why he was so set against her now—the depot had come just a week after that breakfast. She'd shattered his image of her. A fall from grace made harsher by contrast with his dawning enchantment. Still, it wasn't deceit like cheating on him, was it? Her dishonesty—except for claiming she was nineteen and making up a Soc project on Election Eve—was just omission, right, not some sort of planned evil trickery. She hadn't deceived him on purpose! She hadn't meant to hurt him!

But he acted betrayed in that horrid diner.

Maybe he was right. She *had* lied, easily. He'd believed her.

So maybe he felt used. Maybe he thought she was making fun of him. But he had to know how helplessly in love she was.

Didn't he?

Oh, this was torture.

And who was comforting him now? What friends did he have, to surround him with love and feed him crackers and wine and distract him with Hearts? Who was handing him Kleenex and making sure he drank water?

I have to go see him. I'm the only one who can ease his pain. He was in pain, she knew from his shocked look, she'd never forget that look as long as she lived. And he had no best friends, that she knew of; Troy was back East, and his Poli Sci people were the sort you'd trade mere paragraphs with, never confidences. Aimee wouldn't rush to his side, not with her husband on campus, and anyway Lowell wasn't the kind of person to be easily distracted from this major life tragedy by some floozy sex symbol. Or was he?

How well did she really know him, anyway?

She twisted and turned on every awful alternative until her agony felt like its own terrifying trip—from which sleep was a final and welcome escape.

SEVENTEEN

A T BREAKFAST the next day, Jenny and Ginger flanked her, protectively, at the cafeteria table and pressed for information they hadn't sought the night before but that she still couldn't begin to supply.

"Is it another girl?" asked Ginger.

She shook her head.

"Was he bad to you?" asked Jenny.

"No. What happened was my fault." She couldn't tell them why. They had no idea about her involvement in the depot graffiti, although the audacity of the act was still the talk of the town—along with the surprising election of the new third-year law-student mayor—or her bust, or that she'd lied to him. Nobody could console her in this. Nobody but him.

"Are you sure it's really over?" Jenny spooned sugar into her coffee. "Sometimes the first serious argument seems like the end of the world, like some insurmountable barrier, but it can actually serve to deepen the relationship ... "

"Makeup sex can be the best ever," Ginger chimed in.

Sitting there a second longer was impossible. She fled to the cocoon of her bed again, where she stayed until another day and night passed. Jenny brought her sandwiches and more water. Ginger brought weed and wine.

With Sunday came a dusting of snow. The rare quality of daylight brought Clare from her bed, to look outside, where the Jordan made a sinuous silver reflection of the white sky. The snow on the long silent lawn looked new and hopeful. A clean slate.

I'm going to see him.

She took a shower even though the doctor had said to wait a few more days. She bundled up in her new maxi coat, a birthday gift sent from Mom and her sister Claudia, a rust-colored wool that felt as warm as their love—but fought tears at this thought. She put on her flimsy maroon suede boots and quickly ruined them, tramping over the snowy slick sidewalks, up through the rising woods surrounding Tulip Tree and beyond, to his apartment building.

She buzzed his doorbell and, when there was no answer, banged on his door as if babies needed to be rescued from a fire inside.

It took awhile for the door to open. He leaned on it and scowled like she held religious tracts or some kind of threatening summons. His unshaven, wild-haired, bleary-eyed appearance made him a risky stranger even though he wore the familiar black Moroccan dress. He finally straightened up and said, "No."

She pushed on the door he was closing. "Yes. It's only fair to let me talk."

He walked into his apartment, leaving her to follow. He slouched in one of the armchairs next to the fireplace—filthy, she saw, with embers and half-charred scraps of the newspaper he used for kindling—folded his arms and watched her with narrow unfriendly eyes.

She reached into the strength she'd used to shake the status quo in high school, foment the antiwar movement in Merrillville, carve away The Weight, and climb the barbwar. She stared back. "I didn't mean to hurt you. I lied about my age because I wanted you to think I was old enough to be with you. It didn't feel wrong to pretend to be … more sophisticated."

His deep skeptical frown wasn't encouraging, but she went on. "Maybe it was stupid but I don't regret it."

He didn't respond.

She didn't try to get closer but stood straight in the middle of the room with her cold-mush boots dampening his pale thick rug. "I *never* accepted that dumb bet, by the way, please realize that, even if you don't want to hear anything else from me. That was all Ginger."

Finally he said, "But the two of you are best friends."

"She's the first real friend I made here, but we're very different. I like her sense of fun. We love the same music. I *don't* share her attitude about—about having lots of guys. That's her, not me." She recalled his saying this about Debi of the red nails

91

and jangly bracelets in the library. "And you know that's true. You know *me*."

"I thought I did," he muttered.

"I wanted to apologize after the hospital, for dragging you into my troubles, but you were so fucking aloof and I was all drugged up. I couldn't get the words out."

His exhalation seemed to come from a place as deep as the Wishing Well. "I didn't mind sharing your troubles, Clare, but I still don't understand your deception." He sighed again. "I feel bad you got hurt. I wanted to kill Henderson."

His cold eyes and voice didn't soften this statement or the invitation he offered next. "You might as well take off your coat. I'll make you tea."

So she peeled off her birthday coat and wrestled her boots away while he went to the kitchenette to put on the kettle. She perched on the couch edge like the first time, but now pulled the wool throw around her as a mantle, against the cold inside her and in his apartment. His plants needed watering, and papers were scattered in uncharacteristic disorder on the floor, along with his leather jacket and two lonely-looking empty whiskey bottles. No music played.

She couldn't tell where her heartache ended and his began.

His tray was a sparse echo of her initial visit: one plain mug, tea bag dangling over the side, no cookies or brandy to sweeten their conversational prospects.

"Can I ask you something? You said you treated Ginger's contest as a way to get lucky with me on the hayride."

He sank into the chair again and dropped his forehead into one hand in an attitude of extreme fatigue. "I did."

"So, you thought I was using you, but you were using me too."

"We both got what we wanted."

"I need to know, though, just for my own sense of ... reality. Would you have asked me out if you didn't hear about that idiotic bet?"

He raised his head, stiffly, and inspected her as if for the first time, absent the courtly admiration he'd used so skillfully on her then. He seemed to need a long while to come up with an answer as he assessed what felt like every part of her. In his broody

92

disarray, with purple-brown smudges under his eyes, and scruffy beard, he looked like some jaded rocker, ready to snort cocaine off the bare asses of his groupies before trashing his hotel room. As in the beginning, she forced herself steady, and returned his suddenly dangerous-feeling regard.

Finally he said, "Knowing what a liar you are? No."

Without thinking, she launched toward him and tumbled him onto the floor. She shook him so hard his head thudded on the carpet. The sight of his flying hair brought her to her senses and, horrified, she patted his head with tentative fingers as if she could stuff the enraged genie that had possessed her back into its jar.

"What the *fuck!*" He twisted, flinging her to his side, and grabbed her arms. "Is this what you came for?" He rolled on top of her. "This is what you want?" His kiss was like a bite, his stubble scratched her face, his hands were hard and he reeked of smoke, sweat and bourbon, but her hopeful excited grasp was even tighter than his. *Yes, come back to me, yes.*

But within seconds he wrenched away. He stood up and whisked himself as if brushing off snow. Then he crossed his arms and glared. "I asked you to stay away."

She slowly leaned to her good side and sat up. Her stitches were pulling, now that she was noticing, and her hitching sobs made the pain worse. "Okay." She stood to pick up her coat. "I didn't mean to—attack you. I came to say I'm sorry."

"Are you ... all right?"

She turned, sleeve half on. "Don't be polite *now.*"

"You look like you're hurting." His tone was still chilly.

"I *am* hurting." She wanted to shake him again. "And it's all your fault!"

"*My* fault—"

"You're so mean! You let me suffer all alone this week. You left me flat in that horrible diner—you're a *bad* boyfriend!" She collapsed in the puddle of her maxi coat. "And you tell me I'm a liar and you think I came here for—was trying to—I hate you." She covered her face with her hands. It hurt so much to cry it made her cry even harder.

After some time she felt his arms encircle her and she pressed her wet face into his shoulder.

EIGHTEEN

"I'M NOT used to this," he said into her hair. "I'm sorry." He stroked her as her sobs subsided. Then he leaned back to look at her. In his eyes was all the tenderness she'd been seeking, finally, but a regretful nostalgic glisten kept him distant still.

"I'm not used to it," he repeated. "I don't meant to hurt you more when I know you're already hurting, honey. I *never* lose control like this. It's just not me." He tightened his arms around her again. "We can't do this anymore."

"Won't you forgive me?"

When he didn't answer she thought her words had soaked into his shoulder so she asked again. "Please, Lowell."

"It doesn't matter, if I do, or whether you forgive me for being such a jerk, leaving you alone all week and getting so rude just now. We have to let go anyway."

"But we love each other."

He dropped his arms and slowly stood. "But you can't come with me."

"I could if we got married—"

"*Married!*" he exclaimed, with such alarm that she felt each vessel of her heart constricting, shrinking in retreat. "No no no. This is"—he lifted his shoulders searchingly—"it's just ... an episode." He frowned down at her and she looked away.

"C'mon, you know what I think of marriage, don't wish that on yourself." She felt his hand patting the top of her head. "If it's what you really want, I'm sure you'll find someone—but that's not me."

Her face crumpled into tears again.

"Hey now. I'm just your first. You're going to have so many others—"

"You're the only one I want in my life!"

"And how do you think your life would be, if we were crazy enough to get married? I'll be moving every two years. Not much time for a wife to settle in, make friends, find a job—it's a tough life for women years older than you, how do you think it would be for a young girl who's only lived away from home for three months?"

"Three and a *half*," she said sullenly.

"Now you sound like your age, Jesus, seventeen! If I'd known what a kid you really are I'd *never* have hit on you. I'd've looked away."

"That's why I didn't tell you." But she hurried past this little point. "I don't care about friends or a job, if I've got you."

"You're wrong, Clare, but I know you're too young to realize it—"

"—you erase everything! I hardly do any work now, I hardly see any friends—"

"—I'm sorry about that too," he said, slowly. "I realized, this week, we got too intense too fast. I should've cooled it. It wasn't good for you."

She gesticulated wildly around the room. "This *is* good for me! All I want is *right here*. All I need is you."

"Not true. You need your activism, you need your French House buddies, you need your singing, and there are a thousand guys on campus who'd jump at the chance to be your boyfriend." He smiled. "A *good* boyfriend."

"I don't want them!" Thoughts tumbled frantically and she snatched the tail of one. "I could join Peace Corps in Senegal and live with you."

"One thing I have observed about relationships." His mouth drew into a flat line. "The giving has to be equal, for it to last."

"You don't think we would last?" She rubbed her hands over her arms, cold under her sweater, shivering as if the snow covered his carpet and was creeping up the walls. "You don't trust our love?"

"I wouldn't trust a situation where you'd give up college just to be in the same country with me. Peace Corps sends people to the boonies, even if they accepted a dropout. Chances are we wouldn't even be near each other. Anyway, you told me Peace Corps is a government mouthpiece." He actually had the nerve to smile again, provocatively. "And you're *too young* to join up, baby."

"I could just come with you anyway—I could teach French, or work in a restaurant, I have lots of experience in that—"

He was shaking his head. "*Listen* to yourself. You're a bright girl with a bright future. You're going to finish your education, be a leader in social justice, not a waitress in some foreign restaurant. Besides, you wouldn't even get working papers."

"I don't care!" she wailed. "I don't care what you say! I love you and I won't just let you disappear. I won't."

He knelt and took her face in his hands.

"I want you to remember what I'm about to say when I'm gone and you're mooning over might've-been. Okay, Clare?"

"Okay, *okay,* dammit. I'm listening."

"I don't *want* to marry you. I'm not ready and you're not either. And anything other than marriage won't work, not in the countries where I'll be serving.

"If you just hung out with me, like a hippie, people would see you as—some cultures are so judgmental. You wouldn't stand it. I wouldn't stand for it. And you'd grow to resent it, and you'd wonder why you were shuffling around the world after some guy, just because"—he suddenly laughed, shortly—"just cause he's a good lay. Of course he'd be working, you understand, not lying around in bed with you."

He dropped his hands. "And forget about your revolution, outside the States. Repressive regimes deal with that kind of talk so badly. You have *no* idea." He sat back. "Are you getting the picture?"

"It's a horrible picture, it's not how I'd feel—"

"I've been around State people all my life. The wives are— God, I can't see you giving up your youth for that. Tea parties, ladies' lunches. Not a one of em ever heard of Lenin or your other old Russians." His half-smile twisted, sarcastic. "Or would care to."

"You want to just throw me away?" She could hear the note of hysteria creeping into her voice but was powerless to stop it. "Forget all about me?"

"I won't forget you, Clare, and I'm not throwing you away. I'm letting you *go*—so you can get on with your life and I can get on with mine."

"Just because I don't fit in with your fucking plan."

"Hey! I don't fit into *yours*, doll. Not enough for you to have trusted me with who you really are." She had no defense against his calm deliberation. She couldn't even feel gratified that he'd obviously given their relationship so much thought this week. "But I hope you hear me now. There's no way. It's best we make a clean break. No contact."

"It doesn't matter how we feel?"

He shook his head.

"So this is it, this is goodbye, and I'll just see you in class? And not speak?"

"Actually, no," he said slowly. "I'm done here. I'm leaving as soon as I can get my head together enough to sober up and pack."

"You're ... dropping *out*?" There were still three weeks in the semester.

"No. My thesis is finished, I've got the credits for the master's. I cleared it with Simmons to drop the TA-ship. I'm driving back East next week. Thanksgiving."

"Were you even going to tell me you're leaving?"

"I was working up to it, yes."

"Working with whiskey." She kicked out at one of the bottles.

"You have more courage than I do, coming here now. I wasn't ready to come to you."

"You're running away from me."

"Oh Clare. As if leaving here could take you from my mind." His tone was so despondent, and so final, she ran out of words.

She let him drape her coat around her, let him tug up her boots, and watched as he threw his leather jacket over the Moroccan dress and put on his own boots, obviously uncaring how peculiar he looked. He led her to his Corvette, and drove her back to French House through a series of white blizzardy veils. Only the susurration of tires on snow broke the silence.

NINETEEN

THE REST of the term passed quickly. It was just bearable, not having to see him and maintain some pretense of civilized distance, but it was not easy. She kept her head down, burying herself in long-neglected classwork and doubling up on her library hours so she'd have no time to think.

Her nights were miseries of memory, longing and tears. Lowell did not get in touch with her, and she didn't ask anyone if they'd heard from him. She couldn't bear to hear his name.

During Christmas break, however, her brother Andy took her aside one evening during the week he visited from grad school in California.

"So this guy Lowell from Virginia called while you and Claudia were out shopping this afternoon," he said. "He wanted to know how you were. I told him fine."

"How did he sound?"

"Pretty subdued." Andy studied her kindly. "Seemed like a decent guy. Left a number in case you want to call him. Took our address so he could write to you. He sounded like he might be someone ... important. In your life."

"He dumped me, Andy," she replied. "Anyway, he was too old for me."

She didn't save the paper with Lowell's number, afraid to keep it in case she got panicky and was tempted to call him. Pride was the only thing that would get her through this, she knew; if they had no future then he was right, no contact was cleaner.

Back at school in the new year, after a long talk with her mom, and then with Ginger, about careers, she switched her major from French to Spanish, where she thought there would be a lot more job options. She moved to the Spanish wing of the dorm but made no new friends. She studied hard, determined to offset her mediocre grades of the first semester, grateful her

French background made Spanish an easy acquisition and the Linguistics Department accomodated her.

She served out her community service sentence, working on a cleanup crew around Bloomington with the other underage SMC kid. Steve Henderson and three older cell members were facing jail time but Lowell's lawyer friend was brokering some deal for them with Student Legal Defense.

One stoned afternoon, Clare and Ginger decided to go together on the university's Mexico program. They would share an apartment, buy lots of good weed, and have fun. Ginger had been in Mexico the previous summer and promised it would be a blast.

Clare hoped a new country would erase Lowell for good. She made the applications and arranged her plans to spend the next year in Mexico.

TWENTY

Beirut, 1973

A HMED WAS driving past St. George's Bay while Low leafed through a file of papers en route back to the embassy. They'd lunched at the ambassador's house in the hills outside the city, his thanks to the staff for an under-secretary's recent, successfully concluded visit, and they were both sleepy from rich Arabic food and excellent wine.

"Fuck the office, Ahmed, let's go to Summerland instead." Low yawned, mentioning the seaside club frequented by international expatriates and upper-class Lebanese.

"Don't I wish," said Ahmed. He was a thin-featured, sleek-haired, impeccably dressed youth, recently returned from graduate studies at the Sorbonne. He worked in the Commercial Section as a liaison between the embassy staff and local businesses. Low struck up a friendship when he discovered they'd both lived in Paris.

Lebanon was a surprise, after expecting Senegal, but surprises were routine in the Service. He'd been given several months' intensive Arabic before starting work in July. Beirut, bathed by sea breezes, blooming with intense life and color, was dazzling after the somnolence of a Washington summer. The city reminded him of Paris, with fashionable style and cuisine, shops and boulevards, but there was warmth in the people that was unique, in his experience. And the coastal scenery was stunning.

But the job was fucking *boring*! He was a lowly assistant in the Consul's office and work consisted of processing the visa applications of students, tourists and businesspeople who wanted to visit the States. His days were a shuffle between file cabinets and the Xerox copier; monotony relieved by stultifying sessions learning how to operate the telex machine.

Occasionally he interviewed applicants: none of whom, he

100

was sure, had any interest in oil-based emerging economies since their gaze was fixed so determinedly westward; all of whom, he suspected, were amused by his hesitant attempts to engage them in Arabic. Allah knew he wasn't much of a natural linguist.

He gave himself pep talks to stave off disillusionment: everyone started at the bottom, he had to work his way up the chain before he could fully develop his talents, he was very lucky to be posted to Beirut—it was an important Arab-world city. He refused to complain openly to his father, who might pull strings on his behalf, if he made a solid case that he wasn't learning anything; but the last time they'd talked, he'd delicately hinted at wanting more.

"It's so routine, Dad, so paperwork-oriented."

"You're learning the ropes."

"Extremely quotidian ropes ... "

He heard James' sigh even through the thousands of wire-miles separating them. "You have to *find* meaning in the quotidian, son, it's one of the most important skills you'll ever learn—uncovering your significance and value to the routine, ordinary, dumb stuff you have to do every day. That dumb-seeming stuff is why it's called work."

Low's silence probably spoke for itself.

"Lowell." James' voice became stern. "If you can't find something to absorb you in what you're supposed to do every day, then at least make yourself useful."

Make myself useful.

He began to deliberately solicit Ahmed's insights and introductions to local society, since this was a sensitive area, hard to penetrate by most diplomatic Americans. Ahmed explained the bitter infighting which grew daily more violent between rival political and religious factions. He outlined Lebanon's tormented history since World War Two, blaming the French for setting up a constitution which did not divide power equally amongst Christians, Sunni and Shiite Muslims, and Druze tribesmen.

According to Ahmed, the Shiites in South Lebanon were resentful of increasing Palestinian domination of their region; not only had they lost economic and political power to the refugees, but they were subject to Israeli raids because of relentless Palestinian attacks back across the Israeli border.

101

Sunni Muslims tended to support the Palestinian cause while Christians did not. Tribal leaders, who controlled the rural areas and whose feuds and loyalties went back hundreds of years, were mobilizing their own militia, as were the refugee camps backed by the Syrians and the Palestine Liberation Organization.

The central government's power was eroding since it could not minimize confrontations amongst the various factions. Just last month an agreement was signed that gave the PLO virtual autonomy in certain areas of Lebanon. In South Lebanon, as well as in the poorer sections of West Beirut, there was an atmosphere of armed camps. Ahmed warned against going into any of these neighborhoods without a guide.

"Just like D.C.," Low joked, but he took notice of the tension underneath the city's glamour and encouraged Ahmed to elaborate his lessons with frequent outings.

"Where to tonight?" he asked as they walked into the embassy, after the ambassador's lunch.

"Someplace new." Ahmed winked. "I'll show you the real Middle East."

"About time, man, I knew most of this was fake."

Ahmed laughed.

Since it was Wednesday, the beginning of the Muslim weekend, Low left work early. He drove to his tiny fourth floor walk-up studio, all he could afford on his modest first-job salary. He was grateful Dad had sprung for the used Puegeot he drove. But he liked his open-air courtyard; he liked waking to the sound of excited voices, of children getting ready for school and the street vendors hawking their wares, and to the homey smells of breakfast cooking.

He'd lived in a similar setting in Paris, but Beirut was so much friendlier he didn't feel the same big-city anonymity. When he tried using Arabic in the neighborhood, people responded with delight and encouragement. He got such a kick out of it. Listening now to Arabic music wailing from a neighbor's radio, he stretched out on his narrow bed.

Back in Bloomington, he's with her on the carpet in front of his fireplace. Firelight glows on different parts of her hair and body as she undulates in his grasp. In his absorption he doesn't feel the veil forming between them, transparent but impenetrable. His arms loosen and she melts

102

away.

He jolted awake, heart pounding.

Clare had a hold on him like the old Beatles song. She inspired tantalizing possibilities at first sight.

Long hair was the trend, but he'd rarely seen hair like hers—waist-length ripples lit with damp-looking dark-honey color: imagine this hair slipping over her naked body, whose opulent curves were so obvious in her braless tee shirt and tight jeans. Her full breasts just asked his palms to lift, his thumbs to tickle, as her lush lips just asked for his deepest kiss. And how she *stared*: eyes so dark a brown they looked black in their intensity, swallowing the entire Assembly Hall the afternoon they met, as if she wanted to reach into his soul. Mesmerizing.

What fun to find her in French, and catch her always eyeing him, so hungry yet so shy. He'd been touched by her confiding her political genesis, after the demonstration. Her espousal of revolutionary talk didn't hide her anguish over Joe's death. He usually avoided radicals—little humor, lots of work—but the fervid way she watched him was so provocative. When someone joked of Ginger's and Clare's silly bet—"I hear you can just pick whichever one you want"—he figured the Language Units hayride, conveniently the weekend after the protest march, was his chance to explore the likelihood of casual sex.

When she'd sung those wacky ditties about Lenin he about fell off the truck in surprise. Under the severe party-line front, she was witty and open minded.

Her virginity also surprised him, given her radical hippie vibe and the alleged bet with Ginger. Of course he hadn't realized, their first bewildering night, how young she really was. But experiencing her naïveté transforming into trusting, reckless ardor was the most erotic turn-on of his life: sex with Clare was never casual.

He shivered, hardened by memory of languid hours passed showing her how often and how many ways he could make her come; or make her laugh; or in just stroking her soft vanilla-scented skin, suspended by her enthralled regard. He had never known such sated peace, nor felt so swimmingly lost to lust: once they were lovers, her every move stirred him to constant, helpless, unexpected excitement.

His helplessness kept him on edge, fighting to keep distant, so he could produce his thesis and stay focused on his goals. Other girls might have sensed his vulnerability, and extracted obligations, but Clare was too inexperienced to do more than express her own bemused longing and heave lovelorn sighs.

Keeping his cool with her had been so easy he regretted it, now, staring at his pale plaster studio ceiling, feeling the sweat from arousal and this sad dream chilling his skin. He should have told her, every time, how incredible she was. He should have told her, at the end, he forgave her deception, even though learning her real age had freaked him out. Hiding her cell was part of the drama, no doubt, for a budding "revolutionary."

At this remove, her defiant persona-building seemed courageous and endearing. He'd almost always mocked a deep-South accent at Indiana as a lark, responding to students' reaction when they heard he was from Virginia; he knew what it meant to pretend to be someone you weren't. The impulse was not necessarily malicious.

She was well read, in spite of her stated disdain for formal scholarship. How many Indiana teenagers quoted Nechayev? And she was fearless, a brave fighter for that misguided SMC outfit. When he pictured her teetering on the wire while her cohorts fled, he still felt outrage, still felt the barbs piercing his own skin. He still blamed the asshole Henderson.

How was she expressing her activism now the war and its protest movement were finally beginning to wind down? Was its conclusion any solace to her, for losing Joe? Doubtful. That loss was inconsolable. Did she still consider herself a revolutionary?

He twisted around to face the wall.

God, how awkward he'd been at the end. Fleeing the diner? Drinking whiskey for days? Getting rough when she showed up? *That just wasn't me.* No relationship had ever unraveled him this way. She was the brave one, coming to face him after his weeklong hangover.

He'd broken his own rules trying to contact her at Christmas but realized, ruefully, that she'd taken him at his word and would stay out of touch. So he made the effort to push her from his thoughts. But he'd been tense for a long time, had trouble sleeping, didn't concentrate well. Stupidly, he'd begun smoking more heavily. The dream persisted for months.

Early in their friendship, Ahmed had asked casually if he had a girlfriend, and Low surprised himself by talking about Clare. Ahmed, whose calm manner inspired trust, was the only person Low'd confided in besides Troy. But he didn't tell anyone about the dream.

"I think you did the only honorable thing, under the circumstances." Sympathy softened Ahmed's narrow face. "You had to let her go, if you really didn't want to marry her."

This had the ring of benediction. Low felt eased, a little.

"I suppose she is very beautiful."

"No." She wasn't even a type he noticed. He usually went for sleek, petite, well-groomed and snooty. He enjoyed making them melt for him and regret their snootiness. But Clare was untamed—bare faced, weird shoes, drab uniform of worn jeans and tees, hair tangled. She was tall and sturdy; she wore his clothes on occasion, at his place. If memory served, she didn't even shave. And it didn't matter. The one time she dressed up, for Simmons' party, she'd converted herself into conventional prettiness; but he recalled feeling swollen with heat and suffering under the burden of his own good manners the entire evening. He'd barely heard Simmons' thesis comments since he just wanted to get her alone and naked again.

"I mean, you'd never see her in a magazine." Unless it was *Mother Jones*. "She looked ... old fashioned." He didn't know how this came to him, but her face fit on one of those Victorian-era Christmas cards, starry dark eyes gazing at him adoringly, pink lips opening like a flower, peachy cheeks blushed with ersatz cold, under a fluffy white hat.

"Then what makes her so difficult for you to forget?"

He scrubbed through his suddenly-itchy hair. "She was ... unusual."

"Haven't you seen other women since then?"

He'd been at loose ends in Virginia before his training started, uneasy over leaving Clare, uninspired to seek out new companionship. His old girlfriend Karen, whom he normally would've looked up, had moved to a commune in Vermont. He'd had a short thing with a British translator this summer in Beirut. But Clare stayed in his mind and the dream persisted.

105

"If you think of her you should tell her," Ahmed offered. "Write to her."

Low remembered his unreturned call. "Not worth it."

"But she made a profound impression on you ... "

"It was only a few weeks." Mid-September to mid-November. He'd driven back East in a grey fog: mile after cold flat midwestern mile, missing her more with every desolate rain-splattered road sign, unable even to listen to music. He'd been a ghost at Thanksgiving and again at Christmas, earning the irritation of his father and sister and assorted expectant guests.

"A short time can inspire a long love."

Was it love he'd been so lost in, with Clare? He'd always been cautious about the word; people used it too easily, in his experience. "Absolutely not. She was way too young, a child really, but I didn't understand that. I didn't know her well."

"Sometimes confessing love can release us from its weight."

"I'm not the confessing type. I'm over her."

Ahmed had just looked at him steadily, with his deep eyes.

"What about you, Ahmed, do you have a girlfriend?"

His friend had given a half-shrug. "Nobody serious, certainly not here, not now." His tone precluded further personal questions.

Now, in his room, Low got up to splash cold water on his face and change his shirt. He poured himself some Johnny Walker and took a swallow. Better. Clare—he'd never forget her, but she'd made it clear, by her silence, that she was lost to him. And the dream? Just a dream.

He lit a cigarette and went onto his tiny balcony, which endowed an expansive feeling because of the view it commanded of the western half of the city.

Sunset was coloring the sky in streaks of orange and pink. A prayer call sounded at the mosque on the corner, imploring the faithful to worship; then another sounded a few blocks away, then all over in echoing waves that moved him with their eerie beauty. Time stopped. A few figures moved between the buildings, hurrying on their way to the nearest mosque.

He took a deep breath. A slight sea breeze cooled his face and curled his cigarette smoke away, and he felt cleansed. He put his ashtray and glass of Scotch on the balcony floor so as not to offend any passers-by who might glimpse him, smoking and drinking, on their way to salat.

After the prayer calls ended, the soccer game in the alleyway next to his building resumed as the players drifted back from the mosque. Low smiled at a couple who waved at him. He joined them when he could for evening games. It was a great way to practice Arabic, repeating ingenuously all the scatological phrases they foisted on him, and he relished playing hard soccer again for the first time since St. Paul's.

At Georgetown and I.U. his primary physical activity had been lots of sex.

Here there'd been only Pamela, the British translator he'd met at an embassy party his second week in Beirut. She was elegant, slim, clad in cream linen, with light red hair, big blue eyes and pale skin. She'd seemed amusingly prissy to him, in that upper-class British way, like someone he could tease, and she came on strong—staring into his eyes when they were introduced, pretending to brush something off his lapel, holding his hand when he lit her cigarette. Wanting a woman as he did—it had been many months since Clare—he quickly responded and they left the party to go to her apartment.

She was an avid lover, so although he didn't try to jolly her out of her prissiness once he perceived it was innate, he kept seeing her for a few weeks before her next post.

He was surprised when, on their last date, she suddenly got sentimental.

"I shall miss you, Lowell. I was crushed when they said I had to leave." As he looked at her, at a loss for words, she covered her face. He handed a napkin when he saw tears running through her fingers. "Bloody hell. If only you didn't *touch* me the way you know how to do, or *look* the way you do, this'd be easier."

He'd heard variations on this theme about his looks for years.

She sipped her G and T. "You must have Irish blood. The Irish are the only truly sensual Northern people."

He barely stemmed a snort of laughter at this nonsense. Yet his mother Lydia's amused voice came to him, blaming her Irish ancestry, whenever he behaved badly as a child.

"When Irish eyes are smiling," Pamela sang. Should he call

for the check? But she quickly broke off. "You've no idea what I'm talking about."

"I realize you're upset," he said cautiously, not wanting to provoke a bigger scene.

"You must have had a very intense love affair, and it ended badly, and you've vowed never to repeat it. Or else, perhaps, it's something to do with your mother?"

"Why are you analyzing this?"

"Because I'm keen to know what makes you tick. You fascinate me." She put a hand on his cheek and he twisted away. "I was over the moon about you until I realized you were only interested in the physical aspect of our relationship."

"So were you—"

"I'm not accusing you, darling, I know you're young. I'm simply trying to understand who you really are. If you're as cold as I suspect." She gazed at him so intently he had to look down. "What makes you fall in love? Surely one or another girl has come fairly close, with all the attention you must get—"

Low shook his head. He was as terrible at this kind of conversation as he was, he thought, good at seduction.

Pamela persisted. "Well, what attracted you to me?"

I was really horny. "You're smart, pretty ... "

"And I nabbed you as soon as you arrived here."

So I'm easy. "Didn't we both get what we wanted?"

"I just wish I could've elicited the real man underneath. If there is one."

As if he was some kind of phony, to take what was offered freely! Women: rarely hard to get but always hard to get rid of.

Celibacy was acceptable. With Ahmed he was in the predominantly male Lebanese world. Beirut women—some, incredible beauties—were impossible to get to know, since even the ones who showed interest, with their eyes, were surrounded by watchful family or friends so he didn't want to acknowledge them. Western women—it amused him to already think 'Western'—paled by comparison, overly aware of their surroundings, fidgety as Pamela.

Clare, he knew, would have embraced Beirut with open eyes and an eager heart, finding adventure in every new smell, taste, sight and encounter. She'd be perfect company. Unsettling, how he yearned for her, after that dream. *But she's history.*

Low finished his cigarette, locked the balcony doors, rinsed his glass and ashtray out in the sink, and went downstairs to wait for Ahmed.

TWENTY-ONE

THE BAR was narrow, dark, crammed with men who hunched over tiny coffee cups and hubbly-bubbly—colorful glass multi-stemmed water pipes. The rich, familiar smell of hashish struck Low, reminding him of college days. "This is an American tradition too."

"*Tak arabi, ya sadiki,*" said Ahmed. Speak in Arabic, my friend. He led them to a corner table and called for coffee and a hubby bubbly.

The hash was powerful and Low felt instantly removed, as if he were watching the room from far away. He saw himself down the strong coffee, in slow motion, and shake the little cup for more. He saw Ahmed greet men at other tables and one youth rise to join them. Ahmed did not introduce them; he glanced at Low and ordered more hash, called 'shishah.'

Low smoked and idly listened to their conversation, of which he understood about two-thirds. They discussed their families' health and then the current ever-splintering divisions among Phalangist, or separatist, Christians. Low caught the word 'assassinated' and saw Ahmed's face darken. Their voices lowered.

The boy wore an old flak jacket with some kind of insignia on it—like so many in Beirut these days, essentially a gang sign—and a pair of battered jeans. He sported a heavy beard although he looked no older than a teenager. Odd: this scruffy gangster was a friend of the ever-dapper Ahmed. Low studied him, surreptitiously, committing the insignia to memory.

As Low bent to the pipe again he saw the friend gesture toward him, speculatively, and saw Ahmed's quick head-shake. The ambiance seemed to sour after that; the kid went back to his table and Ahmed slapped some money down.

"*Yullah,*" he told Low. Let's go.

110

The crisp night air was a tonic to Low's smoky head. Ahmed drove to the tourist district where the nightclubs were, and although he didn't talk about whatever was worrying him, his mood seemed to lift as he wove madly in and out of his lane on the corniche.

"Oriental dancing. You'll like this, Lowell." He had been promising the Oriental dance show for some time, but summer was slow in Beirut and the best dancers toured Europe. Now in late September people were coming back to town.

The nightclub was one of the newest, with a flashy mirrored décor and a polished parquet dance floor. A band played mediocre jazz in one corner. The prices were astronomical. It was cheaper to buy a bottle than a series of drinks, so they ordered Scotch—the ubiquitous Johnny Walker Red Label. Low saw a few familiar faces, from the embassy, and he waved. He hoped he did not look as stoned as he felt.

"Terrific hash," he told Ahmed. "Why didn't you take me to that place before?"

"Americans can be … judgmental." Ahmed had told him about spending a couple of years at a New England prep school, another experience they had in common, where he hadn't liked being viewed as an oddity, an "A-rab," who probably rode camels and lived in a tent. Girls, he complained, had acted as if he was dirty, or an exotic treat to be added to their collection.

"Not me, buddy, I'm not judgmental," Low said, surprised that Ahmed would still wonder about their friendship. "We're pals, remember?"

Ahmed gave him a long look, but before Low could query him further, the room darkened, the band switched from jazz to popular Lebanese, and one dramatic red spot lit the dance floor as a woman glided out.

She bent her head almost to her knees, long black hair covering her face. When the tempo quickened she flung back her hair in a dark fountain and moved just her hands to the rhythm. Her control was perfect. As the music rose in volume and intensity she threw different parts of her body into motion, creating a sensuous counterpart to the beat, jingling the bells on her hips and feet and fingers in a hypnotic performance.

When at last she dropped her head and her luxuriant hair fell

111

forward there was a still moment and then a roar of applause. She smiled widely, flashing white teeth, and walked swiftly and gracefully among the tables, collecting tips in a black velvet folder.

When she came to them, Low leaned back and fixed her with a frank stare, while Ahmed added to her folder. She returned Low's look and touched his temple with one long finger.

"Nice eyes," she said in English, with an amused lilt. "Cute boy."

Low jerked his head away and she laughed and went on to the next table.

"What the hell *is* it with Lebanese women?" he asked Ahmed. "I've never had trouble before. But here, even if I manage to get one alone long enough to talk, all they do is giggle. Or else they treat me like a kid. I keep striking out."

"You're American." Ahmed shrugged. "They like your looks, but you're too direct. You have to be subtle here, very discreet." He nodded toward the dancer. "You're aiming too high. Women like her always have a wealthy older man. A jealous older man."

"So I'll wait a few years. I'll be older." Low watched the dancer, her curvaceous form stirring him to moodiness, weave her way back behind the stage. "Maybe even wealthy."

"I'll find someone for you. All my friends are coming back from vacation now."

"Like that guy at the café? He looked like he could *use* a vacation."

Ahmed threw him a wary look and spoke rapidly in Arabic.

Low frowned. "Try me in the morning." He gestured to his glass. "Drinking's supposed to make languages easier, but it's never happened to me yet." A window of caution flew open in his head: Ahmed had asked him if he recognized the friend's badge as the Mourabitoun's—one of the most extreme Muslim groups.

Ahmed's narration of the different gangs and their causes was not flavored by approval or disapproval for any particular Lebanese faction, although Low knew he was a not-very-devout Muslim. Sensitive to admonitions against talking too-personal politics, Low had always refrained from asking about Ahmed's own affiliations.

This now seemed an error.

It was turning into a late night. Low felt too tired, suddenly, to deal with the implications of Ahmed's broaching a taboo subject in such a clandestine way. "I'm heading home," he declared, draining his glass. "A taxi's safe from here, no?"

"Sure." Ahmed's eyes were on the musicians. "But you'll miss the next act, Lowell, and I hear she's fabulous—"

"Another time, pal." He patted Ahmed's shoulder and found his way out through the glittery crowd. A taxi swung past and stopped for him.

TWENTY-TWO

FROM THE back seat of the taxi he stared at the lighted streets, teeming even at this late hour, with small groups clustered in front of stores, at outdoor cafes, sitting on the curb. It was the aspect of the city he liked best.

But tonight, surfeited with Lebanon momentarily, he was remembering Indiana.

IU's Political Science department was excellent, but he'd chosen the school mostly to see a new part of the country after what he knew was a lifetime of privileged Northeast homogeneity. Bloomington was quaint, reminiscent of New England with its neat town square and wooded hills, and tolerant of the huge university in its midst. The students were milder-mannered than on the East Coast, even those from out of state, as the Hoosiers' natural amiability rubbed into them on campus.

In his mind's eye, Low watched Ginger and Clare perform one of their guitar and dulcimer duets at the Language Units variety show. The poignant Leonard Cohen melody, "Sisters of Mercy," threaded from his head into the streets and turned them strange and sad. There were a couple of lines about traveling so long and needing comfort.

He saw Clare's sweet face as she sang, lit by the simple tune, eyes closed, cheeks flushed, betraying her reserve in performance. She was an amazing singer, her voice high and true and shiver-producing. Damn that fucking dream—it made him ache for her steady warmth. He felt so cold tonight.

Climbing the four flights of stairs to his studio, he recalled Ahmed's suggestion that he write to her. Had Clare cooled down enough to acknowledge, now, a letter from him? What the hell. It was a way of shaking his unease. He took out a pad of paper and another glass of Scotch onto his balcony. The streets below were still alive as he began to write.

114

Clare,
I think often of you and of our time together. Leaving you was so hard.
I hope you remember the good in what we shared. By now you're back in
French House for your sophomore year. IU seems far away but I miss the
ease of those Bloomington days. I trust you're enjoying them as you did last
year.
Things are strange in Beirut tonight, as they have been for some time. I
suspect my closest friend here might be involved with an extremist group.

Writing that gave him a jolt. Just because some barroom acquaintance wore their badge, it didn't mean Ahmed was involved with the Mourabitoun. But then why had he asked, in such a rapid dialect, if Low recognized the insignia? *Testing me.* Testing his understanding of what? The language or the reference? Why the fuck would Ahmed put distance between them like that? Low had widened the gap by pretending not to understand, an instinctive self-protective impulse, disturbed by the very name Mourabitoun.

The political groups here are like street gangs in the States, turf wars
included, but their violence is more organized. The Mourabitoun are
notorious, powerful quasi-Marxist Sunnis, supported by the PLO who have
all the weapons and money. Their nickname is 'loony-tunes' because they're
so vicious.

He didn't want to describe, to Clare, the loony-tune torture stamp, levied at perceived enemies: cutting off a victim's genitalia and stuffing it into his mouth. He crossed his legs tight and took a healthy swallow of Scotch.

One of them being so openly friendly toward Ahmed, with me right
there, means he's either related or useful to them. Ahmed didn't want to
introduce me when the kid came over to sit with us, and when the kid asked
about me Ahmed ignored it. So what's Ahmed doing at the embassy, you
might ask? He's a translator and Commerce Department assistant. Nothing
too interesting to internal Lebanese politics in that. Could he consider our
friendship any kind of access? Not likely. I'm just a junior lackey here,
without any power or influence.

It bothered him to admit his lowly status, even in a letter he already suspected he wouldn't send. He stared at the last line and then out into the night.

The loonies were of great interest, it was reputed, to the senior political officer, a man several reporting structures above him.

Should he try to uncover more about them? Make himself useful, as James advised?

He could tell Ahmed they should revisit the shishah bar. It might look odd if he went alone; he'd been the only foreigner in the place. He could pose as a curious innocent if they saw the scruffy youth again, and he could charm the guy but keep pretending his Arabic was poor. He'd have to find a good reason to befriend the kid. Ahmed might find such an overture suspect after his furtive question about the Mourabitoun insignia.

Who was Low, exactly, to Ahmed?

He paced the tiny circles proscribed by the balcony's small footage.

He'd never wondered about anyone's friendliness. He was used to being as direct as he wanted to be, and used to having people like him, seek him out, invite him. Had he taken his bond with Ahmed for granted, by trusting him from the beginning, heedlessly sharing frank observations of the city and of their colleagues?

Ahmed was the only person in Beirut he'd call a friend.

For the first time that struck him as odd. Why should he not have been closer to the American community here?

"Because they're a bunch of drags," he said aloud.

His colleagues were mostly married, tired-seeming, locked in a small world of socializing frequently with each other and talking about the same things at every gathering—State Department office politics, the latest party, who was balling whom, what was happening in the States, how inconvenient life was in Lebanon since the Troubles. There weren't even any good-looking women in the diplomatic community.

Foreign Service officers shifted so, it was hard for them to build relationships, and many became desensitized to local culture outside of their embassy work. Maybe that was just true of expatriates—Americans in Paris had been much the same. He'd grabbed then at Aimee's overture since he recognized she was the only way he'd ever really get to know France.

But his dismissive attitude toward Americans here was probably a mistake.

Wasn't there some coolness toward him, now that he was

thinking about it, hadn't their drawing away become more obvious, the more time he spent with Ahmed? Ahmed had no interest in going to the official functions or casual gatherings either; he agreed with Low they were deadly dull. They now skipped all but mandatory social events in the expat group.

But his colleagues seemed increasingly offended when he turned down invitations to their dreary barbeques and cocktail parties.

What a novel sensation: he was *disliked*.

But so what? He wasn't in this to make friends with expats. He was in this to influence opinion on the ground.

And Ahmed was a hell of a lot more interesting than any official American. He'd traveled, he was open-minded, he had a quality of listening that induced comfort. And he'd made himself completely available to a newcomer, offering the famous hospitality of his culture, making Low feel at home. Going to that hash place was a measure of confidence in their friendship, wasn't it? Unless it *was* some kind of test.

During training in the States, they'd been warned against fraternization with foreign nationals, warned against romance and sexual temptation. Low knew sexual behavior—no woman in the world could play games with him. But Ahmed was a guy. Low hadn't thought twice about hanging out with him. No way was this fraternization. Was it?

He stared at his letter to Clare, not really seeing it as he folded it and stuffed it into his pocket. He swallowed the last of his Scotch and went back inside.

He'd use this unsettling encounter as a way to test Ahmed right back, if a test was what the hash bar had been, and as an opportunity to explore the shadowy Mourabitoun, if he could.

Make myself useful.

He was certainly tired of spinning his wheels here as a glorified file clerk.

TWENTY-THREE

THE NEXT week, Low approached the political attaché, Allen Guthery, a greyhound of a man with eyebrows the size of his mustache. Guthery regarded him with some wariness, not only, Low knew, because of Low's distance from official Americans, but because Guthery had worked under Low's father during the early Sixties.

"What's up, Goodenow?"

Low briefly sounded him out on the idea of learning more about the loonies.

"How'd you meet this kid?"

"A shishah place."

"Why the hell were you there? Don't tell me you were alone, please, I don't want to have to lecture *you* on basic protocol."

Low shrugged. He wasn't going to bring Ahmed to Guthery's attention.

But Guthery did it for him. "Did Badawi take you?"

"We were hanging out," Low admitted. He supposed their friendship was no secret.

"Did you get the feeling he had you meet this kid on purpose?"

"No. He seemed nervous that I was there."

Guthery nodded. "We'll play it like this. Continue hanging out, as you call it, business as usual. Get him to take you back there. Same time, on a Wednesday. These things are usually routine. Then be friendly to the other fellow. Your Arabic's good enough to chat with him. Let me know where it goes." He sat back and spread plate-like hands against the edge of his desk, signifying the end of the conversation.

This was not what Low expected. "That's it?"

Wasn't Guthery going to describe the intricacies of the Mourabitoun hierarchy, advise him of their exact city geography,

118

clue him into what to look out for, specifically?

"Look, Goodenow, there's no surveillance in my operation. State doesn't want our people getting tangled up in internal movements. I'm certainly not going on record to advise you to infiltrate a local militia. But it's only sensible to use this link, if you truly believe there's something to learn." He leaned forward again. "Sometimes, you know, our government positions foreign nationals with us, trained to conduct this kind of intel. It's entirely possible Badawi is one of them. I'm not informed of who's who. Their identities are protected."

Guthery meant CIA. "Ahmed doesn't strike me as that type."

"First lesson of diplomacy, Goodenow, assume nothing."

"But no smart Agency hire would want to get close to the loonies." The penalty for discovery would be too severe. They'd make a horrific example of a spy. They'd make death seem welcome.

"Maybe a really good one would."

Low got the feeling Guthery was dismissing him. He stood.

"Don't let yourself get into any situation where you're isolated with the Mourabitoun youth, Goodenow, I don't need to remind you of that danger."

"No sir."

AHMED RESPONDED readily to Low's expressed desire to spend more time together. Ahmed started inviting him after work to swim in the Badawi's pool and stay for dinner. Low'd been trained since childhood to be a perfect guest. He asked Ahmed's grandfather about Lebanese history, he followed Ahmed's mother, Sonia, into the kitchen to learn her famous makloubeh recipe, he played backgammon with Ahmed's little brother and let him win. At every visit he spoke only Arabic, in a halting manner. He didn't let on how much more he understood than he could produce. He made sure they were all delighted with him.

At the same time, he accepted the next cocktail party invitation he got from one of his American colleagues, and an offer of a tennis game after that, and then went to someone else's barbecue. Each time he asked Ahmed to join him. Each time Ahmed refused. But his friend didn't once question Low's sudden new welcome of embassy functions.

"I feel like getting really high," he told Ahmed one Wednesday afternoon several weeks after his talk with Guthery. "Would you take me back to that place with the dynamite hash?"

"What about Samia?" They had made a habit of catching the dancer's Wednesday night show where Low flirted ritually, and fruitlessly, with her.

"Nah, I'm giving her up. I'd rather do drugs. It's better for my health."

Ahmed laughed. "Okay. I'll pick you up around nine."

That evening Low pretended to get stoned—actually, it was hard to resist the strength of the hash—and studied the men who stopped at their table. Ahmed seemed to be in a hurry to leave, but his sense of hospitality necessarily prevailed as Low ordered more coffee and pastries and sucked away at the hubby-bubbly water pipe. Some unseen DJ kept switching from American rock to Middle Eastern pop. Finally the scruffy youth from the first evening appeared. He sat down next to them, and peered into Low's face.

"I see you again," he said in thick English. "Christian, what you do here?"

Ahmed frowned. "Farouk, this is Lowell, you know we work together."

"I am so very pleased to meet you," Low said in slow formal Arabic. He produced a goofy grin. Absurdly, a Three Dog Night song burst into his brain, "Momma Told Me not to Come," and he had a hard time not snickering. Not the way to have fun, indeed.

Farouk ignored him then, and talked to Ahmed in the same rapid dialect as before. After the usual familial salutations, there was an agitated discussion of a recent street battle and, more generally, the advances and retreats of various militias. Of the three-fourths Low could understand, it all sounded like Sharks versus Jets from "West Side Story," but he noted some names of leaders and locations mentioned, as he observed the two.

"You heard about last weekend," Farouk said abruptly.

Ahmed grimaced. "Don't mention that in front of him!"

"He's too crazy with shishah to understand us," Farouk sneered. "He shouldn't be here. Why did you bring him?"

"He insisted on coming."

"What for?" Farouk suddenly stood, tilting the little table. The water in the pipe sloshed and Low's baklavah slice slid onto the floor. Other patrons glanced over, but their scrutiny did not deter Farouk from grabbing Low's arms and heaving him upright. "I take you from here, Christian," he snarled in English. "You don't get nothing more."

Low yanked away. "I can leave on my own."

"He's my guest," Ahmed hissed, standing too.

"I don't know who is he or why you bring him but he go out now." Farouk gripped Low again and shuffled him through the small smoky room to a back exit. The little fucker was a lot stronger than he looked.

Outside, he pushed Low with such force he crashed against a metal garbage can, spilling its reeking contents into the alley. He kicked at his head before Low staggered up, shoulder throbbing, and threw himself into a hard punch at Farouk's midsection with his good arm.

Farouk doubled over, but then twisted around like an acrobat to wrap Low in a crushing choke from behind. Low parceled his breath down tiny ladder steps to control his crazed heartbeat but spots swam before his eyes and he knew he was about to pass out. Blood pounded in his head as he tried to wrench free.

"*Halas!*" shouted Ahmed. He reached past Low's head to take Farouk's face in both hands and shake it. "Stop. Remember where he works!"

"Remember where *you* work, ya Ahmed." Farouk gave a final vicious jerk on Low's throat before releasing him to the puddled alley ground where he stayed, slumped and gasping. "I see him with you again ... " He cocked his thumb and forefinger into a mock pistol, fired.

"*Yallah.*" Go. Ahmed lifted his chin toward the bar, and Farouk went back in.

Hash, lack of breath and the pain in his windpipe were altering Low's perception so the dank alley had the murky surrealism of a strange dream. And in this dream it was with dismay, but not surprise, that he heard Ahmed mutter in Arabic, "Now I have to kill him."

121

"Goddammit, you're not killing anybody," Low began, before his voice gave out.

"Shut up," Ahmed said tiredly. He leaned to hoist Low to his feet.

As they passed the bar's still open back exit, the incongruous blare of Rod Stewart wailed, "oh Maggie I wish I'd never—" Then Fairuz, the popular female Arabic singer, immediately replaced Rod. Several male voices sang along, loudly.

Low peered inside, rubbing his neck, wanting to get in another punch. Ahmed reached out to grip his arm, nails digging in to show serious intent, and dragged him away. After ten minutes of alleyways they came to a wide well-lit street.

Ahmed faced him. "This is a personal situation for me."

"No shit. For me too."

"Farouk is ... unstable. He doesn't like Americans."

"No shit," Low repeated, hoarse. "That doesn't mean he deserves to be killed."

"He's striking at me by attacking you. So he's my responsibility."

"You want to explain that?"

"No." He took a handkerchief from his pocket and wiped at Low's forehead. Low jerked away and took the bloody cloth, kept wiping until there were no more streaks.

They watched each other for a moment. Low shrugged, finally, trying to express disinterest, since there was no opening for him to speak frankly. Not now. Maybe not ever again. Ahmed laughed softly. "Okay, ya sadiki, time for a drink."

His head was reverberating with alarm, but his feet were already taking him into another bar behind Ahmed, a touristy place. He cleaned up a little more in the bathroom and then drank the fastest whiskey of his life in spite of the wicked burn it made going down his fragile throat.

"Tomorrow night." Ahmed suddenly rubbed Low's back, shocking him sober. "My mother is fixing makloubeh, your favorite." He lowered his brows in a mock frown. "You won't disappoint her by not coming."

"I'll be there." What else was he supposed to do?

"Lowell, anyone who looks at me looks at you, because you're always with me, *n'est'pas?*" Ahmed's smile, for the first time, seemed to show too many teeth. Low yawned hugely, feigning fatigue, and stared into his glass. Soon after, they took separate taxis home.

He couldn't report this to Guthery. He could just imagine the dry way he'd comment, "We can't prove the kid's hostility to you is related to the Mourabitoun, any more than we can assume Badawi is some kind of hit man without local police involvement. Goodenow, *they're* the ones you need to tell, if you really think Badawi meant business."

Yeah, right. He wasn't about to talk to some local policeman. In Lebanon, as in many countries, the mere suspicion of crime resulted in everyone associated—including its reporter—being thrown into jail, for as long as it took to sort things out.

"But be careful," Guthery would say. "Don't be alone with him. Tomorrow should be safe enough. He won't pull anything in front of his family."

Low smoked a final cigarette, thinking of nothing as he lay in bed, as the smoke curled away from his face into darkness. He barely remembered to stub it out in the nightstand ashtray before he fell into a stunned sleep in which different people got shot in the alley, falling sideways into the hash bar: Guthery, Farouk, Ahmed, himself. One by one they tumbled in slow motion, all night long.

TWENTY-FOUR

A T DINNER the next night, four of Ahmed's cousins came, recently arrived from Switzerland. The talk was fashionable and easy. As he chatted, Low felt the previous night's morose weight, but Ahmed's face showed no anxiety. He'd obviously slept well.

Another cousin arrived just as dinner was being served. She was seated next to Low, and in spite of his edginess, he became immediately aware of her. She was strikingly pretty, with a lithe figure dressed in a soft-looking sweater and skirt, shiny straight black hair, and the ardent dark eyes and beautiful skin he had admired in other women here. She smiled at him and put out a small square hand.

"Leila." Her touch was firm, her gaze over him swift. He made polite conversation, careful not to look at her too often, as he recognized the moves. He usually relished this chase from the first spark-filled glances to the final satisfied sighs. But tonight it was no fun. He felt like a robot with Leila, in fact, discordant with the entire tone of the evening. The cousins seemed brittle and jaded despite their youth.

Over their goodbyes, Leila let her hand stay in his a little too long for propriety, but he could only manage a frozen smile. He went to look for Ahmed.

He was in his father's study, already pouring two glasses of Scotch from the crystal decanter beside a leather-bound set of Dickens. Dr. Badawi had spent years as a medical student in England and had, Ahmed said, loved English literature. Sonia had told once Low that she was glad her husband had died before the Troubles. Ahmed handed Low a glass and raised his own with a challenging smile. "To our friendship."

Low put his glass down. "I'm not drinking to that until I have some answers." His regret was instant. *How stupid I sound!*

"You don't want them. Stay out of it."

"I'm already in it, Ahmed, Farouk put me in."

"Farouk recognized you were a threat to him, and feared you were to me by association. He was right to throw you out. This way you can know nothing more, about him or any of us."

"Talk to me."

"You want to get into this, truly, you want us to be honest? *Now?*"

"What are you doing at the embassy?"

Ahmed's laugh sounded cynical. "Come on Lowell, this is me, remember? Your faithful companion? Your drinking partner? Your pal?"

"Not after last night."

Ahmed's expression was clearly a sneer. "You had so much smoke," he said flatly. "Anyone could see that. Maybe you had a ... bad trip?" He walked up close. "If I were you I wouldn't want that getting around. A drug problem? The embassy wouldn't like it. You drink quite a bit as well. If you ever talk about this at work, that's what I'll say."

"Son of a bitch," Low said slowly.

"Who are you calling a bitch?"

"I mean no disrespect, you know that, but *think* about Sonia," Low snapped. He grabbed Ahmed's rigid shoulders. "You're putting her and everyone in your family at risk by getting involved with crazies like Farouk."

Ahmed threw him off with an exaggerated violence Low suddenly recognized as drunkenness. Low stepped back, submissive, holding up his hands.

"You talk about my family? They took you in like a son. And for what? Which of us is the real risk?" Ahmed's eyes were huge and accusing and his hand shook as he poured another drink. "These crazies, you Christians call them, work for the honor of my family."

Christians? Again? "Ahmed, you know I'm not religious." Low hadn't set foot in church in years, not since his last mandatory Chapel at St. Paul's prep school. Episcopalian mumbo-jumbo left him cold after his mother's departure.

"And you know what I'm talking about. Your pro-Christian government supports the Phalangists allowing the Israeli army to invade my country, to murder so many of my cousins, the Phalangists propping up this corrupt excuse for Lebanese leadership."

By now, in late 1973, Christian-based militias acted like an extension of the Lebanese national army, who gave them training and light weapons and, it was rumored, funds channeled from private sources. The Lebanese army had been noticeably absent earlier this year during an Israeli raid in Beirut, in which PLO leaders and Lebanese Muslim militia had been killed. Groups like the Moutabitoun operated closely with the PLO and received financial and military help from Syria, Libya and Iraq, whose Soviet support made them enemies of the U.S.

It was completely clear to Low, now, which side Ahmed was on.

"You work for my government too!" Anger pushed aside Low's wariness. "How can you even associate with the loonies? You're educated, you should have a reasonable perspective, you must see how screwy this whole polarization has become, how manipulated by outsiders—"

"Let me ask you something, Lowell. Has your family ever been attacked? Their homes destroyed? Their businesses ruined?"

"That's not the point—"

"It is exactly the point. Answer my fucking question."

The answer was, not since the U.S. Civil War, where half of Low's ancestral family had been impoverished by the defeat of the South. The other half, on his father's side, had been in New England since 1635. Low shook his head.

"You have no idea what is required to be a freedom fighter in your own country, even if your ancestors knew. The situation here is too complex for any foreigner to understand."

He'd heard some version of this freedom-fighter apologist talk before. "You're right about the complexity here, Ahmed, but I do understand the need for legal solutions to political differences, according to the rule of law, which your government is *still* trying to operate here and which, in my opinion, would be a *lot* easier if the PLO wasn't infiltrating so aggressively."

"Or if the Phalangists weren't now our defacto army."

He wasn't getting anywhere. "I'm sure freedom fighting, as

you call it, doesn't involve working at the American Embassy, not unless you're using your connections somehow."

"As you were trying to use mine."

"Look, Ahmed, I'm only thinking of diplomatic security, where your presence at the embassy is concerned—"

"You're thinking of yourself. You've told me often enough how bored you are, how you want to get ahead more quickly. What better way to do that than supply interesting information? And I—" Ahmed held up a hand to cut off Low's reply—"I was stupid to take you again last night. You shouldn't have been there. Let it go."

"But why—"

"No more," Ahmed declared. "You won't get anything from me, Lowell, I know worse interrogators." He laughed shortly. "And if some embassy boss thinks he can get rid of me I'll remind him any Lebanese who replaces me will also be doing two jobs. America's. And his own." He sank onto the sideboard, shoulders slumped.

From across the room, Low felt he was witnessing Ahmed age. There seemed to be nothing left to say. Low leaned against the wall as if pressed by a huge hand. The ice in his glass appeared to wink, mocking, Johnny Walker's jaunty little man tipping his hat.

"Don't worry, Lowell. Your job, your reputation, your career—all safe. Even if you go back with no information from Farouk or from me."

"What about ... *your* reputation? You've been seen with me a lot."

"Our cameraderie was no risk."

"What did you get out of it? What was this ... show of friendship?"

"It isn't a show. I like you." Ahmed scrubbed his face and rolled his head around on his neck. "We're even, you know, at the embassy, there's nothing I can get from you. The notion of access isn't operative at your level."

Like I need to be reminded.

"I want you to go now," Ahmed said quietly. "On your way out, thank my mother for the meal." Low nodded. "And on Saturday, as usual, Lowell, we'll have lunch."

127

Low left the room. He stopped in the parlor to say his goodbyes to the family, and Sonia came to kiss him in the usual manner, on both cheeks. When she held his face, to his amazement an impulse of tears gripped his throat. He knew this was his last visit. Sonia must have seen what was in his eyes for she frowned suddenly, her gaze sharpening. He drew back.

"Ma'salama, ya uma." Goodbye, Mother.

TWENTY-FIVE

OUTSIDE, SUDDEN autumn had emptied the streets, making them cold and eerie to Low as he drove back to his studio.

He called Guthery once he was home but immediately thought better of it, knowing he was too drunk to talk, staring at the receiver, stuck now in the conversation he'd initiated.

"Goodenow? Do you know how late it is?"

"I thought you'd want to hear my progress."

"What are you talking about? Where *are* you?" Then Guthery added abruptly, "No, don't answer, not on the phone."

Oh bullshit. "I'm home. It's okay. I'm in a pretty low-key building."

"Poor neighborhoods are much easier to corrupt than wealthier ones."

Low wasn't up for further argument tonight, about anything. "I just thought I should let you know what's been going on."

"Tell me Saturday. And if there's been real progress, as you say, take some precautions, you know? Don't get in your car, don't let anyone hand you a package, the usual. Got it?'

The usual? Jesus. How'd this get so out of control?

"But act normal," Guthery went on briskly, oblivious to the absurdity of his suggestion.

Asshole. He's getting a kick out of this. The big spymaster. And I thought I'd be the big spy. That makes me an asshole too. My first posting, distinguished by espionage. In the service of my country. What a load of crap. He knew he was inebriated, still in shock, but couldn't stop listening to this miserable internal rambling.

He lay on his bed fully clothed and stared at the ceiling but saw only Ahmed's face, with its look of cynical comprehension. *He expected me to try to use him. He assumed it all along.* He saw Ahmed's grandfather, his little brother, Sonia. He'd set out to win them over and of course, had succeeded; but this now felt like an irrevocable error, the kind that sent people to hell. And he didn't even believe in hell.

The next day was long and arduous: pacing the room, feeling imprisoned, smoking too much, suffering a massive hangover. There was no reprieve from the lengthy tirade inside his head, calling himself a false friend and the worst kind of opportunist. But the heaviest feeling was disappointment in his judgment. He'd made a rookie's mistake by exaggerating his own importance, thinking he could play some bigshot role. But there'd been no need of his subterfuge. He was no use at all here.

A phone call from Leila, Ahmed's pretty cousin, did little to distract him. He could not very well make a date with her, under the circumstances, and he felt annoyed at her for calling. He was jittery and abrupt on the phone. He could almost see her scowl as she hung up. "What do you expect, James fuckin Bond?" he said into the dead receiver. "Jesus."

He spent a sleepless night and went early to work next day. Having to use the bus made him more irritable. He just didn't think of himself as a public-transportation kind of person. He imagined the other passengers knew how he felt and were staring at him in covert hostility. When he checked a few faces and saw only the tired boredom of ordinary working people it depressed him further. *So this is it. Monday morning, even though it's Saturday here, and I'm just another guy on his way to the office. And this is how it will be, for the rest of my life.*

He wandered numb into the embassy, for the first time feeling no thrill as he flashed his diplomatic ID, no pride as he entered the gates. The secretary's eager smile turned to a puzzled frown when he walked past without a greeting. He huddled for an hour nursing one cup of coffee, going through projects in slow motion, pondering routine items as if they were Sanskrit.

He glanced up when Guthery knocked a little staccato on his desk. Low pawed protectively at his IN box. "Come with me, Goodenow."

In his office down the hall, Guthery shut the door behind them. "I had Badawi checked out, and he's not a threat to you, or to any of us. His pals in the loony-tunes are a different story, of course. He's not running them, so he can't control them. So I advise not spending time with him anymore, certainly not going to the hash bar again."

A sardonic thought shot through Low's funk like a shaft of sunlight: *how fucking long did it take him to come up with this brilliant conclusion?* Imagine: he'd joined the Foreign Service with the aspiration of becoming a senior political officer just like Guthery.

"Can I go to lunch with him?" he asked, bland.

Guthery frowned. "Stick to the commissary."

The commissary cafeteria served food worse than the Language Units fare he'd sampled with Clare in Bloomington. His and Ahmed's favorite place was a shwerma stand several blocks away. On nice days, it made for a pleasant walk, a break in routine.

"Right, Goodenow? Steer clear. Concentrate on those visa applications."

Low went back to his desk, to examine a few more of those visa applications, each one feeling sadder, to him, than the last. He wanted to reject them all and tell the applicants, *The grass isn't greener, people, stay here. Solve the problems. Make things better for your own country. Lebanon needs you.*

It was a relief when Ahmed stopped by at twelve thirty. "Coming?" He cocked one eyebrow, challenging Low to break their routine.

Low stood, staring at his friend, hoping to find in these warm-looking dark eyes the ease he'd found before, or at least some kind of closure.

Ahmed clapped his arm around Low's shoulder. "It's okay, Lowell."

They strolled out in what would have looked to anyone like relaxed amity.

"Where's your car?" Ahmed stopped, peering at the rooftops glittering in the sunlight of the embassy parking lot.

Low thought fast. "In the shop. Tuneup. But let's walk, it's a nice day."

"I don't have time to walk today. My car's around the corner."

Ahmed's Volkswagen was parked under a tree. He unlocked his door and climbed in, then reached across to unlock the passenger side, glancing up at Low with a smile of affectionate rue. Low just had to grin back.

As Ahmed turned the ignition, Low opened the door and was blinded by what seemed to be a flash of sunlight on the windshield. The door flew off and flung him backward.

TWENTY-SIX

Mexico City, 1974

THE PLANE descended into the valley—a bowl of lights, glittering like diamonds on the black velvet of the surrounding mountains. Looking out, Clare felt a thrill of excitement mixed with apprehension. Her stomach, empty except for several gin-and-tonics, contracted. Ginger was chatting with their seat-mates, a boxy-dressed Midwestern tourist couple in their fifties. She cadged Valium from the woman by pretending to worry that her guitar might be damaged down in the luggage hold.

"It's the cold," she said tearfully, after seeing the woman take out a container of the familiar yellow pills. "The wood will crack and the strings will break."

Clare smiled. They'd loosened their instrument strings well in advance of getting on this flight at Chicago's O'Hare Airport. But the woman was all sympathy and handed over a couple of pills. Ginger regaled her with stories of Mexico's tourist attractions, the best places to stay, the best bargains, how to avoid getting "turista." She left out the details she'd shared with Clare: current dope prices, negotiating deals, whom to suspect.

"It's not Spanish House," she'd cautioned. "Let me do the talking at first."

"Yeah I know man," Clare said in her hippie voice, and ironically quoted the U.S. Customs slogan. "If you get busted down there, you're in for the hassle of your life." They'd laughed: immune to such admonitions.

Once off the plane, Clare was struck by the flow of rapid Spanish around her. Ginger propelled them through the airport procedures and outside to where taxis queued in the balmy air. As the cab sped into the city, Clare stared at the Spanish signs

133

and said them aloud as they passed. She was feeling the giddiness that comes from being surrounded by a strange language for the first time. She laughed, and Ginger jabbed her with a sharp elbow.

"Be cool," she said. "He'll get the wrong idea."

Indeed, the taxi driver was eyeing them with a knowing leer, in the rearview mirror. "Tourists?" he asked, in accented English.

"Students," Ginger replied firmly, in her clear Spanish. She fixed him with a stern look. "Never say you're a tourist here," she told Clare. "They'll walk all over you. And if you don't understand, don't let on."

They entered a quiet neighborhood of tall metal walls. Trees stood in squares of earth embedded at precise intervals in the sidewalk. They drew up to the number Ginger indicated; this was the boarding house set up by their departmental advisor.

Ginger rang the doorbell and a dog barked deeply within. A little window slid open in the gate, and a small dark woman in an apron peered out at them. A sharp-faced blonde was looking over her shoulder.

"We're the American students," said Ginger in Spanish.

"Welcome. I am Señora Lopez," said the blonde, opening the gate. She told the servant to bring in their bags, and ushered the girls into the kitchen, where she served them hot chocolate with sweet breads. It was the traditional Mexican evening snack, a welcoming gesture, but Ginger hurried them through it by telling the Señora they had to get downtown to see friends of her parents.

"But it's too late," exclaimed the Señora. "Nearly ten. How can I let you go out alone?"

"They'll really worry if they don't see me tonight," Ginger said sorrowfully. She showed the Señora the business card the couple on the plane had given her. "I promised my parents."

"But you can telephone—"

"They're waiting outside the hotel, near the fountain. They'll be frantic."

"But let me call a taxi, the metro won't be safe at this hour." She eyed their jeans and tee shirts. "And you'd better change your clothes so you don't look so—" She shrugged, and led them to their apartment behind the house.

134

The apartment consisted of a living room, a tiny kitchen, a bathroom and a flowery pink and white bedroom with twin beds. In one poster on the bedroom wall, Zefferelli's version of Romeo and Juliet stared entranced at each other, while on the opposite wall Ryan O'Neil and Ali McGraw gazed mournfully into the camera. Clare contemplated these girlish artifacts as Ginger whipped on a minidress and did her makeup.

"We'll go to Cero Cero," she said gleefully. "It's *the* disco. Hurry up!"

Clare had only brought one dress, not the discotheque type, but she put it on dutifully, still in a daze. She didn't think she looked as good as she had a year ago, since gaining back about ten pounds, but Ginger assured her blondes attracted men. They secured their key from the still-disapproving Señora, promising to call if they got lost, and to speak to no one except their parents' friends. Clare got the distinct idea the Señora thought they were sisters. Maybe all gringas looked alike.

"See how easy?" Ginger grinned as they sped away in the taxi. "It's a matter of establishing who's boss. We're lucky we have rooms separate from the house."

The taxi moved from quiet streets to crowded ones. The tourist, or Pink Zone, was a dizzy blur of lights, fountains, traffic circles and statues on wide boulevards, and galleries, boutiques and restaurants on small European-named cobblestone streets. Crowds strolled, dodged manic drivers, lingered in outdoor cafes. *Far out.* Chicago, the only city Clare knew, was grey and circumspect in comparison. She followed Ginger into the big hotel where the Cero Cero club was.

They sat at a sunken, circular booth. Blue lights lit the heavy glass tables from underneath. Well-dressed couples swayed to loud unfamiliar music.

"No carding." Ginger was looking around with a vivacious smile. "No bouncers. All the gin and tonics men can buy us. Beats Bloomington, eh?" Clare wasn't sure.

Soon the girls were asked to dance. It was the first time since Lowell that Clare had been close to a man. Her partner was thin and graceful, in a dark suit. He moved her around the floor, not speaking or smiling, pulling her closer until she could feel his erection. Putting space between them made her stumble. When

135

the dance ended he led her back to the table and sat with one arm tight around her. He stared into her face.

"*Rubia. Hacemos el amor?*" Blonde. Shall we make love?

She laughed nervously. "Ah, no, no thank you."

He leaned away, took out cigarettes and, still courteous, offered her one. She took it and they watched the dancers. *Jesus, how do I get rid of this guy?* He was good-looking in a gloomy sort of way, and he smelled nice, but she was not in the mood. It was all too much—the long flight, the gin on an empty stomach, the effort of Spanish, the unaccustomed altitude, getting dressed up for the first time in so long.

She suddenly missed Lowell. Again. If he were here he would be sharing her amusement at the blue lights, joking with the stiff young man and teasing Ginger. She felt desolate in this silly setting and was angry at him anew, irrationally, for abandoning her to a fate of unwanted Mexican suitors. She stood, bumping her knees on the little round table, but as she was awkwardly getting out Ginger appeared with another fellow in tow.

"Where are you going? We just got here."

"I know, but I'm splitting. This isn't my scene."

"Wait." Ginger spoke to her partner, who sat down, and took Clare's arm. They went out to the ladies' room, as surrealistically decorated as the main floor.

"Now." Ginger looked at her. "You need to get high. I know you're freaked out, it's all new and strange, but don't be a baby." She took the two hits of Valium out of her purse and they each swallowed one. They looked at each other in the mirror. Clare thought she looked pale and puffy next to Ginger's vivid coloring.

"Let's fix you up." Ginger pulled out her little makeup kit. "You're gonna go back out and dazzle those pachucos. They won't know what hit em."

"But I don't want to dazzle them. I miss Lowell."

"Stop!" Ginger barked. "I heard enough about him back in Bloomington. You are *not* dragging that name down here. Keep it in the past where it belongs. We're here to have a *good time*, Clare, even though you forgot what that means." She snapped the kit shut and glared. "You coming?"

"Like I have a choice."

Ginger pursed her lips for a moment and then crooned hoarsely, in her best Dylan imitation, the song about being lost in the rain in Juarez at Eastertime.

It was the song they'd done, preparing for their Mexico sojourn, and Clare laughed to hear it again in the blue and silver Cero Cero ladies' room.

"That's better," said Ginger. "Now let's go and boogie."

They stayed at the club until it closed, dancing with a variety of men and letting them buy the drinks. Ginger was right— they seemed entranced by Clare's hair and squeezed her amorously. She managed to ward them off, even in her hesitant Spanish and her altered chemical state. Ginger begged taxi fare from her last partner, a middle-aged businessman who pressed his card into her hand along with the money.

"Call me at my office," he said as he put them into the taxi. "I'll take you wherever you want to go."

"*Muchas gracias, senor.*" Ginger batted her lashes at him. "And go fuck yourself," she added in English as they pulled away.

TWENTY-SEVEN

THAT NIGHT set the tone for one aspect of Mexico City for Clare with Ginger. They collected cards. They accepted meals and tours from whoever seemed to promise a good time without too much hassle. Most of them seemed old to Clare, at least mid-twenties to mid-thirties, possibly married, too polite and schedule-bound to force sexual liaisons but eager nonetheless.

Clare knew the persona she put on for these club-met dates was artificial, but she figured it was Experience: this was her taste of urbane sophistication. She bought a red minidress at one of the flashy shops, like the girls at the Cero Cero wore. It wasn't really her style, but it suited the occasions, and it was not easy to undo. That proved valuable on several nights when a struggle went on: hostile teeth might mash against her unwilling lips, but no roaming hand could unfasten her dress.

After one such outing she mentioned her frustration with the struggle to Ginger.

"It's a tradeoff." Ginger shrugged. "You let them have a thrill in return for the date. It's like the Fifties."

"But I never feel like giving them a thrill."

"You don't pick the cute ones."

"They don't pick me, not when I'm with you."

Ginger smiled. "Have you gotten laid at all since we arrived?" Clare shook her head. "I hope you're still on the pill. You know what they say, kiddo, use it or lose it!"

Clare saw no need to confide that, pill aside, she still wanted only Lowell.

Classes at the college were as easy as Ginger had promised. Clare signed up for subjects that turned out to be mostly slide shows—Mexican Art, Folklore, and Pre-Columbian Architecture. The fourth course, amusingly entitled Mexican-American Affairs, was their liveliest, taught by a friendly, rotund Cuban named Miguel, whose trademark was taking the class out for beer and political discussion, at the little Café Verona across from the college.

The Mexican art students she met in class were more to her liking than the dates, especially the few who were bold enough to joke about the decadence of the imperialistic North, and make fun of the girls—Yanqui gringas—for their outings with materialistic businessmen.

"It is my political strategy," she told them solemnly, as her Spanish improved. "I will corrupt the system from within." She enjoyed their hoots of sarcastic laughter. Unfortunately, they did not live close, so she couldn't see them often enough to truly befriend.

Living in the Señora's house were two other American girls—Christine, from upstate New York and Beryl, from Manhattan. Christine was slight, pale, with long brown hair and big light-blue eyes she blinked slowly when she wanted to make a point. She called herself Cristal, ever since one of her dates told her she had eyes like crystal. She was the most popular gringa at the college, with dates booked early and late every night.

Ginger and Clare, trying to figure out Cristal's appeal to Mexican men, other than her eyes, pinned it down to her small size, her mini dresses and her sweet, helpless manner.

"They feed me." She shrugged prettily, when Clare asked her directly how she handled so many dates. She'd come up to their apartment to give Clare advice on how to dress, and act, to attract boys. Ginger lolled on her bed, smirking, during the wardrobe inspection.

"You do realize we have it *made* here," Cristal told them, a bit severely, as if they were inattentive children. "In the States, there are so *many* pretty girls." She stood in front of the mirror, twisting a strand of hair, blinking leisurely. "And I mean ... really beautiful. So that a girl who's just—nice-looking—doesn't stand a chance." She turned and gave them a slow smile. "But here, we can have whoever we want. Just because we're Americans."

"Yeah, tell me about it," Ginger said in her hippie voice. "What did the chavo say to the blonde hippopotamus walking down the street?"

139

"What do you mean?" Cristal frowned.

"*Chula*," answered Clare. "He told her she was cute." She and Ginger had made up a bunch of what they called gringa jokes, which made as much fun of the men chasing them as the gringas themselves.

"Oh." Cristal's smile seemed uncertain. She picked up a passport photo of Lowell, which Clare had stolen, lying on top of the dresser. "This guy's an outrageous fox," she remarked. "Is he someone's brother?"

Ginger snatched the photo and thrust it into a drawer. "He's nobody," she growled. "He's ancient history."

Clare could not suppress a smile.

Beryl, older than the rest by several years, also had long dark hair, long enough to sit on, which was much admired, and in that fabulous New York way made herself more chic than any of them. She had a job lined up after graduation as a translator at the United Nations and did not bother dating. Ginger and Clare wondered how Beryl could stand sharing a room with Cristal, but Beryl was mature enough to keep her own counsel.

The Señora was an upperclass widow of Spanish ancestry. She had strict rules about male visitors, so Ginger was obliged to carry on her sexual exploits away from the apartment, much to Clare's relief. In most ways Mrs. Lopez was a proper matron, but she had one eccentricity—she believed there were rats in the alleyway between the house and the apartment, and she had trained her German shepherd to attack them.

"Suzi! *Matalos!*" Kill them! She would drive the dog into a frenzy of barking. Nobody knew for sure whether Suzi had ever killed a rat, or even actually seen one, but her training provided some strangely exciting moments.

The Señora's grown children lived away from home. The only one who visited often was Alejandro, who managed the family ranch in Michoacan, a hilly state to the south. He was smoothly handsome, and he occasionally deigned to flirt with Cristal, but ignored the rest of them. Ginger and Clare, whose living room windows looked down into the Señora's kitchen across the alley, liked to watch him eating breakfast unaware and giggle, "Oh, Ale*jan*dro," as they smoked their first joint of the day.

The procurement of decent weed—The Endless Search, Clare called it—gave them a view of Mexicans unlike what they saw at school, on dates, or at the Señora's.

Their technique was crude but effective. They looked for long-haired, denimed hippie types, rare in Mexico, on the street or in the metro, and said, "Que onda," what's happenin. If they got an enthusiastic response, they steered the conversation to dope. Ginger was particularly adept at spotting unsavory types or seeing through an act. Clare was the straight man, driving a hard bargain by expressing horror at prices quoted.

They never bought more than a few joints' worth at a time. Ginger wanted to buy a kilo—so much cheaper—but nobody carried that much at a chance meeting, and they hesitated to solidify these shifty relationships by planning further encounters. So they were always in short supply, and this perpetuated The Endless Search. They dared not probe their club dates or anyone at school, because of the negative attitude among most Mexicans about marijuana use.

"We need hip friends," Ginger sighed in frustration, after one fruitless afternoon wasted on the metro. "Where are they?"

141

TWENTY-EIGHT

SURPRISINGLY, The Endless Search conclusion appeared in the Señora's kitchen in the form of her eldest son. Ginger, Clare and Beryl were having coffee when he strolled in, dressed in baggy pastel cotton pajamas. His brown hair waved past his shoulders and a long filigree earring dangled from one ear. His face was intense, with dark eyes and thin features; "El Greco," thought Clare. He slung a canvas bag onto the countertop next to the coffeepot. The girls stared. He calmly got out a mug and poured himself some coffee.

"Where's Mrs. Lopez?" he asked in perfect English after a considering sip.

"She's upstairs," lied Clare, ready to dash to the street screaming, "Policia!"

He shook his head. "No, she's not here, I already looked. It's okay, don't be nervous, I am her son Jesus. Maybe she told you about me, I just got back from India." He smiled, a little sardonically, and indicated the chair next to Ginger's. "May I sit down?"

"Of course, it's your house," declared Ginger. Then conversation flowed, and before they left for school, Ginger and Clare invited him up for a visit.

"He's the most intriguing guy I've met in Mexico," Clare said as they walked to class. "Imagine him in the same family as the Señora and Alejandro!"

"Not to mention Suzi," said Ginger. "No wonder he had to escape."

Jesus, whose name suited his appearance so well, talked eloquently that evening about the philosophy that had drawn him to India. He showed them a few yoga positions and encouraged them to meditate daily, to dispel the bad vibes inherent in Mexico City air.

142

"Pollution?" queried Clare.

"Death," Jesus said seriously. "From the Aztecs onward, it is a valley of death."

"Heavy," intoned Ginger, taking a long hit.

Jesus grinned at her and his face took on a sudden worldly attractiveness. "Of course I don't expect you to understand. You Yanquis are insensitive to matters of the spirit. It's your materialistic culture. It blinds you."

"Hey, I read Carlos Castaneda last year," Clare protested comically.

Jesus raised an amused eyebrow. "And you learned ... what?"

"How to come down to Mexico and get really stoned," she said, drawing out the word in her Dylan voice.

Jesus laughed, but shook his head when they passed the joint. "I gave all that up."

"All what?" Ginger asked.

"Drugs, alcohol, tobacco, red meat, sex ... "

"Jesus, Jesus," Ginger said mournfully. "You might as well be dead."

"So The Endless Search continues," muttered Clare. She'd hoped Jesus might be a way out. He looked at her, questioning, and she explained how they propositioned hippies. He found this very funny. She liked that he kept a sense of humor after giving up so much. He told them, grinning, he knew some trustworthy people who might help them.

So Jesus became their first solid weed connection in Mexico, and their first real male friend. As they got to know him better, the house gringas began to look on him as a confidante; as a joke they pronounced his name Jesus like the Anglo Christ. Even Cristal got over her initial distrust of his eccentric appearance. He did not judge them as they suspected the rest of his family did, indeed his whole society; and the fact that he was avowedly celibate removed any sexual tension they might otherwise have felt with an attractive young man living in close proximity. When they told him their love problems he made Zenlike pronouncements which Clare suspected were a gentle put-on, but always made them feel better, since at least he listened.

His insights into the Mexican psyche were scathing and

143

profound. He really did believe the city was spiritually unhealthy, and planned to settle in Cuernavaca once his transactions for buying a house were completed. Meanwhile his old friends, mostly artists, came to visit him and marvel at his Indian transformation. The Señora's kitchen was often filled with colorful characters discussing philosophy well into the night, drinking wine, pots of coffee (Jesus' one vice) and smoking whatever was around.

The Señora was remarkably tolerant of all this. Jesus was her firstborn, he explained to Clare one day, and she believed both that he could do no wrong and that he would soon grow out of his *jipi*—hippie—phase.

To Clare, Jesus' presence was a welcome change from her dreadful dates, but he was not around very often. She dated less, tired of the effort, and was thus left by herself when the other gringas went to the clubs. She missed Ginger's rowdy company.

She got into the habit of going out alone to explore, belting the collegiate trench coat her mother had given her, against the beginning of the rainy season and the unwanted stares of men. She pretended she was a reporter whose beat was the city, all its beauty, all its ugliness. Certain scenes stood out. Some haunted her dreams.

In a local bakery at closing time, customers snatched pastries with clattery metal pincers. Outside the bakery a man with similar pincers, in place of an arm, clacked them aggressively at passersby and shook his tin beggar's cup with his good hand.

A speeding car struck a boy as he ran across the teeming streets in the Zocalo square downtown. Traffic did not even stop as the boy's body was bumped, hideously, by car after car until a policeman finally came running out, blowing his whistle. Cars swerved past. It was real trouble to hit a policeman. Nobody stopped, knowing they'd all be tossed into jail, for even being near the scene of a crime. Clare could not stomach going back to the Zocalo.

While walking through dingy side streets one dusk, watching for the approach of alleyboys who swooped up silently to grab a purse or a feel, Clare heard a commotion and turned a corner to see what was going on. A raggedy crowd surged under a streetlight where a young boy, lithe and skinny as a cat, was shimmying to grab something attached to the top of the lamp-post. Clare peered up in the gathering twilight.

Swinging on twine were a box of Saltines, a bottle of dishwashing liquid, a bag of flour. People cheered when the boy snagged the Saltines, but began to boo and pelt him with stones when he reached for the dishwashing liquid. It was another child's turn.

She watched as boy after boy tried his luck. A burly man with a ladder and a sack replaced items as they were snatched. Was it a promotion for a new supermercado, a block party, charity, some political ploy? She never found out, for she felt the tug of an alleyboy at her elbow and, not wanting to see another hungry, leering face, hurried to the broader well-lit streets.

In Sanborn's, the Americanized coffee-shop refuge for gringos, Clare liked to eavesdrop on funny conversations among culture-shocked tourists. She also witnessed the desolation of fragile pastel-haired ladies who sat in solitary booths sipping watery tea served by indifferent waiters. These elderly Americans lived on Social Security and cheap South-of-the-Border dreams. They counted out their change with careful arthritic fingers.

She strolled though Alameda Park Sundays, where balloon vendors, clowns, street artists, and brilliantly dressed children provided a riot of color. The feeling was as old-fashioned as in a French impressionist painting, and everyone's faces glistened, to Clare, with nostalgia.

Jack Kerouac had wandered Alameda Park in the Fifties, taking photographs and writing poetry. She felt his spirit. From the abundant fragrant metal carts, she bought corn on the cob slathered with mayonnaise, grated cheese and chili powder, and ate while admiring the white and gold rococo splendor of Bellas Artes, the fine arts auditorium. Street food never made her sick.

After a bus journey out to the Pyramids of Teotihuacan, she sat away from tourists to ponder the chilling habits of the Aztecs. The place seemed haunted and she thought of Jesus' sober assessment of the environment. With a shiver, she recalled the stark poem carved on a wall at the Anthropological Museum:

Cuando aun era de noche, cuando aun no habia dia,
Se convocaron los dioses, alla en Teotihuacan.

145

"When it was still night, when there was still no day,
The gods met, there in Teotihuacan."

Looking at the hulking Pyramid of the Sun, the poem
sounded completely plausible. No way would she be here after
nightfall, not even to catch the much-touted Sound and Light
Show.

Racketing through tunnels on the metro alone, she always
looked at either the ceiling or floor, since if she glanced at the
other passengers she invariably found their implacable dark stares
all focused on her. They looked sad to her, but maybe this was an
effect of the rainy season. Maybe it was her own deep sadness.
At the station she followed the crowds flowing up the escalators,
but never felt so out of place as when she glimpsed in the
mirrors her lone pale head bobbing in a sea of black.

Sometimes then she thought of Bloomington, with
melancholy, of the simple warm belonging embodied in French
House. But those memories usually brought Lowell, making her
even lonelier. She would retreat to the ruffled austerity of the
pink and white bedroom and smoke until she saw faces in the
flowery curtains.

Once, after making and consuming an entire pan of hash
brownies, she and Ginger had hallucinated the Kennedy brothers
in the curtains. John F. Kennedy was still much revered in
Mexico and one could buy souvenirs—cigarette lighters, ashtrays,
cups and saucers—with his picture on them. Thereafter Clare
took comfort in their remembered benign presences in the
drapery, smiles intact, hair waving vigorously. She hoped, as long
as they didn't speak, she was still mentally fit.

TWENTY-NINE

ON A FRIDAY evening during the worst of the rainy season, Clare was lying on the couch listening to one of her favorite radio programs, *'La hora de los Rolin,'* Rolling Stones Hour, and getting high, when there was a knocking on the downstairs door.

"Clare?" Jesus' voice called.

"Hi Jesus," she answered, rising as Jesus and another man came up the stairs.

"I saw a light and thought someone might be in," said Jesus. "I wanted to introduce you to Julio. He's the only one of my friends who is still politically active, so I thought you might have some ideas in common." He sniffed the air and smiled. "And I thought you might give him some smoke."

Julio was already at home, stretching out his long form on an armchair and planting his booted feet on the coffee table. His shoulder-length straight black hair, mustache, sharp features and severe expression reminded Clare of a slender Pancho Villa. He only needed a belt of cartridges slung over his chest. His eyes were closed but his first and second fingers felt warm and supple as Clare pressed the joint between them.

Jesus sat on the floor in a yoga position. "What were you doing tonight?" he asked in Spanish. "Thank you for letting us interrupt you."

"You're always welcome to interrupt me, Jesus, all I was doing was communing with the Kennedys," she answered in English. Jesus translated, telling Julio the bedroom was haunted.

Julio slowly opened large black eyes on Clare. *"Que imaginacion."* What an imagination. His voice was low and resonant. He continued to look at her, without expression, until Clare felt uneasy.

The instantaneous-seeming international camaraderie of

dope and music was a façade, she decided. She was so stoned, Julio and even familiar Jesus suddenly seemed to be from another planet. "Let's Spend the Night Together" came on with a tinny clamour. At once the walls looked too white. Clare switched off the overhead light and lit a candle.

"I need to either smoke some more or go to sleep," she announced, ignoring her dope paranoia, pretending she was back in French House with a couple of buddies.

"I'll smoke some more with you," said Julio in Spanish, smiling for the first time. "Then I'll put you to sleep, little girl."

The glint of humor in his eyes increased her discomfort, yet illuminated its source. He was the first guy to look good to her since Lowell. His skin appeared warm, his hair gleamed, his lips, sipping the joint, were well-shaped; and he sprawled so comfortably she sensed it would feel easy to settle next to his blue-jeaned flannel-shirted length. He looked like an album-cover hippie, of the type so popular now, a pseudo-chic emulation of some Old West that never was.

He held her gaze and smiled more broadly, showing a white flash of teeth and a twitch of tickly-looking mustache. How would it feel to kiss a man with a mustache?

"Jesus tells me you were active in the antiwar movement," he said in Spanish.

"Yes, in the States."

"Have you joined any of the student groups here?"

"No."

"Because your soldiers are finally leaving Vietnam?"

"Because I am a foreigner here, it seems … not right to me." What was the Spanish word for unethical?

"But the movement is global. And it's more than anti-Vietnam-war, you know, it is the struggle for justice against the oppressors in every country."

She remembered when feeling that way was her primary emotional state.

"You're politically active how?" she asked him.

"We want to identify all the *desaparecidos*."

"Who?"

Julio's eyes widened. "You don't know what is happening here? All political opposition is aggressively, systematically, illegally repressed. Didn't you hear about Tlatelolco in '68?"

She knew there had been some kind of rally put down by the police, brutally, much worse than the Chicago demonstrations during the Democratic Convention that year, with many Mexican students shot or imprisoned. "That's still going on?"

"Of course."

No wonder there were so few students at her college who really wanted to discuss politics, in spite of the exhortations of their professor Miguel, the jolly Cuban. No wonder their joking about Yanqui imperialism was tinged with bitterness. She sat back, feeling foolish, berating herself for ignorance.

What had happened to her political awareness?

Lost, here, in a cloud of smoke, gin-and-tonics, and idiotic club dates.

Lost, before, in a Lowell-whirlwind of love and pain.

Lost during her time on the depot wire.

"We want the release of all political prisoners and we want justice for those who were killed," Julio was saying.

She forced her ears open to understand his rapid Spanish. *Justice for those killed* resounded within her, the thud of soft earth filling an open grave. There were so many: the Kennedy brothers. Martin Luther King Jr. Kent State. Jackson State. A few had foreign flags, tilted askew: the Red Brigade. Prague. Santiago.

She didn't have the heart to prop up headstones, anymore, except Joe's.

However, as if he'd seen her glimpse of a Santiago marker and intended to spotlight it, Julio went on, "And we are commited to supporting our brothers from Chile."

Rumors about Chilean refugees, who were flooding Mexico, floated like zephyrs streaming off the far twin volcanoes dominating Mexico City's skyline.

In the wake of Salvador Allende's doomed Socialist experiment more than two hundred thousand people fled Chile following the September 11, 1973 right-wing coup against him— and many countries refused to accept the refugees, fearing the wrath of the United States, who labeled them dangerous Communists. So many had disappeared there was no way to accurately count them. Leftists blamed the coup on the CIA, who they claimed acted on behalf of corporations threatened by

149

Allende's industrial policies.

Shame was creeping in.

She'd deliberately compartmentalized her political feelings since her night on the wire. She'd steeled herself against the Nixon re-election and against what she felt, still so hurtfully, was Lowell's rejection of her due to that night. She'd kept going to meetings, of course, finding irony in her arrest-related cachet and visibility in the SMC—visibility being what she'd thought she wanted—but once Nixon declared the war over, she'd dropped out with a sense of sad relief.

Many of her erstwhile compatriots around the U.S. also abandoned their political stances, almost in unison last year, in what she suspected was the same gloomy resigned mood.

Yet injustice still raged.

"And we want to replace this government with one that is more suited to the economic realities here, to create an equal distribution of assets."

Julio was a Marxist? That was brave of him, if Mexico was as repressive as he indicated. "So you're a revolutionary." This used to sound so thrilling.

"And an artist," Jesus added. "He paints."

"I'm just a worker. From each according to his ability, you know." He reached again for the joint, this time lightly touching Clare's fingertips. She felt a tickle of excitement unrelated to his political passion. Julio leaned back and closed his eyes. She watched him for a moment before closing her own. The Stones spun into the druggy reaches of "Their Satanic Majesties' Request" and she spun along.

Sometime later Clare felt gentle hands stroking her hair. She opened her eyes to Julio's, who was kneeling beside her, gazing at her with a contemplative expression. Jesus was gone. The room was silent.

She sat up and pretended to be a hostess. "Shall we, um, would you like some ... wine? Or maybe tea?"

But she was speaking in English. Julio was stronger than he looked—he pressed her down and kissed her, sweeping clear her months of mourning Lowell. His mouth took her tongue as his fingers slid into her flannel shirt. When his lips brushed her neck and below she said, "Yes ... *sí*," and moved her hands into his shining hair, letting hunger overtake caution, surprised by how easy it was. His mustache lent a little frisson to his caresses.

As they lay on the couch afterward, with Julio's arms around her in a loose hug, Clare heard Ginger's quick steps on the stairs. She pulled her flannel shirt over them.

"*Buenas Noches!*" cried Ginger with a trill of amusement. She was flushed and disheveled, clutching a bottle of whiskey. "Look what I won at the Cero Cero dance contest!"

She plopped onto the floor with the bottle. "Let's have a swig." She peered at Julio. "I don't believe I've had the honor?" Then she winked lewdly at Clare. "Congrats, finally."

During this performance, Julio raised his eyebrows and linked his hands behind his head. "My clothes," he told Clare at last, in Spanish.

"Oh excuse me!" Ginger rose and scooped up his shirt and jeans. "Here, *senor.*" She dumped them on top of him and walked down the hall to their bedroom.

Clare watched Julio dress. His face was closed and unreadable as if they had never touched. "Don't go," she said. "Stay tonight."

He looked up. "And—" he jerked his head in the direction Ginger had gone.

"She won't mind. We can stay in here." The Señora couldn't see them.

"You are a little girl," he said softly. *Niña*, in Spanish, was a common term of endearment for a girlfriend, but she wondered if Julio meant she was childish. She frowned at him. His smile grew. "I'll stay."

Clare took out glasses and snacks, and Ginger brought back the bottle, and Julio became talkative as they drank, telling them with a wry self-deprecation about his efforts to sell his paintings to tourists at the Sunday art fairs around the city.

When Ginger flirted he eyed her, smiling, keeping one warm hand on Clare's hair, her thigh, or her hand. But as much as she liked this sensation of being claimed, in spite of Ginger's provocation, she had the curious feeling of watching herself from the outside. She felt Lowell's presence.

"This guy's an ahhhtist? A Communist?" she imagined him drawling. "You think he'll teach you anything?"

151

EMMA GATES

Stop it, she told herself, or him, fiercely. *I deserve another boyfriend! I can't be fixated on you forever. Like some stupid bird too strongly imprinted in infancy. Some dumb duck. Leave me alone!* The image of Lowell receded.

THIRTY

BEING WITH Julio freed Clare from artificial dating and from her solitary wanderings. Her Spanish improved immediately, since he spoke no English, but she didn't get the political involvement she had expected from him. He said it would be too dangerous to introduce her to his cell. She understood that from the SMC.

Instead, she tagged along with him to gallery openings and parties. Julio was achieving some buzz in the art scene. He did enormous canvases in silent white with seemingly random slashes of color, which he said represented the desaparecidos. His work was attracting the attention of serious collectors and their trendy hangers-on, whom Clare observed as that silent reporter who wandered the city during the rainy season.

Wagner, a wealthy German exile retired from a corporation he didn't like to reveal, about whom all sort of rumors swirled, gave fabulous parties at his villa in the south of the city. People said he was pathologically afraid of being alone. He was Julio's first and most loyal buyer.

A beautiful Brazilian rock band went everywhere, even on the metro, painted and costumed as if for Carnival. They didn't care that Mexico City was not Rio, that under its picturesque European veneer brooded a dark intolerant judge. They didn't care that nobody knew if they were men or women. They assumed Julio's political convictions meant he was socially progressive, and so were happy to invest in him.

There was a puppet maker, a wicked craftsman who fashioned grotesque, larger-than-life caricatures of notables as the black-and-white skeletons of folklore. His work sold for sums Clare found phenomenal. He wanted to collaborate on a show with Julio, but Julio was a loner.

Mario owned five light planes that departed weekly from the

153

mountain town of Oaxaca, loaded with Acapulco Gold, headed for Kansas cornfields, producing the income that allowed him to invest in Julio's art. He was an understandably nervous youth, fidgeting constantly, doing up hits of mescaline on the occasion he found a flat surface to snort from. He told Clare he could replenish hers and Ginger's supply at cost, which she accepted, and offered to let them trial some other "interesting things," which she politely refused.

As in most cities, the artistic community was small, and frequented each other's events. It was more fun being a voyeur in their world than observing the streets alone. She even made a friend, Wagner's girlfriend Grace, a slight woman in her thirties with curly red hair and green eyes, whose feminine appearance belied her booming voice and loud Texan laugh. She drove a gleaming yellow Triumph and Clare enjoyed stares from the students when Grace sometimes picked her up at the college.

Toward the end of the semester Julio proposed she move into his three rooms in the artistic old neighborhood of Coyoacan. It was too much of a commute to come and get her every weekend, he said, a two-hour metro and bus trip. He was working on an upcoming solo show and had little spare time. She already spent most weekends at his place anyway; glad to get away from the hothouse girlishness of the gringas together and from the Señora, who reverted to shrill once Jesus moved to Cuernavaca.

His request wasn't romantic. They weren't in love. There were none of those luxurious Lowell-esque orgasmic sessions she remembered so vividly. The language barrier between them did not always disguise the fact that she and Julio didn't have much in common. He was kind, however, and she was sure that was more important than sex in a mature relationship. Lowell laughed, in her mind, but she banished him.

Clare told Ginger about Julio's suggestion the morning after he mentioned it.

To her surprise, Ginger vehemently opposed the idea. "Why the fuck go through the hassle? You'd get all the drudgery of marriage and none of the benefits."

"Benefits! A relationship isn't a matter of benefits. When two people are on the same wavelength they don't worry about who's getting what."

"Bullshit. That's *exactly* what they should worry about. That's what makes relationships succeed or fail."

"What a calculating idea!"

"Don't kid yourself you're madly in love with this guy," Ginger said shrewdly, pouring Karo syrup onto her Cornflakes. They were going through a lean condiment time, having blown a month's food budget on one of Mario's excellent kilos, and made do with whatever was left in the cupboard. "I remember how you were with what's his name, Mr. Prep, and this is obviously not the same thing."

"Of course not! I would never put myself through that again."

"Would you marry Julio if he asked you?"

"No—"

"Then why live with him? What's in it for you?"

"It's an opportunity for … a unique experience," Clare said hesitantly, trying out how it sounded. "I want to see what it's like, living with a guy."

"Ha! See what it's like to wash his underwear."

"He doesn't wear any."

"He might start, once you're around to wash it!"

"Ginger, get off my case. I don't need your approval!"

"You asked for my opinion. And I think you're wrong to move in with some drug addict Commie artist just to prove how hip you are."

"Look who's talking about drugs—" Clare indicated Ginger's water pipe, filled and at the ready next to the bottle of Karo. "What a hypocrite!"

"I may play with those types," Ginger said coldly. "I don't live with them. This is my *time* to fuck off. I won't be doing this once I'm not a student."

They stared at each other, surprised by the sudden hostility, breathing hard.

Clare said softly, "I think you don't like Julio because he doesn't pay any special attention to you."

"And I think you can't handle yourself with men, so you stick like a burr to the first one who comes along. Or, excuse me, the second."

155

Ouch! *Is that true?* "I didn't know you were so conventional," Clare sneered finally, as nastily as she could manage.

"I didn't know you were such a fool!" Ginger snagged her water pipe with a two-fingered loop and left the room. Clare heard her rattling hangers in the bedroom closet.

"Fuck off, Ginger!" she yelled.

"Don't come crying to me when it ends this time!" Ginger yelled back.

A week later, Clare skipped classes to pack up her things. She stood for a moment in the bedroom, staring for the last time at Olivia Hussey as Juliet. They'd replaced the "Love Story" poster with the Grateful Dead, to the Señora's dismay.

"You would have moved in with Romeo, right?"

That Julio was no Romeo was beside the point. She was doing this to prove she was capable of taking this adult step alone, into the post-graduacy of womanhood. Ginger would be sorry when she saw how Clare's life was filled with interesting people, who had important things to say, in Julio's trendy artistic neighborhood.

The horn blared outside—Julio had borrowed a friend's car—and Clare lugged her suitcases away. "So long, Suzi," she muttered as they drove off. She was irritated the Señora demanded rent in full until she got a replacement gringa. Ginger flat out refused to help her find one ("I don't want some new chick invading my space," she'd stated).

That night Julio cooked, to celebrate her arrival. He knew how to make tortillas from scratch, how to prepare beans, how to make an authentic chili sauce. It took hours, but everything was wonderfully fresh and tasty. She raised her beer to toast the chef.

"And to you," Julio responded. "You'll do this next time, Niña."

"Oh no." She laughed, shaking her head. "I can't even boil water."

Julio just smiled. The expression did not really translate.

THE LAST weeks of school were hectic. The metro and bus commute from Coyoacan to the college was indeed exhausting, and she arrived at each destination weary from battling the crowds and the heat. To add to her discomfort, Julio's building had periodic water outages and they had to make do with cold-water baths from buckets collected when the water was on. She stayed up several nights in a row finishing papers she had not bothered to work on earlier, having realized, too late, what a shocking amount of research the amiable professors of her slide-show classes actually expected. And all in Spanish! *Híjole chihuahua.* Someone really should invent technology that made it easier to learn, and produce, in other languages quickly.

Julio helped her with the art reports, but she was on her own for Mexican-American Affairs since he refused to analyze that poisonously colonialist relationship. She turned everything in at the last possible deadline, knowing with a sinking feeling she had not done her best. How she *hated* school.

The fashionable art history teacher, picking up her mail, raised elegant eyebrows at Clare's disheveled appearance and accepted the paper gingerly. Clare shuffled out of the office feeling awful. She was wearing the same tee shirt and jeans for the third day.

In the grassy, sunlit courtyard sprawled a group of gringo acquaintances, Ginger among them. They were laughing in a way that seemed distant to Clare as she stood watching. They were discussing the trips they would take, now that classes were over for a few weeks.

"Hey Clare!" Cristal sang out. "How's the love nest?"

Clare walked over to them slowly. Ginger glanced at her, and went back to her conversation. She was wearing a pretty white sundress Clare remembered, with a pang, their buying together during a Bloomington pre-Mexico shopping spree.

"So, is it fun being a Mexican hippie?" Cristal looked Clare up and down with a smirk. "You sure look the part."

Clare tried to laugh but her throat was too tight.

Beryl walked up. "Come out for a farewell beer. We're leaving tomorrow."

"You buying?" Clare asked, grateful.

"Sure."

They trooped over to the Verona Café. Miguel, their young Cuban prof, came along. He seemed quite smitten with Ginger in her sundress and she flirted saucily back. School was out, after all. Clare downed her beer, dazed with sleeplessness and the unexpected ease of being surrounded by English speakers again.

"Here's to the good ole USA!" roared a red-faced boy after the third pitcher. "Where the water's hot and the meat is wrapped in plastic!"

Everyone added comments.

"To the folks who brought us to Vietnam!"

"And Cambodia!"

"And Watergate!"

"To Nixon!"

"To Ford, you ass, to Ford!"

So it went. Toward evening, they crowded into the metro and went to the Plaza Garibaldi, a square where strolling mariachis serenaded camera-wielding tourists, and lethally strong drinks were sold at outrageous prices. Some of their group joined in the mariachis' sentimental songs, and Ginger persuaded one of the musicians to lend her his guitar. She looked over at Clare.

"Come on, pal, for old times' sake."

They sang their travel favorites, "Sisters of Mercy," "Tom Thumb's Blues," "Leavin on a Jet Plane," and the Stones' "No Expectations." The group moaned along, swaying in alcoholic affinity. Afterward, Ginger lurched to give Clare a hug.

"To friendship!" she crowed, raising the guitar. The mariachis cheered. But it was late, and Clare had to make her way back to Coyoacan.

"I'll give you taxi fare," said Ginger, one arm around Miguel. "Don't take the metro alone at this hour."

"You sound like the Señora." Clare smiled, remembering their first night in Mexico. "And Ginger, about what I said to you that day ... "

"I'll forgive you if you forgive me."

"I'll letcha be in my dream if I c'n be in yours," Clare said in her Dylan voice.

"How is it with Julio? You look wasted." Ginger whispered, "Too much sex?"

"Too much commuting. Now I know why he didn't like it."

"You guys should move closer when school starts again, it's not fair to you."

"Come visit sometime, okay?"

158

"*Simon, limon,* next semester."
"Give my regards to Suzi."
"And Ale*ja*ndro." They both snickered.

THIRTY-ONE

S HE DIDN'T travel during break; she still had to pay rent to the Señora, and contribute to food at Julio's. It was warm, and opening the windows brought in all the noise and smells from the street: alleyboys playing endless soccer games, vendors crying *"El gas!"* or *"Nueces!"* or *"Duraznos, muy frescos,"* in nasal chants, tortillas frying, sewers not functioning, neighbors fighting, customers carousing at the local tavern. Well, this was Experiencing the Third World. Too bad there was no college credit for it.

It was impossible to eat simply without a refrigerator and oven. No more grabbing a yogurt or splashing milk on cereal or cooking a frozen pizza. Julio didn't believe in convenience foods anyway. He thought they were expensive, loaded with preservatives, a harm to local farming communities, a rape of the environment by corporate thieves.

This kind of life required daily shopping, water collection if it was being rationed, transport of cooktop and water heater gas in heavy metal cylinders, which, purchased from the "El gas" man, had to be lugged up five flights to the building roof for hookup.

She realized most families in their building shared small rooms, without major appliances, and she felt a little ashamed of her discomfort. But Julio had started making money with his art. He could afford to buy a refrigerator and a real oven. He disdained this, since he easily cooked three-course meals on his one gas ring with two pots.

"The art money supports my cell. That's the only reason I paint," he told her sternly. "I thought you were beyond materialism. I don't need to live better than this."

"But how much easier life would be. You'd have more time to paint."

"I paint when I'm doing these chores, I'm thinking, I'm

160

seeing," he said. "Maybe housework wouldn't bother you so much if you developed more of an inner life."

She worried over this for a time.

Julio was certainly self-disciplined. Contrary to the myth of the excessive artist he was not moody, nor was he a pothead, as Ginger had assumed; to her chagrin they rarely got high. He told her his success depended, besides talent, on his capacity to work methodically and live an orderly life.

Clare was torn between admiration and resentment. She admitted to herself, as she was not ready to admit to him, that living with him disappointed her. She could not seem to get to the heart of Julio, whether because of her inadequate Spanish, her lack of experience with men, or his dearth of verbal expression. Maybe his weekly meetings with fellow revolutionaries gave him the emotional interaction she would have wanted from him.

Nechayev would have categorized her role—"the Revolutionary's woman"—as simply supporting. Ergo, deeply unsatisfying. But this felt like a course she wanted to pass, and she told herself it was the experience, more than the man, which mattered, so she struggled gamely with the inconveniences of life in old Coyoacan.

She caught on, through repetition, to the delight of perusing the open-air market: the careful inspection of fresh fruits, vegetables, breads, and meats; and the slow-paced give and take that pervaded the ambiance. She paid attention to the talk around the produce stands and realized everyone was trying to find the best ways to cook, to present, to enjoy the production and the consumption. A revelation: she'd feared food for so long as either an enemy or a rigorous cure, she had never learned to simply savor.

She'd started overeating around the time her father got so sick. Peter Meredith, a lifelong steel man, had worked his way from line worker to foreman. He'd always been a smoker, and his coughing was accepted as commonplace to those who knew him, until he was diagnosed with lung cancer. After he died, Clare's mother Ellen drew steadily inward until she reached some kind of core, and only then was able to radiate outward to her children again. That took some hard years. She went back to fulltime nursing work and was exhausted much of the time.

Clare had been the darling baby sister, showered with affection by her noisy siblings Andy, Claudia and Joe. Peter's death stilled the household. That summer everyone worked, sensing Ellen's wordless fear and responding to it practically, with the energetic sympathy of youth. They all pitched in to synchronize chores at home with their jobs and they all grew up quickly. They became Clare's parents when she was ten years old, even Joe who was only twelve and took on two paper routes.

Clare had necessarily been alone while they worked, but she had neither resources nor experience to enjoy solitude. She'd never had to initiate friendships at school—pretty, amiable, and eager to please as a typical youngest child, she was always accepted in children's groups. But she had no one best friend. So she stayed in, too shy to go to the community pool or playground alone. She read, watched TV and listened to her siblings' rock records, responding to the beat, thrilling to the exciting words. And she ate. She always had a sweet tooth and that summer her hunger ran rampant.

Her family didn't notice right away. When her sister Claudia took her shopping for school clothes, Clare's size had surprised both of them.

"I guess you're growing up, honey," Claudia said, standing behind her in the mirror and studying Clare with a puzzled frown. Sixteen, stylish in her long straight hair and mini, she had looked light years ahead of her no-longer little sister. "Don't worry," she added, patting her own non-existent hips and approving her own reflection, "it'll drop off. It's just baby fat."

It did not drop off until Clare decided to take action during her senior year of high school, when she despaired being left out of the sexual revolution. She engineered her weight reduction with the same determination she'd put into the fledgling political movement she'd created in Merrillville. At seventeen, she'd been eager to experience all she missed, and figured college would be the place to enjoy it.

She'd fallen directly into Lowell's so very capable hands.

But Lowell was dangerous to recall too often or too clearly; she could not afford this indulgence if she wanted to make a go of her present life. It wasn't Julio's fault that he could not live up to Lowell's brilliant memory.

She pushed aside, too, the recollection of Ginger's pointed discussion about benefits. A radical artist should not be expected to adhere to some bourgeois definition. If she could not uphold revolutionary principles in her own society, she'd support them, for Mexico, in him.

But it was lonely. When Julio was working, he easily swatted aside the swarm of gaudy people who buzzed around him. As much as they intrigued her, Clare was not important to them, and none of them came to see her except Grace, occasionally.

WHEN JESUS visited from Cuernavaca he told her, once Julio had left for his studio, she was crazy to be living like an old housewife when she was not yet twenty.

"Jesus, Jesus, not you too. I want to do this, okay, it's *experience*."

"You don't have to contribute to the revolution here. It isn't even safe for you to be involved. You have no idea how repressive our government is."

This sounded like something she'd heard before. "I don't make much of a contribution. He tells me nothing."

"You love Julio so much you can't live without him?"

Jesus was Julio's friend, so she didn't want to confide in him too closely, but he looked at her with kind knowing eyes.

He'd brought her the new Dylan album, "Blood on the Tracks," and its wry lyrical sagas spun behind them on the record player she'd insisted Julio buy, since she'd had to leave Ginger's radio back at the Señora's. Jesus, as little time as he'd spent with her, knew she loved Bob Dylan. Julio did not listen to music.

"I just feel I need to keep this commitment."

"You mean you'd rather live with Julio than at my mother's house."

"It's more the whole gringa scene," she began tactfully.

He unfolded himself from his lotus position on the floor. "I understand your desire for independence, hijita—"

"Why do you say that? You and Julio, you both call me little girl, or little daughter." She could explore this concept with Jesus, whose English was fluent, whereas Julio had been puzzled by her asking. "Do I seem so childish?"

163

Jesus studied her. "Clare ... in Mexico, you're a child until you're married. I know it's acceptable in your culture for an educated girl to have sex with a man, to live with a man, when still very young, but here it's ... unusual in Julio's and my class."

"You mean improper."

"Yes, although some people are starting to do this. But they are considered rebellious. Bohemian."

She flashed to Lowell's last speech, about judgmental cultures.

Jesus' features crinkled up in his rare smile. "But you don't care!"

This kind of observation was pure Jesus. "Which means?"

"I mean you American students, excuse me but I will make this generalization, since I saw the same behavior so often in my mother's house with the gringas. You live here as if you are in some kind of cinema inside your heads. As if what you do here doesn't matter in your real life. This experience is ... a fiction, to you."

An uncomfortable chill crept up her back. "I do sometimes feel kind of ...removed, like a reporter," she said. "But when I'm alone, it's just the way I talk to myself about what I see. I don't make it up, it's all real, what I observe, how I feel."

"You are lonely."

She didn't need his sympathy. "No! Being alone a lot doesn't mean I'm lonely—"

"You are lonely." He was smiling as if this were not a pitiful judgment. "Clare, you chose this path for a purpose not related to Julio or your relationship, but it will illuminate your life. All you learn here will lead you to your future."

She folded her arms. "Deep, Jesus, deep."

He ignored her sarcasm. "You should live alone, to experience the power of your own observation. You deserve real independence."

Before she could react, he clutched her in an uncharacteristic embrace. He smelled of Patchouli oil and lemon. She was startled by the sudden closeness and by the contrast with what was now her familiar male scent: Julio's turpentine and sweat. She wasn't used to thinking of Jesus as huggable and was about to push away when he let go.

He walked to the door. "Think about it, hijita."

AT LAST Ginger came to visit, fortified by the supportive presence of Cristal and her current well-groomed *popof*, an elite boy who recoiled at Julio's appearance. They sat on the floor awkwardly, making very small talk, consuming cheap red wine and the humid Saltines and manchego cheese Clare bought from the corner store.

Julio only spoke when asked a direct question. Clare covered his silence, babbling inanely, but her attempt to be a gracious hostess was foiled by the water's going off, so she was obliged to ask everyone not to flush the toilet. Among friends this would have been good for a few laughs, and Ginger, at least, snorted sympathetically, but any possible jokes died in the face of Julio's impassiveness and the obvious disconcert of Cristal and her date.

When Miguel came to collect Ginger, the party picked up a little as Julio identified Miguel's Cuban accent. They commenced an impassioned discussion about political realities in Latin America: the unique experience of Cuba and Chile, the unreliable financial support of the Soviets, the ever-present threat of CIA-backed militias, propaganda campaigns and coups, and most of all the fluctuating nature of agricultural economies and the state's inadequacy to address natural consequences.

Clare had to insert her own opinions forcefully, even in her still-hesitant Spanish, since the men did not bother to include the gringas in their discussion. Probably the built-in nature of Latin machismo made revolutionaries here as obtuse as Movement men were, Stateside, about women's participation.

Ginger motioned her aside to ask for more wine. "Jeez, are they gonna yap like this all friggin night?" she asked, uncorking the bottle Clare brought out in the tiny galley kitchen. "I wanted Miguel to take me to Beatriz." Clare's mouth watered at the very name of the famous taqueria. They had the best chilaquiles. She couldn't afford to go there anymore. "He was already late getting over here."

"Julio sounds like he's into Marxism," Cristal said, joining them. "Doesn't he know how dangerous it is to talk about revolution in Mexico?" Her boyfriends' opinions gave her a certain authority in stating this. Indeed, in the main room, her popof date looked wide-eyed from Miguel to Julio, increasingly alarmed as their voices rose.

Clare wasn't about to divulge the reality of Julio's political activities. She poured more wine, passed more crackers when the cheese was gone. When Ginger prevailed upon Miguel to leave, Clare watched them go with a mixture of relief and regret.

"You call them friends?" Julio remarked as he stacked empties in the box for a glass recycling project they'd joined. "They drank all that and didn't bring any replacements. Typical bourgeois. The Cubano's okay, though, I like him."

Naturally.

THIRTY-TWO

SOME TIME after that disastrous visit, a letter came to the school from Clare's mother. At the end of class she took it over to the Verona to read over a glass of beer, as a little treat. It was Mom's first letter since Clare wrote she had moved and needed money. She'd given her new address only as 'in care of Julio Mendiron,' not wanting to clarify their relationship.

Dear Clare,

I assume the change in your address means you are living with Julio Mendiron. Is he a boyfriend? I don't see why else you would leave the family situation you had before. If you are enough of an adult to live with a man, you should be enough of an adult to tell me about it honestly. And to earn your own way now. I don't approve of that kind of living arrangement, so I am not obliged to support it. When Claudia moved in with Phil, I didn't help her. I did appreciate her telling me about it, though.

I am disappointed in you, if you tried to hide this from me as the reason you moved, and I suspect, by your silence about moving, that it is. But I do love you, very much, and I believe you'll benefit from having to work through this experience on your own.

Write soon. At least tell me who he is, what he does for a living, how you feel about him. As always, call collect if you have serious trouble.

Love from Mom

Guilt and tenderness braided into a tight knot inside her as Clare looked at her mother's careful handwriting. Mom would have composed this letter slowly, looking up from time to time over her half-glasses, debating the best way to put things, wanting to sound as reasonable as her final words reflected.

"I am disappointed in you." Clare had always been a Good Girl; she'd never heard this from Mom before. *Oh Mommy.*

Oh hell.

She had to get a job.

When she looked up she saw Grace entering the dim space.

"There you are! Ginger said she saw you heading this way."

"Hi Grace."

"What's wrong?"

Clare handed her the letter and finished her beer while Grace read it.

"That's all? You think it's the end of the world? Poor baby." Grace shook her head.

This didn't reassure Clare. "I need a job but I don't know what I can do. I don't have working papers, my Spanish is not expert, and I have class every day this term."

"Teach English. That's what I do when I need extra funds. I can put you in touch with the InnerLanguage people if you like, over in the Zona Rosa."

"But I wouldn't have enough regular hours to teach English."

"So drop a class or two. Just show up at the end and take the exam. Sounds like those clowns would never notice." She laughed at Clare's expression. "It's either that or go back to Suzi, or tell Julio to support you. Can you do that?"

"No way."

"Well, at least I can buy you dinner."

Grace drove her to Coyoacan after a quick meal.

"Where's Julio?"

"He's staying at his studio." His opening was tomorrow night and he was in a single-minded state that ignored the absence or presence of anyone around him.

Grace wandered over to the window and looked out. Teenagers were playing soccer even at this late hour and their rough voices echoed through the alleyway. Grace wrinkled her nose. "All very picturesque, but doesn't it get old?" She didn't wait for an answer, but settled herself in a corner piled with cushions. She put on the new Dylan record Jesus had brought. "Got anything to drink?"

Clare found a bottle of red and poured two glasses. They both sipped.

Grace made a face. "Where do you get this vinegar? How can you stand it?"

It was better than Ripple. "It's cheap."

"That's one thing about aging," Grace said. "Poverty loses its panache. What the hell does Julio spend his money on?"

"He doesn't believe in modern conveniences."

"No shit." Grace sipped again. "Wagner heard some talk about Julio's politics. Maybe he's funding the rebels." Her tone was casual but the subject had Clare suddenly hyper-alert.

"What rebels?" she asked.

Grace shrugged. "Any of em, pick one, there are so many, Wagner says." She stood and walked around to flip through canvases stacked against the walls. "So these are his rejects, huh, the ones he isn't putting in the gallery."

"I guess,"

Grace turned to laugh at her. "You guess! You don't sound too sure. How long have you two been together?"

"A few months."

"He doesn't talk to you about his art or his politics?"

"No."

"So, what, you guys just have sex?"

This was none of Grace's business, but Clare found herself blurting, "Not much."

"So, really, you just like living in Coyoacan." Grace laughed again. "Funny how you young gringas seem to dig this groovy old art scene. Not me. I like the modern conveniences of Wagner's villa. Give me south of San Angel, please!"

A sense of surreality was covering Clare's thoughts like a dark cloud, hastened by the late hour, Julio's absence, the menacing prehistoric-birdlike cries of the soccer boys, the mournful Dylan songs and Grace's pointed comments. If she were to write back to Mom, she'd have little to say. Grace was right. She knew nothing about how Julio made his art, nothing about what he did with his cell, nothing about the certainty of her situation with him. Jesus and Ginger were right. She was living in a cinema to prove her independence.

Grace pulled on her jacket. "You don't seem to be in the mood for company."

"Sorry, Grace." Clare opened the door and made a lame joke to cover how profoundly disturbed she felt. "It's like one of those Fellini movies, where everything gets all weird and Latin after midnight—"

"That's Bunuel, dear, this hemisphere." Grace kissed Clare's cheek. "See you tomorrow at Julio's gallery opening."

Clare closed the door and sighed, leaning against it for a moment, before going to the window to watch as Grace, five floors below, got into her Triumph and drove off. She could see the busy warrens of the neighborhood twisting away toward the major highway.

At first, here, she'd found the sight of so much open life enthralling and vivid, containing as many worlds as an Octavio Paz novel brought to garish reality, but right now the barrio looked dusty and alien. She knew if she descended into one of the alleys she would not discover any new "worlds"—she would simply be investigated and harassed by the young toughs who ruled the streets. There was no true intrigue in it, no more fascination.

She thought back to the girl who'd roamed Mexico City alone months ago, seeing it in dramatic shadows and light, the film Jesus rightly identified.

That girl was gone.

Maybe it was time to go back to the States once this term was over. Her Mom was right, too: if she couldn't support her present situation by herself then she had no business trying to continue. She had a year's worth of credits left to finish her BA; she could get a student loan, finish her time in Bloomington and quit school forever at twenty. That sounded good: she was getting tired of inhabiting what felt, more and more, like someone else's life.

She cranked shut the casement windows, to block the street noises, left on the record player to repeat Dylan's wistful tunes. Too tired even to brush her teeth, she fell asleep with the sour taste of Bull Blood wine still in her mouth.

THIRTY-THREE

THE OPENING was all Clare expected from a Zona Rosa gallery—white-coated waiters bearing trays of canapés and Champagne, sharp-eyed critics from the local art press, rival artists and gallery owners, and the usual throng of tourists, trendsetters and sycophants. Clare glimpsed Mario in a corner, talking intently to a rat-faced man in an electric blue suit. Elizabeth Taylor's Mexico City hairdresser nodded briefly as he brushed past; he'd given Clare's hair a look, once, and quoted a styling session, but she'd just laughed.

The serious buyers and collectors circled the paintings, alone, speaking to no one. From time to time, they stood in front of one piece, absorbing, adding and subtracting with their eyes as the party eddied around them.

Julio sat on a stool in a corner and chatted with those who approached him. He wore his usual paint-spattered jeans and flannel shirt, sipped his usual herbal tea and seemed not to realize what the fuss was. It always surprised Clare to see how casual he was with art-scene people. His agent hovered nearby, clutching plump little hands as he watched the buyers frown or smile.

Wagner and Grace arrived about an hour into the show. They shook hands with Julio and his agent before Wagner moved to inspect the paintings while Grace stayed to talk to Julio. Clare sipped Champagne as they made polite conversation.

"Where's the hard stuff?" Grace asked Clare in an aside.

Clare led her to the back bar where she knew the agent kept the whiskey. Grace poured herself a healthy glass.

"You look good, Clare."

Clare had taken time with her clothes and makeup, for once, wanting the gallery visitors to see Julio had a presentable companion. She wore a black skirt and sweater with a brightly patterned Guatemalan belt, her hair in a smooth ponytail, gold hoops in her ears. She'd decided, last night, she didn't want to look like a hippie anymore, or a polyester disco dolly.

"So how many paintings should Wagner buy this time, hmm?"

Clare shrugged.

"He's making your boyfriend rich." Grace set her glass down. "Even though he isn't spending on that temporary-feeling place, or on you, on even on a car, for God's sake, the man lives like he's taken a vow of poverty."

"That's none of my business." She made her tone imply "or yours." "Oh look, there's the Secos y Molhados lead singer, I've got to say hi."

The singer's skin-tight sequined jumpsuit outlined his muscular, unmistakably masculine form, even as his makeup and long hair emphasized his feminine beauty. He was effusive toward his fans, and his Spanish was intriguingly flavored by a delicious Brazilian accent, so it was easy for Clare to lose herself for a moment in his amusing penchant for flirtation with men and women.

Beyond him she noticed Wagner, hands folded behind his back, studying a particularly large canvas which for once was crowded with Julio's multi-colored slashes—"that's what it's like in prison," he'd explained to her, the only time he opened up about a painting.

Wagner set off in a determined-looking pace toward Julio's agent.

Clare followed Wagner. Grace had left, she assumed for other openings; the Zona Rosa was brimming with art tonight.

" ...such a wonderful patron! We are eternally grateful," the agent was saying. Julio was shaking Wagner's hand. As Clare approached, she tried to read what was in both mens' expressions: Julio regarded Wagner, who was half a head shorter, with what she knew was a totally phony smile, and Wagner was nodding vigorously at the agent, not even looking at Julio.

"I've been thinking about that one since I first saw it," Wagner said. "It represents such variety of life, such a spectrum of color, so many facets of wisdom."

"Mmm." Julio inclined his head. *So many political prisoners,* Clare imagined him adding, *Thanks for your donation to their cause.*

Where had Grace's comment about rebel support come from?

Art people tended to take a leftist view of current events but spoke of them specifically only as they affected funding and censorship. Poets and singers were more easily riled than painters, and dancers seemed oblivious to all but earthquakes, but everyone talked about the refugees from Chile and the desaparecidos from within Mexico. Maybe it was easy for Grace, or Wagner, to take a wild guess in that direction, regarding Julio's use of art money.

When Julio caught sight of Clare he motioned her over.

"What's on your mind, niña? You're not an investor or a critic, you don't have to look so solemn. Have fun. It's a party."

"Does Wagner know what he's investing in?" she whispered into Julio's ear.

He laughed. He muttered a reply that was so fast, so low, she could not understand him, but his agent was already towing him into the middle of the gallery, calling for quiet, so he could make an emotional speech about the discovery of a great new talent. Everyone applauded, signifying the end of the official opening.

After the doors closed, someone brought out a joint, someone else passed the guest book to which all added personal messages, and more Champagne was opened. A photographer rapped on the window and pressed his ID against the glass, and since he was with an international newspaper the agent let him in, and they all posed in front of the prisoners' canvas. Julio was thus confirmed for posterity as the artist of the era.

Clare did not get another moment with him until the last of the guests were clustered by the doors. "Julio. Do you know Wagner's talked about your politics with Grace?"

He looked at her with more concentration than she'd received in weeks. Maybe now his show was over he was free to see her again. "Nena, I just told you. I'm sure that's why he buys from me. It's his way to clear his conscience. He carries a lot of guilt."

"About what?"

"What his company did in Chile."

"Chile!"

"Querida, this isn't your concern."

173

"You're not ...worried?"

"Worried?" He laughed. "I just became a national asset! I'm in a position now to make a real statement." He patted her arm. "Everything I do is intended, you'll see."

"I don't like the way that sounds ... "

He wrinkled his mouth in a smile that caught in his mustache. "I'm sorry," he murmured. "You'll understand ... " His agent and the gallery owner came up to them, interrupting whatever it was he meant to say.

"*Vamonos, maestro*. Come, Clare, we're celebrating at El Coyote Flaco."

"You go ahead," she told them. She could not face another late night. "I'm too tired to keep up with the party. I'll see you at home, Julio."

THIRTY-FOUR

WHEN JULIO didn't come back that night, as she sat listening again to "Blood on the Tracks," Clare figured he'd had too much to drink and stayed at his agent's house.

She was having a strange dream about a Beatles song when a slice of mid day light broke through the curtains and woke her. It was nearly one in the afternoon. His agent must have kept him for Sunday brunch. Either that or he went to his studio, which was his normal Sunday hang-out unless, as sometimes happened, he was able to borrow a car and drive to Bosques del Pedregal, at the foot of the mountains south of the city, where there was a large forest preserve perfect for hiking and picnics.

Massing clouds indicated today wasn't a good picnic day.

She sat at the rickety little card table and drank her coffee, looking around at the shabby room, which had never been hers. Grace was right. It *was* temporary feeling. Funny how this had never before struck her as so wrong. Its only adornments were Julio's paintings, hanging and stacked, and their stark character did little to relieve the bleakness chilling the afternoon.

When the door shuddered its metallic clang, and the key subsequently turned in the lock, she sprang up, anxiety rioting with relief as she admitted how frightened for him she'd been, how glad he was okay, they just *had* to get a telephone—

It wasn't Julio opening the door, it was Jesus, and Mario behind. Jesus gave her a hug but Mario pushed past to grab a stack of paintings leaning against the far wall. He hoisted them, with gloved hands, and beelined out the door.

Clare flung Jesus' gloved hands from her arms. "What the hell …?"

"Clare, Julio has been taken, we have to get you and his paintings out before the DFS arrive. Hurry, hijita, take anything you need from here and we go now, fast, Mario has a van—"

175

She whirled toward the nearest stack, witlessly galvanized although she did not know who the DFS were, or what Jesus was talking about—

"No, I'll take them." Jesus shouldered her aside. "I've got gloves, we don't want them to track fingerprints. Get your things and meet us outside."

Mario was already back for another batch of paintings, did the man fly? He existed on mescaline so he probably levitated through the window.

Jesus shook her and repeated, "We need to go!"

She raced to the bedroom and threw some clothes and books into a backpack, stood for a moment thinking, dashed into the bathroom to collect her pills, toothbrush and shampoo. Of all stupid things, she marveled, she was gaping at the medicine cabinet, while Jesus and Mario heaved the last of the art away. Not knowing why, she took Julio's toothbrush.

Jesus grabbed her arm. He slammed the door behind them. They fled down the five flights headlong—in the history of her life here, the ancient cage elevator had never once worked—and Jesus hustled her around the corner where Mario sat in a panel van with his black sunglasses on, revving the engine, tapping nervous fingers.

She stopped short.

"Jesus." She wheeled on him, looked into his mild brown eyes. "Is this some drug thing? Because if it is, I'm not helping you guys. Julio—" But she didn't know what Julio wanted. She didn't know where he was. "Let's stop at the studio, I'm sure he's there—"

"He's gone, Clare, we have to go too, now." Jesus pushed her into the van and she was wedged between the men as Mario drove like a maniac, like everyone else did, through the sidewinding barrio traffic circles and alleys until they reached the Avenue Insurgentes, the main highway bisecting the city.

I'm glad I got dressed, she had time to think as they careened northeast. She had three long Mayan dresses she liked to loll around in during weekends, still hanging in the closet—

"Jesus! I didn't lock the door!"

"No importa," Jesus said, so preoccupied with Mario's driving he did not bother to answer her in English.

"What do you mean, Julio's been taken?"

Mario shot her a glance as his wiry arms wrenched the wheel back and forth. "Desaparecido," he said briefly, and the chills started up her arms and down her back.

"Why?" As if she didn't know, fighting horror: his cell must have been busted.

"He's with a group called the *Liga*, the 23rd September League," Jesus said.

"23rd September ..." This rang a faint bell.

"*Guerrilleros,*" Jesus went on. "They kidnapped an industrialist last year, it went wrong and the *tipo* was killed in a shootout between his bodyguards and the police. They're underground now."

"What do they want?"

"They're revolutionaries, Clare, they want release of all desaparecidos, they want their manifesto published, they want to overthrow the government. Julio told you a little, I remember, the night I brought him to meet you. They're Communists."

"He never wanted to talk about it again."

"Probably he wanted to protect you."

"Did Wagner engineer this?"

Jesus looked at her. His lemon-patchouli scent permeated the van. He was wearing pajamas, his usual baggy Indian getup, which somehow irritated her.

Clare went on, "Did he? I *knew* he and Grace were acting weird! I tried to protect Julio from them, last night, but I didn't know what I was doing or what they were up to either—"

"I don't know Wagner or Grace." Jesus, she remembered, had not been at the opening. "I don't know how they found him. You should be glad you were not with him."

"*Simon,*" said Mario, the slang equivalent of yeah, man.

She slapped hands on her eyes and bent to her knees. Her mind filled with rampaging images of Julio being thrown against the walls of some filthy cement-block blood-stained basement, his fingers stomped on by thuggish soldiers like they'd done in Chile to the musician Victor Jara, ruined his hands so he couldn't play guitar, before they shot him.

"*Basta,*" said Jesus. Enough. "You can't get hysterical now, Clare, you are the *mujer de un martir.*" Martyr's wife—how did they know he was a martyr already? "You have to hold up an example of dignity."

"*Simon,*" Mario repeated.

"Why are you taking his paintings?" She didn't know how she could still speak Spanish with any clarity.

Mario glanced at her. "So the state can't get them, *nena*, he wants his assets distributed for the cause." He grinned suddenly. "And I'm just the chavo to move them on the market."

She twisted to look at the bundles of art, covered with blankets, wound with rope. The van, the rope, the gloves: discordantly premeditated for an always-wrecked super-dealer and an "only-now-exists" Zen practitioner.

"You guys know more than you're telling me. Where is Julio?"

"We don't know, Clare."

"Who are the...the DSS, or whoever you said was coming to his rooms?"

"Direccion Federal de Seguridad. Secret police." Jesus touched her shoulder. "He told me when this day came, I should get you away. And take his artwork. He didn't want them to destroy it, or sell it."

"He wants the profits for his cell," she guessed.

"He knew this was inevitable. The *Liga* has been targeted by the state for a long time. He made his preparations and he was ready for his martyrdom. More ready than ever, now that he's famous, all the world press will notice. He makes a good ... how you say, statement."

"I'm in a position now to make a real statement," he'd told her last night.

They came off the *pereferico* into a new neighborhood of high-walled pastel buildings and water-washed tree-groomed sidewalks, where Mario pulled into a spotless garage. He and Jesus unloaded the paintings into a storeroom off the garage that Mario secured with a heavy padlock. They peeled off their gloves and grinned at each other.

"Tell me the truth," she said quietly, unconsciously speaking English. "You guys wouldn't be so happy if he really was desaparecido."

"I am happy to the commission I make of the *pintura*," Mario said in his stiff English. "This *vale mas que nunca*, the artista Julio is *famoso* after last night. I am happy the money go to the *causa* that he, he believe this can to be ... *realizado*."

"So how's the money getting to the *causa?*" she asked.

"Not for you to know, nena, he want that you don' have *problema* for this." Mario yawned hugely, the first indication he needed a fix, she recognized.

"Fine." She folded her arms and leaned against the van. "What now?"

"I'll take you to my mother," said Jesus. "You'll be safe there. DFS don't know you. You can go to school as usual."

"So, as the *mujer de un martir*, I'm not supposed to be part of this statement?"

Jesus looked at her for a long moment. "You want to be?"

"We can do that, mano, she stay in Coyoacan, give a *presentacion* for *la prensa*—"

"We can't protect her in Coyocacan," Jesus interrupted.

"Where is Julio?"

Jesus glanced away.

Mario sniffed loudly. "I'll be upstairs, en mi casa, come up when you like."

In Mario's absence she felt comfortable enough to reach forward and slug Jesus on his bicep. "What the *fuck* is going on?"

He stepped back, wary, rubbing his arm. "Clare—"

"You prefer I think he's being tortured than tell me the truth?"

He sighed. "Okay, yes, you're very quick. He disappeared himself."

"He *what?*"

"He's underground now. If everyone thinks he's taken by DFS, desaparecido, the news will get a lot of sympathy for the left. Mario can sell his paintings, they'll bring more money than ever, now he's famous. Mario knows how to get the money to his compadres. This was his dream, he told me, but I don't know where he is, truly."

"You mean he ... engineered his own disappearance."

"Yes." Jesus suddenly looked as tired as she felt.

"So ... there's no DFS, no real crisis here."

"They really are going after all the Liga members. He was

179

working to get his show done as fast as possible before they catch up to him."

"Can I can get in touch with Julio if—"

"—you should know, his real name is not Julio." Jesus had the grace to shrug, sheepishly. "Sorry. I can't say more."

As if I want to hear it. She felt empty as a husk, a dry cornhusk of the type she remembered from late autumn in Indiana, where she wished she was right now. "Jesus."

"I regret, Clare, I know you loved him—"

She didn't love him. She never had loved him. But she was glad he was safe. She looked at Jesus. "Tell him I'm okay. If he asks."

"I don't have any way to talk to him—"

"Just tell him," she repeated. "Now take me to your mom's. I've got a degree to finish."

THIRTY-FIVE

Virginia 1975

IN THE smoochy, boozy aftermath of the Happy New Year screams, a woman with too much makeup was putting the moves on Low. She had him effectively cornered, since he had tried to retreat by edging backward on his crutches.

Her boss was a lobbyist, she told him, as if he'd be impressed. The way she looked right now—lipstick smeared, eyes glassy with lust and Champagne—she'd be better off claiming anonymity. She slipped her arm around his waist and leaned against him heavily, making him stagger a little. Her hand crept down to cup his ass.

"I don't usually behave this way." She breathed into his ear, "Where've you been hiding?" She squeezed him and he moved away. He had done the same things to women he was pursuing but never, not even when very drunk, had he the poor taste to hit on someone as obviously turned off as he was.

It was amusing, to be on the receiving end of the pursuit, but enough was enough. He put one rubber-tipped crutch on top of her foot and shifted just a little weight onto it as if by accident. She yelped.

"Gosh, I'm awful sorry," Low said. "I keep losing my balance this time of night." He gave her a smile and moved away. Time to find his father and go home.

HE'D BEEN living at home for nearly a year.

After a ten-day coma in a Beirut hospital, he'd been transferred, through Landschul air base in Germany, to Washington's Walter Reed Army Medical Center for several months—months of pain so intense that his first thought on waking was regret that he'd survived the car bombing.

181

The door's blowing him back had spared him all but superficial burns, and he was fortunate—they told him—not to have cracked his skull, but both legs and feet were broken in several places, as well as his left arm and collarbone. His jaw was broken and both shoulders dislocated. They said he was suffering traumatic brain injury, whatever that meant. They said he was lucky to be alive.

Had he already been in the car with Ahmed, he would have exploded—a quick messy death that would have been preferable, he believed for a long time, to the torment of repeated surgeries to set his bones straight.

His only relief was in periods of drugged stupor. The drugs did not remove the pain, but put it at a distance so he could contemplate it, as if looking at a man-eating lion in a cage, to observe the true nature of the beast. But soon the lion sprang from its cage and began again to maul him, twisting and worrying him like so much raw meat.

His doctors, wary of addiction, prescribed minimum dosages. Low submitted to the pain with fevers, sweats and a loss of appetite so profound they kept having to hook him back up to the IV for feeding even when his jaw was healed enough to chew.

He hated feeling like a lump of useless flesh, hung up in traction, kept alive through tubes, prodded and poked and turned around, stuff put in and stuff taken out, just a bag of garbage not yet rotten enough to be tossed away.

Throughout, his father visited almost every afternoon. Low could see how James worried about him, so he tried to rouse himself when he knew his father was due. At first he could only relay fragments of what had happened, because his mind was so cloudy and his mouth was so uncooperative, but as time passed he told more.

One day James came in and gave him the official story.

"Guthery says they're stating it was your own car that was wired. The embassy has to hush this up and forget it, was the gist I got."

"You call him?" He remembered Guthery's moustache. "He still asshole?"

"He sure was this morning. He says they don't want to reveal the extent of your friendship, that he's not sure if you were the real target or Ahmed was. If you were the target, he says it was random. Mourabitoun don't do car bombs."

"They want. Hurt worse than explode," Low explained through thick-feeling lips, so slowly. "They like. Rip apart. Bit by bloody bit." His mind produced these images effortlessly now. Who knew he had all this gore inside?

"He says if Ahmed was the target, it was reprisal for some tribal thing. Sounds like "The Godfather." Vendettas, feuds, no end to it. Guthery says a civil war is breaking out now. I gather that's his excuse for your being almost killed. He sent you on a covert mission, essentially, with no training and no backup." James' voice was gravelly with rare anger. "I'm thinking about getting him canned."

"No, Dad. Barn door, horse gone. Not his fault."

James eyed him, his face still cold for Guthery. "He doesn't want Ahmed's family to claim the embassy owes blood money. No way he'll pay. That's why he's not letting them know you survived, by the way, your supposed death gives a reason not to extend any help other than life insurance for Ahmed."

Sonia. Samir, the little brother. The sweet-eyed grandfather with his carved Damascus chessboard, waiting patiently for a game, cooking thick fragrant coffee in his own little brazier on the third floor of Ahmed's house.

Would he never stop seeing them?

"Oh fuck me," Low mumbled, trying to twist his head away so James wouldn't catch his eyes' useless watering.

"What's that?" Low knew James hated hearing the F-word.

"My fault."

"No sir," James stated in a loud firm voice. "Absolutely not."

"Because I was bored. Dad." He could not make the words sound as disgusted as he meant them to be. He slurred, now, there was no punch in his speech, no fluctuation: he was rendered monotonous. And his throat was so fucking dry it felt like the goddamn Grand Canyon. He preferred not talking at all.

"You were an innocent bystander—"

"Not innocent."

"Guthery says you were well liked. Respected. Doing a fine

job."

"Lying. Asshole. I hated job."

"He says your colleagues appreciated you—"

"Pack of. Bores. He's lying," Low said again, spitting in his effort to snarl. "I never gave em. Chance know me. I wanted. Drama." Worn by the attempt to explain, he tried to turn, to push his face into the pillow, but he got stuck with the weight of his body cast and IV entanglements. "Fuck me," he repeated, his body alight with spangling pains like some freaky sparkler as James repositioned him. "Too bad. Ahmed. Wander into my show."

He felt his body heating, prickles and then bursts of furnace blast; the fever always shot up when he got upset or tried to move. It was meds time.

When he lay on his right side, the uninjured-arm side—even though he craved the change, longed for it, welcomed it for a glorious moment of relief—the cast soon pressed on him like a suit of cement, pressed so hard he forgot to care about Ahmed, as a hallucination of Mafia-style drowning appeared: slipping quiet into a river of murk, body cast ensuring an easy glide to airless depths.

Maybe it wouldn't be so bad. Maybe he'd float through patches of watery sunlight on his way down. He closed his eyes. He didn't even have the strength to ask James to turn him again.

"Your guilt is misplaced, Lowell. You wandered into *his* show." James' voice brought him back, and he didn't want to be back.

"Spying," Low gasped with what felt like the last of his air. "Got him killed."

"You're not making any sense." James stood. Low felt his perplexed concern, pressing heavy as the cast. "You need to get over this."

Well, that was James: a quick-fix kind of man, puzzled by lack of spirit or enthusiasm, impatient with laggards. Until now, Low knew he'd never been a laggard or a mystery to his father, but he could only spare that a couple of seconds' meager thought before drowning.

Next time he woke, a woman was seated where James had been. He wasn't sure if it was tomorrow already; when it was bad he lost time. He glanced at the IV pole; bottle hanging meant he still wasn't going to be able to eat, fuck it. At least the fever was gone. He looked at the woman.

She didn't say anything. She studied him as if she knew him, though, her light brown eyes gazing steady, seeming to hold him. Maybe she was a former teacher; he'd had a lot of visitors, he didn't always recognize them. Maybe she was one of his friends' mothers. She had smooth dark hair curled around her ears, gold studs, nice makeup, little glasses perched on a small nose. She wore a crisp red shirt and a khaki skirt. He rested his eyes on the red shirt, its pointed collar, its stiff fabric. It was good to see color.

"Hello, Lowell, I'm Dr. Grant. Elena Grant."

He didn't know her. "Hey."

"I've come to talk to you, see how you're feeling."

"Feelin shit, doc, tell truth."

She didn't smile the way the nurses did when he said this, when they thought he was kidding, or ignore him the way the other doctors did, the ones who looked like doctors.

"I want you to talk, if you're willing. I'd like to hear about what happened in Beirut, how you feel about it."

How I feel? Beirut? Jesus please us. "I can't talk much."

"I know, Lowell, we can take this as slowly as you need to. I can ask the questions, if you like, and you can just blink. One for yes, two for no."

Was she for real?

But what else did he have to do in here? He hated TV, he couldn't move, he couldn't read, so what did he have to lose? He liked the way she looked, as if she belonged outside in the hurly-burly working world, not stuck in the tense grey-green-white of hospital people too busy saving lives to crack a joke or even look him in the eye. Her red shirt said she was alive.

He blinked, once.

"Do you blame yourself for what happened to you?"

Well, duh, one blink. It was his choice to *use* Ahmed! His choice to seduce the whole family into accepting him. His fault that now, after the loss of Dr. Badawi so long ago, they'd lost Ahmed too, Ahmed who would have provided for them, the hope of Sonia's heart, Ahmed whose grandfather would always wait, forlorn, on that third floor ... Jesus. His blink turned into so many, burning, that he had to turn his head away from Dr. Grant.

"If you had died, and Ahmed had lived, would you feel better?"

What kind of stupid fucked question was that? If he was dead he wouldn't care, that was the point, he wished he was dead! Dead was better, dead was no pain, no caring, no longing. He glared at her. He knew his eyes still worked, he could still stare down some candy-striper volunteer girl, he hadn't lost all his power.

"Let's suppose you died, okay, Ahmed's alive, and he's then able to carry on with what he was doing before.

"Let's suppose the bombing—it was his car, remember— was just a warning for him. So those people who wanted him dead will keep trying since, in this hypothesis, you died and he didn't. Do you suppose those clever people will find him, in Beirut today? Of course they will. You had nothing to do with this."

She was talking too fast.

"He was my friend." He could not emphasize, only slur.

"You shared a unique experience, both of you new at the embassy, you just from Indiana and he just from Langley—"

Was he hearing this right? "No."

She nodded. "Guthery didn't know enough to name him, and you'll have to pretend you never heard this, but it's true. Although he had family connections to the Mourabitoun, Ahmed was supposed to be working for us."

Who was she calling us?

But he remembered Ahmed saying, "The people who hired me knew what they were doing," and, "Anyone who replaces me will be doing two jobs. Yours, and his own."

Fuck me twice! Ahmed's being CIA made him an even more vulnerable target, with Low hanging on him all the time; no wonder he'd been taken out. *I might as well have pinned the goddamn bullseye on his back.* This felt worse than being lion meat.

Elena Grant patted his hand. Hers was cool, dry, and her fragrance was sweet as she leaned toward him, and her voice was soft and her red shirt seemed to shine. "Lowell. Get rid of your guilt about Ahmed. What happened had nothing to do with you."

"He wasn't. CIA. Loonies would. Do worse."

"We put him there."

"Who. Took him out?"

She had the nerve to smile as if it didn't matter. "That's being investigated. But I wanted to make it perfectly clear to you that he knew the risks of supporting his tribe."

"Then I shoulda. Kept clear of him."

"In fact, befriending you provided him perfect cover."

He couldn't show his scorn for this notion with even a shrug.

She took off her little glasses to peer into his eyes. "Don't be an egotist." She shook the folded glasses at him, a strict teacher's admonishment, but he couldn't even flinch, he was that constrained. "This was *not* your fault."

"Bored was. My fault," he managed. He had an irresistible tickle in his throat to cough, but not the mastery of his muscles, so it felt like drowning once more. He wheezed and felt tears rolling down his cheeks, and heat crowding his entire body, as his throat ached for release.

"Bored," she repeated. She wet a washcloth at the corner sink and mopped his face. The motherly touch made him want to grab her and wail all over her nice red shirt. Then she held a cup of water to his lips with a straw. Bliss. "You were overqualified for that particular position. We can fix that."

Who was she calling we?

"And, Lowell, since trauma like this tends to make other losses re-emerge? I'd like to talk to you about your mother, Lydia, next time we meet."

Lydia had flown in to coo over him just last week. He closed his eyes.

187

THIRTY-SIX

AFTER HE was liberated from the body cast and his limbs healed, a new torture began: physical therapy. He was told, first gently and then forcefully, that he was lucky to be alive and that the only way he would walk again was by devotion to therapy. When he argued that he didn't care, he wanted only to sleep, they dragged him out of bed and set him to the exercises.

James equipped the house with therapeutic machinery and a hospital bed, and moved Low home as soon as the doctors approved it. But as Washington's late summer pace picked up and James' own schedule got more hectic, he had less time to spend with Low and less patience.

"You have two choices," he said one afternoon. "You can stay an invalid. Or you can work at recuperating."

"For what?" snapped Low. "All I ever wanted was to join the Foreign Service just like you. Now what am I supposed to do, go back and be a better spy? For the good of my country? That's fucked."

"Listen." James lifted Low's chin so he was forced to look into his father's eyes. "Whatever mistakes you think you made before, you're responsible for yourself, now. You're twenty five. How will you spend the rest of your life?"

"What does it matter?"

"It does to me. Because I'm not interested in harboring an invalid. If you want to stay one, we'll find a nice institution for you."

Fuck!

"That's right. You want to live here, you work at putting yourself back together."

"Shit."

"And no smart talk."

IT WAS a difficult fall. Low chafed at his slow recuperation and resented having to live at home again after years of independence. It was only his determination to move out that propelled him to the exercise room day after day. His father was curtly approving of his efforts and left him alone to get on with it. Low saw only Dr. Grant, biweekly, and his coach. Marlon had been a basketball player, but after being injured in a car crash and learning to walk again, he turned his energies to becoming a physical therapist. He worked with many vets and made fun of Low's depression.

Marlon's hands were as compassionate as his manner was jeering, and Low knew he couldn't have tolerated anyone else witnessing the depth of his weakness. Marlon was matter-of-fact about his legs. "They'll work when you do," he stated, and finally Low believed him as he progressed painfully from leg casts to walker to crutches.

His first time out alone was terrifying. Marlon drove him to the middle of populous Georgetown, familiar to Low from his undergraduate days. "I'll pick you up in an hour, gimp, if I remember what you look like."

Low slumped on his crutches, trembling on the corner, shaken by the traffic and the crowds, frightened that someone would knock him over. It was a steamy September day and he stared at the girls breezing by in their light clothes, impossibly alluring to him, their glances slipping past him as if he were invisible.

Unable to stand longer, he crutched into the nearest open doorway: a bar. He hoisted himself awkwardly onto a stool and ordered a beer. The beefy, bearded bartender watched him and said abruptly, "It's on me, man."

"Thanks," Low answered. "Uh, why?"

"You're a vet, aincha? Me too. What company you with?"

"Ah. I wasn't exactly. I was in Beirut."

"Oh yeah?" The bartender still looked puzzled.

"Lebanon. The Middle East."

"Oh I dig. One a them embassy guards."

"Sort of."

"So who hit ya?"

"I don't know," Low said slowly as the guy slid a beer into

189

his hand. "I really have no idea."

Other customers had already claimed the bartender's attention.

Low sipped his beer. Marlon only allowed him one a week so he was trying to enjoy it when he caught a glimpse of himself in the facing mirror. He gazed at his unkempt visage. His eyes were sunk in dark circles and his lips were cracked and dry from muscle relaxants. He was emaciated, his skin was an unhealthy white, and his hair was past his shoulders, uncut all these months. His tee shirt hung on his bony frame. It was the first time he'd really looked at himself, aside from a small mirror to shave, in longer than he could recall.

I look like a fucking junkie!

He had not set out to deliberately avoid the draft, but he'd assumed, as an outstanding scholar, he was too smart to be caught in a foolish war. Troy's experience had taught him how arrogant that attitude was. Troy had been just as bright as Low, their freshman year at Georgetown, but less interested in studying than in exploring the Sixties cultural revolution. The draft had snatched Troy as soon as he dropped out.

Low raised his beer to the ghost surveying him in the mirror. Here he was a vet, a cripple, just as out-of-it disoriented as the stereotypic "grunt" who lost a year of innocence, or worse, in Vietnam. He recalled Clare's outrage at the waste of Joe and for the first time really understood her fury. He could not hold his own gaze.

"Whatcha lookin at?" Marlon was suddenly leaning on his elbows next to Low.

"I thought I was supposed to get on alone for awhile here?"

"A baby like you? Wobbling around on those crutches like you do?" Marlon imitated his shaky stance, cruelly, and Low laughed through the sting.

"Fuck you, coach."

"That's better. Thought you were gonna cry into your beer all day."

THIRTY-SEVEN

ONE DAY not long after the Georgetown outing, Marlon didn't show up at his usual time. Low sat in the formal living room, looking outside, feeling bereft as a small boy whose buddy missed a playdate. A car came into the circular drive, not Marlon's, and a young woman got out. She pulled on a white lab coat over jeans and tee shirt as she crossed the veranda.

"Hi, I'm Tracy," she said musically. She had bright green eyes and shiny brown hair. "I'm Marlon's sub. He couldn't make it today."

Low wasn't sure he could do his therapy comfortably with this strange girl, but he led her to the gym anyway.

She put him through a few of the floor sets and said, "You're so tense. You're hurting your muscles this way."

Low stared up at her from the mat, sweating, breathing hard. He suddenly felt furious at himself for being weak, at Marlon for not showing up, and mostly at this Tracy with her healthy good looks, her curvy body and her casual manner. He was powerless when she flipped him over, easily, and started to give him a brisk massage. She was good, but he couldn't relax to enjoy it. Her proximity made him too uncomfortable.

"Okay, hot shower." She stepped toward the shower in the stall at the end of the room James had equipped as a gym, turned on the jets, came back to where he lay, panting. "Come on, Lowell, let's get you massaged another way."

He didn't want some girl looking at him naked! He pulled away from her, but she grabbed his arm and repeated, with some ire, "Let's get you massaged this way."

She helped him in and turned away, to let him get undressed. Once in the shower with the jets blasting, soothing his aching limbs, he finally relaxed. He closed his eyes.

"Do you ever smile?" She was standing right outside the

191

frosted shower door.

"What am I supposed to I smile about?" he snapped. Who the fuck *was* this chick?

"Well, this," she said, and peeled off her lab coat, tee shirt, jeans. Her high round breasts brushed against his chest when she stepped into the shower. She turned off the water and cupped his face as she reached up to kiss him and press close.

Through his surprise Low felt himself get instantly, painfully hard. Lust roared in his ears and pounded his heart. But he pulled away and looked at her. "This is part of your therapy?"

"Uh-huh." She rubbed herself against his arousal. She kissed him again and now he kissed back, remembering how, just starting to get into the feeling of her mobile, slick mouth, when she tugged him to sit on the tiled bench inside the shower.

"You do this to all your patients?"

"Only the sexy ones."

"Come on, the way I look? Marlon sent you, didn't he?" Low pulled away again. "Fuck, he thinks I can't get a girl on my own?"

"Honey, I'm sure you can," Tracy purred, sliding onto the floor and gently pushing his thighs apart. "I just wanted to be one of them." She opened her hand, unwrapped the condom there, stretched it over him and fastened her soft, warm mouth on his erection. He had forgotten how exquisite this felt.

Anger and humiliation evaporated. His hand felt boneless, caressing her head, until he exploded in what felt like the most powerful orgasm of his life. Sweet, heavy languor flooded his veins, and his muscles and nerves went completely limp for the first time in months as pleasure replaced pain. He rocked back against the wall as if it was down-filled.

After awhile he opened his eyes and reached to stroke Tracy's cheek. "Sorry I was so unfriendly, before. Thank you."

"Oh, I'm not done." She used her hands and lips and tongue and he responded with more strength than he realized he had, as this familiar dance came back to him. They danced until he was weak with exhaustion. Tracy smiled as she helped him dress.

"Feels good, doesn't it?" she said, a little smug.

"Mmm." He smiled.

"Thought it would. Just what you need."

"You're not really a therapist, Tracy—"

"Call it what you like. I'm better for you than those machines."

"Come back some time."

"Sure I will." She kissed him. "Whenever I can."

"You sent me a hooker," he jibed to Marlon the next day.

"A what?"

"It's okay, as long as I don't get VD," Low said, watching for Marlon's reaction. "I did appreciate the gesture."

"Looks like you did more than gesture. You look almost human today."

"She *is* a hooker."

"She's a part-time assistant masseuse at the clinic. But she does a little work on the side, for a select clientele. She goes for the goodlooking vets."

"That's not me." Not anymore.

"Poor baby. You got all your limbs, doncha, which is what she noticed in your picture, not your pretty face." Marlon stared at him critically. "Which by the way would look better if you eat like I tell you. You wouldn't be such an ugly dude if you got some sun, a haircut, put on some weight—"

"Who are you, Elizabeth Arden?"

"Self image is an important part of healing," Marlon intoned. "A poor self image detracts from the benefits of therapy—"

"Send her back, then, I feel a poor self-image attack coming on." Low grinned. "I suppose her line of work is a natural outgrowth of massage."

"Natural outgrowth! Somebody's comin back to life."

"So what do I owe you for her visit, coach?"

Marlon just laughed.

WITH MARLON'S regimen now including laps in the heated outdoor pool, and a few Tracy visits—mostly massage but with a couple of very instructive sex sessions where he felt like a new student—Low improved as fall progressed. As his muscles hardened the pain of movement receded, and he no longer thought of himself as lion meat.

Beirut was still a black hole of remorse. He could not absolve himself from his moral weakness in deciding to exploit Ahmed's nearness to Farouk. His friendship with Marlon and

Tracy, whom he would never have known in his normal circle, made him realize how he'd taken privilege for granted. Maybe expecting life to be easy had made him think he could shortcut his way up instead of working like an ordinary guy. Fatal mistake.

It was time for a new kind of life. He'd been spared so his eyes would open. To see what, he did not yet know.

THIRTY-EIGHT

LOW'S VISIBILITY within the diplomatic community was boosted by the car bombing, since he was seen as a hero, wounded in action. President Ford wrote a letter of commendation; he was an old golfing buddy of James', and Low had escorted First Daughter Susan to one of her debutante events a few seasons back. The State Department conveyed its regular regards through James, expressing their eagerness to have Low back in the fold, at a higher level.

"It's bogus, Dad," Low told him one morning in October. They'd been discussing Low's plans, or lack of them, as James put it. "I don't feel like being rewarded for my own stupidity by people who are even more stupid."

"Admirable." James' tone was dry. "But achieving an ambition can, honorably, include taking advantage of opportunity when it presents itself."

"Not when the opportunity is based on an action I'll always regret. I won't do it that way. No more shortcuts."

James looked at him. "You know, Lowell, you were always an easy child."

I guess this is payback, Dad.

"Your only awkward time was when your mother left."

Not again. Dr. Grant made a big deal of this, and she'd been triumphant to eke out from him the earth-shattering admission: his mother's departure had fucked him up.

"But, aside from that, and your too many girls and drinking and pot-smoking in prep school and college, you've always kept commitments. You've never had those kinds of life-wrecking episodes like some of the families we know. You've always held a steady course, one that I've been proud to observe."

How did James know about all his youthful partying?

"So now, when you've had this ... setback, it's natural that

195

you might feel a little ambiguous. A little reluctant to get back on the horse, so to speak. Entirely understandable."

Low had enough equine analogies to last him a lifetime of ribbons. "I am never getting back on that particular nag. I won't go into this country's political arena."

"It might surprise you to know that I really do understand." James stood and walked to the window. He was the kind of man more comfortable, with certain topics, addressing landscapes than faces. "You know, when your mother left I had to examine what in my own behavior might have ... contributed to her dissatisfaction. I had to realize that my sense of standards might be experienced, in others, as a kind of rigidity. That not everyone is cut out to follow a straight line."

James had never spoken this way.

When he turned back from the window, Low studied his sharp features, the keen white-fractured grey eyes like his own, the silver-streaked hair, the crisp blue-and-white striped shirt under an impeccable navy pinstripe. James was always buttoned-up. To admit to soul-searching was as unlike him as wearing purple tie-dye. *Dude*, Low wanted to say, *heavy*. He wasn't ready to talk with James, yet, about possible root causes of Lydia's departure. Elena Grant's explorations were painful enough.

James reached to scrub at his head. "You need more time to think things over," he said. "I'm glad to see you doing so much better, Lowell, you're getting stronger every day."

"Are you actually gettin laid back in your old age?"

James gave him a wintry smile. "Get a haircut." He tugged at Low's long locks. "Have George drive you to the barber in town."

"You've been saying that the last ten years."

"Probably will for the next ten, too."

After James left, Low sat looking at the forested hills surrounding their house, where gold and scarlet were just staining the leaves, feeling he was really seeing it for the first time. It was unusual, having this leisure to review his life, remembering people and events and searching out meanings. He thought about his family and the trauma of his mother's desertion. He thought about his best friends, Karen in Vermont and Troy wandering wherever. He thought of the only lover who had touched him deeply, radical Indiana Clare, a haven of unexpected ease in an otherwise rushed and driven time. She'd made him want to stay put when his prerogatives were hurrying him forward.

And look where they got me! He laughed at himself a lot these days.

He moved to the stereo and put on "Blood on the Tracks." Troy had introduced him to Dylan some years back, and Clare had been such a devoted fan he'd made fun of her. But this album held up to repeated listening.

It seemed fitting when an hour later a familiar, beat up white VW bug drew up to the drive and an equally beat up figure emerged. Low stared, and got to the door as fast as he could.

"Son of a bitch, Troy, what took you so long?"

"Low, what did they do to you!" Troy flung his arms around Low and hugged hard. The crutches clattered away and Troy helped Low to a chair.

"Sorry I couldn't make it sooner! I just found out last month, when my letter to you in Beirut was returned. What the hell happened?"

"It's a long story. Good to see you, man. Can you stay awhile?"

"Sure." Troy grinned. "I'm, ah, between jobs."

So he was dealing again. "Well, got something for a cripple?"

"Tokin cripple," Troy joked, and pulled out a bag.

They had a smoke and Low talked, briefly, about Beirut. When he finished Troy frowned into the ashtray, twirling the roach around in its little clip and knocking off miniscule parts of ash. Copper hair scattered like flames on his shoulders and, watching him, Low had the sensation of looking at a very old photograph.

"Way for you to start out in the Real World, Low." They had used to jest about the Real World as freshmen at Georgetown. "What now?"

"Good question." Low took the roach and inhaled the last of it. "My dad told me to take my time, but I can tell he'd feel good if I went back to the Service."

"Long as I've known you, that's all you wanted."

"Not anymore. I used to believe effective diplomacy could

really change foreign opinion of us, maybe even change policy. But what I saw in our embassy was a bunch of people very out of touch with what was happening. A civil war broke out right under their noses and all they focused on was their own little world." He grimaced. "Not that I was so aware, either. My mistake."

"Well, look at it this way," Troy said. "Most people spend years achieving their goal, and if they find out it wasn't worth it after all, it's too late for them to do anything else. You might've just saved yourself some time."

"I haven't completely given up on the idea of foreign service. There's a commercial side I might explore. But right now I'm just ... taking a breather."

"Why not take it with me? I'm due for some visits to the New England schools."

Low thought about it. He'd have to get Marlon's okay. He still had therapy three times a week. He'd have to take some hand weights. He wouldn't be able to drive.

"Low." Troy's hand was on his shoulder. "I didn't mean to be insensitive. I guess travel's not a hot idea for you right now."

"I'd like to go, it's just a matter of arrangements. I can't drive, not yet—"

"I'll drive! We'll take it slow!"

"I've got another operation scheduled for after Thanksgiving."

"We'll be here."

"Let's do it!"

James approved the idea. He knew Troy came from a good Boston family; Low was sure he had no idea Troy supported himself as a dealer. James insisted they sign on with AAA, stay in decent motels and rent a fullsize car. "Fuckin boat, man," Troy said.

Marlon agreed. He and Troy hit it off, since they had some D.C. vet friends in common, and he put Troy through the exercises with Low so Troy could be the coach on the road.

Marlon and Tracy came over the night before they left. They sat in the leather-clad den drinking and sampling Troy's latest consignment. When Low got up to refill his glass at the recessed bar, Troy rose to help him.

"I like your new friends," he said in a low voice. "They're a lot more fun than those horsey types you used to hang out with. Or those snooty intellectuals, Jesus. What happened to them? Did they all drop you now you're no longer a rising star?"

"They come by sometimes." Low, unoffended, poured himself a whiskey. Marlon had just okayed his having anything stronger than his weekly beer. He took a healthy swallow and looked at Troy. "I don't have much in common with them anymore. I can't ride, maybe never. I donated Midnight to a therapeutic riding program."

"You were crazy about that animal!"

"I was a kid. Now other kids can enjoy him." He took another sip. "As for intellectuals, remember Whittaker from Georgetown?"

"The economics whiz," said Troy. "The Communist."

"Wall Street." Low smiled. "And Karen? My Republican squeeze? First Ms. President?"

"I knew someone was missing. Thought she'd be living with you by now."

Low shook his head. "That was over a long time ago. She joined some commune in Vermont right after Watergate. I guess she got disillusioned."

"A commune? That straight-laced gal? Too much!"

"They believe in all kinds of hocus pocus. She calls herself a witch." Low laughed. "Not so different from party politics!"

"She had a mystical side before," Troy said. "She told our fortunes here one New Year's Eve, remember? She predicted disaster if you didn't marry her."

"Didn't they all."

"Maybe she was right?" Troy raised his eyebrows. "A witch? Maybe she put a curse on you." He considered Low for a moment. "But that wouldn't work on you buddy, would it."

"Nope. I am not superstitious. I got into this all by myself."

THIRTY-NINE

IT WAS a beautiful time of year for New England. They wound their way through postcard towns where the white church spire, the square, the Revolutionary War statue, small lake, bucolic hills and above all the splendid trees surrounded their laconic inhabitants and lent them grace. The colors drew the eye up, away from evidence of hardship at ground level, where farming and industry had been hard hit by the oil crisis.

They visited their old prep school, now coed, where they remembered escapades from ten years past and noted sadly that kids today didn't have as much spirit, although that didn't prevent Troy from coming on to a winsome senior girl who sneaked out for a smoke with them.

They stopped to see Low's sister Elise at her college in Vermont. It was late in the evening when they arrived. A sweet-faced blonde in a long thin tee shirt opened El's door, and started at them. Low saw Elise inside, sitting at a prim student's desk, also in her nightclothes. He crutched past the startled blonde and collapsed onto the narrow bed next to the desk.

"Low! What are you doing here!" Elise jumped up to give him a hug that nearly knocked both of them off the bed.

"We heard you were having a slumber party." He eyed the blonde's shapely expanse of bare leg. "Too bad I forgot my PJs, have to go commando."

Elise laughed. "Betsy, this is my brother Lowell and his friend Troy. Divide everything they say by at least ten, and don't let either of them get you alone."

Betsy's blue eyes widened as Troy lounged in next to Low and, leaning on the desk, began to roll a jay. The two friends exuded an aura of vagabonding freedom that banished the studious atmosphere of the little room. Elise snuggled close, face shining.

"Just in time, dudes," she said. "My supply was getting thin."

Low glanced over at Betsy, enjoying the scenic view. "How about havin one small toke with us, darlin?"

She tried to pull down her shirt and stared at the floor while pink color rose in her cheeks. "I've got mid-terms. I have to go."

"Mid-terms." Troy groaned. "Spare me."

"Okay, Bets, see you tomorrow."

"Too bad," Low remarked, leaning back on the pillows. "She was cute."

"You scared her off." Elise giggled. "But you came to see me anyway, right? Or did you run out of girls back home?"

"Elise, I haven't chatted up a girl in so long I wouldn't know what to say."

"I don't believe it," said Elise.

Troy asked, "What about Tracy?"

Grinning, Low told the story of how he'd met Tracy.

"You! A sexual charity case! And you're laughing about it." Troy shook his head. "You have really changed, man, you are a different dude entirely."

Low shrugged. He suddenly felt his nightly weariness.

"Time to go," said Troy. "We'll come by tomorrow, Lise."

At the Holiday Inn they sprawled on their beds, having a Heineken nightcap.

"That Betsy," Low said suddenly. "She reminded me of Clare."

"Her? She went to Mexico," Troy said, his eyes on the TV. "She's living with some guy down there."

Ouch! "How do you know?"

"Lee and I keep in touch, after we hit it off that time I visited you in Bloomington." Troy was a prodigious correspondent, much more talented than Low at ever-widening his circle of acquaintances.

"But, why Mexico?"

"Remember her hot-bod friend Ginger? They went together."

"I thought she'd go to France." Stupid, he knew, but this news stung. "What guy?"

"What are you, jealous?" Troy laughed.

Low shook his head.

"You're better off. Lee told me she got real testy after you left."

"She was never testy with me."

"Are you *still* in love with her?"

"In *love* ... " Low frowned. "I just think of her."

"Why?" Troy looked over at him curiously. "You've moved on, right?"

"Yeah, but she was ... special."

"Sounds like unfinished business. You better call her."

"How?"

"I'll get her number from Lee."

"But she's living with someone."

"So? You're an old college friend. You can call her. No big deal."

"When we broke up I told her no contact. You know my policy. But I called her house afterward, talked to her brother. I wrote a couple letters, even in Beirut. I didn't *send* the letters. But she was on my mind." He lay back. "She doesn't want to hear from me. It's over."

"Not for you, buddy," Troy said softly. "And I've never known you not to get what you want. I say call her up."

Low stared at the ceiling. "No."

"Then write to her." Troy pulled open the nightstand. "Do it courtesy of the Holiday Inn." He tossed a sheet of paper and a pen over to Low.

Dear Clare,

I'm very sorry our relationship ended the way it did. I think of you often and I wish I could hear from you. I know you're living with someone, and perhaps you don't think of me, but I'd like to know how you're doing. If you don't respond this time I will not try to reach you again.

Sincere regards from Lowell Goodenow

"You sound like a fucking lawyer! Put some romance in it!"

"Romance? She might not even remember me."

"Are you kidding? That gal was gone, man, Lee told me she was totally hung up. Tell her, baby, I am still smokin hot for you—"

"That's not the point—"

"At least sign it, "love"—"

"Why don't *you* write it?"

"You're the stud around here, I'm just the sidekick, living vicariously through your endless conquests." Troy ducked as Low tossed the pen at him. "Seriously, make it a little more appealing. Use that famous *ole South'n chahhm* you always used to fake out there at Indiana."

"It's quite sentimental enough. I have *some* pride. If she's interested, she'll write back."

"Meanwhile you'll end up alone, old, decrepit—"

"Shut up—"

"Oh Clare!" Troy minced around the room, Heineken in hand, fluttering his eyelashes.

"You fuck—" Low threw a pillow this time. "I bare my soul and you make fun—"

Troy grabbed the pillow and flopped onto the other bed. "Just make it sexy. She'll come around. They always do, for you."

Low finished his beer. "Who'm I kidding," he said, humor draining from his mood. He hated nights, even these nights on the road with Troy. "This is just idiotic nostalgia. Clare's closed this book." *Some guy. Some Mexican guy.*

"Send it," Troy said firmly. "Find out. If she doesn't answer, then you close the book too." He lifted his palms. "There are so many women, Low, and—"

"So little time. I know, I know."

PART OF that maxim was proved true the next night, when they went to a student house party with Elise. Halloween was a few nights away so it was a costume party, and Elise fixed a fake moustache and a patch over one eye, to make him a peg-leg pirate. Troy, the hippie, didn't need a costume.

When everyone started dancing, Low sat in a corner armchair to watch the obvious queen of the party. She wore a red satin Playboy-bunny outfit, complete with ears, bow tie, fishnet hose and rhinestone-studded red heels. Her Harlequin eyemask sparkled with red sequins. He hadn't seen anyone so tempting since Clare, whose appeal had been her air of stern-politico reserve as contradicted by the innocence with which she sneaked those smoldering glances.

But this red satin party girl was the opposite of innocence. As Low studied her he felt himself get hard. She reminded him of his first lover, a busty townie cheerleader two years older than he, first in line to seduce the new fourteen-year-old preppie. Lusty Linda.

What a shocking thrill it had been to discover he could turn girls on just by looking at them. At about age twelve, he'd become pantingly aware of the delicately groomed girls at his fortnightly dancing classes, but the setting was extremely formal and he was so formal himself he never even tried to hold one close. He didn't know what to do with their stares and smiles. Yet within weeks of starting at St. Paul's, crudely enlightened and boldly encouraged by older boys, he lost his virginity at a party with his new friends and local girls. Thereafter, greedily exploiting his attractiveness, he had thrown himself into constant sexual adventures with a vengeance.

He had never bothered to wonder, until recently, just where that vengeance came from or why he never let any girl get too close. Dr. Grant quickly drew the connection—between his desolation at losing his mother to her adulterous affair, and his so-easy enactment of power over women—and suggested gently that he back off sexual encounters for awhile, to let this insight settle and to see how it felt for him to relate to women without that focus. "It's cheating yourself, Lowell, seeing through this single lens, cheating potential partners too. Give yourself a chance to look beyond. You're so much more than that sexy teenage boy."

But turning his analytical abilities inward was too new an exercise to feel natural.

So here he was still going through the motions, still throwing out his net of arrogant availability to see if anything of interest came swimming by. For a moment it felt pointless and he had to agree with Dr. Grant. *I'm too old for this, and these kids are way too young for me.*

But why be at this party? What else was he going to do tonight? Ponder his tragic past? Go back to the hotel and watch boring TV like some tired old loser? Bullshit. He looked again for the girl in the bunny suit and mentally tugged on his net.

One advantage of being on crutches was he didn't have to

make the first move. He waited for her. Soon she stood in front of him, dancing to the horny Bad Company song, "Can't Get Enough of Your Love." Her partner kept trying to grab her but she deftly twisted away.

When the song ended somebody fussed with the stereo so there was a break in the dancing. She sent her partner off and leaned casually against the wall next to Low, who did not acknowledge her until she put her hand in front of him, cigarette in the first two fingers, signaling she wanted a light.

He put her cigarette between his lips, lit it, and pulled on her hand so she bent to him. He placed the cigarette between her lips, his fingers pressing them gently. Then he slid the mask up from her forehead and sat back appraising her face, smiling a little and letting the mask dangle from his fingers. She snatched it away and he smiled some more, watching as she smoked in silence. When the music started again she turned to him.

"So do you dance, or do you just watch?" Her voice was rich, slightly British in the Boston way, enhanced by petulance.

"I can only dance with you lyin down, Sugah," Low said, letting his eyes wander all over her and insinuation flood his tone.

Red stained her cheeks and her mouth tightened. She seemed about to speak when Low slid one crutch out from under the chair. She glanced at it and then at him, looking still irritated but now embarrassed too. She opened her mouth but he spoke first, patting the wide arm of the chair. "Sit this one out and keep me company."

She perched on one cheek, crossing her legs to keep balanced. "You don't look comfortable." He circled her waist and pulled her onto his lap. She looked down at him, still put out, but obviously wanting to meet his challenge. He'd known so many girls like her, wealthy East Coast prepschoolers used to always getting their way. *Just like me.*

"You have some nerve," she told him coolly.

"That makes two of us. What's your name?"

"Alicia Bradford." Her announcement was haughty, as befitted one of the oldest names in America. He nodded. D.A.R. Junior League. Deb parties long out of date for most of the country. She'd marry well, spend money wisely, and in fifteen years be seducing her tennis coach. Well, maybe twenty. She was a stunner.

"What's yours?"

"Lowell Goodenow."

"Goodenow! Oh, you're Elise's brother!"

"You sound relieved." He grinned. She leaned back against him, ready now to chat amiably about people they knew. He tightened his hold, and stroked her thigh as if absent-mindedly, amused by how her manner changed once she knew he was one of her own kind.

"So how'd you break your leg?"

"Dumb accident."

"So were you like skiing or what?"

He looked into her eyes. She was completely drunk, or stoned, he saw. The excitement fled his body and he became aware, abruptly, of the familiar nightly ache in his back. She felt heavy all of a sudden.

"Guess not, huh?" She laughed a little. "Seeing as it hasn't snowed yet." Her foot jiggled in time to the music and if he concentrated on her ankle, leg, thigh, the way she squirmed on him, he could feel himself revive. It seemed important to make the effort; he'd never lost interest so fast before and it scared him a little. You're gettin past it, geezer, he laughed to himself; but it was more than this.

When he got overtired, just beyond his ability to clearly perceive it, lay the abyss in which Ahmed still beckoned, despite Dr. Grant's spotlight down there. If he could really move, if he could run or ride or play soccer or dance, he could work it out. He could lose it in painkiller pills or drinking but he paid for that the next day.

He wanted sex. Dr. Grant was right, it was one of his favorite pursuits, but so what? What was so wrong with needing a healthy outlet? Of course he brought himself off, regularly, but it wasn't the same. Tracy had helped, but she was bought. He had to do better, God, he used to be able to. Here was his chance, right now, on his lap. Was he up to this?

He paid attention to her thigh. The fishnet felt strange and he poked his finger into one of the tiny diamonds and wiggled it.

"Hey, you'll tear them." She shifted and then stood, twisting around to check the back of her thigh, in a provocative pose.

Low watched, feeling his erection grow again, and he said, "How come you chose this costume, anyway? I mean, I like it, but I thought young women are feminists?"

"Who cares?" she whispered, settling back onto his lap and putting one fragrant arm around his shoulder. She smiled, jiggling a little against his hardness, but the heat of her body still did not dispell, for him, the glaze in her eyes. "Take me somewhere to get a real drink. All they have here is cheap beer and wine."

This wasn't working. He wanted sex with somebody he could actually talk to.

She peeled off his eye patch, pressing her breasts against him. "You're handsome," she cooed. "Will you buy me whiskey?"

But what a squeeze! He restrained himself from clutching her. The old Low would have taken her back to the Holiday Inn for a rowdy all-nighter. He'd play pirate and she'd play Bunny. Her costume looked easy to unzip, and he'd trace the lines it made on her body with his hands and mouth before he used his fingers the way Tracy had shown him ... but, dammit, he guessed the old Low was gone. He could have this peach and pretend nothing had changed. But she didn't feel right, even though she felt good, and he didn't feel right pretending.

I'm done pretending. The sigh coming up from his depths nearly dislodged her from his lap.

"Alicia." He dropped his hands along with his Southern. "I'm not up for an evening with you. I got hurt not too long ago and I'm still trying to recover. Can you understand that?"

She wriggled again and pouted. "Feels like you're up to it."

He produced a final grin. "You could bring the dead to life, beautiful, but I'm not ready for strenuous exertions. You go find yourself another guy."

She flounced off him, hard enough to cause serious twinges, confirming he'd made the right choice. She might be what he wanted, but she was not what he needed. Not anymore.

FORTY

H E WOKE to the telephone's shrill ring. Troy lay as if dead on the other bed. Low reached for the phone, almost falling on the floor.

"Low?"

"Elise, hey." He tried to wake up.

"Low? Sorry. I thought you'd be up," Elise was saying. "I have to see you."

Alarm stabbed him. "What's the matter?"

"I don't want to tell you on the phone. I'm at the library on campus. Can you meet me?"

"I'm on my way, honey, don't cry. I'll get a cab. Wait outside for me—"

"—don't tell Troy," she sniffed.

He pulled on his clothes, scribbled a note for Troy, and then crutched out to the lobby to get a cab. He still felt asleep. What was with Elise? It had been years since he'd heard her crying. Of course, it had been years since he'd lived with her.

Elise was huddled on a low stone wall by the bicycle rack on the side of the library, half hidden in the evergreen shrubbery. Low sat close and hugged her to his side. She pushed her blotchy face into his shoulder.

"What, what is it?"

"I'm pregnant. I just got the test results over at the clinic."

He held her in silence, rocking gently, compassion knotting his throat. Elise was just eighteen; this was her freshman year. It didn't seem fair. He thought back. There'd been some boyfriend last spring; he remembered a masculine shape next to her in his hospital room. She'd spent the summer on a European art study tour. She hadn't mentioned any special guy when she'd come home, just madly unpacked, shopped for college, and left.

He could not claim to be surprised or outraged. He could

208

not offer to beat up the perpetrator as he'd been able to do when she was in kindergarten. He'd been away from her life for so long that he didn't even feel he had the right to offer advice.

Her smile was weak but real. "I'm glad you're here. I'm glad you've changed."

"Oh?"

"You're nicer than you used to be. Just in time. There's no one else I could talk to."

"Your friends?"

"I don't have any real friends here."

Low digested this. She'd always been popular, cheerful, surrounded by kids. "Why's that?"

She shrugged. "Bunch of gossips. Assholes."

"I see." He didn't. "Anyway, let's get coffee somewhere. We can talk."

At a local diner, he led the conversation away from her situation, chatting about his and Troy's trip so far, how it was tough doing exercises in hotel rooms, but how it felt so good to be away from the confinement of the summer and to be moving again.

"Let me come with you."

He broke off to stare at her. She played with her spoon, not looking at him.

"You don't mean that, Elise, you just got started here—"

"I hate it here. I'm dropping out."

He waited, and then said carefully, "Sometimes when one part of life gets problematic, it seems the solution is to change everything, but that usually just screws up things even more, I know—"

"No." Now she glared at him. "You don't know. You've always had it so easy." He was silenced by her vehemence. "You were always Father's pal, his best boy. You didn't have to stick around and take his shit after Mother left, you went off to prep school and you never came back either. Just like her. Father and I were trapped in that mausoleum and he hated me for being around, for being his responsibility when he just wanted to forget he had a family. And he saw her every time he looked at me! It made him despise me, Low."

She had their mother's face, true enough, Low thought as he

studied her, the same small-boned delicate beauty, the same fine dark hair and huge blue eyes. He could suddenly see James behaving exactly as she described. But how sad, Elise hanging onto this, all these years.

"It wouldn't have been his intention to hurt you. He wouldn't even have realized what he was doing."

"But I was just a kid! And he was always leaving me with the housekeeper, ignoring me. I remember trying to get his attention and he'd just say, 'that's enough now, I'm busy.' He was always so fucking busy!" Tears spilled down her cheeks and Low put out his napkin to catch them. "I wouldn't do that to my little girl." Her voice broke.

"You're still a little girl, yourself," he said softly. "Is that what this is about, honey? Still trying to get his attention?"

She jerked away angrily. "What are you, some kind of shrink?"

"You wanted me to know. I'm just trying to figure out how you let this happen—"

"Let it! Jesus, just like a man! As if it's my fault!" She tried to sneer through her tears. "When you take girls to bed do you bother to find out if they're on the pill?"

"Absolutely. I'm always careful." Very careful, but he supposed he was lucky none of his partners had gotten pregnant. That he knew of. Troy hadn't escaped: a dismal business.

"You're probably the only one then. Most men don't care," Elise went on bitterly. "He didn't care at all."

"Who is he?" I'll kill him, he wanted to say, but it was not funny. Ahmed would have meant it, and acted, if he'd had a sister in a similar predicament.

"Just a guy," she said guardedly. "Do I have to tell you?"

"Why not?"

"He's married, I don't mean anything to him—"

"How'd you get hooked up with a jerk like that?"

"He was our tour leader last summer." She stared up, challenging.

"What the hell were you thinking?"

"It just happened! And don't presume to give me any lectures on love, I know you, screwing everyone in sight, married or not, you know you have *no* right to say anything about my behavior."

"Why did you tell me then?"

"I don't have anyone else," she said, her voice wavering again. "And you're not cold the way you used to be, you seem to have mellowed—"

Low shook his head, beginning to feel irritated. "So you don't plan to tell him."

"No."

"You'll just disappear with us and never return, like magic, huh? Then what happens?"

Her mouth set in a look he remembered from her childhood. "I think I'll have it."

Low sighed. He sipped his coffee, glad it was strong and hot. He was so tired. His eyes felt rimmed with rust and his back was aching from not exercising this morning.

Elise toyed with her sweet roll. Her fine hair slipped down in two sheets on both sides of her face.

The friendly clatter of the diner surrounded them, the waitress' broad Vermont twang booming across the counter where a single grill man was working. He never missed, Low noted, his movements were almost choreographed in a studied frenzy—a shake of salt, a flip of pancake, a stab of the waitress' order onto his little spike, a push of his chef's hat further up his bony brow. His face wore a look of passionate concentration.

"That's Bruce," Elise said, following his stare.

"Bruce?"

"It's Bruce's diner," she explained, tapping the greasy menu with her finger.

"Oh."

"Some kids made a movie of him. Like you know, that white haired guy? The one with the soup cans?"

He watched her becoming a little girl again, twisting a strand of her hair, tilting her head and smiling as she tried to distract them both and push away her pain for a moment. She looked so young and unready. He wished he could have protected her from this. But he had not in years spent any time alone with her. It had been easier to assume she was okay and James was okay and the only thing worth thinking about was his own ambition. Cold, she'd said, he used to be cold. Someone else had said that about

211

him—Pamela, the translator.

"That New York guy, the artist?"

"Andy Warhol," Low told her.

"Yeah. It was so cool. They showed it on local TV a few weeks ago, and you can see it brought in the business." She indicated the line of customers forming at the door.

"They all come to see Bruce, huh."

"And eat his *brains*," Elise said in a hollow spook-voice. Sure enough, "fried brains" was prominently featured on the chalkboard menu above Bruce's head.

"Jeez, Elise, puh-leez," sprang from Low's memory of teasing her years ago.

"No dice, Ice," she delightedly finished, using her old childhood nickname for him. They grinned at each other for the first time that morning.

FORTY-ONE

ELISE PROVED implacable in her insistence on having the baby—no amount of argument could dissuade her. She packed her things, wrote notes to her professors to secure incompletes, tied up business at the Bursar's office. Her efficiency impressed Low and convinced him of her intent. He and Troy waited out the week for her at the Holiday Inn.

They resumed their New England travels. Elise made up road games and songs, helped with the driving, put Low through his exercises. Her buoyant excitement touched him, but beneath it Low sensed her fear and, deeper, a fatalistic gravity. He connected the fear to James' reaction—they had not told him—and the gravity to the awesome fact of harboring life. He noticed that Troy was as careful with Elise as he was, both of them keeping a reverent distance.

They tooled scenic highways like leaf-peeping tourists. Troy knew of Bob Dylan's Rolling Thunder Tour and they followed it loosely for a couple of weeks, lucky to catch shows in a number of towns. Low thought of Clare every time he heard "Knockin on Heaven's Door" and wondered how Dylan knew about her, when he sang "Shelter from the Storm."

They made one last stop before returning home to Virginia—a visit to Karen's commune, back in Vermont.

"You say she's a witch?" Troy asked as he maneuvered up the winding gravel road to the farm.

"I'm sure she's a good witch. White magic. Fortune cookies. Love potions."

"Aphrodisiacs." Troy grinned at him in the rearview. "Trust you. But tell me, if this is a women's commune they may not welcome us horny dudes. They gay?"

"Don't know." He'd spoken briefly to Karen on the phone, to say they were in the area and to get directions. She'd sounded

213

pleased, if surprised, to hear from him, and said they'd be welcome to visit.

"But we keep farmers' hours," she'd warned, laughing. "Don't expect any parties—we don't drink, don't stay up late, don't have any men around to distract us."

"Prep school again, Kar, are you regressing?"

"Just the opposite," she'd answered firmly."Come see for yourself."

The Karen he'd known was a strong, outgoing girl whose attitude was personified by her wild red hair and clear, piercing green eyes. From their first meeting—he in fourth grade, she in fifth—they forged an allegiance that thrived through horse worship and tennis lessons, languished during the awkwardness of early adolescence, and blossomed into a mutually satisfying sexual exploration Karen initiated in their late teens. "I want to get this sex thing right," she'd said. "My other experience was awful, but I see how you are with girls so I figure you're good at it."

With easy accord they'd solidified their relationship during vacations, in spite of frequent political arguments. Karen was a staunch hawk—her father was a cold warrior, a Republican leader in the Senate, and she'd grown up in near John Birch-state of awareness of the Red menace. At one point she'd given Low, then eleven, sheets of stamps that read "Help Stamp out U.S. Trade to Communist Countries." He'd pasted them all over the stable. The horses remained unenlightened.

Low recalled the last time he'd seen Karen, the summer he returned from France. She'd been distracted, on edge, snapping at him for no reason. She claimed to be unwilling to have sex, but after a few hours' proximity in riding, swimming or tennis, he'd always won her over.

He'd imagined they'd go on enjoying one another's company indefinitely. He liked her mind, her humor, her body, the sense of history he had with her. But that summer, as Karen became increasingly obsessed with the upcoming Presidential election, she grew distant and treated him with something like impatience. He hadn't been overly concerned. He was working on his thesis and preparing for his final semester at Indiana.

The week before he left he'd gotten a late night call from

Karen. She told him, shortly, that she'd had enough of election politics and quit her job on her father's staff. She was moving to a farm in Vermont with a girl she'd known in college. She'd given him the address—"Not that you'll ever write me, Goodenow, of that I am sure"—and said goodbye. He'd mulled it over for a day, thinking the times were a-changin.

Later he wondered how much she knew about the Watergate break-in; how that might have contributed to her disillusionment. He *had* written to her, abeit sporadically. He still thought of her as one of his best friends.

They pulled into a scrubby yard laden with a few unidentifiable pieces of farm equipment. The door of the low rambling white house opened and a woman came out. Low hardly recognized Karen. Her hair, which she'd always tried to control by keeping very short, was long and heavy on her shoulders and gleamed russet, no longer the carrot he remembered from childhood. She'd put on weight and it looked good—her body had lost the tight angularity that so quickly became tension when she was riled, which in his memory was much of the time. As she walked toward the car, smiling warmly, Low felt a stir of arousal. She looked earthy, sensual, a medieval fairytale in her long green cloak.

"Hey Karen," Troy said as he got out to greet her. "Lookin real fine, mama."

She gave him a push that dismissed her inviting aura. "You too, daddy-oh," she mocked in her strong rough voice. She gave Low a bear hug that swayed him, crutch-bound, too quick for him to kiss her. She linked arms with Elise and walked them into the farmhouse.

They met her commune-mates in the huge homey kitchen. There were five women in all—"not enough for anyone to get a real rest from farm work," Karen said—and the congeniality among them was palpable. Everyone squeezed around the table for a hearty vegetarian supper. Carob brownies and herbal tea were brought out after the meal.

Elise, sensing a sympathetic atmosphere, revealed her pregnancy over her second cup of tea. Karen jumped up to give her a warm hug. "To think the last time I saw you, you were just a kid," she marveled. "Now you're nurturing a new life. What an honor." Elise smiled seriously as the other women similarly praised her and began to ask questions and give advice.

Troy and Low, sharing a glance, moved in unison to the small parlor down the hall. Troy produced his bottle of whiskey. After half an hour or so, Karen joined them. She refused a drink, but sat on the couch next to Low for conversation and studied him as he gave his version of the accident. He leaned against her shoulder. The heavy food, the whiskey, his ever-present fatigue and her round warmth made him want to put his head on her lap and snooze.

She felt as right as Alicia felt wrong. He could pursuade her into a night's idyll for old times' sake, couldn't he? Just to ease him back into some kind of normalcy? They could do this as dear friends. He smiled into her eyes.

She blinked and sat up straight. "I'm going to do you a favor, Lowell."

"I was hoping so," he murmured.

"Not that kind," she said patiently. "I'm going to do your cards. Come sit at the table here." She walked to a small round table in the middle of the room. She lit two fat white candles on opposite wall sconces and took down a box next to the candles.

"What's up?" Troy grinned.

"You can watch, but no editorial comments. I know you're a skeptic."

"And I'm not?" said Low, shooting Troy a gleeful glance.

"Not as much as you once were," she answered cryptically. "Come on." He pulled the second chair next to her, awkwardly dragging it behind his crutches, and sat. As she laid out the tarot cards Low saw down her dress, a lowcut rust-colored paisley Indian gown that showed her deep cleavage. When he brushed against her arm she glanced up sharply.

"Lowell! Sit across from me, that's how it's done."

Rolling his eyes at Troy, he moved around the table.

"And concentrate on now," she said stern. "Think about your present condition."

"Yeah." Low sat back and folded his arms across his chest. In my present condition you're turning me on, he told her with his eyes. But she was frowning at the cards, which to him were nothing more than a jumble of strange pictures.

"You've had this … trauma in your recent past."

"No shit."

Karen shot him a silencing look. "The hanged man was involved. See, right here. He represents … some kind of betrayal, in your case."

Oh fuck.

Karen went on. "This female figure is very prominent, both in your past and in your future." She looked up. "Are you involved with anyone?" She didn't wait for his answer. "Silly question. You've always got someone." She tapped the card. "She represents … redemption. See this light she's holding? She's very powerful, or let's see, she will become a very powerful influence in your life."

"She a redhead?" Troy had ambled over and was leaning his elbows on the back of Karen's chair. He flicked one shining lock of hair off her shoulder. She knocked his arms away impatiently.

"Come on, you guys, I am not in the mood for your macho crap."

"I just thought, you know, maybe it's you, Karen." Troy winked at Low. "You two have always been such an item."

"Cut it out."

Low studied her expression and realized, abruptly, that she was about to get angry. He remembered the signs. "What else do you see, Karen?" he asked in a serious tone.

Troy snorted a derisive laugh and left the room.

"Good riddance," Karen muttered. She looked at the cards. "You've been in a state of psychological chaos. There's a whole mixture of symbols … Lydia's here, as well as James and Elise. That is, I see them, because I know you so well."

"Lydia came to see me in the hospital." Karen looked at him. "And I have this … relationship, I guess you'd call it, with a doctor at the hospital. Elena Grant." Karen's brows rose. "She's a shrink. We talk a lot about things I didn't really look into before." He shifted, uncomfortable under her scrutiny. "I mean, just to get me out of a funk I was in, after the bombing. I was so fucked up."

"Good for you, Lowell," she said softly. "I remember when Lydia left, how it was for you, and Elise, and your Dad. It's good you had a chance to hammer that out."

He dropped his eyes. This seduction was taking a turn he hadn't counted on. She leaned forward to take his hand in her strong grip. "I'm your friend, remember. Next time you talk to Lydia, ask her how it was for her, how she came to her decision. Find out. You're not a kid anymore. You can handle her now." Her gaze was steady and commanding. "I see a lot of murk in these cards, Lowell, a lot of business you need to clear up. You have major decisions ahead. You can make the right ones if you straighten out what's around you right now."

"I'm doing okay," he muttered, put off by her tone and by the galling idea that she could sense so much through what he saw as such bogus means.

Karen smiled. "You always do okay on the outside."

They looked at each other. Low tightened his hand on hers to turn the moment in spite of, maybe because of, her unsettling insights. He lowered his gaze to their hands. "Can you read my palm too?"

Karen turned his left palm. "Not upside down."

He rose and crutched to the couch. "Sit next to me? I get tired in a straight chair."

"Sure, Lowell." He watched the graceful way she blew out the candles on the wall sconces and came across the room, gown swaying around her, diaphanous.

"You're so pretty in that dress."

"Thanks." But she was all business as she bent to his palm. She pointed out the various lines. "Your life starts out deep and strong, childhood, I would say. Then it gets way too shallow, your accident, maybe. You nearly ... died?"

"Ah, Kar, isn't this stuff supposed to be some kind of comfort?"

Her straightforward analytic gaze lightened to a surpised softness. "You're finally admitting you actually need help with a feeling of *dis*comfort?"

Just want to get back to normal! "I'm ...recovering."

"I'm sorry you were hurt." Finally she leaned into him, but he knew it was companionable. She took his hand again. "Then it deepens and gets thick. See these little lines? Some say those indicate the number of children you'll have, it's three for you, but I don't guarantee those lines are particularly significant."

"Can you tell the near future?"

"Like what?" She looked up at him expectantly and he saw that, witch or not, she had no idea what was on his mind.

He put his arm around her, caressed her shoulder, and looked intently into her eyes. "It's time for me to rest. Come lie down with me."

She stared at him as slow disappointment dawned in and then narrowed her eyes. She moved away and sat very still.

I blew it. The old normal just didn't work for him anymore.

"Don't I deserve better than that, from you?" she asked in a low voice.

"Kar, it's been so long since we've seen each other, and I feel close to you—"

"Can't you possibly relate to women any other way?" She stood and glared down at him. "Christ, Lowell, have you no imagination? Will you never grow up?"

This hit annoyingly close to the unnerving self-awareness he was developing. "It's not an *insult* I want to be with you again! It's a tribute. You mean a lot to me."

"Goddess." She looked at him with a pained expression. "There was a time I would have been so glad to hear this from you. There was a time I got stuck on you, like a fool, and I couldn't wait for break so we could see each other again, after that summer we were lovers for the first time, remember?" She shook her head sadly. "The most wonderful summer of my life. I'd loved you as a friend forever, but to discover how—how you were in bed, how you made me feel, that was such a shock.

"I wasn't disappointed when you didn't answer my letters that semester afterward. I knew that wasn't your style. But I did expect that I'd become special to you somehow, since I was a real friend first. I couldn't wait to see you at Christmas."

Low raised a hand to massage his brow. He knew what was coming.

"You showed up the Saturday after you arrived, same as always. There was a beautiful snowfall, I thought we'd go hiking in the woods, resume our romance." She laughed bitterly. "But you had that girl in tow, that little blonde. Melinda something."

"Melissa."

"Whatever. You wanted to fix me up with her brother! You

thought we'd all go skiing at their place in New Hampshire, one happy foursome." She gathered the cards carefully on the table and stacked them with a slap. She looked up. "I wanted to kill you, but I was too sick in love with you by then, and besides, we were still friends. So like a crazy idiot I went along."

He nodded, remembering how quiet she'd been on that trip.

"I had to listen to you wooing Melinda that whole time, knowing you were fucking her silly every night while I suffered with Dirk—"

"Dick."

"Ah yes," she said dryly. "Aptly named, that boy. He wasn't a bad lay, really. And you had certainly taught me how to enjoy myself, sexually. So I did." She slid the Tarot deck back into its box. "And when you got tired of her stupidity, and wanted to ditch them both, you did. And put the moves back on me without a wasted motion." She shook her head. "And it's been like that ever since, between us. I was always willing. I don't blame you. But it hurt me.

"I do love you, Lowell. I'm probably the only real woman friend you have. Oh, of course, you get accolades from the world. But I know you. And I love you anyway." She folded her arms. "The last time we had sex was the last time."

A contraction twisted him inside, he could not identify the exact location, but it felt like the weird growing pains he'd endured in his knees as an active youth. "I'm sorry, Karen. I never meant to hurt you. You and Troy are my best friends."

"Thank you." She smiled, finally. "It was partly my fault. I never told you I was in love with you."

He had to admit, "It might not have made a big difference to me."

"I think I knew that. Maybe that's why I didn't want to risk telling you. At least you're honest."

"I'm trying to be, now," he confided. "But I should have realized—"

"We should have just stayed friends, I suppose. But I really liked our physical relationship. I don't even regret falling in love." She frowned at him. "You've made quite a career out of breaking hearts, haven't you?"

He shrugged.

"Yeah, I know, you're one of those guys who always claims to need space or time or other women or something. Right?"

"Well, I usually do—"

"Ha! Just wait till *you* fall in love. You haven't met your match. But, no—" She looked at the cards—"you did meet her. She's past and future. Not someone current."

Should he tell her about the white-veiled Clare dream?

No, Karen was already too woo-woo about this stuff. "Maybe it is you," he said, trying for chivalry. No way Clare could be in his future. Not unless he conjured up some hocus pocus more powerful than even a Vermont white witch could access.

"Not bloody likely, pal. I'm over you." She grinned at him. "Still friends?"

"Yeah," he agreed, feeling an ache of loneliness even as he acknowledged the wisdom of her conclusion.

"Don't look so sad. You can sleep in my bed—I can tell you do need me—but no sexy stuff." She laughed. "Just sleep, like when we were kids, remember?"

Low could not imagine not reaching for her if she was in bed next to him. "No."

"Oh come on Lowell. We'll wear pajamas, eat crackers, tell ghost stories. I know some real ones now." She ruffled his hair. "We'll be kids again, best buddies."

"Well, okay, but if I get excited, let me get you excited too. Let it happen."

"It won't," Karen said with conviction.

And it didn't. They lay chastely side by side—Karen, taking no chances, lay on top of the covers—reminiscing about their shared childhood, their families, and their old country day school. Low barely registered the soft kiss Karen placed on his lips before he fell asleep.

The next morning Troy woke Low early, to get on the road before the snow accumulating in the top-heavy grey clouds fell and stranded them. Karen made a healthy whole-grain pancake breakfast. Troy grimaced at the chicory coffee but Low politely asked for more. Another housemate gave Elise packets of teas for her pregnancy, and made Elise promise to try for home delivery with a midwife rather than submitting her body to the male-dominated butchery of modern hospitals.

Elise made wide eyes at Low. "I can just see Father letting me use the Monticello table in the dining room for the delivery."

"We may have to get him a temporary offshore posting."

"How about a permanent one," she said morosely.

"Hey." Low put his arm around her, leaning on his good leg. "Nothing he does or says can hurt you, unless you let it. You made this choice. You're sure. Nothing can change that."

"You know, it's providential you were here to help me, Ice," Elise told him quietly, using her old nickname for him. "I mean, if you'd still been in Beirut, I'd have been all alone with this." Low kept quiet, unwilling to explore any more "providential" connections.

"You'll change a lot together, this winter," Karen told them, watching them both. "You'll grow. You'll help James grow too."

"That's for damn sure." Low grinned.

"Can I come back here if it gets too heavy?" Elise asked the women.

"Of course." Karen put an arm around each sibling. "But I don't think you'll need to. You've got a strong friend here." She patted Low's shoulder.

"This is all very tender," Troy said, standing. "But we've gotta hit the road."

Karen stood waving at them for a long time. Elise sighed and settled in beside Low in the back. "She's terrific," she said with emotion. "You should get back with her."

Low met Troy's knowing eyes in the rearview mirror. "It ain't in the cards, sis," he replied, and Troy laughed over that down the long road to the highway.

222

FORTY-TWO

IN THE months that followed, James, Elise and Lowell had to create a different way of being with each other as they shared a home for the first time in ten years. James, once he realized she was resolute, surprised his children by treating her with an almost courtly deference and confined his exasperation and worry to private sessions with Low.

They refused Thanksgiving invitations by mutual accord. Low was an okay cook, but the naked cold turkey intimidated him, early on the morning of Thanksgiving Day, as did his mother's scrawled recipe for stuffing which inexplicably called for lots of bread slices laid out all over the kitchen the night *before*. He passed on the stuffing, of course, but the meal wasn't complete without it.

At dinner, Elise fled upstairs, unable to stomach the sight of the bird being carved, and James got drunk for the first time in Low's memory. He and Low picked at the food silently.

This is how WASPs cope with stress, he thought in the kitchen afterward, pouring himself another glass of James' fine old whiskey as he cleaned up. *We stop eating, and drink instead.* Intimate family life, he was noticing as an adult, seemed fraught with these uncomfortable little revelations.

They all convened in the kitchen late that night to snack on cold leftovers and trade ideas for hangover and morning sickness.

Lowell's third and last operation, to put permanent steel rods in his shins, was a success, and by Christmas he was easily wielding his crutches again. The holiday was more natural than Thanksgiving had been. James felt secure enough by then to talk about Elise to a few old friends, who were warm and gracious at his annual eggnog party.

"Your father looks more relaxed than I've seen him in

years," John Andexter, one of James' colleagues said to Low. "It must be doing him good, to have you two around."

"It's doing us all good," Low said, still surprised by this.

"And your sister looks lovely," said Andexter's wife. "She is just blooming." Elise was acting as hostess and her womanliness had never been more apparent. "We'll give her a shower in the spring," Mrs. Andexter continued. "I think she's very courageous. And I commend you and James for being so supportive."

"We're looking forward to you rejoining the team as soon as you're able," Andexter said. "We think with some training, some years, you'd make a first rate political attaché." Andexter sipped his bourbon and watched for Low's reaction to this unorthodox direct approach.

"I appreciate your confidence in me. And I'm still interested in diplomacy. But before I presume to take that up again I need to learn more about the world and how I can be useful to it."

"You lived in France."

"For a semester, as a student. I was so wrapped up in my thesis I didn't really see France at all." Remembering Aimee, he shook his head. "I knew one French person well. A woman."

"Only one?" joked Andexter.

"I didn't learn anything about France or about Americans. Beirut wasn't much different. I met one family."

"That's typical of the Foreign Service, son. You knew that."

"It's not enough for me."

"Well. When you finish your wandering, come talk to me." Andexter patted his shoulder. "Your kind always returns to the fold. I'll welcome you back. Merry Christmas, Lowell. And be sure to come to our New Year's Eve party next week."

FORTY-THREE

Kuwait 1983

THEY WERE three hours from Kuwait City, post-movie and pre-snack, and everyone was stirring. Clare peered out the window and saw, with a shock of excitement, the brilliant blue of the eastern Mediterranean giving way to the dun-colored rocky plains of the Middle East. She pressed her head sideways against the double-paned oblong, trying to see straight down—and was rewarded by the sight of the Sinai Peninsula, clear as a map and as evocative, making her laugh aloud.

She savored her impressions from visits to other places: Paris was haughtily splendid, achingly nostalgic, pastel-washed. Barcelona was a medieval monk on perpetual holiday. London was monumental and mundane, its too-familiar history lurking at every brass-plaqued corner, every slap of the Thames on its muddy banks, every Cockney accent wafting through the fog, and even in the confines of tea rooms to which Clare escaped when she needed to hush the clamour of the past outside. Greece was reminiscent of Mexico: sun-splashed exterior masking a traditional, suspicious, argumentative essence. But these grand locales did not inspire the thrill of travel in the Arab world.

Going to Egypt on her first Saudi school break was an even greater adventure than going alone to teach in Saudi Arabia. In the Kingdom, foreign professional women were seldom at liberty to experience Saudi life without some kind of official filter. But in Egypt she'd been free to explore alone. Cairo was as vivid as Mexico City, just as smoggy and teeming. The *dioses* of Teotihuacan and their Mayan counterparts would have saluted the stately Valley of the Kings. She was touched by people's weary, humorous, larcenous hospitality. She felt brave, negotiating her visit entirely in Arabic and avoiding any unpleasantness of thievery or lechery, proud of herself in a way she never felt when merely flying around Europe.

The Arabian Gulf region was both clear and opaque. Its native men and women, whose private lives were shrouded from view, stood out in white and black against a backdrop of bright blue sky, beige earth, colorful foreign workers, wild traffic and ubiquitous clouds of construction dust. Clare enjoyed, without understanding, her affinity for the region. She must have lived here in a former life. She didn't believe in mysticism, but nothing else could explain why, in spite of its numerous irritations for a Western woman, she felt so at home here.

AFTER LANDING in Kuwait City, Clare sailed through immigration and headed for baggage claim and customs. She'd made sure the proper documents were prepared and translated in the States, so she could show the prototype, but audiovisual equipment occasionally generated new red tape on arrival and there was always the possibility of a screw-up: laws changing overnight, someone wanting a bribe or just being in a bad mood.

The Kuwait Customs official went through her things, and when he opened the computer case, she handed the documents to him. He ruffled them and gave her a questioning stare.

"Duty stamp?"

"It's all right there." Clare indicated the papers in his hand.

"No duty stamp here." He patted the keyboard, nestled next to the monitor in its customized case.

"It's not necessary," Clare explained in Arabic. "We have an exhibitor's license. No duties are charged."

"No stamp," he repeated in a maddening monotone.

Clare forced a pleasant smile and shrugged openhandedly. They looked at each other for a short, wary time, during which he seemed to be mulling his options while the impatient line behind her pressed against Clare.

Then he dropped his gaze and shook his head. "No pass," he said, and pointed to a bench against the wall. "Wait here."

Damn. She watched him disappear into a back office and another clerk take his place at the customs table. *I should have let my hair down and flirted with him. Or else worn a long skirt and a head scarf in case he's a fundamentalist.* Her face felt hot. All those Western-suited *men* were being waved through without any hassle. Naturally there were only a few Western women. She leaned back, closed her eyes.

"Ms. Meredith?" said a cheerful Southern voice above her. "I'm with the local office representing U.S. commercial concerns. Just a few questions for you." The speaker was a tan, sandy-haired boy in a green Lacoste shirt and khakis. "Jeff Hunter."

"There's a misunderstanding, Mr. Hunter. We have an exhibitor's license. We don't need to pay duties." She was glad her voice sounded level, with just a touch of we-know-these-crazy-things-happen irony.

"I'll need to see your documentation, ma'am," he said politely.

Ma'am?

"That fellow took it," she told him coolly, indicating the small back office. "But everything is in order."

"You had your equipment certified?" Jeff Hunter was studying her rather more carefully than she thought the circumstances warranted.

"We have the standard temporary import license. I'm exhibiting the equipment at the EduGulf trade show, and then I'm taking it back to Chicago in exactly the same condition. It's a prototype. We don't need a Certificate of Origin." Clare kept her voice clear and low. She couldn't afford to lose her temper with this teenage civil servant.

"Is the software encrypted?"

"No, it's commercially available. We've modified it to include a video portion." A trickle of perspiration in the middle of her back had her sit up straighter. "Is there some problem? We've taken this to the educational shows this year in Europe and Asia. Our agent here is well known, he reps us for the whole peninsula—"

"You haven't sent any other shipment into the Middle East recently?" He was older than she'd first assumed. There were lines around his now narrow eyes. *What the hell!*

"We ship here all the time. InterTech has been selling into the region for years."

"Have you, personally, brought anything into Kuwait

recently?"

"No, EduGulf is my first visit to Kuwait." Frustration choked her words. "Maybe I should call the consul." The implied threat seemed not to register in Jeff Hunter's suspicious eyes.

"I'll make a call for you. Please bear with me, Ms. Meredith, I'm sure you understand security precautions are for everyone's safety."

Of course Clare realized how rigid anti-terrorist scrutiny had to be, in many parts of the world where InterTech did business, but such scrutiny was not the purview of U.S. commercial officers. Kuwait Customs was the in-charge entity. Being questioned like this was an anomaly she wanted to contest. But she knew no official, from any country, had an iota of logic or irony or even humor at airport customs.

In a final lame protest she stated, "They let all those *guys* go—" She nodded toward the last passengers from her flight.

"I'll be right back. I'll have them get you a soft drink." He gave her a look that he must have intended to be reassuring. "Don't worry. Consider this a routine check."

Routine, right. She drank the juice brought by another official, and rolled her head around on her shoulders to relieve her tension. Worst case: she'd never get out of the airport, and simply have to fly back to Chicago, as had happened to her Asian counterpart at a trade show in Beijing last year. The culprit then was an obscure piece of equipment whose Taiwanese origins, boycotted in China, had been revealed deep within the documentation.

She categorized these glitches as Adventures in International Trade, one of the stories she kept telling herself she'd write someday. She'd learned to at least try to exert flexibility and hang on to a sense of humor even if circumstances made her want to jump out of her skin. It would be pretty funny if, after twenty-four hours of angst over meeting Lowell Goodenow again, she wouldn't even have to see the man. Not so funny for InterTech, of course, or for her agent here—

Jeff Hunter reappeared, trailed by the first Customs inspector, with her folder and her computer case. Clare's relief was immediately replaced by fury.

"Now can you tell me why I had to go through that b—"

She bit off 'bullshit.'

"It really was a random check!" His tone was irritatingly cheerful. "You're free to go."

Clare stood, wanting to loom over him, but he was just that much taller that she couldn't. "So how did you get me cleared?"

"I called my boss."

"And he is?" Naturally any boss in the Gulf, even for the U.S. Government, was a 'he.'

"Lowell Goodenow, our regional Commercial Attache." *Oh, of course. Perfect.*

"What made him think my company was okay after all?"

"He didn't say," was Jeff's smiling response. "You can ask him yourself tonight at the reception. He told me to remind you all exhibitors are welcome."

"Delightful."

So far there were no good omens for this show, Clare thought on the Hilton shuttle. *Hassled by pen pushers from two countries, bailed out by the guy who dumped me in college, the one guy I've never forgotten, who I have to face tonight.*

How could there be anything wrong with her documentation? She'd ask Khaleedy to double-check, make sure she could take the prototype back to Chicago without repeat scrutiny. As if they didn't already have enough to do!

Once in her room, she called Khaleedy, but got no answer at his office. He was probably at the exhibit hall in the lower level of the hotel. She should get down there too. But for a moment she stood at the corner windows, which gave views of both the corniche and the hotel courtyard where a swimming pool glittered invitingly. As in Saudi Arabia it was surrounded by men. Not a woman in sight. Waiters held trays of soft drinks. Kuwait was dry.

What I'd give for a cold beer and an eight-hour nap. She closed her eyes and listened to the whoosh of the air conditioner. I'll take a shower, have some lunch, and then go down to the exhibit hall, she decided after a few peaceful seconds. As soon as she took off her jacket, the room phone rang.

"Miss Clare? This is Ibrahim. How was your flight?"

"Fine, thanks. I'm glad you called. I tried your office."

"I'm in the lobby. Would you like to rest? I can inspect our booth while I wait for you."

"I'll be right down."

Khaleedy, InterTech's Gulf States rep for years, was a portly, soft-spoken Palestinian in his late forties. She'd met him twice at company headquarters in Chicago. She appreciated him especially because of his gracious welcome of her new VP status; not every Arab man would be so respectfully accepting of a young American woman's direction.

After exchanging polite regards for each other's health and families, he clasped his hands together and said heavily, "I have bad news. We were unable to clear the show cartons of videos and language tapes without your signature. They are still at the port, with our language lab equipment."

Clare stared, speechless with dismay, as he shook his head and continued, "Believe me, I have tried everything."

"But you are the consignee—"

"The address labels were damaged on the voyage somehow, some leak, it's hard to tell. All they have is the return address with your name on it."

"But the show opens this afternoon! We should get right out there—"

"No, it's too late today. The port closes at two and it takes an hour to get there."

"God damn it!" Clare exclaimed, and then quickly added, "Sorry," at Khaleedy's reproachful look. "It's been a long night. Morning. Do you think this has anything to do with the new freight forwarder I used?"

She'd been so proud to save InterTech money by researching an outfit they hadn't tried before, one who came highly recommended by cohorts in Chicago's international trade community; what a painful lesson this would be, if she'd made an error in judgment.

"I doubt it. You know how damage can occur in any shipment. But at least you have the demo videos with you."

"Right here." Clare indicated the wheeled cases she'd brought from her room. She'd trained herself to travel like an executive, displaying sharp attentiveness and even-tempered pleasantry, no matter the time zone or city or her own exhaustion from jet lag. But she'd just lost it in front of Khaleedy, swearing like that; a measure of how rattled this show was making her.

After setting up the equipment there was only half an hour before the show began. At least this first afternoon was given over to tours of educators and students from local schools. She didn't have to sell to anyone, merely explain, and keep children from making off with the expensive color catalogs. She'd save those for the big guns tomorrow: government ministers, central school purchasers and major buyers looking for new lines.

Looking around, Clare saw familiar logos throughout the exhibit hall and checked them off mentally, recalling which sold products she evaluated superior or inferior to InterTech's. She noted she was one of only three women in the booths. This was normal for Gulf States business and one of the reasons she'd lobbied to do the show herself. A woman attracted attention and in a competitive market, why not use that edge?

She was busy non-stop once the hall doors opened. She fielded questions, gracefully snatched catalogs away from rowdy schoolchildren, wrote down names with promises to send information, and gave away an entire box of business cards. Khaleedy worked alongside her, translating on occasion when the dialect got too thick for Clare, making appointments with every school board director who stopped by.

They took turns running the computer through its interactive paces. Clare had triple-checked there would be no hardware or software glitches. The exhibit across the way was not so foolproofed: two young Western men sat glumly on their counter, swinging their legs and handing out brochures, surrounded by silent dark equipment. Her impulse of sympathy didn't trump her relief at the blackout of what looked to be a formidable display.

When the school day ended, and the hall emptied, there was almost a perceptible sigh from the exhibitors. School groups were dreaded visitors, always packed yet rarely profitable, but it was a traditional demonstration of goodwill to open this show to them first. Around the hall people straightened up their booths. Clare gratefully sipped the Pepsi Khaleedy bought her.

"I've had so much caffeine today I'll probably stay awake the whole trip."

"You must be tired. You should have come yesterday to

sleep before the show."

"It didn't work out that way. But if you don't mind, I'll take a break now."

She ducked out of sight behind one of the booth panels to sit for a moment, to massage her aching feet and scrunch her shoulders. It felt so good to take off her shoes! One of the worst parts of trade shows was the unforgiving cement floors exhibitors had to stand around on—Clare froze as she heard a shockingly familiar voice greeting Khaleedy outside their booth.

His trace of Southern had vanished but she knew his timbre viscerally. Her muscles tightened and her skin tingled in a tidal wave of sensual memory. She flattened against the paneling, heart pounding, unable to force her frozen body to emerge.

"I'm Ibrahim Khaleedy, InterTech's Gulf agent."

"Sure, I recognize you from last year's trade mission in Oman," Lowell said amiably. "I trust business is coming back for you since the adjustments?" Kuwait's stock market had taken a dive two years ago. Companies at this show were only now regaining ground as educational project budgets stabilized.

"Much better, especially since the new five-year education plan was announced."

"Glad to hear it. Did your supplier arrive safely?"

"She'll return ... in a moment." Clare was sure Khaleedy was too polite to call to her, since she didn't reappear on her own, although he probably wondered what she was doing. "I'll tell her you're in the hall."

She heard Jeff Hunter's eager voice. "Mr. Goodenow, this is the computer Customs had the issue with at the airport this morning."

"Jeff, this is Ibrahim Khaleedy, the company's Gulf sales agent. Jeff Hunter, from our office. He alerted me to the matter of your documentation—"

"What matter?" Khaleedy's confusion was apparent in his anxious voice.

"Probably just Custom's usual formality." Lowell was bland. "I'll take it up with your supplier later. Please remind her I'm hosting a reception this evening."

"Thank you, Mr. Goodenow." Footsteps faded, and there was a light knock on the panel framework. "Miss Clare?"

She snatched an acceptable excuse for disappearing. "I was just pinning up my hair." She tucked a stray lock behind one ear. "Thanks for handling that."

Khaleedy said in a low voice, "What was wrong with the import license?"

"It was just an irritating random check. Hunter took it too seriously."

"So the license was correct?"

"Same as all the others I've used. Temporary, for showing the demo. I validated it with Commerce's district office." The U.S. Department of Commerce kept an office in Chicago.

"They are being too careful, this show," Khaleedy said. "It isn't good for business."

"It's always something," Clare murmured. She was used to friction between national importers and the U.S. Department of Commerce, who tended to cross-check each other to a degree guaranteeing duplicate time-wasting. Local Customs was a useful scapegoat.

"Goodenow gave this to you for the American reception tonight." The card had the same message as yesterday's telex—just yesterday!—with a line added: "Hilton pickup 5:45 pm."

"I'll pick you up at seven tomorrow for the port trip."

"Thanks, Ibrahim."

FORTY-FOUR

CLARE TOOK a reviving shower and put on a long-sleeved black dress, appropriate for a Western businesswoman in the Gulf. She added a light pink scarf to soften the severe neckline. She looked at her shoulder-length hair, finally deciding to leave it down, held back on one side with a trio of slim black velvet clips. Black-tinted stockings and heels completed her outift.

She met the small group of American exhibitors in the lobby, and exchanged greetings with Michael and Frazier, Californians who'd had the blackout across from InterTech. They sat near each other in the embassy van.

"Kudos on getting your stuff to work," Frazier said. "Who'd you bribe?"

"No bribes needed. I'm tech savvy."

"If you don't mind my asking, isn't it a little intimidating for you here? I mean, being a woman?" Michael asked. Indeed, she noticed, she was the only woman on the van.

"Actually, I consider it a competitive advantage." She grinned.

"You weren't anxious, coming to Kuwait alone?"

She was used to this sort of question. "I taught for two years at Riyadh University. Kuwait's a piece of cake compared to the Kingdom."

"Wow, what was that like? Did you have to cover up?"

People were always fascinated by Saudi clothing strictures. "My hair, yes, when I left campus. We wore the abaya too, that's kind of like a black graduation gown."

"Why would an American woman want to work in Riyadh?" Frazier wondered.

"I thought it'd be interesting."

"Jeez, I guess it must've been! That's some kinda place to call interesting."

"So how'd you end up in business?" Michael asked.

"The University sent me to a local trade show to scope out a new language lab. I clicked with the folks doing the InterTech exhibit, ended up buying equipment from them, then accepted their job offer to work at headquarters in Chicago, three years ago. They wanted me because I could reach women's schools in the Kingdom."

"Smart. Why don't *we* hire a woman to sell for us in Saudi girls' schools?" Michael asked Frazier. "Once we earn the riyals to afford their show fees."

"Let's just dress *you* in one of those getups, Mike, hide your ugly face, who's to know? You can finally learn to act like a lady."

"A wiggle in the walk, and a giggle in the talk … "

Clare wanted to enjoy their banter—she suspected it was for her benefit, the lone female, a mixed blessing in the Middle East—but her heart was pounding too hard for her to focus on their ensuing discussion, as the van pulled past a security gate and into the embassy surrounds. The residential buildings spread out across several blocks, whose grassy yards gave a look of bucolic California suburbia. She felt her stomach clench as they stopped in front of a house toward the back of the compound.

In the foyer they were greeted by Jeff Hunter, who brought them into a long formal living room. Clare saw Lowell immediately. He stood at the foot of a staircase, looking up at a woman and child leaning down to him. The woman laughed, grabbed his head to kiss his forehead, and ran upstairs. The child, a girl with long hair in Lowell's ebony shade, followed her mother.

Oh my God he's married and a father.

Of course this inevitability had occurred to her, as she'd indulged herself in sixteen hours' flight time dwelling, *obsessing* actually, on their college romance. Just because *she'd* never found another lover as enthralling didn't mean he'd experienced a similar lack. In fact, she remembered him saying, in spite of his professed cynicism, he'd certainly get married since wives were 'useful' in the Foreign Service. But seeing the reality made her throat tighten. She pressed her lips against the ache and spun away as Lowell came toward the exhibitors.

"We've gotten lots of business in the Kingdom through shows," she told Frazier brightly.

Lowell was approaching her trio too soon.

Frazier asked, "How long did it take you guys to find a good agent there?"

She didn't answer. Lowell was right in front of her.

It was the same striking face: hypnotic eyes, patrician nose, sharp chin and sensuous lips. *How many kisses did I enjoy with this mouth?* The shiny black waves of his hair were crisper, and his jawline was marked by a faint thin line she had not noticed in his youth. He wore a stylish charcoal suit and red tie, with a U.S. flag lapel pin.

As she stared, he gazed back, for what felt like a long time.

Clare realized that Jeff Hunter was speaking. "Ms. Meredith! We meet again. This is our Attaché, Lowell Goodenow."

"We know each other," Lowell said. "Do you remember me, Clare? I.U., fall of 72. French class." His voice was smooth and friendly, but his perfect white smile didn't light his eyes, which fixed on hers with cool curiosity.

"What a small world!" Hunter said.

"*Don't know much about the French I took*," she heard herself quipping, quoting the funny old ode to being stupid in love, "What a Wonderful World This Could Be." "But I certainly recall that semester."

The corners of his mouth lifted as if he was about to laugh. Clare didn't know what else she might have babbled, but someone hailed him, and he moved on.

"You guys have more than French together?" Frazier was asking. She looked at him, numb. "He seemed kind of ... observant," he went on, eyeing her.

"Oh really?" Clare murmured. "Funny, I can barely place him."

"I could use a beer," Michael said. "I hear the diplomatic corps gets all the booze they want."

As if on cue, Jeff Hunter addressed the group. "This is the equivalent of your traditional first night of show Hospitality Suite." He grinned. "We figured you'd appreciate a little refreshment, American style, so come on out to the patio and help yourselves." They started to follow him outside. "And don't forget Mr. Goodenow and I are here to assist in any capacity. Good selling."

"Just show me that keg," Michael said under his breath.

The moon was a pale sliver in a sky still dusky with faded sunset colors. Fairy lights twinkled in palm trees, white clothed tables held shining bottles and chafing dishes, and low chairs were grouped in conversational clusters around the soft lawn.

Clare found a stone bench beside flowering shrubbery and gratefully took the Chardonnay Frazier brought. "I'll rest a sec," she told him. "I'm jet lagged."

"Mike and I are schmoozing the competition."

Clare took a delicious sip and closed her eyes for a second. The chilled wine, soft breeze, and flowery scent induced unexpected ease. Maybe present could balance past somehow ...

But she became aware of a presence beside her and opened her eyes to Lowell.

"I don't want to disturb you." His still expression, perfect posture and sharp dark suit introduced a serious mood to the sweet air.

She sat up straight and stared until she realized his statement was actually a question. "You're not disturbing me," she lied.

"The first day is the most demanding, isn't it." He sat next to her. "What a surprise to see you here, Clare." His smile was easy but still distant. "Welcome."

She spread her lips in a tentative answering smile, not trusting her voice to be steady. Close up, she saw faint lines flowing from each of his eyelids, another set on his forehead.

He was surveying her openly too. "You cut your hair."

"You're not using your accent."

"Ah bring it out on special occay-sions," he drawled.

She yearned to search out meanings behind his watchful eyes, to memorize the contours of his composed grown-up face—but she couldn't reconcile this yearning, or the erotic memories inconveniently crowding the forefront of her brain, with the fact of his being married.

She looked instead toward the gathering, heard the clinking of ice against glass and a few bursts of laughter amid low conversations. She noticed the American flag billowing down its pole. An unseen caretaker lowered it while night fell over the embassy grounds.

She began to formulate a friendly comment to fill their awkward silence.

"So, how did you—" they both began.

"You first," said Clare.

"Ladies first," he said. "InterTech's an interesting company. How'd you join them?"

Disconcerted by his matter-of-fact tone, Clare took a sip of wine, organizing her reply. "I was hired in Riyadh. I met them at a trade show."

"What made you choose work in the Kingdom?"

"Adventure," she said, looking to see if he would react with the same disbelief as all the other Americans she told.

He nodded as if not surprised. "That sounds like you. Did you find it?"

"Sometimes." She sought a different topic, not wanting to confide yet, if at all, in the face of his cool demeanor. She gestured to the lawn, lights, palm trees. *Looks like you got what you wanted, Lowell, en route to that ten year plan.* "Nice setup."

"It has its moments." She saw his eyes, too, following the last flap of Old Glory as it was bundled away for the night. He looked at her again. "I'd like to catch up with you this week. Do you have any open time?"

"Some." If she could trust herself alone with him. Maybe a public place. Maybe he'd bring his wife, or she could bring Khaleedy.

His smile now brought out one exclamation-point dimple, and he lightly touched her hand, resting on the bench between them, for a shocking second. His hand was tan against the white cuff. His fingers were warm. She recalled their sure strength, all over her, and fought the unruly flash of desire. He didn't wear a wedding ring. Probably felt he was above such sentiment.

A married flirt. She ran into plenty of them.

"Tell you what—come here for dinner tomorrow night. We're having a few of the local lights and some other EduGulf people. You might make good contacts."

"I'll see what my agent has planned for me," she said, looking away.

"Oh, bring him along if you'd like. Ibrahim Khaleedy." He

spoke as if weighing every syllable. "By all means. Bring him."

Clare looked up sharply at his tone but fell, heedless, into his stare.

His scrutiny was as probing as the first time, long ago under the trees of Bloomington, his eyes lit with the same curiosity and what felt like the same sensual speculation. In 1972 he'd doubtless been intrigued by her mention of Nechayev's Catechism and by her so-obvious attraction to him. But now, in 1983, what could provoke this intensity in a married man except some kind of meaningless nostalgia? *Meaningless to him, I'm sure.* She dropped her gaze as their moment was broken by the arrival of his daughter.

"I've been looking all over for you!" she exclaimed. "We have to put the candles on Mommy's *cake*." She tugged at his arm. "Come on!"

She looked about eight years old. It certainly hadn't taken long to find his marriage of convenience. Maybe he'd already known his wife when he met Clare. *He musta been through about a million girls* ... the old R&B song ran in her head.

"Julia, this is my friend Clare Meredith, say hi."

"Hi!" The resemblance was astonishing: eyes, hair, dimples. Clare just had to smile at the adorable girl. "It's my Mommy's birthday, Clare Meredith. We have a secret cake."

Lowell asked, "Would you like to join us, Clare?"

As if she could face his cosy family celebration! "Oh how sweet! But no thanks, I need to mingle with the folks here."

"I'll see you later, then. Don't forget tomorrow night."

"She's so beautiful," Clare murmured as they walked away. "Just like you." She put her glass onto the bench. Then she made her way quietly out of the villa, through the embassy compound, and back across the corniche.

Alone in her blissfully comfortable hotel room, she let out one deep exhausted sigh and then, sooner than she'd expected, she fell into a ten-hour dreamless sleep.

FORTY-FIVE

THE COASTAL highway to the port was desolate but not empty, its surrounds littered with parts of twisted cars and other debris. Clare recalled similar highways in Saudi Arabia, where the idea of salvage was alien, and it was routine for wrecks to be dragged to the nearest desert and left to disintegrate.

Sharp salt odor penetrated the closed car. To the right was the Gulf, shimmering flat in the heat, dotted with fishing boats out for the morning's catch. She saw the ribs of abandoned dhows—fishing vessels—sticking out of the sand like prehistoric bones, causing her to flash on the dinosaur skeletons at the Field Museum of Natural History back in Chicago. Large shrill-voiced dark birds, also prehistoric-looking, wheeled in the glaring blue sky.

They passed a group of men milling around a flatbed truck where a robed figure stood with a bullhorn. Clare heard angry shouting and whisked her window down to get a clearer impression. She caught a glimpse of an Ayatollah Khomeini poster being hoisted in the crowd as the shouting got louder, and a partition in her mind opened to capture the scene.

"The war's heating up," she said, referring to the Iran-Iraq nightmare that raged to their northeast. In Kuwait, as in many Gulf countries, there was a fissure between Sunni and Shiite Muslim populations, mirroring those who were at war with each other right now.

"Three years and no end in sight." Khaleedy sealed her window with the controls on his door. *"Mashallah,"* he said, meaning *what a shame.*

"How are the Kuwaitis taking it?"

"As you might expect." His eyes flicked to hers in the rearview mirror. It was customary for unrelated women to sit in the back. "It's too close."

"I'm sure it can't be … comfortable, having a pro-Khomeini demonstration here."

"I didn't see a demonstration," he said, watching the road again, adhering to the safe adage of avoiding political discussion. Clare could accept this. She was used to such denial from living in the Kingdom. "Here's the entrance to the port. Get your passport ready."

Armed guards stood at the gateway. Once cleared, Khaleedy drove into the huge fenced-off enclosure where containers were stacked five and six high in front of an enormous warehouse.

Khaleedy opened Clare's door for her. He seemed tense; maybe he was afraid they wouldn't release the cartons even with her say-so. A woman's presence in this part of the world never facilitated official matters. Briefly she wondered how, if the shipping labels had been damaged, the return address stamped all over the boxes was still clear. But she'd seen it all, in ocean freight; anything could happen to cartons even in well-sealed containers.

In a far corner was InterTech's cage, its floor littered with brochures and cased audio and videotapes. Clare wanted to get in there and wipe them all off. She glanced at Khaleedy, who looked as pained as she felt. "I told them to repack everything," he muttered, and added an unflattering noun, in Arabic, to describe his evaluation of port authority.

Clare signed the waybill while a couple of Yemeni workers stacked the pieces into new cartons and loaded them on dollies to wheel out to Khaleedy's Suburban.

"That was quick," Clare commented as they drove away.

Khaleedy gave a thin smile. "We'll find a way to invoice the baksheesh." Greasing wheels was a baked-in part of commerce, one that required creative accounting in order to comply with the U.S.' strict Foreign Corrupt Practices Act.

The crowd of demonstrators had dispersed. A mirage, she thought wryly, as they sped back to the Hilton.

Clare let Khaleedy open the booth while she quickly went to her room. A message light was blinking on the phone, so she called the hotel operator. "Two calls, both from a Mr. Goodenow," she was told. "One last night when your phone was on Do Not Disturb, and another this morning."

Probably repeating his dinner invitation, she thought as she went back to the exhibit hall. *No way can I handle sitting next to his wife and daughter all evening. Maybe Khaleedy can be my excuse not to go.*

"Anything going on tonight?" she asked him at their booth.

"No, we thought we'd wait until the weekend to invite you to dinner. My wife is looking forward to meeting you. She'll cook a Middle Eastern feast on Friday."

"Wonderful! I'll bring my gifts—just simple souvenirs from Chicago," she told him, seeing his face begin to wrinkle in protest. "Things I thought your children would like."

They talked about his sons and daughters until the appearance of the delegation from area Ministries of Education and Information, accompanied by representatives from various regional embassies. EduGulf was not only a trade show but a forum on education, with well-known pedagogical speakers, panels, and programs that showcased everyone's Five Year Plans.

She saw Lowell, the picture of urbanity in his official role, wearing navy pinstripe, somber navy tie, another flag pin. It really wasn't fair that he still looked so good to her. His Arabic was excellent as he chatted with the GCC ministers. Clare wondered how he'd polished it—the Foreign Service people she'd known in Riyadh could barely string a sentence together.

The interactive video worked perfectly for the visitors. Clare gave her accompanying presentation with the the Arabic-enabled keyboard. She wound up her performance and was surprised and pleased by their little burst of applause. Khaleedy moved rapidly among them, shaking hands, making appointments, collecting and handing out cards.

Lowell approached. "This keyboard overlay is a nice innovation," he remarked. He picked up a brochure and leafed through it. "You say your system can be adapted for any training program. We could use something like this at the embassy from time to time." He glanced up, lips in a small smile. She could smell, faintly, his same intoxicating cologne, and was transported to those long hours spent breathing him in. She forced her eyes to stay open rather than closing for a long lovely inhale. "How about a discount for an old friend?"

How glittery his eyes still were, and how thick his lashes. "If you're serious about placing an order locally, you can work through Ibrahim."

He huffed out a short sigh. "Clare, I know how busy you are, but I have to talk to you privately. I was hoping to catch you again last night."

"I don't think there's much to say." She began arranging catalogs.

"There is. I wouldn't have called you twice, otherwise."

"For *old times'* sake?" She tried for sarcastic but it came out snippy.

"No." Then he seemed to change his mind. "At least ... not yet." He turned his frown into a quizzical solicitation. "Have lunch with me?"

"Alone?" Did he regularly lunch solo with women? What did his wife think? *Oh grow up, Clare!* How many lunches had she taken with married men, business or sociable? *But none of them made me as nervous as he does.*

His raised eyebrow told her how silly her question was. "Okay," she said, as Khaleedy joined them.

"It went very well, Miss Clare. Mr. Goodenow, hello again." They shook hands.

"CIA," said Khaleedy once Lowell rejoined the ministers. "Don't mention those damaged cartons to him."

"Why would I? But why not?"

"He's already suspicious about our import license. His office is making a lot of trouble to the Palestinian and Lebanese agents. Extra documents, ID cards—" He spread his hands. "Did you go to the American Embassy last night? You see it's like a fortress?"

Clare barely recalled the security check. She'd walked out of the compound with just a wave at the guard shack; it was right across the corniche from the Hilton. "But it's logical, after the Marine barracks bombing in Beirut two months ago—"

Khaleedy shook his head. "They are too harsh. Giving a hard time to honest businessmen. Some of my friends haven't gotten equipment cleared in weeks. They're losing all their clients."

"That's Kuwait Customs. Nothing to do with the U.S. Department of Commerce, or the State Department, who he works for—"

"The embassy helps its own people, yes? Like for you

yesterday, at the airport, that one's office. They let you pass."

That hadn't felt like help. More like a roadblock. "What are you saying?"

"Look around. See those empty booths? They were supposed to be staffed by Lebanese agents. Goodenow doesn't trust Lebanese, I heard."

Clare was used to the suspicious political dialogue flowing throughout the Arab world, just as in some Mexican circles, and to the familiar claim that U.S. Embassies were hotbeds of covert CIA activity. Plots were always suspected on all sides and were, of course, sometimes real. She remembered the darkness of the CIA's activities in Chile.

There had been enough recent terrorist attacks in this region to warrant tightened security all over the Gulf. But she wanted to reassure Khaleedy. She needed him to keep focused on business as she was trying to do.

"Ibrahim, InterTech has complete confidence in you. If you feel you've been bothered by any American officials here, I'll make sure you get an apology. You're one of our most productive agents. I want you to feel comfortable."

"Thank you, Miss Clare. I appreciate."

"Why don't you take your lunch break now, and I'll take mine in an hour."

Only a few visitors trickled in after the final white-robed ministers wafted away. Clare was unpacking a new batch of catalogs behind the paneling when she heard a child's excited voice exclaim loudly, "Look, Mommy, Doofus!"

Clare came out with a smile that sagged when she saw Lowell's daughter and wife standing in front of the computer, which was running an interactive Dearly video.

"Go on, Julia, answer the question," her mother encouraged. "See, you just tap out yes or no—is it okay if she does it on this keyboard?" she asked Clare.

"Sure, that's why it's there."

While Julia ran through the program her mother glanced at a catalog. She was a delicate, fine-boned woman, with flawless skin, large blue eyes and her daughter's black hair. But, *Oh sure, some diplomat's wife!* Clare could not suppress this snide inner comment, remembering so clearly Lowell, pacing in his long dress that final afternoon, the austere snowlight underscoring their heartrending goodbye as he told her, "The wives are—God, I just can't see you giving up your youth for that."

His wife wore a tight denim miniskirt showing off long tan legs, and a huge yellow sweatshirt, silkscreened with the image of a barely-clad Sting. She looked both totally out of place and totally at ease. Clare acknowledged her confident beauty and fought a rush of pain. *I loved him first, but I was just too young*—even though this woman looked about her own age. Which would have made her, what, barely twenty years old when she bore his child? Strange.

"Is there anyplace locally we could buy these videos? We're only here for a couple of weeks but she misses her cartoons."

Clare gave her the list of retail outlets that Khaleedy supplied, pasting on a phony smile, hiding her reaction. A couple of *weeks*? Did they not live with Lowell? How he must resent not having his family around! Maybe his wife just couldn't handle the strictures of Kuwaiti life. Some Western women—the more shallow, closed-minded, hysterical types—simply did not tolerate the mores of Gulf culture—

"Thanks. I don't think we met last night—I'm Elise Goodenow."

"Clare Meredith."

"*You're* Clare! I'm so glad to meet you! Low told me you were here." Elise's smile was broad, welcoming. Taken aback, Clare said nothing. "He couldn't believe it was really you—"

"Mommy! I got a perfect score!"

"She looks like her father," Clare said politely.

"Her *father*?" Elise asked sharply.

"Like Lowell," Clare said, confused. "She looks just like him—"

Elise snorted. "Low's her *uncle*, not her father."

Clare tried to recover quickly. "I saw you all together last night and you looked like a family. A nuclear family," she concluded awkwardly. "I assumed he was married."

"Low?" Elise grinned. "Maybe you forgot he is *not* the marrying kind." Her expression was just like one of Lowell's, from the old days, alight with wicked amusement. "Too funny. He wanted to introduce us at the reception, after this little family birthday thing for me, but you'd already gone. He was so bummed."

"Happy birthday."

Khaleedy came up, said hello, and told Clare she was free to take her break.

Elise continued as they followed Julia to the lobby. "I'm sure you know what an impression you made on Low. I think you were, for him, the one who got away."

"Oh I doubt it," Clare automatically negated. "We haven't seen each other in eleven years." She felt Elise's stare but could not elaborate. *The one who got away?*

"As it happens, we're having lunch. Business," she added firmly, to banish, for herself as much as for Elise, the specter of lovesick teenage Clare. "He needs to verify my import license."

"Is *that* what it's called these days?" Elise shot her another teasing Lowellesque grin.

"I see you've met." Lowell intercepted them at the lobby fountain. "I'd have you join us but Clare and I have to talk shop—"

"I don't like the food here," Julia chimed in. "It's Turkish Week. Yuck."

"We'll go find that Hardee's," Elise promised, putting her arm around the child.

"My driver knows where it is." Lowell smoothed a lock of hair from Julia's forehead. "Have fun."

FORTY-SIX

"I WANTED you to meet Elise last night." Lowell didn't walk toward the hotel coffee shop, where other exhibitors were thronging, but opened the door into a small dining room overlooking the courtyard. She passed right next to him to enter and caught his fresh scent again. "I reserved this after we spoke earlier, it's less ... public."

"I should have known you and Elise were family—you look so alike!" She might have realized they were siblings, last night, if she hadn't been so jet lagged and jittery.

But she felt even more nervous now, knowing he was single, seeing the exclusive space he made for their lunch together, and hearing again Elise' blithe comment, "You were the one who got away." Elise was wrong. *He* was the one who got away. She was sweating inside her snappy grey suit, dammit, she didn't bring enough clothes to afford this anxiety.

She peeled off her jacket and hung it behind the chair he'd pulled out for her. She wanted to pluck her blouse to fan herself, clutch her hair away from her neck, wipe her forehead with a charmingly folded Hilton napkin—and held still when she saw how he was observing.

"It's a little *close* in here, hmm?" He slid open the window and a welcome breeze blew through, but his knowing grin, when he sat, heated her skin again. He doffed his own jacket, yanked at his collar and tie, and chuckled. "Sitting with you like this takes me right back, Red."

Their last meal out together: brunch following her flu week, when every shared glance and even chewing and swallowing were suffused with eroticism that time had not erased for her nor, if she could believe the intimate twinkle in his eyes, for him. *Have some pancakes.*

She fixed on a bright social expression. "Is Julia's father—"

247

"History. Elise raised Julia on her own, mostly. They've lived with me sometimes."

"Not here—"

"Cairo," Lowell recounted. "Tehran—"

"Tehran!"

"My first serious job in a Commercial Attache office. Seventy eight, seventy-nine. The good years!"

"Were you a *hostage?*"

"I finished my posting just before the embassy takeover. A number of my colleagues stayed on longer than they'd planned."

"So then you went … ?"

"To Egypt. And now here."

"I'm sure it's been satisfying." Being the U.S. Commercial Attache to the Gulf Cooperation Council was a bigger deal, more exposure, than being ambassador to a single country: a role fitting the oil-oriented MA thesis she recalled. He'd done well.

"It's been … interesting. How about you? You were telling me last night how you got started with InterTech."

"I did some freelance work for them at first. They needed someone to help develop a software program teaching ESL to Arabic speakers. When my contract expired at Riyadh University, I went to work for InterTech headquarters in Chicago."

"Does your mom still live in Merrillville?"

He remembers where I'm from. She nodded.

"Must have been good for you to be near family again after being so far away."

A waiter came in, wearing a red vest and fez. "It's Turkish Foods Week," he announced. "We have special menu."

Lowell did not take the folder the waiter tried to hand him. "Chicken sandwich and Perrier. Clare?"

"The same." This lunch was not about food.

"Turkish Week," Lowell repeated, after the waiter's departure. "Marketing." He moved flatware aside, threw an arm behind his chair, leaned back to consider her.

"You must travel all over for InterTech. You enjoy it?"

"Very much."

"What's your title again?"

"Vice President, Middle East Division." She liked saying this out loud, and saying it to him made her feel they were at last of equal stature. 'Vice President' had such a fine ring. She handed one of her cards over the table.

He examined it and looked up. "Have you had the position long?"

"A while." She didn't have to admit she'd only recently convinced her boss to give her the title in order to impress clients during this business trip. "I report to the president. Our company owner."

"I've heard of him, of course. Belgian, isn't he?"

"American, for some time now." She gave her PR speech. "He built the company on his knowledge of educational technology after working years in the field, in a number of universities around the Middle East. We won an E award a couple of years ago." The E award was a high honor, conferred by the U.S. Commerce Department on the most productive exporters.

"I remember. It's a fine accolade."

"You know us, then."

"We've been mandated for some time to facilitate export promotion. I've met some of your people in the Kingdom. Your predecessor, I suppose." He studied her. "When I saw your name on the show list I couldn't believe it might actually be ... *you*."

"Because I'm a big business tycoon?"

"Oh, I knew you'd do well wherever you went." He smiled briefly. "Although, as a businessperson, I'm sure your ideas about Marx's dialectic might have changed some."

Marx! She hadn't thought about the dialectic in years.

"Your crusading is something I could never forget," he went on. "You were so committed. Have you stayed politically involved?"

"Not the way you remember." She'd never gone back on that wire. "I guess in Mexico I got a different view of what I used to call the Revolution."

"You knew leftists there?"

She nodded. Julio's 23rd September League had long since disbanded, but its brutal scattering by secret police still generated sporadic news.

"How'd you handle Riyadh? It's repressive, for an outspoken person like you."

249

"I wasn't outspoken in Riyadh, nobody gets politically active there, not if they want to keep their head. But in college? I wanted to speak for Joe—you remember, my brother—and I was sincere about wanting to end the war." She was able to admit, "I've realized, since then, being politically extreme as a teenager gave me ... an identity." She did not add, "to hide behind," since this recent self discovery still felt private.

"Interesting insight." His scrutiny made her feel as uncomfortably disarmed as if she were still that naïve teen, new to her unveiled body and unused to its power and its demands regarding him. "You seemed genuinely dedicated, to me."

"I was, about Vietnam. The Nechayev thing ... didn't stick."

"Not being active doesn't mean you gave up your ideals. What'd you do after IU? I tried to find you, you know, I was so curious." Now his eyes lit and both dimples bracketed willing-looking lips. "Troy told me you went to Mexico."

She saw red hair sweeping a shoulder as Troy perused the end of SMC's courthouse demonstration, while a blushing young girl quivered for Lowell to sit next to her, shaken as much from the excruciating agitation of first-ever desire as from the demo's hasty demise.

"The vet from Boston. You knew each other ... in college?"

"Prepschoolers at St. Paul's, undergrads at Georgetown. He's partner in a D.C. law firm now, if you can believe it." His grin was still so infectious. "So, Mexico?"

"I spent my year abroad in Mexico, after changing my major to Spanish. Started teaching English there. Did more of that in the States after my BA and got a job offer to teach in the Kingdom." She shrugged. "Pretty simple story."

"Nothing about you is simple." He was now looking at her as if searching for some kind of clue. "I'm curious about your coming to the Gulf. At this time."

She wasn't wrong—the penetration in his gaze was keenly measuring. "Why would you wonder? This is the biggest show, I'm the regional VP—"

"The very new VP, with a new relationship to the InterTech agent—"

"Khaleedy?"

"How well do you really know him?"

"I've met him in the States." Why was she feeling defensive? "He's solid, Lowell, we stand behind our people. We check them out very carefully."

"Go on."

"We wouldn't have any sales here otherwise!" she retorted. "Look, I think you should level with me. If you guys have some problem with InterTech. With Khaleedy. With our bloody import license." She drew up straight as she saw him begin to frown. "With my political history, damn it, I can guess this isn't idle chatter."

"You're right. That's why I wanted privacy for this conversation." He reached forward as if he might take one of her hands, but she quickly folded them in her lap.

"Well, lay it on me! I'm a big girl now, in case you didn't notice! I can take it!" The more she spoke, the angrier she felt, strangled by the need to keep her voice even.

"Can you?"

What the hell!

"A shipment was intercepted during a routine Kuwait Customs spot check at the port last week. In that shipment was a carton of audiotapes. Shiite propaganda, in Arabic, but Iranian-made. That's not illegal here, not yet, but it's very ... *interesting.* To the Kuwaitis.

"So Customs asked us to examine the waybill, since it was from an American show exhibitor. When I recognized *your* name in the documentation, I volunteered to ask you about this, after we realized "Clare Meredith" was indeed the same person I knew so well once upon a time back at Indiana U. Imagine that, Sugah." His flash of practiced smile chilled her more than his words. "You answer for InterTech activity in the Gulf. What do you think's going on?"

"Going *on?*"

"Are pro-Khomeini tapes part of your product line?" He actually laughed.

"Of course not!"

"So how'd they get into your shipment?"

"I have no idea!" But at once she recalled Khaleedy's request that she not mention the damaged cartons at the port, and had to drop her gaze.

She heard the sudden intake of his breath. A moment passed. Then he asked in a low even tone, "Can you tell me how the cargo was routed?"

She outlined, fingering the tablecloth as a map, still reluctant to look at him.

Athough her cherished Chicago River ritual was to look northeast toward the Atlantic route, the Great Lakes were closed to shipping November to April, so she had InterTech use the inland waterways to reach the venerable Mississippi, departing U.S. shores from New Orleans.

From there it was water straight to Beirut, for first-stop unloading and reloading, then through the Suez Canal to Jiddah where the ship made final dock. The last leg was terrestrial, across the broad bosom of Arabia, to reach this particular trade show in Kuwait City.

She'd priced out the wet route all around the Arabian Peninsula and up through the Gulf, thinking it might be cheaper than by land through the Kingdom. But given the war, insurance rates for any passage near the Strait of Hormuz were through the roof, so she'd stayed with the Jiddah landing.

"So Beirut was the first stop." She finally glanced up. His accusing frown skewered the tablecloth where her route map left a glaring trace. "When Khaleedy picked up the consignment, were the contents intact, I mean, aside from the box Customs opened?"

So then she had to tell him about this morning's trip to the port, not leaving out the demonstration or Khaleedy's dismissal of it. "He was being protective of me. I understand that. In my experience, probably yours too, local businesspeople never talk politics. He can't discuss the war when even Kuwaiti Shiites and Sunnis are at each others' throats—"

"—exactly why we're so concerned about propaganda right now."

She finished, "That stop yesterday at Customs felt like a last straw, but now it seems no more than an irritation, really, I never thought things could get worse—"

"We told them to stop you."

"You—!"

"We had to know who you really were."

She could only shake her head.

"There's no immunity when it comes to security. A show like this, full of Westerners looking for business after the stock market crash, at the same time as an escalating pattern of anti-Western attacks in the region—it's a soft target.

"And I knew the depth of your activism, how you used to call yourself a revolutionary, so I couldn't help but wonder if you were supporting the Shiites here, for some reason."

"*Seriously?*"

His response was cold. "Seriously."

"I do not support either side. I'm smart enough to recognize an internal struggle that no sensitive outsider would mess with." She felt heat rising and knew color was staining her neck and cheeks. "You still judge me for that depot paintjob, and the way I hid my age. You still think I'm ... *deceptive!*"

"Clare. Please." He held up his hands in a gesture of surrender. "I don't know you now." His expression softened. "I'm not *judging*. You risked real danger, then, for a cause you believed in, even if now you seem to see that time in a new light. Your courage is one of the aspects of your character I admire most, when I think of you."

Hearing him say this partially loosened the kernel of lonesome injury lodged in her heart since their last meeting. "But you were so ... disapproving," she had to point out.

"Well ... you really shook me up." He glanced down. "I overreacted." He took a breath and leaned back. "In any case, regardless of that early activism, your history didn't show any tie to Middle East political movements. But I still wanted to talk to you upfront."

The warmth she'd felt an instant ago cooled. "My ... history?"

"Of course we ran your background, and Khaleedy's, and the other InterTech officers."

The waiter entered with a flourish and set out lunch for which she had no appetite.

As soon as he left, Lowell said, "Don't look at me that way. You vetted clean, but Kuwaiti security will keep inspecting as long as there's a war up north. No stone unturned."

"Consider me turned." Turned inside out. "I'll get to the

bottom of this thing with the cartons. I'm not letting InterTech's name, or mine, be tarnished."

"I advise you to stay away from it. And I'd appreciate your not confiding in Khaleedy until we know more."

"But it's my business, mine and Ibrahim's, and our freight forwarder's." *My new forwarders. My find. But Ibrahim and I agreed, they weren't at fault for the damage, if it really was damage and not deliberate tampering … this is so fucked up!*

"Clare, please understand, our concern is protection."

"And you call that export promotion?"

"Making this trade show safe for businesspeople? Absolutely. Making it safe for you, so you can keep expanding your InterTech empire here in the Gulf." He had the nerve to show his charm once more in a warm smile. "I can tell you're *very* good at your job."

"You too." She took her glass, wanting to toss it at him. "Here's to us," she sneered.

"Ouch." He laughed. "I deserve that."

"I hope you believe I had no knowledge … "

He held his palms up. "I believe you. I'm sorry I had to ask … like this. But I didn't want pretend, with you, or let anyone else ask. Your company wasn't the only exhibitor exploited. There's a lot of examining going on. We can analyze U.S.-based elements, but there's too much out of our control, as you can imagine." Hearing him admit this allowed her to recognize his sincerity. "And, Clare, I'm also very sorry to tell you the rest of InterTech's shipment will likely remain at the port for further inspection."

"My language lab inventory."

"Whatever came on that container."

Fuck, fuck, fuck. Delayed delivery of orders meant delayed payment, disgruntled customers, bad ratings …

"I've already initated fast-track clearance for you with Kuwait Customs," Lowell went on. "But our reach only extends so far."

"I have to tell Khaleedy about this!"

"Of course you can tell him there's a delay—he'll be notified this afternoon anyway, that the entire container batch from that shipment is being held. But, in spite of the fact I know you trust him, I'd advise not telling him about the propaganda. Just in case he's somehow a link to whatever's going on."

Makes sense. No reason to add to Ibrahim's paranoia. She put on a gracious face. "Thank you for giving me a heads up, Lowell."

"Look." He seemed about to reach across the table again, but stopped his movement. "Can I send my driver to bring you to dinner at my house tonight? Good food, decent wines, interesting people. And I'll be nicer, I promise."

"How much nicer?"

His apologetic smile grew. "As nice as I possibly can be."

"You won't lock me up in the basement? For more interrogation?"

"Lock you up? . . hmm." A flicker of amused interest lightened his face further as he shook his head. "There are no basements in the Gulf."

"So ... is it Turkish Food Week at your house, too, or are you strictly patriotic?"

"Come find out." He glanced at his watch. "I'd better let you get back to the show."

"I guess I should say thanks for lunch."

His wry expression acknowledged her tone. "I guess I should say it was my pleasure."

FORTY-SEVEN

THAT AFTERNOON, Clare went through the motions of exhibiting, mechanically setting up the program and running through it repeatedly, endless as the replay of lunch in her mind. She watched Khaleedy work the show, milking every contact, nailing every chance for further discussion, tirelessly helpful. No stone unturned.

Only the most reliable and productive agents reached his level. If he had been used, she was sure he was not aware of it. He was on edge—she'd witnessed his worry about the other agents' being under surveillance, his suspicion of official scrutiny, and his nervousness at the port—but at this show, and in all her prior dealings, he was an absolute professional.

She snatched a moment to exchange a few chagrinned comments regarding their inventory's delay. At least she could reassure him that Lowell's office was trying to help.

She trusted Ibrahim. But she wondered if he had enemies.

Did *she?* She looked around the exhibit hall, where everyone was as busy as flies at an ice cream social, as her Dad used to say.

Who would want to damage InterTech's reputation? And how had the cartons been infiltrated? For that matter, how had they been intercepted during a routine inspection? Someone wasn't being straight, somewhere. Maybe she could figure this out by keeping her eyes open.

Michael and Frazier's booth across the way was up and running, all the bells and whistles making passers-by stop. She watched them for a moment. She'd heard stories of equipment sabotage amongst rivals at less-organized trade shows. Messing with electronics on site would be easier than messing with shipping where documentation was so strict, every bit had to be accounted for, by both exporter and importer, and customs brokers on both sides.

Michael caught her eye. "Come on over and check out your newest competitor, Clare!" he called. "Get ready to post some losses."

She crossed the thin carpeting and looked at their computers. "You call this interactive? Just because the user has to push a button?"

"Hey, we deal in the real world of education, where the average school board still wants interactive on the playground. Slow and steady wins the race."

She'd feared they were hipper than that. She smirked. "Depends where the racetrack is, boys, don't choke on InterTech's dust here in the Gulf." She left them to handle their visitors and to give Khaleedy a break.

At six she went to change for dinner. She was glad she'd packed her most smashing silk suit, flame-red, her best color. She took care putting her hair up, doing her face, fastening on pearl earrings and necklace. Classic, she thought, studying the mirror, understated since the suit's sober cut contained the passionate hue as did her pearls and clean chignon; but this suit was her favorite because of its confidence. She was neither the teary college girl nor the flustered stammerer of today's lunch. She'd hold her own, she told herself on the short ride over to the embassy, adopting an aloof gaze. She'd *shine*.

She recognized deep appreciation when he opened the door and considered her. How fine to receive this again from him! "You look ... amazing, Clare. It's so good to have you here."

"Thank you." She kept her cool by not smiling back.

Lowell ushered her into the foyer, where another woman stood; a young woman with huge green eyes and ice-blonde hair, dressed in a white satin pantsuit that outlined her little body. *Just because he's single, you wanted to assume he's unattached?*

"Clare Meredith, Loren Webb. Clare's the Middle East VP with InterTech, one of the exhibitors at the trade show. Loren's father was our last ambassador to Saudi Arabia. He's traveling in Qatar right now while she visits here."

"Why, I met your father in Riyadh," Clare remarked, pleased to identify herself as a person who met ambassadors. "He's a gracious host." She need not add she'd been one of hundreds of Americans invited to a post-election party in 1980, nor that as

257

the only Democrat she left early, disgruntled, feeling there was not enough free-flowing booze in all the Kingdom's diplomatic corps worth celebrating a victory she would never believe in.

She smiled sweetly at Loren, who was murmuring, "How nice, I'll pass that on, Daddy will be so pleased." Lowell indicated they should follow him to the main living room where a few other guests mingled.

"How'd you get a visa to go to Saudi on business?" Loren asked.

"I was teaching at a university then."

"My, that's impressive," Loren said, eyes wide. "I know how hard Saudi is on working women." Suddenly it was easy to chat about Riyadh, and Clare forgot to stay aloof.

Twice more Lowell answered the door and brought in other guests, and when they were ten, after they'd been served drinks, he led them into a formal dining room where a long, beautifully laid table waited. There were colorful little bowls of meza and steaming platters of broiled lamb, rice, vegetables and fresh flat bread.

"You always were a good cook." Clare could not resist ribbing Lowell, in a low murmur, as he pulled out her chair to seat her. "You've branched out."

His hand spread on her upper back, briefly, and his knowing grin hit her skin and scattered inside to light her up here and there. "I had a little help with this, Clare, but I'd be happy to cook just for you, if you're free another night here."

Before she could think up a response he was introducing the people next to her, a Kuwaiti woman contributor to an Arabic women's magazine, and a deputy from the Kuwaiti Ministry of Information.

"How is business so far this week?" asked the deputy, on her left.

"Thank you for asking, sir, I'm impressed with the quality and quantity of visitors, and with the facilities. Everyone is so hospitable."

"Is this your first visit to Kuwait?"

"Yes." She quickly thought of a few positives she noticed about his country. "It's quite a change from Saudi Arabia. I like seeing women driving, and the number of healthy small businesses, and … the fishing boats."

"When did you see fishing?"

She told him about her trip to the port.

"And how do you know Saudi Arabia?" asked the writer.

"I taught in Riyadh for two years." After the usual exclamations of wonder over this, the talk turned, as it invariably did in the Gulf, to Saudi Arabia and its handling of its providential—most non-Saudis said its completely undeserved—wealth.

Clare had to state her opinion. Her experience in the Kingdom had been positive. "When you consider that only a couple of generations ago, theirs was a nomadic culture, I think it's pretty impressive the way they've managed to build a cohesive society."

Kuwaitis thought of themselves as vastly more sophisticated than their neighbors to the southwest, so she tactfully added, emphasizing the difference between the two countries, "With such a widely scattered population, in such harsh geography."

Nobody argued with that.

"But didn't you feel repressed, as a Western woman?" asked Loren. "Whenever I visited Daddy I always felt so … confined."

"You know, when Riyadh University offered me the job, I decided not to judge," Clare told her. "I think I knew it would be so different, from anything in my experience, I'd just pretend I was on another planet." She grinned. "I did feel like E.T. sometimes!"

Loren giggled. "A blond E.T.! I know what you mean."

"How would you compare the Kingdom to Mexico?" Lowell asked.

She had pondered this for years. But he was the only person who'd ever asked. She stared at him for a moment, wondering *Do you know how unusual you are?* before addressing the group. "It fascinates me how Latin American cultures' linguistic and other roots, from the Arab colonization of Spain, inform some of their attitudes. About family. About authority. About religion, even though those differ in content. Even some of the food, the use of color, the weaving and pottery designs … I found more similarities than I would have expected, once I was in Riyadh, remembering Mexico City." She had to add, "I felt like an E.T in

Mexico too, sometimes. Always a gringa."

This brought a little ripple of laughter.

"We liked a phrase in Mexico, "So far from God, so close to the United States," " she said, taking the risk of poking fun under U.S. Embassy auspices. "So in the Kingdom I said, "So close to God, so far from the United States"."

"I suppose you wrote some songs describing your experience." Lowell's amused glance took in the entire table. "I knew Clare in college. She's very skilled at musical comedy."

She had to laugh. "I am *not* singing the Saudi songs here."

"So close to the Kingdom, hey." His affectionate smile telescoped him so powerfully into her vision, blocking everything else, she had to look away. She turned to the Kuwaiti writer and they talked about Gulf women's issues. They soon uncovered common contacts from Riyadh's active women's business and academic community, and enjoyed a lively exchange.

When the writer turned to chat with her companion on the right, Clare was free to watch Lowell again. He directed the server to attend to parts of the table, with a gentle nod, while his hands were busy with the guests near him, passing dishes, lighting cigarettes or filling empty glasses. He focused when spoken to, and was quick to contribute to the talk, or get it moving again by bringing up a new topic. He seemed to hear five conversations at once while giving each person the impression he was listening only to them. You really became a diplomat, Clare thought, enjoying her study. *Aren't you something. Aren't you even more beguiling.*

The meal concluded, they went into the living room until about ten thirty, when a few guests started a flurry of departures.

"Thank you," she told him, standing at the door in a small clutch of leave-takers. "This was a special evening."

"Wait," he said, putting a hand on her shoulder. "Let me walk you back."

He still had guests. "You don't have to."

"I want to, Clare."

He said goodbye, shook hands, nodded with promises to accept return invitations.

When everyone had gone, he called into the living room, "I'm seeing Clare to her hotel, Loren, let Elise know if she wonders."

"Okay," came the reply.

In the balmy evening, ground-level sprinklers swished over the dark lawns, lending a feeling of summer as they strolled through the compound. Lowell's was one of about fifteen or so modest villas clustered in the blocks behind the main U.S. government buildings.

Are we really in Kuwait?

This reminded her too much of their first walk in Bloomington, after he'd plucked her from the demonstration and treated her to her first bar, when in the woods she'd stopped by Adam and Eve, and wielded Nechayev to combat her ineptitude at dallying with newly met so-smooth Lowell. She glanced at him, struck anew by the weirdness of this reunion

"Can I see you again this week?" He didn't let her answer. "About lunch—I figured you'd rather have *me* question you, than some official you don't know."

"Even if I resent you?"

"I can handle it." He took her elbow, a light touch, just enough to be gentlemanly. "I'd love to hear some of those Saudi songs, Clare, we're far from anyone else hearing."

"You don't have to flirt with me."

He stepped closer, unmistakably breaching the polite space between them. "I don't know *how* to flirt with you." His arm slid around her and she felt his warmth—so naturally—again. "I don't even know what to say to you."

She pulled away. "I don't know either. I can't tell if I'm in the clear now, since you invited me to dinner, or if you're still trying to get information, or if you're just into some kind of reminiscence trip like me, since I saw your name on the list—"

Under the streetlamp the clarity of his features stood out like a photographic negative: sharp planes, glittering eyes, soft mouth. He looked at her for so long, without moving, she began to regret having been 1972-era direct. He was a stranger now, after all, they had *nothing* in common except a two-month youthful addictive sex session and a current working knowledge of the Arabian Gulf countries' business climate.

"You're right, of course." He started to walk again.

She didn't move. "About which part?"

When he turned she saw anxiety and amusement squaring off in disparate folds on his features as she felt they struggled inside her. He held up his hands. "Clare, can we start over? Can we—I don't know, pretend we just met?"

"No. We can't do that."

Amusement won. "Then let me see you again. Say … Thursday? I'm taking Elise and Julia to the beach. Come with us, and afterward I'll take you out for a … *Pepsi.*" His grin poked fun at the Arab boycott of Coca-Cola and the official alcohol-free ambiance, which she recalled so well from the Kingdom and did not mind. "Or there are terrific restaurants here. One's in an old dhow. Fresh delicious seafood, interesting atmosphere, indigenous music."

"So … this is like … a date?" She was trying to imagine going to the beach with him. The bathing suit she'd brought was a utilitarian workout number.

"Definitely a date. You're not married."

He sounded so sure she figured it was part of his background check. "No."

"Engaged? Boyfriend? Anyone serious?"

"Not at the moment," she murmured, wanting to keep him guessing. "But what about you? What about Loren?"

"Loren?" he repeated, as if it were a foreign word. "She's a visitor. A family friend. I'm not attached. At all."

"And where was Elise tonight?"

"She and Jul are watching videos on the Betamax upstairs because my entertainment evenings bore them, why, do I need their permission to ask you out?"

"I should set up meetings with clients on Thursday."

"People don't work Thursday afternoon. You know that." Thursday and Friday were the Muslim weekend. "The beach would be a nice break. I know how tiring these shows can be."

When she still didn't answer he said, "The alternative Thursday afternoon activity here is the goat market, unless you'd rather nap, in which case I'll ask you for Thursday night."

"I've never been to a goat market. I might like it."

"I'm starting to know just how those goats feel." He took her hands in both of his, a promise of heat. "I won't let you say no. I'll pick you up Thursday in the lobby at one."

"Does this mean I'm in the clear?"

The amusement drained from his expression. His sigh seemed drawn from the waves breaking on the cold sea side of the corniche. She felt a shudder of unease and straightened away from him, from their banter, and removed her hand from his.

"It means I want to see you again."

"Okay, Lowell," she said, making up her mind. "I'll come to the beach."

FORTY-EIGHT

THURSDAY, IN her room, she suffered a fit of edginess getting ready for the beach outing. Although she walked, rode her bike, and went for regular swims at a nearby health club, she was statuesque. She'd learned to appreciate her curves, to feel she was a sensuous odalisque, but compared to women like Elise and Loren, she was *full*. And her navy bathing suit was exactly like a grandmother's, appropriate for the strict Gulf.

Oh fuck it. At least she had a blue-striped gauze skirt and top. In her EduGulf bag she packed a towel and miniature shampoo and soap from the bathroom. And a hairbrush. And some competitors' brochures to glance through. But what about tonight, when they went out for Pepsi? Should she bring a dress?

The phone rang. "Clare? Lowell. I'm in the lobby."

"I'll be right down." She hurried out, almost forgetting her bag. Her pulse picked up as the elevator descended.

Lowell appeared, the perfect beach date in a simple blue oxford shirt, white jeans and topsiders. Wraparound sunglasses hid his eyes but his grin shone just for her.

His long Land Rover was parked in the circular drive. Julia bounced in the passenger seat, so Clare climbed in the back. "Hi!" cried Elise. Loren smiled. For a few moments the women made small talk about the show, the local sights, and souk shopping, but it was hard to hear with the noise of traffic, the rush of breeze coming in the open windows, and Duran Duran blaring through the speakers. After "Hungry Like a Wolf" the music stopped.

"But it's my favorite!" wailed Julia.

"Not mine," Lowell said. "Now it's the driver's choice."

"You prob'ly want that ugly old Bob Dylan."

Clare smiled to herself.

"I just don't want any more Duran Duran."

"This is Radio Kuwait, where the hits just keep on happening!" A cheery announcer's voice rang out from the vehicle speakers, with the careful enunciation of a Gulf Arab whose English was patterned after Britain. "Springsteen fans, here's the latest from the Boss!"

"Born in the U.S.A." blared out.

At the beach, there were showers and changing rooms, a snack shop, a playground, picnic tables with barbeque grills. Hard to believe they were in this peaceful enclave, where not much further north on mine-filled waters loomed Iran and Iraq, locked in their terrible war.

Jeff Hunter came loping up, in shorts and out of breath. "It's too cold to swim. But some of us are getting up a volleyball game. Come join us!"

"Not me," said Elise. "I'm going to lie down and bake and think of nothing."

"Me too," murmured Loren. Jeff looked abashed.

"I'll play!" Julia shouted. She grabbed Lowell's hand and dragged him behind her. Clare followed the example of Elise and Loren, who spread towels on the sand and stretched out. She felt laughably upholstered in her matronly suit when she saw the tiny bikinis they were wearing, but she enjoyed the feeling of peaceful somnolence that crept over her in the sun, and the hypnotic slap of long, lazy waves. She closed her eyes.

A shadow crossed the hot blue beyond her lids, and she opened her eyes to see Lowell standing beside her. "Want to go for a walk, Clare?" She stood and fastened her skirt.

They didn't talk at first. It was easy just to walk, feeling the light cool sand under her feet and the sun's heat on her bare back, watching bright-sailed boats on the sparkling water. A dune rose sharply to their right.

Lowell said, "Let's climb."

On the steepest part he took her hand. All her concentration was suddenly in her palm and fingers, warm where he clasped them. Sensation flared from her hand up her arm, around her breasts and through her body. She hung on, breathless with exertion and excitement.

At the top they stopped, in a shelflike dip, hidden from view of those on the beach. A breeze dried Clare's brow and ruffled

Lowell's hair. He opened his shoulder bag and took out two sweating bottles of Heineken.

She smiled as he opened one and presented it to her. "Great. Thanks, Lowell."

The strong cool taste was just right. She looked down at the beach. Below to their left was the small area they had climbed from, to their right past further dunes she saw more picnickers, some in the distinctive black and white robes of native Kuwaitis.

Beside her he lay down, linking hands behind his head. His squarish bare feet, so well known from long ago, dug his toes into the sand. She noted white streaks of scars across his ankles and wondered. She tried out a few sentences, something about the setting, or his work, or the show, or even about that shipment, but rejected them. Their silence was enhanced by the faraway waves, faint cries of seagulls, children on the beach and the wind's soft sloughing on the hard sand. She finished her beer and set the empty bottle into the sand.

He asked, "Did you think about me, after we broke up?"

She glanced at him.

"Just yes or no." The sun glinted on his glasses as he tilted toward her.

"Sometimes." How could she confess years of remembering? She'd sound pathetic!

"I thought of you. I wrote you some letters, you probably never got them, there were others I never sent." He sighed suddenly. "I used to have this crazy dream about you."

"You *did*?" How funny, to imagine him writing her letters, dreaming of her. Funny and astonishing. A rush of pleasure tingled her skin.

"For a long time." He sat up and dusted sand off his hands. She saw herself reflected in his sunglasses, hair unraveling, cheeks flushed in an expectant smile.

She looked away fast to fix on a cooler look, so was unprepared for the touch of his fingers on her head. He removed her clip and pins, one by one, until her hair fell around her shoulders and was promptly lifted away to float on the breeze. He dropped his hands.

"Take those shades off, Lowell. I want to see just what you think you're doing."

266

He removed them. His wide eyes moved from hers to her floating hair, to her mouth, and back again to her eyes. He was so close she saw his pupils dilate.

"Well?" she asked sternly, not knowing what she wanted to hear him say.

His dreamy look vanished. He took her hand, palm up, to his mouth. His lips were cool and damp with beer but his tongue was warm as he kissed her.

Instant arousal shocked up her arm and deep inside. She snatched her hand away and closed her palm around his kiss by instinct and not intent. "It's not that simple! A long time has passed. I'm not ... so easily moved. And I'm here just a few days—"

"Let's make the most of it," he interrupted.

"What?"

"You're exactly how I imagined you'd be, at home in any setting, when I was remembering you in Beirut."

"Beirut?"

"I saw this at dinner the other night too. Even with people you've never met, you fit in and charm everyone. I'm sure you were the same in Mexico, in the Kingdom, everywhere you go. Do you realize how unusual you are?"

"What?"

"You're smart and funny and unique." His pupils widened further. "And beautiful."

"What if I'm not ready to reconnect with you?" Heat was smashing disorientation but she shot out her last defense. "You *left* me!"

"My mistake, then. But we're here *now*." He took a long sip of beer, squinting at the sun as he tilted the bottle. His throat moved as he swallowed. He put the bottle into the sand and smiled again. His body had scarcely changed; his Levis snugly encased his legs and thighs. He scooted close for another moment of careful scrutiny. Then he enclosed her.

His lips were warm, smooth, his tongue hot and quick, his embrace enfolding and, she admitted, familiar and welcome, heating her in all the places he'd turned on first. She wanted to clutch him tighter and fan the fierce surging inside.

But what about how she'd feel later, when he was a distant

stranger again? She leaned away even as her mouth was still fastened to his.

He straightened up then too, murmuring, "Let's consider this time a gift."

"A *gift* ... "

"From the wild and generous universe."

"What exactly are you saying?"

"I'm saying "thanks." "

Behind them came faint music. Without hurry he turned to see who was coming. Clare kept her eyes on his face, immobilized by their kiss as by some powerful narcotic.

A *gift*.

"Hi, Jul, you having fun?"

"You hold my radio so I can roll down."

"It's too steep to roll, you'd get stuffed with sand, but you can jump."

"Sure I can roll! It'd be easy!"

"You'd better not roll, Jul. You know I can't run after you," he warned.

"Maybe Clare can." A pout came over Julia's perfect features.

"I want her to stay right here with me." Lowell patted Clare's shoulder. "She's enjoying the view. Why don't you tell us what *you* see?"

"No, I wanna roll down the dune."

"Do *not* test me," he said, staring into Julia's eyes.

"Okay, okay, Jeez." She thrust the radio at him and plunged back down the dune, taking the long leaping steps necessary to keep her balance. They heard yelps of laughter, and a few moments later saw her running toward the beach, hair streaming behind.

"How old is she?" asked Clare.

"Eight. Going on twenty, fast." Lowell shook his head. "She can be difficult."

"She has presence. She looks like you." She laughed. "I thought she *was* yours."

"Really!"

She nodded.

"Funny," he murmured, beginning to smile again, caressing

her back, spreading ripples of ease up and down her spine. "So at the reception, no wonder you seemed reserved. You thought I was *married.*"

"You were reserved too. You thought I was a political agitator."

"Pure conjecture." He encircled her waist.

"Could have fooled me."

"Just mah trainin, Sugah," he drawled. "Had to know who I was dealin with."

"What would you have done if you'd found out I knew what was in that shipment?"

"You don' wanna know."

She stared at him, but a shout from the beach below made them both peer over to watch Julia do a cartwheel on the flat sand. She waved up.

"She's very attached to you."

"I've been pretty constant in her life."

"I can't picture you changing diapers." Several of Clare's friends had children. She'd glimpsed some of the chaos and trauma as well as joy entailed in raising a child.

"Picture it." He grinned. "You name it, I've done it. I was even the labor coach, since Elise was alone. I've done everything for Julia except nurse her."

"You were all living together?"

"We were at my Dad's, in Virginia."

"You took time off to help Elise?"

"I'd been injured. I had to stay at home awhile to recuperate." His shoulders hunched as if against wind. "A story better left for later."

"Is that why you don't run?"

"I can't run for long, or on uneven surfaces. I keep fit in other ways."

She outlined one of his ankles where scars circled like bracelets. "You can tell me."

"We both have a lot to tell. It's a long time. How come you're not married? Those guys in Chicago blind, deaf and stupid?"

"I never looked for marriage." She decided to admit now, quietly, "After my time with you, nobody got that close, even though I had some serious relationships."

"Why didn't they get close?"

"Maybe I was trying to recreate what we had. But it didn't happen."

"My relationships haven't been serious." He pulled her tight so she could feel his thudding heartbeat. "Sometimes I wondered why none of em stuck."

"So ... did you figure out why not?" she murmured into his neck.

"Well, now I'm with you again, I think I know, but I might need ... more analysis." One hand cradled her head while the other moved lightly down her back, up her arm, around to her breast. He kissed her again and she kissed back with all of herself. He pulled away to breathe, "Stay with me tonight."

"Not at your villa. You come to me."

"As soon as I saw you again—" he broke off to push his feet into the sand. "You have the same effect on me."

"I missed you for *years,*" she finally confessed.

"But you didn't want to talk to me, honey, you blew me off when I called your house."

"You said no contact," she reminded him.

"I should have stayed with you when you got hurt at the depot. I let you down." He drew her to him again. "I wish I'd been better for you."

"You thought we had to break up anyway," she mumbled against his cheek. "You were probably right. What could we have done?"

"Stayed in touch. Tried to keep on enjoying each other."

"You *had* to leave."

"I should have been smart enough to find a way to keep you in my life."

"Now I'm the one who has to leave," she began, but he put a finger on her mouth.

"Shh," he whispered. "We'll figure it out like grown-ups this time."

FORTY-NINE

A S CLARE followed Lowell down the dune, a bristling rush of excitement past-and-present jangled inside, warming her skin and tightening her stomach and racing her heart. Halfway down they met Julia. She heard the girl's sprightly chatter and Lowell's crisp replies. She felt the warmth of his hand in hers. She saw the sun, Day-Glo pink, slip beneath the calm water. She smelled enticing grilled meat.

She walked to the people mingling around a bonfire—Elise grinned, Jeff Hunter handed a beer, Loren passed a bowl of guacamole. Lowell went to the van to carry out folding chairs and blankets and she felt most of herself trailing after him.

"Knockin on Heaven's Door" rang in her ears, a boy singing while a wild-haired girl, innocent as milk and lost in love, kissed an ardent, leather-jacketed youth in a grey limestone archway under autumn-gilded leaves.

Snap out of it, she told herself, and went to help Elise make salad.

"Nice lettuce. In the Kingdom it cost seven dollars a head."

"Low talked about you, Clare," Elise said as if reading her mind. "He tried to find you, but I guess you moved around a lot." She smiled. "He's *so* glad you're here."

"Me too," Clare admitted.

She enjoyed seeing, again, the easy way Lowell engineered an evening. From what she remembered of the diplomatic corps in Riyadh, the life was an endless round of work, including near-constant entertainment. Did he get tired, the way she sometimes got tired, of being 'on?' Did he ever want empty time? She asked, when he sat with her.

"This is easy. These people are closest to me, here. But if I could snap my fingers and make em disappear?" he said. "I'd be alone with you on this beach, the sun setting—"

271

"The moon rising," Clare added.

"The breeze blowing—"

"In your hair, can I touch it in front of everyone, maybe like this?" She reached up.

"Let's just go behind that dune. The gulls are so noisy nobody will hear us."

"They'll just hear the Iranians' shelling—" There was, indeed, a distant sound like thunder.

"Right now? That's the Iraqis."

"Oh, whoever."

"It's always something," he agreed, sadly, as their mood lost buoyancy. "And most of the time Americans get the blame."

She tried to lighten up. "And all we want to do is make a few sales, snag a few markets, twist a few government arms—"

"You're in business now and you still feel that way?"

"I'm a realist. My view of the way we manipulate things hasn't changed that much, even though I'm idealistic about global education and excited to help facilitate it with what I know are quality products. I'm proud of what we do at InterTech.

"But, Lowell, hasn't your specific experience shown you we *do* manipulate, throwing U.S. weight around however we can?"

"You think others don't?" He gathered a small handful of sand and let it trickle between his fingers. "In my experience not much can be explained simply. Sometimes the good guys and the bad guys end up working for the same goals, strangely enough, and sometimes not at all."

"But you work for the good guys, right? White hats?"

"I still don't see things in black and white. We ... work." He smiled. "As do you, Clare. But I'm off duty tonight."

Time passed for Clare in a blur of anticipation as night fell, fast and black, and the picnic group packed into their vehicles. Loren left with Jeff Hunter for a party at a nearby British compound. Lowell drove back to the city on the coastal road where the scenery flew. They stopped at his villa to let Elise and Julia out, and for Lowell to get a change of clothes.

As soon as they were alone on the Hilton elevator, he wrapped her tight, kissing her with slow thoroughness and disengaging, unruffled, when the elevator doors opened on Clare's floor.

As soon as they were inside her room he drew her top off and swimsuit down, pinning her arms, and took her breasts in hot hands to his hotter mouth. Her heart slammed against his cheek as he suckled. Not being able to move her arms made his hunger even more exciting.

He covered her breasts with his hands, keeping them warm, as he straightened up and spoke low into her ear. "I wanted to grab you just like this when I first saw you back at IU. But you deserve Champagne and silk sheets and Leonard Cohen or whoever you like serenading from some distant balcony."

"I like being grabbed by you." Her mouth was so dry she could barely say this.

He grinned and took a bottle from the bag he'd set onto the floor. "I did bring bubbly at least." He conjured two glasses and held them toward the spacious bathroom. "Let me serve you in the bath, Mademoiselle, before I grab you again, let's take our time now."

She laughed, still breathless, as he turned on the taps, emptied in the bath-wash miniature, and poured wine. He stripped. He was stronger-looking than in his youth, with the sculpted muscles of dedicated workouts, but there were scars, long and jagged, on his legs and ribcage. She fingered the lines on his torso even as she hesitated to bare her own body. "I'm not seventeen anymore, Lowell."

"I'm not twenty three."

So she had the courage to peel off her swimsuit. They sank into frothy water.

After a couple of toasts he set the glasses on the floor. "You were perfect to me before, Clare, but now—you're a goddess." He slid toward her and clasped her on top of his lap in an embrace so tight, so intimate, she felt dizzy with lust. Then he moved behind her, cradling her between his legs, fondling with slippery hands, practiced and easy, roaming all over for a delirious time before finally opening her and moving his fingers with rythmic intent.

"Oh Lowell," she panted, twisting her head to catch his mouth for an open kiss.

Then he helped her out, wrapped her in a towel, and walked her to the bed where they fell together. When he finally pushed inside, still rubbing with his clever fingers, she was so ready she tightened, throbbed, and exploded into liquid. She thrust against him as every nerve was lapped in a warm phosphorescent sea.

He sank beside her. She felt his breath on her cheek, first rapid and then slowing. She lay cocooned in glow, eyes closed, muscles singing. Finally, she felt able to take a deep breath, and let it out in a long sigh.

Then she turned, slowly tumbling onto him, and snaked her arms to pull him tight. She kept her eyes closed, pressed her face into his neck and licked. He tasted like home. She clung to him as on their first night together, savoring the warm dark and the feeling of him contained in her arms, pressed into near discomfort. He did not move.

FIFTY

SHE WOKE in darkness, heart pounding. Beside her Lowell thrashed, making anxious noises, struggling as if held down. She turned on the lamp. She tried to put her arms around him but he pulled away. His eyes flew open and he took a deep gasping breath.

"Clare, stay." He reached for her. "Stay here."

"I have to," she reminded him gently. "It's my room."

He sat up straight and pushed his hair back. Then he looked at her and told her about his old nightmare where they were snow-veiled apart.

"Maybe your dream relates to that last scene we had? Maybe it represents the end of passion, the way that snowstorm put a ... white-out on our love." She used the word unconsciously and looked to see if he was still so shy of it. He was staring at nothing. "Something ... allegorical," she tapered off.

"Why now?" He turned his vacant gaze to her and it sharpened into alarm. "Clare, it's been years since I had that dream. I never told anyone about it."

"It's been years since we were together. Maybe ... being close to me again disturbs you."

He shook his head.

"Don't dismiss the idea. I never fit into your plan. I was too radical." She plucked at the bedspread. "Maybe a threat."

"You were an unexpected experience," he said slowly. "You made an impression on me like no one else. I think the dream let me know how sad I was to leave you."

I love you for saying this.

He drew her with him as he lay down. "I want to hold on tight, now I found you again." She felt his deep sigh echo her own. "I don't know why this dream came tonight, but I attend to my instincts better than I used to. I'm attending now. Let's trade

275

life stories and see what we turn up."

"Life stories?"

"Tell me something I didn't get the chance to learn about you."

She had to think fast. "I like horror stories!"

"We have *so* much in common, babe, I am a true Stephen King fan."

"Really? Me too!"

"He's a New England classic. Picks up where Washington Irving left off." He shifted to look into her eyes. "I want to hear about your last ten years. Best concert."

"Um ... Bob Dylan, 1975, Chicago. You?

"Stones, '78, London. Worst album?"

"Anything disco—except Donna Summer. She's great. Even in the Kingdom I heard her all the time on the underground stations, and at every party."

"Good answer. What's your favorite *new* music?"

"You know I could talk all *night* about this." She nibbled his chin. "I'm sure they're your favorites too, we shared similar taste ... Michael Jackson, of course, everyone loves him, especially region rats like me."

"Yeah, I remember."

"The Jackson Five are from Gary. We *love* them."

"Clare the Red region rat." He smiled. "Other bands?"

"Some Fleetwood Mac. Dire Straights. Men at Work.. Suzanne Vega. The Police. Bruce Springsteen, of course. Ramones. The Cure. Boney M are a funny trip and so are Talking Heads. Bob Seger—"

He kissed her mouth as she was still naming great talents. "As usual, your musical taste is impeccable. But I want to hear more about you. Best accomplishment?"

"Going to the Kingdom—knowing no one—to take the Riyadh U job. You?"

"Recovering from a bad accident without permanent neurosis. At least I hope not." He grinned. "Best lover?"

You were the best! But his eyes' brightness wanted to tease out truth or dare. "Pass," she told him primly, and enjoyed his laughing squeeze.

"At least *I'm* fessin up. You're my best ever, Clare. What was your worst experience?"

This required a more serious mode. "Definitely that time in Mexico when I realized ... " She recounted, hesitantly sometimes, what her life had been, while he watched her. When she got to the part about Julio, he asked, "Did you ever find out where he disappeared himself to?"

"I just wanted to forget when I got back to the States."

"We could have some people check it out."

"Creepy, Lowell, "people" like the thugs who busted up his cell. I put that episode behind me when I got over feeling disillusioned."

"I understand." He took a deep breath, and told her the story of Ahmed. She listened in mounting distress as he spoke.

She outlined his scars with a light fingertip. "You earned your stripes."

"That's what the doctors said."

"Don't blame yourself."

"I still do," he said quietly. "And I could never go back to Beirut to tell his family how sorry I was. They thought I was dead too." He caught her hand, tracing his ribs, and caressed it. "I learned something I needed to know from that time."

"I guess we were both innocents abroad."

"You might have been innocent, although you understood the concept of global revolution. But I was ignorant. I was so consumed in Lebanon, trying to get ahead, I didn't observe the environment as I'd been trained. I didn't do my job."

"You paid too high a price for that."

"Not as high as some. I think ... Americans have a tough time grasping other people's political motivations. They're more severe, depending on the country, than we're able to fully imagine."

"Mexico showed me that. And Chile, in its way." They lay a moment in silence. She tried to lift the somber mood. "How did you come to switch from politics to commerce, anyway? And bypass being ambassador to France?"

"I took a long time after Beirut to think about my goals. When Julia was about a year old and Elise had settled down with her at my Dad's, I just ... took off. I traded my diplomatic passport for an ordinary one, and I worked my way around the world."

"You? *You* dropped out?" She laughed. "How?"

"I took odd jobs everywhere I went. Part time, low wage, communicating in sign language, you name it. *Lots* of restaurant and hotel work." His rueful grin conceded the way she'd lassoed her ambition to his, during their breakup conversation, and the way he'd dimissed restaurant work then. "I started by driving down to Mexico. I thought of you, wondered if you were still there." He hugged her. "But by then I'd given up the idea of contacting you. I got as far south as Argentina, where I visited my mother."

"How was that?"

"Irritating, but necessary. I was so pissed at her for so long it was a relief to have a big shouting match. It allowed us to be natural with each other again."

"Did you ... like her husband?"

"I hated his guts, and he knew it. He stayed away from me." He grinned. "But he gave me the fare to fly to London." She listened, fascinated, as he relayed his two year journey throughout Europe, Africa and Asia.

"It's so unlike you!" she exclaimed at the end of his narrative. "I mean, I remember you on a straight track. You were so ... ambitious."

"Arrogant," he corrected. "After Beirut I had to start over. I had to know what life was really like outside the States, outside the viewpoint I always had the luxury of holding."

"But when you came back, you joined the Foreign Service again."

"The commercial section. I decided trade makes better allies than official diplomacy. But my first posting was to Tehran." There was a faraway look in his eyes. "That was ... a trip and a half, as we used to say. Confirmed my choice to stay out of politics. I didn't like the way we handled ourselves there, ditching the Shah—who was our own creation as a tyrant—and then scrambling around for favors from Bani Sadr since we were so clueless about Khomeini. I got as disgusted with the government as you were, when we met."

"But you stayed with it. You went on to Egypt."

"I decided to be optimistic. And I liked learning more

Arabic." He leaned on his elbow to study her. "How'd *you* get so fluent? Aside from being a natural linguistic genius?"

She poked him. "In the Kingdom, the university gave us lessons. It was hard getting Arabic down, after how easy Spanish was, even thought they do share some cognates ... but I persevered. I'm comfortable with the language now."

"So you started using it right away with InterTech?"

"Yes, in the Kingdom it was easy to practice with people I met selling into womens' schools."

"For a gal who hates to study you've sure done wonders in the field of international education, Red." His grin came with a little tickling poke of his own. She squirmed away, giggling. "And in Arabic, no less, *ya salaam*. How'd you keep up in the States?"

"I hired a tutor in Chicago."

"Is there much of an Arabic-speaking community in Chicago?"

"Small. My teacher's Syrian."

"Syrian," he repeated. The remote look came into his eyes again as he fell silent.

279

FIFTY-ONE

"LOWELL?"

He blinked, got up to fetch the bottle of Champagne, took a gulp. "You know how edgy this show has made some of us. It's just a tense time. I didn't even want Elise and Julia to come for this visit, but she's incredibly stubborn. Insists on giving me "Christmas in Kuwait"—as if I care!

"And now we're even more anxious, trying to figure out the sabotage of five different shipments."

This wasn't what she wanted to think about.

He pulled on his jeans and drank again. "When I heard about those bloody tapes ... with you as the sender!"

But if he wanted to talk this over again, maybe she could help him think it through. "Lowell, I didn't mention ... I used these new forwarders ... "

"You *what?*" His alarmed exclamation startled her.

"They saved us a lot of money," she explained. "Commerce vetted them in Chicago before I signed them. Ibrahim said they weren't a likely cause of the damage. I really don't think—"

"Changing forwarders is significant! It opens a door to ... vulnerability."

She found herself scrambling to diffuse his agitation. "I can find out if they have an office in Beirut, where the first landing was."

"But you didn't want to tell me about them." His frown cooled into scrutiny as he sat up straighter on the side of the bed. "Yet you said, before, you said you knew nothing."

"I didn't think of this in time to mention it." She didn't need to feel defensive; she'd evaluated the forwarders' records and gotten plenty of references. "But I stand by my choice."

"But ... what else might you not be telling me? What else might you have ... overlooked?" His tone chilled further with each slow word. "What if this change allowed someone to access your container? If someone might have used you without your being aware? You mention a Syrian tutor, for example. So I wonder if you've ever been involved— in the Kingdom, or in the States—with any Iranians? Palestinians?"

"Sure. I taught English for several years—after I finished my B.A. I taught in Chicago. Most of my students were Iranians then. And there were lots of Arabs too."

"Well ... " His gaze sharpened. "I mean *involved*, Clare. Did you ever have a relationship with one of these guys?"

"A couple of times." She resented his implication. "But it's none of your business."

"Yeah, I know, and I don't mean to be intrusive. But you have to agree, a connection like that is not an unreasonable possibility." The air in the room suddenly felt charged with tension. "So I'm just wondering ... were they politically active? Some Middle Eastern students in the States are. Can you think of any link, recently revived? Are you still corresponding with any of these guys?"

She pulled the blanket around her nakedness, a shield against his obnoxious line of inquiry. She bit back a pissed-off reply to give herself time to think.

"Stop scowling and look at it objectively, Clare. You're in a nice position now to help an old ... friend. Let's say he calls you up and asks for a job. Or if he can send something to his family back home, in your next shipment. Or he recommends his cousin the whiz translator. Or he has this freight forwarder he wants you to try—is that how you got the new ones? Or maybe he has contacts for you to look up next time you're going to Amman."

She hated his tone. "I'm not that naïve," she snapped.

"So maybe no former boyfriend," he said aridly. "What about colleagues in the States? What other Arabs or Iranians do you do business with?"

"You want a *list*? I'm responsible for all our sales to the Middle East. Except Israel, of course. That's the European division. As you probably know already, with your background checks." He nodded. "I have *hundreds* of contacts. Sales reps, purchase agents, clerks, school officials, researchers. Ministers.

Princes. Princesses. Friends of my boss."

"His father was Palestinian."

"But he's—Lowell, come on. He's been an American for years. His mom and wife are WASPs. He sent his kids to Jesuit school. His family's older than God and twice as wealthy." Anger flamed in her chest. "He's also *totally* sincere about education! If I didn't believe that I wouldn't be working for him. I am not stupid."

"I know. But what about other people, Clare? Anyone around you or Khaleedy or even around your tutor." He folded his arms across his chest. *As if he's sober-suited, behind a huge desk, scrutinizing some lowly employee.*

His bare chest was tan, she noted, with more hair than in his youth, hair that ran suggestively downward into his jeans. Amazing to think they had been wrapped together asleep an hour ago. His cold voice interrupted her thoughts. "Any wild guess."

"You make me sound like an idiot. No one makes decisions for me, so why the hell should I guess! I don't live in some paranoid spy novel!"

"It's a dirty job, hey, but somebody has to do it," he said with a humor that did not touch his gaze.

"It's pretty fucking dirty, all right!" Hot indignation fueled her voice. "At least in my line of work I don't have to seduce anybody into giving me information!"

His hands whipped out to grab her shoulders. "*Don't.* I wanted you just the way you wanted me, nothing to do with information, you know that."

"Then act like a lover, not an interrogator! You said we didn't have to talk about this!"

His grip loosened. "I'm seeing you three ways right now, Clare. As my lover, of course, we're still so good together. I don't want to lose you again." He frowned and cupped her face in his hands. "But I wonder if you're a possible connection ... or part of a pattern."

She pulled away. "You don't trust me."

"I do. But maybe not the people around you. And I'm sorry to be trashing our reunion like this."

"Your dream made you suspicious of me."

"Come on. That's irrational."

282

"You still see me as that lying radical kid." To her chagrin, her voice broke.

"Clare, this is not about the past."

"It is totally about the past. If you didn't still think of me as some extremist, you'd never accuse me this way."

"I'm not accusing you! There's no reason to sound so defensive. You're not the only one, I told you, at least four other consignees had this happen and they're all being very closely monitored to figure out where the trails lead."

"So did you ... decide to stick close to me? *Watch* me, see where my trail leads?"

He recoiled. "I don't have to watch you."

"What, you don't mix business with pleasure?" she asked, in sarcastic reproach. "You're above it now?"

"I'm above it," he agreed quietly. "I told you I've been out of the political arena since Beirut." His body seemed to contain the stillness of cold marble as he contemplated her, and the light in his eyes was equally cold, as if he beheld an enemy.

"You took advantage of our closeness to bring this up!"

"It wasn't my intention."

"But it's so much more important than really getting to know me again, right? So ... let me get this straight. You said you see me three ways. One, as a great fuck, just like the old days, hallelujah. It was good for me too, Lowell, you've got even better moves. Two, as some kind of gullible pawn or worse, a frickin *terrorist*." She paused. "I can't wait to hear what the third way is. This is just like getting wishes from the evil fairy."

She got out of bed, drawing a blanket around her, and spoke with all the distance she could muster. "I'm going to take a shower. When I come out I don't want to see you here."

He began to speak, but she held up a hand. "I'll cooperate in every way with your investigation to clear my name, and InterTech's, before I go back to the States. But I don't want to talk to *you*. Let your, your operatives or whatever question me. Since they're the disinterested professionals."

FIFTY-TWO

W HEN CLARE came out of her shower he was gone, and the bed was made, and the room looked as spare and empty as an architect's model in the clean grey dawn. What she wanted most was to throw herself onto the bed in an anguished fit and howl until the pain lessened.

You didn't have to say you wanted to hold on. And making up some moronic *dream!* She ripped his pillow from the bed and flung it with all her strength into a corner. It landed with a satisfying thud. *Straightforward sex would have been just fine. Better, in fact, without the nasty dose of nostalgia. Gift from the universe, my* ass!

She shuddered and closed her eyes for a moment. Then, calmly, she retrieved the pillow, re-made the bed, got dressed, and called for a pot of coffee. By noon she had emptied the contents of her briefcase and gone through each piece of paperwork. She completed telexes back to the States to be transmitted in the business office downstairs. She wrote out invoices and drafted a cover letter to each person who had stopped by the booth. Khaleedy would arrange delivery with the requeste items or catalogs.

Finally she stood, stretched, and wandered to the window. She looked down at the pool again, longingly. How great it would be to have a swim.

On impulse she ruffled through the cards she had collected at the show, and found the one from a woman who'd come with a British publishing company. She was here at the Hilton; she'd scribbled her room number on the back of the card. By lucky chance she was in, and agreed happily to brave the all-male pool area. They spent a pleasant couple of hours sunbathing, doing laps, and having lunch. Clare felt light-headed with the relief of inconsequential chatter and with the exhaustion brought about by sleeplessness and unaccustomed sunshine. By four she was

284

back in her room, asleep.

She got up at six to get ready for the dinner at Khaleedy's house. The relaxing afternoon and the solid nap had eased some of her brittle tension and she felt able to get through the evening with a passable show of good guesthood. She gave her hair a final smoothing in the mirror, collected her bag of gifts for the family, and went down to the lobby promptly at seven.

She was pleased his wife came along. Mrs. Khaleedy, a sweet-faced round woman, smiled at Clare, who took her arm and walked out with her behind her husband, showing respect for cultural dictates.

The Khaleedy home was a comfortable villa like so many Clare had seen in the Kingdom, with a formal living room where they drank fruit juice, an equally forbidding dining room where they ate a savory meal, and an opulent oriental-style family room where, after dinner, Clare sat on the floor with Mrs. Khaleedy, who was Samira by then.

Three of the four Khaleedy youngsters joined them, sprawling on the carpets and cushions, and they watched videos of the family's recent trip to Disneyland, the second son's high school graduation, and a cousin's wedding. Clare watched the screen as the girls in the wedding party danced, throwing their sheets of hair from side to side and gracefully folding and unfolding their paneled skirts, to the rhythmic accompaniment of a women's band.

Then it was time for gifts. Samira presented her with a sheer, beautifully embroidered Kuwaiti overdress. Of course she had to try it on, and had to mimic a few of the dance steps the eager girls showed her after they banished the men from the room, and had to undo her hair so that she could swing it back and forth in the proper stylized manner.

Suddenly in the spirit of things, she was genuinely laughing and clapping at the girls' display. With the resurgence of emotion in her body, she felt tears come to her eyes, but hoped the family would think they were mirth-induced. She handed out her gifts— French perfume for Samira, Bears and Bulls tee shirts for the youngsters.

"I brought one for your oldest son," she told Samira, bringing it out and looking at her inquiringly. "I couldn't remember if he was still at school or working."

"You can give it to Amir yourself," Samira said. "He couldn't join us this evening because he's studying for exams, but I know he'll want to meet you." Clare followed Samira out of the family room and upstairs.

"He's a serious student," Samira went on. "This is his last year at university. He helps his father at the office sometimes." She smiled. "So you could say he also works for InterTech. And Mazen too—his friend."

She knocked on a door halfway down the upper corridor. Faint sounds, some kind of speech, were instantly silenced and the door was opened. Clare took a step back, physically startled. The youth was straight out of the Arabian Nights—the sultriest-looking young man she had ever seen. He blinked enormous black eyes at them, shook back jet hair, and moved aside gracefully to let them enter. He did not speak. He stood tall, imposing in a snow-white robe, while Samira made introductions.

"Mazen, this is Clare Meredith from InterTech. Amir, say hello." Another youth stood, from a desk in the corner. He had the friendly open face of his parents.

Clare shook hands. "Amir, it's good to meet you."

Amir thanked her for the Bulls shirt while Mazen backed into a corner, mute. Samira asked Amir to come to the kitchen for the tea she had prepared them, leaving Clare alone with the silent friend, who kept his eyes resolutely on the floor.

Clare, staring at him, her senses jolted by his sheer beauty and by his silence, reminded herself that she was in the Gulf, where good men are reserved and good women are invisible. Mazen was being polite. He might be one of the new conservatives of the young generation, who were into fundamentalist Islam—the tension within her expanded into alarm.

"You've done some work for InterTech," she remarked courteously. He nodded once, briefly, still looking down.

"He wanted to help pick up your cartons from the port last week when I was in an exam," said Amir, returning to the room with tea and biscuits. "He's lucky enough to have a cousin in Customs." He patted his friend's shoulder, then cocked his head to listen to a telephone's loud ring, and when one of his sisters called him he smiled apologetically. "Excuse me again."

The silence was palpable after he left the room. Mazen's onyx gaze slid inch by inch across the floor as far as Clare's knees before returning quickly to his own feet. Clare took a step towards him.

"Please talk to me, Mazen," she told him quietly. "I have some questions about the cartons you tried to pick up for the show." Still he did not move a muscle. Clare stepped closer. "Don't you speak English?" she demanded.

Finally he gave her a fleeting glance. "I don't speak to women," he said softly.

"Mazen." She spoke firmly and put her hands on his shoulders, deliberately shattering his space. She had to look up to see his face. His fine, thin nostrils flared as he tried to back further into the wall. "Do you know anything about the damaged labels?"

"I don't understand. Please, ask to Mr. Khaleedy." He folded his hands again and stared at the floor. Frustrated, Clare stepped into the hallway. He was about to close the door behind her when she held out a hand to stop him.

"In case you change your mind about talking to me—" She reached into her pocket and took out one of her cards. "I'm at the Hilton this coming week. Call me there, or get in touch through Mr. Khaleedy's office."

She ducked her head under his gaze to force him to meet her eyes, and gave him what she hoped was a meaningful stare. "Think about it, Mazen."

He looked away immediately, but Clare thought she glimpsed a flicker of some emotion—fear, or defiance, or perhaps just mere irritation—acknowledging her words. And his brown fingers closed around the card. This was something, at least.

Clare made her farewells. Again Samira accompanied her husband in escorting Clare back to the hotel, but Clare's attempt to draw her out regarding Amir and Mazen proved fruitless. The woman had nothing but praise for both youths. Amir was a source of pride to the entire family, and Clare was loath to disturb their picture of him. Still, she tried to probe gently.

"Are they very religious boys?" she asked. "They were so quiet and Mazen seemed so ... reserved. A nice quality."

Samira glanced at Khaleedy in the front seat and then leaned close to Clare to reply in a low voice, "Amir doesn't believe. He still goes to the mosque on Friday with his father, so there is no shame to the family, but—" she smiled sadly. "It is a stone in my heart. I know Mazen shares his feeling."

Clare nodded, mind racing. "Maybe they will reconsider," she said. "I thought they were both impressive. Thank them again for trying to help with the boxes."

FIFTY-THREE

B ACK IN her room, Clare collapsed onto the bed.
What a horrible week! Unbelievable: her professional *and* personal lives, which only a week ago had been running smoothly, if without ecstasy, suddenly entwined in the same turmoil.

This is what I get for lobbying so hard to do the show all by myself. Big bad dealmaker me.

There was no one to confide in.

Certainly not her boss Georges—not unless she cleared up the mystery.

Already she was responsible for InterTech's scrutiny by Kuwait Customs—her name on the cartons, her use of new forwarders—and was now also responsible for InterTech's potential alienation from the importantly connected regional U.S. Commercial Attache, dammit.

Of course Georges would not blame her outright, but an aura of incompetence or naivete might make him see fit to name someone else to manage the Middle East Division. Already she'd had to fight to prove she deserved, and could handle, the position: her age, her sex, her nationality and even her hair color all worked actively against her in this job.

There was nobody in the company she could query; eventually whatever she said would filter back to Georges. Anyway, she wasn't close enough to any co-worker to confess her anguish; her persona at work was always upbeat, witty, and professional.

It would be great to chat with her best friend Angie, but Angie spent many winter weekends at her Wisconsin cabin, hibernating with some hunky companion and cross-country skiing. She would not welcome or even understand a teary call from Clare. Besides, she would probably advise Clare to go back to the obvious person right here she should contact.

"Clear the air," she could hear Angie saying. "No matter what he thinks of you, you need his help to straighten out this thing."

Lowell really should be informed about the mysterious Mazen and his cousin at Customs. Maybe she could call Jeff Hunter and leave a message only Lowell would understand—she did not want to upset what was probably a delicate balance of surveillance etiquette and hierarchy amongst spies. She looked up Jeff's number in the show booklet, and quickly dialed.

"Jeff Hunter speaking," his cheery voice answered on the first ring.

"Hello Jeff, Clare Meredith."

"Well hi! That was a good picnic yesterday, huh!"

"Yes—"

"We manage to enjoy ourselves out here in the desert," he said. "Now, what can I do for you at this late hour?"

"Well, it's a bit delicate. I need you to get a message to L—to Mr. Goodenow—"

"Hey, no problem! He's right here."

Be professional, she told herself. *This is business.*

"Yes?" Lowell's voice was wary.

"I went to Khaleedy's to dinner. A friend of his son's tried to help with my boxes at Customs."

"Don't say any more, please," he interrupted. There was a pause and she heard his muffled voice talking to Jeff before coming back on the line. "About this—I need to see you. Fifteen minutes." He hung up.

Oh, God. She straightened the bed, repaired her makeup, ordered coffee and sat at the little table. Then she got up, placed her briefcase and some papers on the bed, as if that could disguise its function somehow.

The first rap at the door jolted her into a stern expression, but it was room service. As she was signing the check a second knock came, on the open door—Lowell.

He had neither slept nor shaved. There was not a trace of yesterday's sexy beach host, nor the suave diplomat, nor the insouciant youth. As soon as the door closed, he walked around the room in some kind of curious inspection, peering into the corners and under the furniture, finally taking the phone receiver apart and re-assembling it. Then he went to the window, twitched the drapes open a crack, and peered into the darkness. Clare stood by the table, waiting.

Finally he turned toward her. He seemed about to reach for her, but his arms didn't even lift as he looked her over with a searching frown. His voice, when he finally spoke, was quiet and serious. "Clare. Last night. I'm sorry."

"What ... exactly ... are you sorry about?"

"I thought I could pick up where we left off. I acted impulsively." His frown deepened so all she saw was regret and distance. "But then I took advantage, as you said, I let my worry outweigh consideration for your feelings. I shouldn't have tried to go back in time, I guess ... "

She nodded quickly, not trusting herself to speak, not willing to show any sign of the sorrow his sober words evoked. She closed herself to feeling, and sat down.

He sat across from her and folded his hands on the table. "Tell me." His gaze didn't leave hers as she spoke, his hands didn't move until she finished, when he reached for the coffee thermos. He poured a cup for each of them.

"The conflict here between Shiites and Sunnis, well, you know already. We're all afraid. But we don't understand what kind of clandestine activity might be going on. I told you, your shipment was only one of a number of unusual recent signs. And although the evidence is pointing to Hezbollah—the pro-Khomeini group—we've no idea who or what their target might be, if there is some kind of plan."

He scrubbed his face suddenly, as if trying to wake himself up. "I told Commerce to cancel U.S. participation in this show, but the ambassador depends on the goodwill of people who want to promote business as usual, boost exports, as you know. If we can just get through this week—" He put his cup on the table.

"Thanks again. You've been very helpful. It may not be the shy boy—it may be the cousin at Customs. This gives us something to go on." He stood.

"*Are* you ... CIA?" The question came out in an unintended hushed voice, and Clare felt irritated with herself.

A tired vestige of smile crossed his face. "We're not spies.We cover them. But I'll get whatever information I can to the right people. You've helped," he repeated. "If you need to speak to me again—" he glanced at the phone. "The hotel switchboard can hear everything you say. I don't mean to frighten you. Just be aware." He walked to the door.

She rose to stand next to him. Could she fix this?

"Clare." His answering look was miserable—eyes hooded and mouth downturned—but ultimately reserved. "You're ... I wish you the best. You deserve it." He turned and walked away. The door closed behind him with a small terminal click.

This time she gave in immediately to her impulse to call Angie, turning from the door to the phone in blind desperation. When Angie's voice answered, Clare gripped the receiver in both hands.

"Angie, it's Clare."

"Well hi! Are you back so soon?"

The pleasure and familiarity in her friend's voice were so comforting that Clare's resolve melted. She bit back a sob. "No, I'm still in Kuwait."

Her anguish made the words dramatic, and Angie asked, bewildered, "Aren't you supposed to be?"

Clare told her the story as best she could, mindful of Lowell's warning about eavesdroppers. The relief of confiding made her tears roll faster and she had to stop talking. Angie's voice, when she responded, was thoughtful.

"I've known you almost six years, and I've never heard you so upset." She paused. "It's significant you met your Lowell again. I remember how emotional you got when you first told me about him. He might be the love of your life! Pay attention."

"But I don't know if he wanted me because of me, or if it was just to get information. Can you imagine a profession where you have to seduce people as part of a job description?"

"Sure. Sales."

"You know what I mean. He didn't have to act like that."

"Maybe he couldn't help it. You seem to see him as such a smoothie, but from your description of the way he's behaving right now, he sounds pretty awkward to me. Emotionally awkward. He can't keep his cool with you."

"He was extremely cool just now."

"Well, duh, he's embarrassed! He knows he was a jerk, and he's sorry. Plus he's got this bizarro business to worry about."

"*I've* got a lot to worry about! I could lose my job!"

"Well, he might too, if things go haywire." Angie chuckled. "Maybe you two can start a Middle East consultancy."

"How can you be laughing about it?"

"You've fallen in love with him again. You better grab him."

"I don't even *like* him right now! Anyway, he's not grabbable." Clare frowned at the floor. "This isn't what I expected from you."

"You want me to say he sounds rotten, and it's hopeless, and forget him. You think you'll do that? You think you'll come back here next week and he'll just fade away? You think you'll never, for the rest of your life, ever wonder what if?"

Angie's vehemence was so clear Clare held the phone away from her ear. She could practically see Angie's dark eyes snapping, her black curls quivering. "I think the chances for real connection with people are rare. Life *is* people, Clare, it's how we are with them and what they mean to us. And I'm tickled to see you getting all hot and bothered. You've always been so ... removed."

"*Have* I?"

"Yes. You're ... guarded. I say, grab him. Take an extra week, tell your boss you're exploring new schools or whatever. Christmas is in two weeks, don't you get some time off? It'll give you a chance to figure out what's happening, both with him and the other deal."

Clare was silent.

"When will you be back in that part of the world? And what is more important here?"

"I wish I *were* there," Clare confessed finally. "I wish I were spending the weekend at your cabin, playing cards, going to that funny little bar—"

"My guest wouldn't think highly of that," Angie teased. "At least he'd better not." They both laughed. "Clare, you didn't get where you are at InterTech by hiding out. I saw you fight up every step of the way. So be bold! Grab the guy, and find the culprit. Think Nancy Drew."

"God it's good to talk to you."

"Anytime. Now call him. I bet he's pining over you."

"He's not the pining type."

"They all pretend not to be." Angie snickered. "Call him."

"Okay. Thanks."

She dialed the number at his villa, not sure exactly what she would say but determined to make it the right thing as soon as she heard his voice. There was no answer. She tried Jeff Hunter. No answer there either. She was wide awake now.

She rose and looked out the window. Her balcony faced the Gulf, a moving black gleam in the night. Arc lights shone on the empty corniche. Precisely placed palms swayed, and she opened the balcony door to feel the breeze, and to look at the waves breaking slowly on the sand. The Gulf reminded her of the Caribbean—calm and shallow for what seemed like miles of coast. She saw the embassy compound across the corniche, the top of its flagpole lit as if to remind all, who might see it, of the meaning of Old Glory. A lone vehicle passed by the security gate.

As she watched, trying to guess which villa was Lowell's, the sky lit up. Before she could decipher its source she heard an accompanying thunderous sound and felt an instantaneous shaking. Her feet knew this feeling from Mexico. *Earthquake.*

FIFTY-FOUR

Virginia 1983

WHY WAS all this snow on the road? And why were all these *mountains* in her way? Wasn't Virginia supposed to be warm? Wasn't it in the South? State geography often failed her; tiny bunched-up New England, the Atlantic coast one long squiggly line, those big squares west of Chicago all alike. She'd traveled more outside than inside this country.

She'd never navigated such a scary road with such manic drivers. Actually, 'navigated' was putting it bravely. She was hugging the shoulder and going as slowly as she dared.

"Can't you see this is a blizzard?" she shouted at the next truck who almost sideswiped her little rental car. "Slow down, for Christ's sake!"

Another rendition of "Deck the Halls" came on the radio and she slammed it off. If she sang along, knowing every word of every festive verse, doing the wonderful harmonies, she might get distracted and plunge into the crevasses which took turns gaping on each side of the highway. She was too frightened to take her eyes from the road for even a minute to look at the directions she'd scribbled during her phone conversation with Elise. She remembered 'just inside Loudon County,' though, and some mention of "several farms up the hill."

They shouldn't call it "Skyline Drive," so lazy and bucolic-sounding. Its name should be "Jagged Cliffs with Falling Rocks. Ice Shoulders. Killer Truckers on Deadline During a Christmastime Blizzard. In Darkest Night." Like some awful surrealist painting.

She knew her nerves were jangly from the drive, from too much coffee and too little space on the too-full flight from Chicago, and the days-long return from Kuwait City with its sleepless nights before that. But she had to admit the biggest nerve-wracker was her own boldness in coming to see Lowell, to whom she hadn't spoken since their last somber parting.

Al Dawa, a splinter group of Hezbollah, had coordinated a series of cab bomb and other attacks on Kuwait City. Both U.S. and French Embassies were hit, along with the airport and key water and oil facilities. There were five casualties as a result, about sixty injuries, and impairment to the airport and Hilton. The U.S. Embassy compound had avoided collapses since the car bomber did not drive into the most populous facility, but there was significant smoke damage throughout the enclave.

Clare and her fellow show participants left Kuwait as soon as transport could be arranged. She stayed several days with the Khaleedy family, who'd welcomed her warmly. After another awkward conversation with Mazen she'd determined there was no shady collusion attributable to his assistance at the InterTech office. But there'd been no way to probe further about his cousin at Customs, nor to query Michael and Frazier or anyone else at EduGulf regarding compromised shipments, in the wake of the assaults.

Elise answered when she'd finally gotten through the embassy switchboard.

"Clare, he's in a local ICU. Smoke inhalation. Pretty bad. He was alone at the office building nearest the site of the blast, passed out, but rescue crews found him." Elise paused. "We're … *really* glad they found him. He's conscious now, being evacuated to the States tomorrow. I'd tell you to go see him but they wouldn't let you in."

Clare took awhile before saying, "Thanks for telling me." She didn't know how to go on.

"He'll be home with us for Christmas." Elise sounded determined. "I've got the house all decorated in my mind. But how are *you*, Clare? How's everyone coping at the Hilton?"

"We're making plans to get out however we can, with the hotel and airport damage. I'm staying at my agent's house until it's sorted." She tried to sound upbeat. "The show must go on, but in different venues now. We're following up with local customers to make sure their orders are filled, that kind of thing."

"So you're okay?"

"My agent and his family have been wonderful. I'm fine."
But her voice must have given away to Elise how unsteady she
was feeling, not because of the city-wide shock, which was
generating city-wide support, but because she was aching so for
Lowell.

"You poor kid! You're probably ready to go straight home
and see your Mom!"

Clare's laugh was still shakier than she could control. "Oh,
yes! I'm seeing her right before she goes to spend Christmas at
my brother's in California."

"But then ... where will *you* be at Christmas?"

"My friends and I usually throw ourselves a great party."

There was a few seconds' silence. Then Elise said, "Listen,
Clare. You are the most important person on Low's mind. When
he was fighting to come back I heard him say your name ... *only*
yours. I'm inviting you for Christmas in Virginia. Fly into Dulles,
we're in west Loudon County—just off the Skyline if you want
the scenic route—you can't miss us."

FINALLY SHE caught a sign looming on the road ahead, and
swung cautiously toward the exit. The "hill" was another
mountain and the "farms" were tracts as big as several city
blocks, but she found what looked like the right place, unless
there was more than one Goodenow in the county. To her relief,
the road leading in was neatly plowed. Her shoulders finally
relaxed as she drove easily down the long, sinuous driveway. She
opened all the windows to take steadying breaths of cold pine-
scented fresh air. *Heavenly.*

So this is where he grew up. The stately brick structure seemed to
flare into the hilly woods around it, spreading elegant wings, yet
for all its size it gave an impression of grace. And homeyness.
The tall spruces leading up the walk were bedecked with
twinkling white lights and there was an enormous red-berried fir
and holly wreath on the door. She could see, behind sheer
curtains on a huge French window in the first left wing, a
Christmas tree lit in riotous color.

"Clare!" Elise opened the door and hugged her. "You made
great time from Dulles. Must've been no traffic."

"Oh, there was some, going pretty fast."

"Cute hat!" The car rental place had been handing out Santa hats and Clare'd put one on to keep warm. "Welcome. Jacket and wet shoes off? Drink? Bathroom? My brother?"

"Yes to all the above."

"Since Low's taking his usual late afternoon nap you can enjoy your first activities at leisure. I'm fixing you a Tom n Jerry. Warm you up." She led Clare into a cozy den.

"Where's the rest of the family?"

"We're in the back, cocktail hour in the greatroom, but Low fell asleep by the parlor tree." She indicated a room across the entry hall, with half-open pocket doors. "Have your reunion and come see us later. Dinner in about an hour."

"Is he feeling more energetic?"

"Since we talked this morning?" Elise smirked as she handed Clare a warm mug. "Go see for yourself."

"And you're *sure* he doesn't mind surprises ... "

Elise gave her a friendly little push. "Make yourself at home. Bathroom's there."

Clare splashed water on her face, dried with an embroidered Christmas towel, brushed out her hair, refreshed her makeup, savored creamy Tom n Jerry. She tilted her Santa hat in a fetching manner. The rim and pom-pom matched her pretty, fluffy angora sweater, its flattering low neckline iridescent with cream sequin braid. She'd deliberately chosen this to disarm his reaction to seeing her. *Don we now our gay apparel, fa la la ...*

Now she was within yards of him. These felt like the last moments of nervous energy she would ever need to expend. She shook out her hands, arms, shoulders, left the bathroom and looked around.

She liked the way the Goodenows lived: though the core of the house appeared to be colonial-era, it was well kept with gleaming floors and woodwork, thick carpets and comfortable-looking furniture in deep colors that complemented the walls and artwork. *So warm and easy!* She recalled his apartment in Bloomington, his villa in Kuwait: this was his model.

She finished her drink, filled the mug with water from the den, and padded in her winter socks to the dim, quiet room Elise called the parlor. The big tree she'd glimpsed from the outside threw colored lightspots onto the gleaming wood floor and filled the room with the rich fragrance of Christmas. Falling snow caught reflections of the lit spruces on the long lawns outside. *Like being in a snowglobe.*

Lowell was draped under a scarlet chenille throw on a couch facing a sizzling fire. She sat in the armchair next to him, watching. The anxiety of that week in Kuwait City wasn't apparent as he slept. His lips and brow were relaxed and his breathing, though audibly labored, was even and deep. There were dark circles under his eyes but his skin held normal color. When he twisted, a lock of hair fell onto his forehead, and she had to stop herself from smoothing it back and running her fingers over his cherished face.

Because she was admiring his hair just then, she didn't see his eyes slowly open. When he abruptly sat up she was startled. The red throw crumpled, revealing a grey sweater that hung on his thinner-looking frame. His beautiful eyes were bloodshot.

For a moment they looked at each other.

"You belong on top of that tree, angel." His voice was so hoarse she barely understood him, but when she realized what he'd said she had to laugh. The relief was so great—he didn't mind her coming—she kept laughing.

"Your silver tongue works even when your voice doesn't."

"What are you doing here? Aside from showing off your Christmas outfit?" His chuckle devolved into a deep cough.

"Don't talk." She handed him the water. "I *had* to come. After the bombing everything shut down and there was no way I could get to you. The Hilton was damaged along with the embassy, you know, so we packed up the show and got out.

"Elise said it'd be okay to barge in on your family Christmas, once you were home. I told her to keep it a surprise ... wasn't sure how you'd feel about seeing me."

In response he leaned forward to put his arms around her. "Glad you're here." She felt his heartbeat increase as his embrace strengthened, felt his respiration drag.

"Easy." She moved next to him. "Breathe easy, love."

He slid off her hat and stroked her hair. "I'm getting better," he whispered. "Relieved there were so few killed. If they'd been effective that day our embassy would've been a parking lot.

299

Kuwait's oil and water supply half ruined. That was the plan."

She wanted to clear the air to make room for what she hoped was a new beginning, now she felt his welcome. "Was there a link from my or other shipments ... to the Dawa group?"

"They all took on freight from the same Beirut warehouse. That's as far as we got." He shook his head and then rested it on her shoulder. "But you have to forgive me—"

"You were afraid of something like the bombing."

"We were crazy with fear. Doesn't excuse how I treated you."

"Something's been bugging me about that night."

"Only one thing, Sugah?"

"You said, that time, you said you saw me three ways. As a lover, and as a conduit, but I was too mad to let you finish. What was the third way?"

His wheeze tickled her ear but she heard every word. "Clare, I see you as ... my wife. I'm supposed to go back to the Gulf when I'm well, to another station while they fix the embassy in Kuwait, but we can work out whatever, wherever you want."

She needed a long time to let this sink in. The fire crackled. The snow fell. The lights twinkled. "You want to get *married?*"

"Would you have me?" His eyes shone, behind their bruised aspect, and his smile contained all the mirth of the wild and generous universe. "I wanted to call you at Khaleedy's or InterTech, after the bombing, but my voice was shot. Elise kept telling me to wait, wouldn't send my letter to you, wouldn't even call you for me." His laugh was a pitiful puff. "Now I know why. She made me shave today. I thought for family Christmas Eve."

"So then, all these years, all this travel of ours, the back and forth in between, was just like ... some series of detours ... "

"That led us back together. Where we belong."

AUTHOR'S NOTE

I began DETOURS years ago while living in Saudi Arabia, where I'd finished all the novels in the small English lending-library in our compound and longed to read a dense romantic saga with characters I could relate to. So I just started writing my own. The first vision that came to me was Clare, Lowell and Troy in that Bloomington bar after the courthouse demonstration. Clare and Lowell stayed with me for a long time, enticing me to find out what would become of them; they sometimes pester me to explore their sequel.

About that fish atop the Monroe County courthouse: it is a true Bloomington icon with various fables surrounding its significance. It was created in the 1820s by artist Austin Seward.

"The Space Between: Adam and Eve" sculpture was installed on the Indiana University Bloomington campus in the 1960s by IU professor Jean Paul Darriau.

Acknowledgements

My thanks go to: My mother who gifted me with rich, deep, strange stories. My sister whose lively imagination peopled our childhood with fabulous characters and whose love of reading inspired mine. My husband who always encouraged me and who has fascinating stories of his own. My children who allowed my writing to eclipse any notion of home cooking (apologies to my hungry eldest son who wanted me to add more scenes of people eating barbecue). My writing collective—Julia Buckley, Elizabeth Diskin, Cynthia Quam—who shepherded my work from the beginning, who are the best editors, publicists and critique partners any novelist could hope for, and without whom I would never have finished a manuscript. Wells Street Press for helping me get from manuscript to publication. Other writers whose generosity has moved me: Karen Osborne, Sam Reaves, Kathi Baron, Jennifer Stevenson, Marilyn Brandt, Erica O'Rourke (the latter three from the august ChicagoNorth Romance Writers of America). Columbia College Chicago for Story Workshop. The beloved denizens of erstwhile Aydelotte Hall (viva La Cucaracha). Cherished friends: aDOORables, NapaGals, YaYas, and Ann L to whom I first declared this novel 'finished' years ago after writing THE END and running to her house all aglow. Snaps to Mary H with whom I cooked up the idea to get serious about writing on a napkin in Canada. Miranda with whom I pounded around the Dhahran compound so many years ago, plotting out Mills and Boon sagas. The Oak Park community whose support has so nourished my family and me during my illness, especially Mary, Fran, Beth, Elizabeth, Kathy and Kathryn. Finally, pulmonologist Benjamin Margolis and Sherrie Majdic, and oncologist Philip Bonomi and Irene Haagopa, whose care has granted me the time to publish before being considered posthumous. Special thanks and love to Sue.

ABOUT THE AUTHOR

Emma Gates was born in New York. She earned a BA in Spanish/Latin American Studies from Indiana University Bloomington, and an MBA with concentration in Arabic/Middle Eastern Studies from Thunderbird. She worked for three years in Mexico and five in Saudi Arabia. She is an international business and telecoms specialist currently living near Chicago with her family and a pair of inscrutable cats.

DETOURS PLAYLIST

I usually listen to music while I write. Often I choose music of the era I am writing about, from my collection, but sometimes my favorite radio station provides inspiration which creeps in to inform the story ambiance (shout-out to WXRT Chicago!)

I smile every time I look at this list compiled from DETOURS. Thanks to my brother, who always shared the best music throughout my life, and to my children who gave me the great compliment of saying they liked my musical taste. Thanks to the artists, whose brilliance so profoundly illuminates my life.

I'll be Waiting – Adele
December – George Winston
Bring on the Dancing Horsemen – Echo and the Bunnymen
Don't You Forget About Me – Simple Minds
Thirty Days in the Hole – Humble Pie
Grazin in the Grass – Hugh Masekela
For What it's Worth – Steven Stills
Season of the Witch – Donovan
Give Peace a Chance – John Lennon
Heart of Gold – Neil Young
One of Us Cannot be Wrong – Leonard Cohen
Tennessee Toad – Leo Kottke
She Belongs to Me – Bob Dylan
Talkin World War III Blues – Bob Dylan
Can't You Hear me Knockin – The Rolling Stones
Reasons for Waiting – Jethro Tull
Sailin Shoes – Little Feat
Suite: Judy Blue Eyes – as performed by CSN
Me and Bobbie McGee – as performed by Janis Joplin
Purple Haze – Jimi Hendrix
Nights in White Satin – Moody Blues
Moonshadow – Cat Stevens
Brown Sugar – Rolling Stones
Attics of My Life – The Grateful Dead
Box of Rain – The Grateful Dead
Knockin on Heaven's Door – Bob Dylan

Willin – Little Feat
Hay Unos Ojos – Ruben Fuentes
You Really Got a Hold on Me – as performed by The Beatles
Sisters of Mercy – Leonard Cohen
Momma told me not to come – as performed by Three Dog
Night
Poeme d 'Amour – Fairuz
Maggie May – Rod Stewart
Welcome to the Human Race – Timbuk 3
Just Like Tom Thumb's Blues – Bob Dylan
Let's Spend the Night Together – The Rolling Stones
O Vira – Secos y Molhados
In Another Land – The Rolling Stones
No Expectations – The Rolling Stones
Leavin on a Jet Plane – Peter Paul and Mary
Mexico Lindo – Vicente Fernandez
Buckets of Rain – Bob Dylan
If You See Her – Bob Dylan
What a Wonderful World – Sam Cooke
Fooled Around and Fell in Love – Elvin Bishop
Hungry like a Wolf – Duran Duran
Born in the USA – Bruce Springsteen
Please Please Please let Me Get what I Want – the Smiths
Deck the Halls – traditional Welsh

"Vladimir: the Musical" lyrics available upon request to Wells
Street Press

Made in the USA
Charleston, SC
25 March 2014